digital
domains

OTHER BOOKS
BY ELLEN DATLOW

———

*edited with Terri Windling

**edited with Terri Windling, Gavin J. Grant, and Kelly Link

digital domains

A DECADE OF SCIENCE FICTION AND FANTASY

edited by

ELLEN DATLOW

PRIME BOOKS

digital domains

Prime Books
www.prime-books.com

ISBN: 978-1-60701-208-5

table of contents

Digital Domains is dedicated to the writers, some of them in this book, who took a chance and allowed their stories to be published on the web, which was a scary place for original fiction back in the mid-1990s.

introduction

ELLEN DATLOW

O MNI *Magazine*, the science and science fiction magazine launched by Kathy Keeton and Bob Guccione in October 1978, was the first slick magazine to regularly publish science fiction and fantasy as part of the monthly mix. It was gorgeous, innovative (look at old issues and you can see how several current genre magazines have taken their layouts and other production elements straight out of *OMNI*) and published some very good stories over the years. I feel privileged to have worked there as fiction editor for almost seventeen years. The print magazine went completely online September 1996, but the year before, as an experiment, Editor Keith Ferrell persuaded Ford Motors to sponsor the publication of eight original novellas (and one reprint) on AOL's primitive website, over a period of a year.

Nine original stories were published on *OMNI Online* between September 1996 and the shuttering of the site March 1998, including three reprinted herein: "Thirteen Phantasms," by James P. Blaylock, first online story to win the World Fantasy Award (also nominated for the Theodore Sturgeon Award), "Get a Grip" by Paul Park, nominated for the World Fantasy Award, and "Mr Goober's Show" by Howard Waldrop. I also initiated a series of online round robins, in which four writers would participate, writing sections of a story arc that continued from the last writer's section.

After *OMNI Online* folded, I and my three former *OMNI* colleagues: Robert Killheffer, Pamela Weintraub, and Kathleen Stein created the webzine, *Event Horizon: Science Fiction-Fantasy-Horror*, with the intent of driving other types of work projects to our web production company, Event Horizon Web Productions. We'd produced two online conventions for Eos Books while still at *OMNI online* and we produced one more under the aegis of *Event Horizon*. The webzine included online chats, superstrings (our new name for round robins), and nonfiction commentary by such provocateurs as Lucius Shepard, Paul Riddell, Douglas E. Winter, Barry N. Malzberg, Howard Waldrop, Jack Womack, and David J. Schow.

Rob edited the nonfiction and I edited the fiction (until I took over both duties when Rob took another job and no longer had time). Among the twenty-two stories published between August 1988 and July 1999 were Kelly Link's "The Specialist's Hat" and "The Girl Detective" (the former, a winner of the World Fantasy Award, the latter, reprinted herein), two stories by Severna Park (one included herein), two stories by Jeffrey Ford (one herein), plus a variety of other new stories and a few of my favorite previously published stories.

SCIFI.COM, the SCI FI Channel's (renamed SyFi in July 2009) website, is a prominent and visible force in the science fiction field and on the web since its launch in 1995. The intention of *SCIFI. COM*, originally called *The Dominion*, was to be an entertaining accompaniment to the SCI FI Channel and evolved by 1999, to become *the* science fiction destination on the web, presenting daily news coverage and interviews with luminaries of the field, book reviews, audio dramas, animation and videos, and by late 1999— when I was hired—a fiction area that would showcase some of the best short science fiction and fantasy (and occasionally horror) being written, and enable readers to rediscover classics of the field. The sub-site was named *SCIFICTION* and was launched May 19th 2000 with a collaboration by Pat Cadigan and Christopher Fowler and a Robert A. Heinlein classic.

For almost six years the site published one original piece of fiction per week, including stories and novellas by an array of talented established writers and newcomers.

Linda J. Nagata's novella "Goddesses" was the first piece of work added by the Science Fiction and Fantasy Association's Nebula award jury to actually win the award. Other stories from *SCIFICTION* subsequently were nominated or won the Nebula award, Japan's Seiun Award, The British Science Fiction Association Award, the Million Writers Award, The Theodore Sturgeon Award, Australia's Aurealis Award, the Hugo Award, and the World Fantasy Award.

If there was still any doubt that online venues could produce outstanding fiction, *SCIFICTION* demolished them for good.

thirteen phantasms

JAMES P. BLAYLOCK

James Blaylock has been a writer and writing teacher since 1976, when his short story "Red Planet" was published in *UnEarth*. Since then he has written seventeen novels and has published several collections of short stories, as well as scores of articles and essays. His novels and stories have been translated around the world. Blaylock is twice winner of the World Fantasy Award, and he received the Phillip K. Dick Memorial Award for his novel *Homunculus*. His story "Unidentified Objects" was included in *Prize Stories 1990, the O.Henry Awards*. According to the *Library Journal*, "Blaylock's evocative prose and studied pacing make him one of the most distinctive contributors to American magical realism."

"Thirteen Phantasms" was the first story from an online publication to win the World Fantasy Award.

There was a small window in the attic, six panes facing the street, the wood frame unpainted and without moldings. Leafy wisteria vines grew over the glass outside, filtering the sunlight and tinting it green. The attic was dim despite the window, and the vines outside shook in the autumn wind, rustling against the clapboards of the old house and casting leafy shadows on the age-darkened beams and rafters. Landers set his portable telephone next to the crawl-space hatch and shined a flashlight across the underside of the shingles, illuminating dusty cobwebs and the skeleton frame of the roof. The air smelled of dust and wood, and the attic was lonesome with silence and moving shadows, a place sheltered from time and change.

A car rolled past out on the street, and Landers heard a train whistle in the distance.

Somewhere across town, church bells tolled the hour, and there was the faint sound of freeway noise off to the east like the drone of a perpetual-motion engine. It was easy to imagine that the wisteria vines had tangled themselves around the window frame for some secretive purpose of their own, obscuring the glass with leaves, muffling the sounds of the world.

He reached down and switched the portable phone off, regretting that he'd brought it with him at all. It struck him suddenly as something incongruous, an artifact from an alien planet. For a passing moment he considered dropping it through the open hatch just to watch it slam to the floor of the kitchen hallway below.

Years ago old Mr. Cummings had set pine planks across the two-by-six ceiling \ joists to make a boardwalk beneath the roof beam, apparently with the idea of using the attic for storage, although it must have been a struggle to haul things up through the shoulder-width attic hatch. At the end of this boardwalk, against the north wall, lay four dust-covered cardboard cartons—full of "junk magazines," or so Mrs. Cummings herself had told Landers this morning. The cartons were tied with twine, pulled tight and knotted, all the cartons the same. The word Astounding was written on the side with a felt marker in neat, draftsmanlike letters. Landers wryly wondered what sort of things Mr. Cummings might have considered astounding, and after a moment he decided that the man had been fortunate to find enough of it in one lifetime to fill four good-sized boxes.

Landers himself had come up empty in that regard, at least lately. For years he'd had a picture in his mind of himself whistling a cheerful out-of-key tune, walking along a country road, his hands in his pockets and with no particular destination, sunlight streaming through the trees and the limitless afternoon stretching toward the horizon. Somehow that picture had lost its focus in the past year or so, and, as with an old friend separated by time and distance, he had nearly given up on seeing it again.

It had occurred to him this morning that he hadn't brewed real coffee for nearly a year now. The coffee pot sat under the counter instead of on top of it, and was something he hauled out for guests. There was a frozen brick of ground coffee in the freezer, but he never bothered with it anymore. Janet had been opposed to freezing coffee at all. Freezing it, she said, killed the aromatic oils. It was better to buy it a half pound at a time, so that it was always fresh. Lately, though, most of the magic had gone out of the morning coffee; it didn't matter how fresh it was.

The Cummingses had owned the house since it was built in 1924, and Mrs. Cummings, ninety years old now, had held on for twenty years after her husband's death, letting the place run down, and then had rented it to Landers and moved into the Palmyra Apartments beyond the Plaza. Occasionally he still got mail intended for her, and it was easier simply to take it to her than to give it back to the post office. This morning she had told him about the boxes in the attic: "Just leave them there," she'd said. Then she had shown him her husband's old slide rule, slipping it out of its leather case and working the slide. She wasn't sure why she kept it, but she had kept a couple of old smoking pipes, too, and a ring-shaped cut-crystal decanter with some whiskey still in it. Mrs. Cummings didn't have any use for the pipes or the decanter any more than she had a use for the slide rule, but Landers, who had himself kept almost nothing to remind himself of the past, understood that there was something about these souvenirs, sitting alongside a couple of old photographs on a small table, that recalled better days, easier living.

The arched window of the house on Rexroth Street in Glendale looked out onto a sloping front lawn with an overgrown carob tree at the curb, shading a dusty Land Rover with what looked like prospecting tools strapped to the rear bumper. There was a Hudson Wasp in the driveway, parked behind an Austin Healey. Across the street a man in shirtsleeves rubbed paste polish onto the fender of a Studebaker, and a woman in a sundress dug in a flower bed with a trowel, setting out pansies. A little boy rode a sort of sled on wheels up and down the sidewalk, and the sound of the solid rubber wheels bumping over cracks sounded oddly loud in the still afternoon.

Russell Latzarel turned away from the window and took a cold bottle of beer from Roycroft Squires. In a few minutes the Newtonian Society would come to order, more or less, for the second time that day. Not that it made a lot of difference. For Latzarel's money they could recess until midnight if they wanted to, and the world would spin along through space for better or worse. He and Squires were both bachelors, and so unlike married men they had until hell froze over to come to order.

"India Pale Ale," Latzarel said approvingly, looking at the label on the squat green bottle. He gulped down an inch of beer. "Elixir of the gods, eh?" He set the bottle on a coaster. Then he filled his pipe with Balkan Sobranie tobacco and tamped it down, settling into an armchair in front of the chessboard, where there was a game laid out, half played. "Who's listed as guest of honor at West Coast Con? Edward tells me they're going to get Clifford Simak and van Vogt both."

"That's not what it says here in the newsletter," Squires told him, scrutinizing a printed pamphlet. "According to this it's TBA."

"To be announced," Latzarel said, then lit his pipe and puffed hard on it for a moment, his lips making little popping sounds. "Same son-of-a-bitch as they advertised last time." He laughed out loud and then bent over to scan the titles of the chess books in the bookcase. He wasn't sure whether Squires read the damned things or whether he kept them there to gain some sort of psychological advantage, which he generally didn't need.

It was warm for November, and the casement windows along the west wall were wide open, the muslin curtains blowing inward on the breeze. Dust motes moved in the sunshine. The Newtonian Society had been meeting here every Saturday night since the war ended, and in that couple of years it had seldom broken up before two or three in the morning. Sometimes when there was a full house, all twelve of them would talk straight through until dawn and then go out after eggs and bacon, the thirty-nine cent breakfast special down at Velma's Copper Pot on Western, although it wasn't often that the married men could get away with that kind of nonsense. Tonight they had scheduled a critical discussion of E.E. Smith's Children of the Lens, but it turned out that none of them liked the story much except Hastings, whose opinion was unreliable anyway, and so the meeting had lost all its substance after the first hour, and members had drifted away, into the kitchen and the library and out to the printing shed in the backyard, leaving Latzarel and Squires alone in the living room. Later on tonight, if the weather held up, they would be driving out to the observatory in Griffith Park.

There was a shuffling on the front walk, and Latzarel looked out in time to see the postman shut the mailbox and turn away, heading up the sidewalk. Squires went out through the front door and emptied the box, then came back in sorting letters. He took a puzzled second look at an envelope. "You're a stamp man," he said to Latzarel, handing it to him. "What do you make of that?"

Landers found that he could stand upright on the catwalk, although the roof sloped at such an angle that if he moved a couple of feet to either side, he had to duck to clear the roof rafters. He walked toward the boxes, but turned after a few steps to shine the light behind him, picking out his footprints in the otherwise undisturbed dust. Beneath that dust, if a person could only brush away the successive years, lay Mr. Cummings's own footprints, coming and going along the wooden boards.

There was something almost wrong about opening the boxes at all, whatever they contained, like prying open a man's coffin. And somehow the neatly tied string suggested that their packing hadn't been temporary, that old Mr. Cummings had put them away forever, perhaps when he knew he was at the end of things.

Astounding . . . ? Well, Landers would be the judge of that.

Taking out his pocket knife, he started to cut the string on one of the top boxes, then decided against it and untied it instead, afterward pulling back the flaps. Inside were neatly stacked magazines, dozens of issues of a magazine called *Astounding Science Fiction*, apparently organized according to date. He picked one up off the top, December of 1947, and opened it carefully. It was well-preserved, the pulp paper yellowed around the outside of the pages, but not brittle. The cover painting depicted a robot with a head like an egg, holding a bent stick in his hand and looking mournfully at a wolf with a rabbit beside it, the world behind them apparently in flames. There were book ads at the back of the magazine, including one from something called the Squires Press: an edition of Clark Ashton Smith's *Thirteen Phantasms*, printed with hand-set type in three volumes on Winnebago Eggshell paper and limited to a hundred copies. "Remit one dollar in seven days," the ad said, "and one dollar monthly until six dollars is paid."

A dollar a month! This struck him as fantastic—stranger in its way, and even more wonderful, than the egg-headed robot on the front cover of the magazine. He sat down beside the boxes and leaned back against the wall so that the pages caught the sunlight through the window. He wished that he had brought along something to eat and drink instead of the worthless telephone. Settling in, he browsed through the contents page before starting in on the editorial, and then from there to the first of the several stories.

When the sunlight failed, Landers ran an extension cord into the attic and hooked up an old lamp in the rafters over the catwalk. Then he brought up a folding chair and a little smoking table to set a plate on. He would have liked something more comfortable, but there was no fitting an overstuffed chair up through the hatch. Near midnight he finished a story called "Rain Check" by Lewis Padgett, which featured a character named Tubby (apparently there had been a time when the world was happy with men named Tubby) and another character who drank highballs . . .

He laid the book down and sat for a moment, listening to the rustling of leaves against the side of the house.

Highballs. What did people drink nowadays? Beer with all the color and flavor filtered out of it. Maybe that made a sad and frightening kind of sense. He looked at the back cover of the magazine, where, perhaps coincidentally, there was an ad for Calvert Whiskey: "Just be sure your highball is made with Calvert," the ad counseled. He wondered if there was any such thing anymore, whether anywhere within a twenty-mile radius someone was mixing up a highball out of Calvert Whiskey. Hell, a hundred miles . . .

Rod's Liquor Store down on the Plaza was open late, and he was suddenly possessed with the idea of mixing himself a highball. He took the magazine with him when he climbed down out of the attic, and, before he left the house, he filled out the order blank for the *Thirteen Phantasms,* and slipped it into an envelope along with a dollar bill. It seemed right to him, like the highball, or like old Mrs. Cummings keeping the slide rule.

He wrote out Squires's Glendale address, put one of the new interim "G" stamps on the envelope, and slid it into the mail slot for the postman to pick up tomorrow morning.

The canceled stamp depicted an American flag with the words "Old Glory" over the top. "A G stamp?" Latzarel said out loud. "What is that, exactly?"

Squires shook his head. "Something new?"

"Very damned new, I'd say. Look here." He pointed at the flag on the stamp. "I can't quite . . . " He looked over the top of his glasses, squinting hard. "I count too many stars on this flag. Take a look."

He handed the envelope back to Squires, who peered at the stamp, then dug a magnifying glass out of the drawer of the little desk in front of the window. He peered at the stamp through the glass. "Fifty," he said. "It must be a fake."

"Post office canceled it, too." Latzarel frowned and shook his head. "What kind of sense does that make? Counterfeiting stamps and getting the flag obviously wrong? A man wouldn't give himself away like that, unless he was playing some kind of game."

"Here's something else," Squires said. "Look at the edge. There's no perforations. This is apparently cut out of a solid sheet." He slit the envelope open and unfolded the letter inside. It was an order for the Smith collection, from an address in the city of Orange.

There was a dollar bill included with the order.

Landers flipped through the first volume of the *Thirteen Phantasms*, which had arrived postage-due from Glendale. There were four stories in each volume. Somehow he had expected thirteen altogether, and the first thing that came into his mind was that there was a phantasm missing. He nearly laughed out loud. But then he was sobered by the obvious impossibility of the arrival of any phantasms at all. They had come enclosed in a cardboard carton that was wrapped in brown paper and sealed with tape. He looked closely at the tape, half surprised that it wasn't yellowed with age, that the package hadn't been in transit through the ether for half a century.

He sipped from his highball and reread a note that had come with the books, written out by a man named Russell Latzarel, president of a group calling itself the Newtonian Society—apparently Squires's crowd. In the note, Latzarel wondered if Landers was perpetrating a hoax.

A hoax . . . The note was dated 1947. "Who are you really ?" it asked. "What is the meaning of the G stamp?" For a time he stared out of the window, watching the vines shift against the glass, listening to the wind under the eaves. The house settled, creaking in its joints. He looked at Latzarel's message again. "The dollar bill was a work of art," it read. On the back there was a hand-drawn map and an invitation to the next meeting of the Newtonians. He folded the map and tucked it into his coat pocket. Then he finished his highball and laughed out loud. Maybe it was the whiskey that made this seem monumentally funny. A hoax! He'd show them a hoax.

Almost at once he found something that would do. It was a plastic lapel pin the size of a fifty-cent piece, a hologram of an eyeball. It was only an eighth of an inch thick, but when he turned it in the light it seemed deep as a well. It was a good clear hologram, too, the eyeball hovering in the void, utterly three-dimensional. The pin on the back had been glued on sloppily and at a screwball angle, and excess glue had run down the back of the plastic and dried. It was a technological marvel of the late twentieth century, and it was an absolute, and evident, piece of junk. He addressed an envelope, dropped the hologram inside, and slid it into the mail slot.

The trip out to Glendale took over an hour because of a traffic jam at the 605 junction and bumper to bumper cars on the Golden State. There was nothing apparently wrong—no accident, no freeway construction, just a million toiling automobiles stretching all the way to heaven-knew-where, to the moon. He had forgotten Latzarel's map, and he fought off a feeling of superstitious dread as the cars in front of him inched along. At Los Feliz he pulled off the freeway, cutting down the off-ramp at the last possible moment. There was a hamburger joint called Tommy's Little Oasis on Los Feliz, just east of San Fernando Road, that he and Janet used to hit when they were on their way north. That had been a few years back; he had nearly forgotten, but the freeway sign at Los Feliz had jogged his memory. It was a tiny Airstream trailer in the parking lot of a motel shaded by big elm trees. You went there if you wanted a hamburger. That was it. There was no menu except a sign on the wall, and even the sign was nearly pointless, since the only question was did you want cheese or not. Landers wanted cheese.

He slowed down as he passed San Fernando, looking for the motel, for the big overarching elms, recalling a rainy Saturday afternoon when they'd eaten their burgers in the car because it was raining too hard to sit under the steel umbrella at the picnic table out front. Now there was no picnic table, no Airstream trailer, no motel—nothing but a run-down industrial park. Somehow the industrial park had sprung up and fallen into disrepair in—what?—less than twenty years!

He u-turned and headed the opposite direction up San Fernando, turning right on Western. It was better not to think about it, about the pace of things, about the cheeseburgers of days gone by. . . .

He pulled into a convenience store parking lot in order to ask directions. There were bars on the windows of the place, and the yellow stucco had holes kicked into it. The newspaper racks outside were full of singles newspapers and giveaway auto ads, and except for a desolate-looking laundromat the rest of the stores in the center were empty, their windows broken or boarded up. Inside the store there was an old Asian woman, very small, standing behind the counter, which was caged with a wrought iron grill. He smiled broadly at her, but she looked at him unhappily, and so out of guilt he grabbed a Nestle's Crunch bar and put it on the counter. Nothing is free, he reminded himself.

"I'm looking for Rexroth Street," he said slowly, then smiled at her again.

"Dirty dick!" she said to him.

He blinked at her, paralyzed with shock.

"Dirty dick!" She slapped her hand on the counter and grimaced, and abruptly he gave up on the candy bar and on any idea of asking directions. His heart pounding, he turned around slowly and stepped toward the open door, one foot after another, willing himself not to run and waiting for her to shout something else at him, some unnecessary obscenity. He climbed into his car, fired up the engine, and backed out fast, then turned up Western again, heading into the hills. To hell with directions; he would take a chance on his memory. He was three blocks north and deep into a residential neighborhood before it dawned on him: thirty-six! The woman had merely wanted money for the candy bar! Thirty-six cents. He laughed out loud, but the sound of his own laughter was unnerving, and he stopped abruptly. Dirty dick! He was still shaking. The incident had cast a pall of uncertainty and darkness over the adventure, and he half wished he hadn't come at all. Why the hell had he forgotten the map? The houses along the street were run-down, probably rentals. There was trash in the street, broken bottles, newspapers soaked in gutter water. Suddenly he was a foreigner. He had wandered into a part of the country that was alien to him. And, unless his instincts had betrayed him, it was clearly alien to Squires Press and the Newtonian Society and men named Tubby. At one time the mix of Spanish-style and Tudor houses had been elegant. Now they needed paint and the lawns were up in weeds, and there was graffiti on fences and garage walls. Windows and doors were barred. He drove slowly, calculating addresses and thinking about turning around, getting back onto the freeway and heading south again, just fleeing home, ordering something else out of the maga zines—personally autographed books by long-dead authors, "jar-proof" watches that could take a licking and go on ticking. He pictured the quiet shelter of his attic—his magazines, the makings of another highball. If ever a man needed a highball . . .

And just then he came upon the sign for Rexroth Street, so suddenly that he nearly drove righ through the intersection. He braked abruptly, swinging around toward the west, and a car behind him honked its horn hard. He heard the driver shout something as the car flew past.

"Dirty dick," Landers said under his breath, and started searching out addresses. The general tenor of the neighborhood hadn't improved at all, and he considered locking his doors. But then the idea struck him as superfluous, since he was about to park the car and get out anyway. He spotted the address on the curb, the paint faded and nearly unreadable. The house had a turreted entry hall in front, with an arched window in the wall that faced the street. A couple of the window panes were broken and filled with aluminum foil, and what looked like an old bed sheet was strung across as a curtain. Weeds grew up through the cracked concrete of the front walk, and there was black iron debris, apparently car parts, scattered on the lawn.

He drifted to the curb, reaching for the ignition key, but then saw, crouched next to a motorcycle up at the top of the driveway, an immense man, tattooed and bearded and dressed in black jeans and a greasy t-shirt, holding a wrench and looking down the driveway at him. Landers instantly stepped on the gas, angling away from the curb and gunning toward the corner.

He knew what he needed to know. He could go home now. Whoever this man was, living in what must have been Squires's old house, he didn't have anything to do with the *Thirteen Phantasms*. He wasn't a Newtonian. There was no conceivable chance that Squires himself was somewhere inside, working the crank of his mechanical printing press, stamping out fantastic stories on Winnebago Eggshell paper. Squires was gone; that was the truth of it. The Newtonians were gone. The world they'd inhabited, with its twenty-five cent pulp magazines and egg-headed robots and Martian canals, its highballs and hand-set type and slide rules, was gone, too. Probably it was all at the bottom of the tar pits, turning into puzzling fossils.

Out beyond the front window, Rexroth Street was dark and empty of anything but the wind. To the south, the Hollywood Hills were a black wall of shadow, as if there were nothing there at all, just a vacancy. The sky above the dark line of the hills was so closely scattered with bright stars in the wind-scoured night that Latzarel might have been dreaming, and the broad wash of the Milky Way spanned the heavens like a lamp-lit road. From up the hall, he could hear Cummings talking on the telephone. Cummings would be talking to his wife about now, asking permission to stay out late. Squires had phoned Rhineholdt at the observatory, and they were due up on the hill in an hour, with just time enough to stop for a late-night burger at the Copper Kettle on the way.

Latzarel took the three-dimensional picture of the eyeball out of his coat pocket and turned it under the lamp in the window, marveling again at the eyeball that hung impossibly in the miniature void, in its little nonexistent cube of frozen space.

There was a sudden glow in the Western sky now—a meteor shower, hundreds of shooting stars, flaming up for a moment before vanishing beyond the darkness of the hills.

Latzarel shouted for Squires and the others, and when they all ran into the room the stars were still falling, and the southern sky was like a veil of fireflies.

The totality of Landers' savings account hadn't been worth much at the coin shop. Gold standard bills weren't cheap. Probably he'd have been better off simply buying gold, but somehow the idea wasn't appealing. He wanted folding money in his wallet, just like any other pedestrian—something he could pay for lunch with, a burger and a Coke or a BLT and a slice of apple pie.

He glued the last of the foam rubber blocks onto the inside top of the wooden crate on his living room floor, then stood back and looked at the pile of stuff that was ready to go into the box. He'd had a thousand choices, an impossible number of choices. Everywhere he had turned in the house there was something else, some fabulous relic of the late twentieth century: throwaway wristwatches and dimmer switches, cassette tapes and portable telephones, pictorial histories and horse-race results, wallet-size calculators and pop-top cans, zip-lock baggies and Velcro fasteners, power screw guns and bubble paper, a laptop computer, software, a styrofoam cup . . .

And then it had occurred to him that there was something about the tiniest articles that appealed to him even more than the obvious marvels. Just three trifling little wonders shifted backward in time, barely discernible in his coat pocket, might imply huge, baffling changes in the world: a single green-tinted contact lens, perhaps, and the battery out of a watch, and a hologram bird clipped out of a credit card. He wandered from room to room again, looking around. A felt-tipped pen? A nylon zipper? Something more subtle . . .

But of course if it were too subtle, it would be useless, wouldn't it? What was he really planning to do with these things? Try to convince a nearsighted man to shove the contact lens into his eye? Would the Newtonians pry the battery apart? To what end? What was inside? Probably black paste of some kind or a lump of dull metal—hardly worth the bother. And the hologram bird—it was like something out of a box of Cracker Jacks. Besides, the Newtonians had already gotten the eyeball, hadn't they? He couldn't do better than the eyeball.

Abruptly he abandoned his search, changing his thinking entirely. Hurrying into the study he pulled books out of the case, selecting and rejecting titles, waiting for something to appeal to him, something . . . He couldn't quite define it. He might as well take nearly any of them, or simply rip out a random copyright page. The daily papers? Better to take along a sack of rotten fruit.

He went out of the study and into the kitchen hallway where he climbed the attic ladder. Untying the last of the boxes, he sorted through the Astoundings, settling on March of 1956—ten years in the future, more or less, for the Newtonians. Unlike the rest of the issues, this one was beat up, as if it had been read to pieces, or carried around in someone's coat pocket. He scanned the contents page, noting happily that there was a Heinlein novel serialized in the volume, and he dug through the box again to find April of the same year in order to have all of the story—something called *Double Star*. The torn cover of the April issue showed an ermine-robed king of some kind inspecting a toy locomotive, his forehead furrowed with thought and wonder.

Satisfied at last, Landers hurried back down the ladder and into the living room again. To hell with the trash on the floor, the bubble paper and the screw gun. He would leave all the Buck Rogers litter right here in a pile. Packing that kind of thing into the box was like loading up the Trojan Horse, wasn't it? It was a betrayal. And for what? Show-off value? Wealth? Fame? It was all beside the point; he saw that clearly now. It was very nearly the antithesis of the point.

He slid the Astoundings into a niche inside the box along with the *Thirteen Phantasms*, an army-surplus flashlight, a wooden-handled screwdriver, and his sandwiches and bottled water. Then he picked up the portable telephone and made two calls, one to his next door neighbor and one to Federal Express. His neighbor would unlock the door for the post office, who would haul the crate away on a hand cart and truck it to Glendale.

The thought clobbered him suddenly. By what route? he wondered. Along what arcane boulevards would he travel?

He imagined the crate being opened by the man he had seen working on the motorcycle in the neglected driveway. What would Landers do? Threaten the man with the screwdriver? Offer him the antique money? Scramble out of the crate and simply walk away down the street without a backward glance, forever changing the man's understanding of human behavior?

He stopped his mind from running and climbed into the crate, pulling the lid on after him. Carefully and deliberately, he started to set the screws—his last task before lunch. It was silent in the box, and he sat listening for one last moment in the darkness, the attic sitting empty above him, still sheltered by its vines and wooden shingles. He imagined the world revolving, out beyond the walls of the old house, imagined the noise and movement, and he thought briefly of Mrs. Cummings across town, arranging and rearranging a leather-encased slide rule and a couple of old smoking pipes and photographs.

The Saturday meeting of the Newtonian society had come to order right on time. Phillip Mays, the lepidopterist, was home from the Amazon with a collection of insects that included an immense dragon commonly thought to have died out in the Carboniferous period. Squires's living room floor was covered with display boxes and jars, and the room smelled of camphor and pipe smoke. There was the patter of soft rain through the open casements, but the weather was warm and easy despite the rain, and in the dim distance, out over the hills, there was the low rumble of thunder.

The doorbell rang, and Squires, expecting another Newtonian, opened the heavy front door in the turreted entry hall. A large wooden crate sat on the porch, sheltered by the awning, and a post office truck motored away north toward Kenneth Road, disappearing beyond a mist of rain. Latzarel looked over Squires's shoulder at the heavy crate, trying to figure out what was wrong with it, what was odd about it. Something . . .

"I'll be damned," he said. "The top's screwed on from the inside."

"I'll get a pry bar," Hastings said from behind him.

Latzarel heard a sound then, and he put his ear to the side of the box. There was the click of a screwdriver on metal, the squeak of the screw turning. "Don't bother with the pry bar," Latzarel said, winking at Squires, and he lit a match and held it to his pipe, cupping his hand over the bowl to keep the raindrops from putting it out.

mr goober's show

HOWARD WALDROP

Howard, Waldrop, born in Mississippi, and now living in Austin, Texas, is one of the most delightfully iconoclastic writers working today. His highly original books include the novels *Them Bones*, *A Dozen Tough Jobs*, and the collections *Howard Who?*, *All About Strange Monsters of the Recent Past*, and *Going Home Again*. He has won the Nebula and World Fantasy Awards for his novelette "The Ugly Chickens."

His most recent book is *Things Will Never Be the Same: Selected Short Fiction 1980-2005*, from Old Earth Books.

Forthcoming are *Other Worlds, Better Lives: Selected Long Fiction 1989-2003*, the novellas *The Search for Tom Purdue*, and *The Moone World*.

"Mr Goober's Show" is a typically strange Waldropian tale of popular culture gone just a bit wonky.

Y ou know how it is:

There's a bar on the corner, where hardly anybody knows your name, and you like it that way. Live bands play there two or three nights a week. Before they start up it's nice, and on the nights they don't play—there's a good juke box, the big TV's on low on ESPN all the time. At his prices, the owner should be a millionaire, but he's given his friends so many free drinks they've forgotten they should pay for more than every third or fourth one. Not that you know the owner, but you've watched.

You go there when your life's good, you go there when your life's bad; mostly you go there instead of having a good or bad life.

And one night, fairly crowded, you're on the stools so the couples and the happy people can have the booths and tables. Someone's put $12 in the jukebox (and they have some taste), the TV's on the Australian Thumb-Wrestling Finals, the neon beer signs are on, and the place looks like the inside of the Ferris Wheel on opening night at the state fair.

You start talking to the guy next to you, early fifties, your age, and you get off on TV (you can talk to any American, except a Pentecostal, about television) and you're talking the classic stuff: the last *Newhart* episode; *Northern Exposure*; the episode where Lucy stomps the grapes; the coast-to-coast bigmouth *Dick Van Dyke*; *Howdy-Doody* (every 8-year-old boy in America had a Jones for Princess Summer-Fall Winter-Spring).

And the guy, whose name you know is Eldon (maybe he told you, maybe you were born knowing it) starts asking you about some sci-fi show from the early '50s, maybe you didn't get it, maybe it was only on local upstate New York, sort of, it sounds like, a travelog, like the old *Seven League Boots*, only about space, stars and such, planets . . .

"Well, no," you say, "there was *Tom Corbett, Space Cadet; Space Patrol; Captain Video*"—which you never got but knew about—"*Rod Brown of the Rocket Rangers; Captain Midnight* (or *Jet Jackson, Flying Commando*, depending on whether you saw it before or after Ovaltine quit sponsoring it, and in reruns people's lips flapped after saying "Captain Midnight" but what came out was "Jet Jackson" . . .); or maybe one of the anthology shows, *Twilight Zone* or *Tales of—*' "

"No." he says, "not them. See, there was this TV . . . "

"Oh," you say, "a TV. Well, the only one I know of was this one where a guy at a grocery store (one season) invents this TV that contacts . . . "

"No," he says, looking at you (Gee, this guy can be intense!). "I don't mean *Johnny Jupiter, which is what you were going to say. Jimmy Duckweather invents TV. Contacts Jupiter, which is inhabited by puppets when they're inside the TV, and by guys in robot suits when they come down to Earth, and almost cause Duckweather to lose his job and not get a date with the boss's daughter, episode after episode, two seasons.*"

"*Maybe you mean Red Planet Mars, a movie. Peter Graves—*"

"*. . . Andrea King, guy invents hydrogen tube; Nazis; Commies; Eisenhower president. Jesus speaks from Mars.*"

"Well, *The Twonky*. Horrible movie, about a TV from the future?"

"*Hans Conreid. Nah, that's not it.*"

And so it goes. The conversation turns to other stuff (you're not the one with The Answer) and mostly it's conversation you forget because, if all the crap we carry around in our heads were real, and it was flushed, the continents would drown, and you forget it, and mostly get drunk and a little maudlin, slightly depressed and mildly horny, and eventually you go home.

But it doesn't matter, because this isn't your story, it's Eldon's.

When he was eight years old, city-kid Eldon and his seven-year-old sister Irene were sent off for two weeks in the summer of 1953, to Aunt Joanie's house in upstate New York while, not known to them, their mother had a hysterectomy.

Aunt Joanie was not their favorite aunt; that was Aunt Nonie, who would as soon whip out a Monopoly board, or Game of Life, or checkers as look at you, and always took them off on picnics or fishing or whatever it was she thought they'd like to do. But Aunt Nonie (their Mom's youngest sister) was off in Egypt on a cruise she'd won in a slogan contest for pitted dates, so it fell to Aunt Joanie, (their Father's oldest sister) to keep them the two weeks.

Their father's side of the family wasn't the fun one. If an adult unbent toward a child a little, some other family member would be around to remind them they were just children. Their cousins on that side of the family (not that Aunt Joanie or Uncle Arthridge had any kids) were like mice; they had to take off their shoes and put on house slippers when they got home from school; they could never go into the family room; they had to be in bed by 8:30 pm, even when the sun was still up in the summer.

Uncle Arthridge was off in California, so it was just them and Aunt Joanie, who, through no fault of her own, looked just like the Queen in Snow White and the Seven Dwarves, which they had seen with Aunt Nonie the summer before.

They arrived by train, white tags stuck to them like turkeys in a raffle, and a porter had made sure they were comfortable. When Irene had been upset, realizing she would be away from home, and was going to be at Aunt Joanie's for two weeks, and had begun to sniffle, Eldon held her hand. He was still at the age where he could hold his sister's hand against the world and think nothing of it.

Aunt Joanie was waiting for them in the depot on the platform, and handed the porter a $1.00 tip, which made him smile.

And then Aunt Joanie drove them, allowing them to sit in the front seat of her Plymouth, to her house, and there they were.

At first, he thought it might be a radio.

It was up on legs, the bottom of them looking like eagle claws holding a wooden ball. It wasn't a sewing machine cabinet, or a table. It might be a liquor cabinet, but there wasn't a keyhole.

It was the second day at Aunt Joanie's and he was already cranky. Irene had had a crying jag the night before and their aunt had given them some ice cream.

He was exploring. He already knew every room; there was a basement and an attic. The real radio was in the front room; this was in the sitting room at the back.

One of the reasons they hadn't wanted to come to Aunt Joanie's was that she had no television, like their downstairs neighbors, the Stevenses, did back in the city. They'd spent the first part of summer vacation downstairs in front of it, every chance they got. Two weeks at Aunt Nonie's without television would have been great, because she wouldn't have given them time to think, and would have them exhausted by bedtime anyway.

But two weeks at Aunt Joanie and Uncle Arthridge's without television was going to be murder. She had let them listen to radio, but not the scary shows, or anything good. And *Johnny Dollar* and *Suspense* weren't on out here, she was sure.

So he was looking at the cabinet in the sitting room. It had the eagle-claw legs. It was about three feet wide, and the part that was solid started a foot and a half off the floor. There was two feet of cabinet above that. At the back was a rounded part, with air holes in it, like a Lincoln Continental spare tire holder. He ran his hand over it—it was made out of that same stuff as the backs of radios and televisions.

There were two little knobs on the front of the cabinet though he couldn't see a door. He pulled on them. Then he turned and pulled on them.

They opened, revealing three or four other knobs, and a metal toggle switch down at the right front corner. They didn't look like radio controls. It didn't look like a television either. There was no screen.

There was no big lightning-bolt moving dial like on their radio at home in the city.

Then he noticed a double-line of wood across the top front of it, like on the old ice-box at his grandfather's. He pushed on it from the floor. Something gave, but he couldn't make it go farther.

Eldon pulled a stool up to the front of it.

"What are you doing?" asked Irene.

"This must be another radio," he said. "This part lifts up."

He climbed atop the stool. He had a hard time getting his fingers under the ridge. He pushed.

The whole top of the thing lifted up a few inches. He could see glass. Then it was too heavy. He lifted at it again after it dropped down, and this time it came up halfway open.

There was glass on the under-lid. It was a mirror. He saw the reflection of part of the room. Something else moved below the mirror, inside the cabinet.

"Aunt Joanie's coming!" said Irene.

He dropped the lid and pushed the stool away and closed the doors.

"What are you two little cautions doing?" asked Aunt Joanie from the other room.

The next morning, when Aunt Joanie went to the store on the corner, he opened the top while Irene watched.

The inner lid was a mirror that stopped halfway up, at an angle. Once he got it to a certain point, it clicked into place. There was a noise from inside and another click.

He looked down into it. There was a big dark glass screen.

"It's a *television*!" he said.

"Can we get *Howdy-Doody*?"

"I don't know," he said.

"You better ask Aunt Joanie, or you'll get in trouble."

He clicked the toggle switch. Nothing happened.

"It doesn't work," he said.

"Maybe it's not plugged in," said Irene.

Eldon lay down on the bare floor at the edge of the area rug, saw the prongs of a big electric plug sticking out underneath. He pulled on it. The cord uncoiled from behind. He looked around for the outlet. The nearest one was on the far wall.

"What are you two doing?" asked Aunt Joanie, stepping into the room with a small grocery bag in her arms.

"Is . . . is this a television set?" asked Eldon.

"Can we get *Howdy-Doody*?" asked Irene.

Aunt Joanie put down the sack. "It is a television. But it won't work any more. There's no need to plug it in. It's an old-style one, from before the war. They don't work like that anymore. Your uncle Arthridge and I bought it in 1938. There were no broadcasts out here then, but we thought there would be soon."

As she was saying this, she stepped forward, took the cord from Eldon's hands, rewound it and placed it behind the cabinet again.

"Then came the War, and everything changed. These kind won't work anymore. So we shan't be playing with it, shall we? It's probably dangerous by now."

"Can't we try it, just once?" said Eldon.

"I do not think so," said Aunt Joanie. "Please put it out of your mind. Go wash up now, we'll have lunch soon."

Three days before they left, they found themselves alone in the house again, in the early evening. It had rained that afternoon, and was cool for summer.

Irene heard scraping in the sitting room. She went there and found Eldon pushing the television cabinet down the bare part of the floor toward the electrical outlet on the far wall.

He plugged it in. Irene sat down in front of it, made herself comfortable. "You're going to get in trouble," she said. "What if it explodes?"

He opened the lid. They saw the reflection of the television screen in it from the end of the couch.

He flipped the toggle. Something hummed, there was a glow in the back, and they heard something spinning. Eldon put his hand near the round part and felt pulses of air, like from a weak fan. He could see lights through the holes in the cabinet, and something was moving.

He twisted a small knob, and light sprang up in the picture-tube part, enlarged and reflected in the mirror on the lid. Lines of bright static moved up the screen and disappeared in a repeating pattern.

He turned another knob, the larger one, and the bright went dark and then bright again.

Then a picture came in.

They watched those last three days, everytime Aunt Joanie left; afraid at first, watching only a few minutes, then turning it off, unplugging it, and closing it up and pushing it back into its place, careful not to scratch the floor.

Then they watched more, and more, and there was an excitement each time they went through the ritual, a tense expectation.

Since no sound came in, what they saw they referred to as "Mr. Goober's Show," from his shape, and his motions, and what went on around him. He was on anytime they turned the TV on.

They left Aunt Joanie's reluctantly. She had never caught them watching it. They took the train home.

Eldon was in a kind of anxiety. He talked to all his friends, who knew nothing about anything like that, and some of them had been as far away as San Francisco during the summer. The only person he could talk to about it was his little sister, Irene.

He did not know what the jumpiness in him was.

———

They rushed into Aunt Joanie's house the first time they visited at Christmas, and ran to the sitting room.

The wall was blank.

They looked at at each other, then ran back into the living room.

"Aunt Joanie!" said Eldon, interrupting her, Uncle Arthridge and his father. "Aunt Joanie, where's the television?"

"Television . . . ? Oh, that thing. I sold it to a used furniture man at the end of the summer. He bought it for the cabinetry, he said, and was going to make an aquarium out of it. I suppose he sold the insides for scrap."

They grew up, talking to each other, late at nights, about what they had seen. When their family got TV, they spent their time trying to find it again.

Then high school, then college, the '60s. Eldon went to Nam, came back about the same.

Irene got a job in television, and sent him letters, while he taught bookkeeping at a junior college.

April 11, 1971
Dear Bro'—
I ran down what kind of set Aunt Joanie had.

It was a *mechanical* television, with a Nipkov disk scanner. It was a model made between 1927 and 1929.

Mechanical: yes. You light a person, place, thing, very very brightly. On one side of the studio are photoelectric cells that turn light to current. Between the subject and the cells, you drop in a disk that spins 300 times a minute. Starting at the edge of the disk, and spiraling inward all the way around to the

center are holes. You have a slit-scan shutter.
As the light leaves the subject it's broken
into a series of lines by the holes passing
across the slit. The photoelectric cells pick
up the pulses of light. (An orthicon tube does
exactly the same thing, except electronically,
in a camera, and your modern TV is just a big
orthicon tube on the other end.) Since it was
a mechanical signal, your disk in the cabinet
at home had to spin at exactly the same rate.
So they had to send out a regulating signal at
the same time.

Not swell, not good definition, but
workable.

But Aunt Joanie (rest her soul) was right—
nothing in 1953 was broadcasting that it could
receive, because all early pre-war televisions
were made with the picture-portion going out
on FM and the sound going out on short-wave (so
her set had receivers for both) *and* neither of
them are where TV is *now* on the wavelengths
(where they've been since 1946).

Mr. Goober could not have come from an FCC
licensed broadcaster in 1953. I'll check Canada
and Mexico, but I'm pretty sure everything was
moved off those bands by then, even experimental
stations. Since we never got sound, either
there was none, or maybe it was coming in with
the picture (like *now*) and her set couldn't
separate four pieces of information (one-half
each of two signals, which is why we use FM
for TV).

It shouldn't have happened, I don't think.
There are weird stories (the ghost signals

of a Midwest station people saw the test
patterns of more than a year after they quit
broadcasting; the famous 2.8 second delay in
radio transmissions all over the world on
shortwave in 1927 and early 1928).

Am going to the NAB meeting in three weeks.
Will talk to everybody there, especially the
old guys, and find out if any of them knows
about Mr. Goober's Show. Stay sweet.

Your sis,

Irene

Eldon began the search on his own; at parties, at bars, at ball games.
During the next few years, he wrote his sister with bits of fugitive
matter he'd picked up. And he got quite a specialized knowledge
of local TV shows, kid's show clowns, *Shock Theater* hosts, and
eclectic local programming of the early 1950s, throughout these
United States.

June 25, 1979
Dear Eldon—
Sorry it took so long to get this letter
off to you, but I've been busy at work, and
helping with the Fund Drive, and I also think
I'm onto something. I've just run across stuff
that indicates there was some kind of medical
outfit that used radio in the late '40s and
early '50s.

Hope you can come home for Christmas *this*
time. Mom's getting along in years, you know.
I know you had your troubles with her (*I'm* the
one to talk) but she really misses you. As Bill
Cosby says, she's an old person trying to get

into Heaven now. She's trying to be good the *second* thirty years of her life . . .

Will write you again as soon as I find out more about these quacks.

Your little sister,

Irene

August 14, 1979

Dear Big Brother:

Well, it's depressing here. The lead I had turned out to be a bust, and I could just about cry, since I thought this might be it, since they broadcast on *both* shortwave and FM (like Aunt Joanie's set received) but this probably wasn't it, either.

It was called Drown Radio Therapy (there's something poetic about the name, but not the operation). It was named for Dr. Ruth Drown, she was a real osteopath. Sometime before the War, she and a technocrat started working with a low-power broadcast device. By War's end, she was claiming she could treat disease at a distance, and set up a small broadcast station behind her Chicago suburb office. Patients came in, were diagnosed, and given a schedule of broadcast times they were supposed to tune in. (The broadcasts were directly to each patient, supposedly, two or three times a day.) By the late '40s, she'd also gone into TV, which is of course FM (the radio stuff being short-wave). That's where I'd hoped I'd found someone broadcasting at the same time on both bands.

But probably no go. She franchised the machines out to other doctors, mostly naturopaths and cancer quacks. It's possible that one was operating near Aunt Joanie's somewhere, but probably not, and anyway, a committee of docs investigated her stuff. What they found was that the equipment was so low-powered it could only broadcast a dozen miles (not counting random skipping, bouncing off the Heaviside layer, which it wouldn't have been able to reach). Essentially they ruled the equipment worthless.

And, the thing that got to me, there was *no* picture transmission on the FM (TV) portion; just the same type of random signals that went out on short-wave, on the same schedule, every day. Even if you had a rogue cancer specialist, the FCC said the stuff couldn't broadcast a visual signal, not with the technology of the time. (The engineer at the station here looked at the specs and said "even if they had access to video orthicon tubes, the signal wouldn't have gotten across the room," unless it was on cable, which it wasn't.)

I've gone on too long. It's not it.

Sorry to disappoint you (again). But I'm still going through back files of *Variety* and *BNJ* and everything put out by the networks in those years. And, maybe a mother-lode, a friend's got a friend who knows where all the Dumont records (except Gleason's) are stored.

We'll find out yet, brother. I've heard stories of people waiting twenty, thirty, forty years to clear things like this up. There was a guy who kept insisting he'd read a serialized novel in a newspaper, about the fall of civilization, in the early 1920s. Pre-bomb, pre-almost everything. He was only a kid when he read it. Ten years ago he mentioned it to someone who had a friend who recognized it, not from a newspaper, but as a book called *Darkness and the Dawn*. It was in three parts, and serial rights were sold, on the first part only, to, like *three* newspapers in the whole U.S. And the man, now in his sixties, had read it in one of them.

Things like that do happen, kiddo.

Write me when you can.

Love,

Irene

Sept. 12, 1982

El—

I'm ready to give up on this. It's running me crazy—not crazy, but to distraction, if I had anything else to be distracted *from*.

I can't see any way out of this except to join the Welcome Space Brothers Club, which I refuse to do.

That would be the easy way out, give up, go over to the Cheesy Side of the Force. You and me saw a travelog, a See-It-Now of the Planets, hosted by an interstellar Walter Cronkite on a Nipkov disk TV in 1953. We're the only people in the world who did. *No one else.*

But that's why *CE3K* and the others have made so many millions of dollars. People want to believe, but they want to believe *for other people*, not themselves. *They* don't want to be

42

the ones. **They want someone else to be the one. And then they want everybody to believe. But it's not** *their* **ass out there saying: the Space Brothers are here; I can't prove it, take my word for it, it's real. Believe me as a person.**

I'm not that person, and neither are you; OR there has to be some other answer. One, or the other, but not both; and not neither.

I don't now what to do anymore; whatever it is, it's not this. It's quit being fun. It's quit being something I do aside from life as we know it. It is my life, and yours, and it's all I've got.

I know what Mr. Goober was trying to tell us, and there was more, but the sound was off.

I'm tired. I'll write you next week when I can call my life my own again.

Your Sis

Cops called from Irene's town the next week.

After the funeral, and the stay at his mother's, and the inevitable fights, with his stepfather trying to stay out of it, he came home and found one more letter, postmarked the same day as the police had called him.

Dear Eldon—
Remember this, and don't think less of me: What we saw was real.
Evidently, too real for me.
Find out what we saw.
Love always,
Irene

So you'll be sitting in the bar, there'll be the low hum and thump of noise as the band sets up, and over in the corner, two people will be talking. You'll hear the word "Lucy" which could be many things—a girlfriend, a TV show, a late President's daughter, a 4-million-year-old ape-child. Then you'll hear "*M-Squad*" or "*Untouchables*" and there'll be more talk, and you'll hear distinctly, during a noise-level drop, " . . . and I don't mean *Johnny*-fucking-*Jupiter* either . . . "

And in a few minutes he'll leave, because the band will have started, and conversation, except at the 100-decibel level, is over for the night.

But he'll be back tomorrow night. And the night after.

And all the star-filled nights that follow that one.

get a grip

PAUL PARK

Paul Park has published a collection of stories, *If Lions Could Speak*, and ten novels, including *Celestis* and *A Princess of Roumania*. He lives in Berkshire County, Massachusetts, and teaches at Williams College.

"Get a Grip" is clever, funny, and nasty and published before a well-known movie used a similar idea.

Here's how I found out: I was in a bar called Dave's on East 14th Street. It wasn't my usual place. I had been dating a woman in Stuyvesant Town. One night after I left her place, I still wasn't eager to go home. So on my way I stopped into Dave's.

I used to spend a lot of time in bars, though I don't smoke or drink. But I like the second-hand stuff. And the conversations you could have with strangers—you could tell them anything. "Ottawa is a fine city," you could say. "My brother lives in Ottawa," I could say, though in fact I'm an only child. But people would nod their heads.

This kind of storytelling used to drive my ex-wife crazy. "It's so pointless. It's not like you're pretending you're an astronaut or a circus clown. That I could see. But a Canadian?"

"It's a subtle thrill," I conceded.

"Why not tell the truth?" Barbara would say. "That you're a successful lawyer with a beautiful wife you don't deserve. Is that so terrible?"

Not terrible so much as difficult to believe. It sounded pretty thin, even before I found out. And of course none of it turned out to be true at all.

Anyway, that night I was listening to someone else. Someone was claiming he had seen Reggie Jackson's last game on TV. I nodded, but all the time I was looking past him toward a corner of the bar, where a man was sitting at a table by himself. He was smoking cigarettes and drinking, and I recognized him.

But I didn't know from where. I stared at him for a few minutes. What was different—had he shaved his beard? Then suddenly I realized he was in the wrong country. It was Boris Bezugly. It truly was.

I took my club soda over to join him. We had parted on such good terms. "Friends, friends!" he had shouted drunkenly on the platform of Petersburg Station, saliva dripping from his lips. Now he was drunk again. He sat picking at the wax of the red candle. When he looked up at me, I saw nothing in his face, just bleared eyes and a provisionary smile.

We had met two years before, when a partner in the firm was scouting the possibility of a branch office in Moscow. Even in Russia he was the drunkest man I ever met. When we were introduced, he had passed out and fallen on his back as we were still shaking hands. Maybe it was his drunkenness that kept him from recognizing me now, I thought. After all, it had taken me a moment.

But we were in New York. Surely running into me was not as strange as me running into him. And why hadn't he told me he was coming? "Sdravsvuytse," I said, grinning. "Can I buy you a drink?"

What passed over his face was an expression of such horror and rage, it made me put up my hand. But then his face went blank and he turned away from me, huddling around his candle and his drink.

He had lost weight, and his black beard was gone. In Russia he had worn a hilarious mismatch of plaid clothes, surmounted by an old fur cap. Now he wore a tweed suit, a denim shirt open at the neck. The cap was gone.

"Boris," I said.

In Russia his English had been absurd. I used to tell him he sounded like a hit man in a cold war novel, and he had laughed aloud. Now he spoke quickly and softly in a mid-Atlantic accent: "I think you're making a mistake."

And I would have thought so, too, except for the strange expression I had seen. So I persevered. I pulled out one of the chairs and sat down. "What are you doing?" he cried. "My God, if they find us here. If they see us here."

These words gave me what I thought was a glimmer of understanding. In Moscow, in the kitchen of his tiny apartment,

Boris once had put away enough vodka to let him pass through drunkenness into another stage, a kind of clarity and grim sobriety. Then he had told me what his life was like under the Communists— the lies that no one had believed. The interrogations. When he was a student in the sixties after Brezhnev first came in, he had spent two years in protective custody.

Now maybe he was remembering those times. "My friend," I said, "it's all right. You're in America."

These words seemed to fill him with another gust of fury. He tried to get up, and I could see he was very drunk. "I don't know you, I've never met you," he muttered, grinding out his cigarette butt. But then the cocktail waitress was there.

"I'll take a club soda," I said. "And my friend will have a Smirnoff's."

"No," he snarled, "that was the problem with that job. Get me a bourbon," he told the waitress. Then to me: "I hate vodka."

Which surprised me more than anything he'd said so far. In Moscow he had recited poetry about vodka. "Yeah," he told me now, smiling in spite of himself. "Tastes change."

Apparently he had reassured himself that no one was watching us. But he waited until the waitress had come and gone before he spoke again. "Boris," I said, and he interrupted me.

"Don't call me that. It was just a job, a two-week job. I barely remember it."

"What are you talking about?"

He smiled. "You don't know, do you? You really don't know. Get a grip," he said. "It's like candy from a baby."

I saw such a mix of passions in his face. Envy, frustration, anger, fear. And then a kind of malignant grin that was so far from my perception of his character that I stared at him, fascinated.

"You never went to Russia," he said. "You've never met a single Russian. You were in a theme park they built outside Helsinki, surrounded by people like me. They were paying us to guzzle vodka and wear false beards and act like clowns. "Sdravsvuytse,' my ass!"

He was crazy. "My poor friend," I said. "Who was paying you? The KGB?"

He knocked his heavy-bottomed glass against the table, spilling bourbon on the polyurethaned wood. "Not the KGB," he hissed. "The KGB never existed. None of it existed. None of this." He waved his hand around the room.

He was in the middle of a paranoid breakdown of some sort. I could see that. And yet the moment I heard him, I felt instinctively that what he said was true.

"They never would have taken you to Russia," he went on. "Not to the real Russia." As he spoke I brought back my own memories— the grime, the cold, the sullen old babushkas with rags around their heads. The concrete apartment blocks. The horrible food.

He put down his empty glass. "Thanks for the drink. And now I'm definitely getting out of here before somebody sees us. Because this is definitely against the rules. "

Then he was gone, and I walked home. And maybe I wouldn't have thought much about it, only the next day I was walking up Fifth Avenue on my lunch hour, and I passed the offices for Aeroflot. I went in and sat down with the people who were waiting to be helped. We were in a row of armchairs next to the window.

This is ridiculous, I thought. And I was about to get up and go, when I found myself staring at a travel poster. One of the agents was talking on the phone, and there was a framed poster of Red Square above her desk. And was that Boris Bezugly in the middle of a group of smiling Russians in front of St. Basil's? The beard, the hat, the absurd plaid?

The Aeroflot agent was a dark-haired, heavy-chested woman, dressed in black pumps, beige tights, and a black mini-skirt. A parody of a Russian vamp. And what was that language she was speaking on the phone? The more I listened, the more improbable it sounded.

I asked the woman sitting next to me. She frowned. "Russian, of course," she said. How could she be so sure? Made-up gobbledygook, but of course once you let yourself start thinking like that, the whole world starts to fall apart. Not immediately, but gradually. I took the woman from Stuyvesant Town to a musical on Broadway. Critics had pretended to like it, though it was obviously bad. Audience members had applauded, laughed—who were they trying to fool?

At work sometimes I found it hard to concentrate. I was representing the plaintiff in a civil suit. Yet no actual client could have been so petty, so vindictive. In my office I sat staring at the man, watching his lips move, waiting for him to give himself away.

And of course I spent more of my time at Dave's. I would go there every evening after work, and in time I was drinking more than just club sodas. But it was weeks before I saw Boris again. He came in out of a freezing rain and made his way directly toward me, where I was sitting at a table by myself.

He sat down without asking and leaned forward, rubbing his hands over the tiny candle flame. "Listen," he said, "I'm in trouble," and he looked it. He needed a shave. His eyes were bloodshot. He wasn't wearing a coat.

"Listen, I can't do it anymore. All that lying and pretending. I've screwed up two more jobs and now they're on to me. I can't go home. Please, can you give me some money? I've got to get away."

"I'll pay you fifty dollars for some information," I said. I took the bills from my pocket, but he interrupted me.

"No, I mean your watch or something. I can't use that bogus currency." He pulled some coins out of the pocket of his pants, big, shiny, aluminum coins like Mardi Gras doubloons. In fact as I looked closely, I saw that's what they were. The purple one in his palm was stamped with the head of Pete Fountain playing the clarinet.

"I don't even have enough here for a drink," he said.

"I'll get you one." I raised my hand for the waitress. But then I saw her at the corner of the bar, talking with the bartender. As I watched, she pointed over at us.

"Oh my God," said my Russian friend. His voice was grim and strange. "Give me the watch."

I stripped it off, though it was an expensive Seiko. "Thanks," he said, looking at the face, the sweep of the second hand. "And in return I'll answer one minute's worth of questions. Go."

"Who are you?" I asked.

But he shrugged irritably. "No, it's not important. My name is Nathan—so what? What about you?"

"I know about myself," I said uncertainly.

"Do you? Jim Brothers, Esq. Yale, 1981. But what makes you think you were smart enough to go to the real Yale? Do you think they let just anybody in?"

Actually, I had always kind of wondered about that. So his words gave me a painful kind of pleasure. Then he went on: "Twenty seconds. What about your marriage? What was that all about?"

"I'm divorced."

"Of course you are. The woman who was playing your wife landed another job. It was never supposed to be more than a two year contract with an option, which she chose not to renew. Last I heard, she was doing Medea, Blanche Dubois, and Lady Macbeth for some repertory company up in Canada."

Again, this sounded so hideously plausible that I said nothing.

"Forty seconds."

"Fifty seconds."

"Wait," I said, but he was gone out the door. He left only his Pete Fountain doubloon, which I slid into my pocket.

Then in a little while the police were there. A man in a white raincoat sat opposite me, asking me questions. "Did he say where he was going? Did he give you anything?"

"No," I said. "No. Nothing."

But then when I was watching TV later that night, I saw that Nathan Rose, a performance artist wanted in connection with several outstanding warrants, had been arrested. There was a photograph, and a brief description of his accomplishments. Nathan Rose had been a promising young man, recipient of several grants from the National Endowment for the Arts. The newscaster's voice was sad and apologetic, and she seemed to look out of the television directly at me. She made no mention of the crime he'd been accused of. What was it—impersonating a Russian?

That night was the beginning of a quick decline for me, because success in life depends on not asking too many questions. The patterns of illusion that make up the modern world require a kind of faith, a suspension of disbelief. The revenge on skeptics is quick and sure, and I soon found myself hustled out of what I'd thought was my real world as rudely as I might have been thrown out of a magic show, if I had stood up in the audience and explained the tricks while the performance was in progress.

But of course at that time I could only guess at the real truth. I conceived the idea that the government had hired an enormous troupe of actors, administered and paid for by the NEA, to create and sustain an illusion of reality for certain people. At first I played with the idea that I might be the only one, but no. That was too grandiose, too desperate a fantasy. So much money, so much effort, just to make a fool out of a single citizen. The Republicans never would have stood for it. Providing jobs for actors just wasn't that important, even in New York.

I lost my job, my friends, and my apartment. I refused to work long hours for play money. And no one could tolerate me. People I knew, I kept trying to catch them in small lies and inconsistencies. I would ask them questions. "If this is just a job for you, why aren't you nicer to me? Surely we'd enjoy it more. How can we turn this into a comedy? A farce? A musical?"

By the middle of December I was living by the train tracks, inside the tunnel under Riverside Park. Maybe it wasn't necessary for me to have gone that far. But at a certain point, I thought I'd try to penetrate down below the level of deception. Because I imagined that the illusions were falser and more elaborate the higher up you went, which is why so many rich people are crazy. Wherever they go, part of their brain is mumbling to the other part, "Surely the actual Plaza Hotel isn't such a dump. Surely an authentic Mercedes corners better than this. Surely a genuine production of Hamlet isn't quite so dull. Surely the real Alps are higher and more picturesque."

But that night in my tarpaulin tent next to the train tracks, wrapped in my blankets, it was hard for me to think that the real Riverside Park was even darker, even colder, even more miserable. I was dressed in a dinner jacket I had kept from my apartment. I was glutted with hors-d'oeuvres, drunk on chablis, because New York provides many opportunities to a man in black tie, especially around Christmas time. I had attended office parties and openings all the way from midtown, pretending all the way. I had been an architect, an actor, a designer, a literary agent. In each place as I grew drunker, the lies I told grew more outrageous, yet people still smiled and nodded. Why not? They were being paid good Mardi Gras doubloons to pretend to believe me.

In my tent, I slid my hand down into my pocket and clasped my hand around my own Pete Fountain coin, perhaps, I thought, the only genuine thing I'd ever owned. Drunk and despairing, I let the cold come into me, let it calm me until I wasn't sure if I could move even if I'd wanted to. My hands and legs were stiff and strange.

As the hours passed, the walls of the tunnel seemed to close around me. But yes, there was some light down toward the tunnel's mouth, too bright, too soft for dawn. Yes, it seemed to fill the hole, to chase away the darkness, and it was as if I had left my body and was drifting toward it, suspended over the tracks. There was heat, too, beyond my fingertips, and as I drifted down the tunnel I felt it penetrate my body and my soul. I imagined faces in the tunnel with me, people standing along the rails, smiling and murmuring. As I passed them I reached out, especially to the ones I recognized: my mother, my grandparents, my childhood friends, and even Barbara, my ex-wife. Yes, I thought, this is the truth.

It couldn't last forever. I was sprawled over the tracks, and the light was coming toward me. I listened to the muffled voices and the creak of the wheels, and the light was all around me. It was so bright, I had to close my eyes. As I did so, I heard somebody say, "That's it. That's a wrap."

When I sat up, I was in a crowd of people and machines. The big lamp had gone out, replaced by a yellow fluorescent line along the middle of the vault.

By its light I could see much that had been hidden from me. For one thing, the entire tunnel was only about twenty-five yards long. I could see the brick ends of it now, cunningly painted to look like train tracks disappearing in both directions.

In front of me there was a lamp rigged to a platform, which ran on wheels along the rails. Now that the lamp was out, I could see the movie camera beneath it, the camera man stripping off his gloves and his coat; they had turned off the refrigeration machines. There was a whole line of them along the wall, and I guess they had been making quite a racket, because now I could hear all kinds of talking from the crew as they finished up. I threw aside my blanket and sat rubbing my hands. Nobody was paying any attention to me. But then I saw my mother coming toward me through a crowd of technicians, and she squatted down. "Congratulations," she said. "That was great."

"Mother," I stammered, "is it really you?" I admit I was surprised to see her, because she had passed away in the spring of 1978.

She was wearing a silk shirt, blue jeans, and cowboy boots. She was smiling. "Yeah, that's great. I tell you, these last few weeks you've made me proud I ever got to work with you. Proud you're my son, so to speak. The paranoia, the anger, the disgust. It was all so real."

"Mother," I said, "I can't believe it. You look so young."

She winked. "Yeah, sure. You've probably never seen me without makeup. But let's not get carried away. Somewhere along the line you must have guessed. That was the whole point of this game."

She stood up. And now others were helping me to my feet. I recognized a few old faces, and then Barbara was there. "Your suit's a mess," she said.

I was stunned, overwhelmed to see her. Her freckled nose. Her crooked smile. She reached up to touch my damp bow-tie. When I'd known her, her breath had always been a little sour, a symptom of chronic gastric distress. Now she was standing close to me, and I caught a whiff of the mints she used—the same old brand. At least that was for real, I thought.

Her little head was close to my lapel. Packed with brains. I'd always said that was the reason she so easily outwitted me. The space inside her skull was so small that her thoughts never had more than an inch or so to travel, to make connections. Her ideas moved faster, like molecules in a gas when it's condensed.

And at the moment when I smelled her breath, I felt a little surge of hope. Even if there was no place for me in her old life, maybe now there might be some new way for us to be together in this new world. Cleverer than me, maybe she had already had the same idea, because I felt her arms around me, her head against my cheek as I bent down. "I'm sorry I was so mean," she whispered. "But I had to. It was the script. Sometimes it broke my heart, the things I had to do to you. I'm not normally so promiscuous."

Mother and the rest had disappeared, and we were surrounded by technicians packing up equipment. "I just wanted to tell you right away," she said. "Before anybody else talks to you. Sex and betrayal are the only things that keep the yuppie games alive. The only reason anybody wants to play. So I had to. That thing where you caught me with your boss's wife—I actually protested to the writers. I cried for days when we were finished."

Then she took my hand and led me outside. It was early morning. We walked through a park that seemed all of a sudden only twenty-five yards wide, and it was rapidly disappearing as people rolled up the astroturf and wheeled away the papier-mache balustrades.

The night before, I had come down to the park the way I always did, along West 98th Street. Now as we approached Riverside Drive, I could see as if from a slightly different angle the painted plywood facades of the buildings, all just a few inches thick. On 98th Street itself there was a huge crew striking the set, so instead of going back that way, Barbara led me north, uptown, and soon we were lost among streets I didn't recognize, although I'd lived on the Upper West Side my whole life.

"Where are we?" I asked faintly.

"Toronto. They always use it for the New York shoots. The real New York is so expensive. It's like American actors—no one can afford them anymore. We use Canadians for everything."

"So what was this?" I asked. "A movie or a game?"

"Both. It's interactive TV. A few hired professionals like me and your mom, and then tons of paying customers. They do most of the minor characters, the extras and what-not. Then the whole thing is broadcast live, with your thoughts picked up on an internal mike as a kind of voice-over. That's what made the show—you were so innocent, so clueless. The show started when you were fifteen, which meant it took you twenty-two years to figure out what was going on. It's a new record. And in the end we had to give you massive hints."

"When I was fifteen?"

"Sure. All the rest was just recovered-memory syndrome. Who wants to make a show about a kid? I mean except for all the shows within the show. Beaver Cleaver and so forth."

"Beaver Cleaver?"

"No expense was spared," said Barbara. "It's the information superhighway. But you have to understand—this was a huge deal."

She was right. By the time we hit Yonge Street a crowd had gathered. Old ladies, teenagers, men, women, all wanting to shake my hand and get my autograph. I was a celebrity, like O.J. Simpson or Woody Allen, except of course I really existed. I was a real person, and not just a collection of computer-generated film clips. "Mr. Brothers," somebody shouted. "When did you know for sure?"

"Show us the doubloon!" demanded another, and when I took it from my pocket, everyone laughed and clapped. An old man grasped my hand. I recognized him as the super of the building next to mine. "I just wanted to say you've given my wife and me such pleasure over the years. Most of the shows should be banned from the airwaves, if it was up to me. But you never even raised your voice. No violence at all. Not that you weren't tempted," he said, giving Barbara a severe look.

Then the limo arrived, small and sleek. Inside I could hear a small hum, as if from a computer. No one was driving. We pulled out slowly into the wide street, and then we were heading downtown. "So what was the show's name?" I asked.

"It was called *Get A Grip*," said Barbara. And when she saw my face, she grinned. "Oh come on, don't take it like that. Sure, you were kind of a wimp, but the guy is right. It was a wholesome show. Every day we found new ways to humiliate you, but you just soldiered on. Most of the time you didn't even notice. I mean sure, you were a total moron, but that was all right. It was your dignity that people loved."

We drove on through the unfamiliar streets. "I guess it didn't keep me from being canceled," I said.

"Well, to tell the truth it was all a little dated. And you needed a good female lead. That fat tart in Stuyvesant Town just wasn't doing it. People seemed to find your life less interesting as soon as I bailed out."

"I guess I felt the same way."

Barbara patted my hand. "But you were still popular among retirees. You have no idea how bad most of the competition is. Like the guy said, they gave over most of the twentieth century to war games. Vietnam, KKK, Holocaust, Cold War, Hiroshima. Those are all the American shows. Kids love them, even the minorities. But I can't stand them."

"Hiroshima?" I asked.

She smiled. "Meanwhile, we thought it was a stroke of genius to work all that into the background of *Get A Grip*. To show what life in America might have been like if it had all really happened. Of course we had to change the footage and the point of view—reshoot a lot of it. Most of those shows are ridiculously patriotic."

"Ingenious," I murmured.

"But that's how we got into trouble. ABC claimed it was copyright infringement, and the American ambassador protested. But *Get A Grip* was a satire, for God's sake. Even the U.S. courts ruled in our favor."

After a little while I said, "So what did really happen?"

"Well, that's what I'm telling you. The Americans were furious for years. So ABC finally made a hostile bid for Ottawa Communication, which produced your show. The deal went through last week, and *Get A Grip* was canceled. But there had been rumors for months, which was why the writers brought back all that Russian stuff last fall. They wanted to take the show to its own end."

"No. I mean, what really happened? In the world."

She squeezed my arm. "Don't worry. You'll soon catch up. Besides, we're here."

We pulled up in front of a hotel. "You'll love it," she said. "Czar Nicholas III stayed here last time he was in town."

So I got out and followed her up the steps. In through the revolving doors. The lobby was all ormolu and velvet and gilt mantelpieces. The elevator ran in a cage up through the middle of the spiral staircase. "What am I doing now?" I asked as we got in.

"God damn it, Pogo, don't be such a dope." I hated when she called me "Pogo." It was a nickname left over from my earliest childhood, and she only used it to annoy me. But as I rode up in the elevator, it occurred to me that maybe no one had ever really called me that. Maybe all those painful memories had been induced when I was fifteen. Maybe they had all been covered in a flashback, when *Get A Grip* first went on the air.

My eyes filled with tears. "What's the matter now?" said Barbara. "Honest to God, you'd think you were being boiled over a slow fire. It's the best hotel in town. I thought you might want to rest for a few hours, take a shower, change your clothes before the reception at the president's house tonight. The Russian ambassador will be there—I tell you you're a star. A symbol of Canadian pride. Come on, is that so terrible?"

Then when we were alone together in the jewel-box room, she said, "Besides, I've missed you."

But I wasn't listening. I was looking at my face in the mirror above the dresser. The same curly hair and gullible eyes, as if nothing had happened. "My whole life has been a parody," I said, watching my lips move. But then I had to smile, because it was exactly what I might have said back in America, back during the salad days of *Get A Grip*.

Barbara was behind me. In the mirror I saw her undo the first few buttons of her blouse, and then slip it off her shoulders. "Let me make it okay for you," she said. Then it was like a dream come true, because she was leading me to the bed and pulling off my clothes. I had thought about this moment so many times since we split up, directing us as if we were the actors in a scene. In my mind, sometimes she was harsh and fast, sometimes passive and accommodating. Sometimes it took hours, and sometimes it was over right away. But none of my fantasizing prepared me for this moment, which was not sublime so much as strange. During two years of marriage, I thought I had got to know her well. But I had never done any of the things she required of me in that hotel room; I had never heard of anybody doing them. But, "Things are different here," she whispered. "Let me teach you how to make it in the real world," she said, before I lost consciousness.

Then I came to, and I was lying on the bed. Barbara was in the shower. I could hear the water running. I sat naked on the side of the bed, staring at the television. It was in a lacquer cabinet on top of a marble table, and the remote was on the floor near my foot. There were hundreds of buttons on it.

Then suddenly I was seized with a new suspicion, and I flicked it on. I flicked through several channels, seeing nothing but football games. But there I was on channel 599xtc, buck naked, staring at myself. Behind me the hotel room, the ripped sheets and soggy pillows. And on the bottom corner of the screen, a blinking panel that said: **PRESS ANY KEY TO CONTINUE.**

Then Barbara was there, toweling her neck, looking over my shoulder. "Okay, so it's not quite over yet," she said. "There are still some things you ought to know."

the girl detective

KELLY LINK

Kelly Link is the author of three collections, *Stranger Things Happen*, *Magic for Beginners*, and *Pretty Monsters* (the last, for young adults). Her short stories have recently been published in *Tin House*, *Firebirds Rising*, *Noisy Outlaws*, *The Restless Dead*, *The Starry Rift*, and *Troll's Eye View*. Her work has won three Nebulas, a Hugo, the Locus Award, The British Science Fiction Association Award, and a World Fantasy Award.

She and her husband Gavin J. Grant run Small Beer Press, and twice yearly produce the zine *Lady Churchill's Rosebud Wristlet*.

"The Girl Detective" remains one of my favorite stories by Link.

The girl detective looked at her reflection in the mirror. This was a different girl. This was a girl who would chew gum.

—DORA KNEZ, in conversation

The girl detective's mother is missing.

The girl detective's mother has been missing for a long time.

The underworld.

Think of the underworld as the back of your closet, behind all those racks of clothes that you don't wear anymore. Things are always getting pushed back there and forgotten about. The underworld is full of things that you've forgotten about. Some of them, if only you could remember, you might want to take them back. Trips to the underworld are always very nostalgic. It's darker in there. The seasons don't match. Mostly people end up there by accident, or else because in the end there was nowhere else to go. Only heroes and girl detectives go to the underworld on purpose.

There are three kinds of food.

One is the food that your mother makes for you. One is the kind of food that you eat in restaurants. One is the kind of food that you eat in dreams. There's one other kind of food, but you can only get that in the underworld, and it's not really food. It's more like dancing.

The girl detective eats dreams.

The girl detective won't eat her dinner. Her father, the housekeeper—they've tried everything they can think of. Her father takes her out to eat—Chinese restaurants, once even a truckstop two states away for chicken-fried steak. The girl detective used to love chicken-fried steak. Her father has gained ten pounds, but the girl detective will only have a glass of water, not even a slice of lemon. I saw them once at that new restaurant downtown, and the girl detective was folding her napkin while her father ate. I went over to their table after they'd left. She'd folded her napkin into a swan. I put it into my pocket, along with her dinner roll and a packet of sugar. I thought these things might be clues.

The housekeeper cooks all the food that the girl detective used to love. Green beans, macaroni and cheese, parsnips, stewed pears— the girl detective used to eat all her vegetables. The girl detective used to love vegetables. She always cleaned her plate. If only her mother were still here, the housekeeper will say, and sigh. The girl detective's father sighs. Aren't you the littlest bit hungry? they ask her. Wouldn't you like a bite to eat? But the girl detective still goes to bed hungry.

There is some debate about whether the girl detective needs to eat food at all. Is it possible that she is eating in secret? Is she anorexic? Bulimic? Is she protesting something? What could we cook that would tempt her?

I am doing my best to answer these very questions. I am detecting the girl detective. I sit in a tree across the street from her window, and this is what I see. The girl detective goes to bed hungry, but she eats our dreams while we are asleep. She has eaten my dreams. She has eaten your dreams, one after the other, as if they were grapes or oysters. The girl detective is getting fat on other people's dreams.

The case of the tap-dancing bankrobbers.

Just a few days ago, I saw this on the news. You remember, that bank downtown. Maybe you were in line for a teller, waiting to make a deposit. Perhaps you saw them come in. They had long, long legs, and they were wearing sequins. Feathers. Not much else. They wore tiny black dominos, hair pinned up in tall loopy curls, and their mouths were wide and red. Their eyes glittered.

You were being interviewed on the news. "We all thought that someone in the bank must be having a birthday," you said. "They had on these skimpy outfits. There was music playing."

They spun. They pranced. They kicked. They were carrying purses, and they took tiny black guns out of their purses. Sit down on the floor, one of them told you. You sat on the floor. Sitting on the floor, it was possible to look up their short, flounced skirts. You could see their underwear. It was satin, and embroidered with the days of the week. There were twelve bank robbers: Monday, Tuesday, Wednesday, Thursday, Friday, Saturday, Sunday, and then Mayday, Payday, Yesterday, Someday, and Birthday. The one who had spoken to you was Birthday. She seemed to be the leader. She went over to a teller, and pointed the little gun at him. They spoke earnestly. They went away, through a door over to the side. All the other bank robbers went with them, except for Wednesday and Thursday, who were keeping an eye on you. They shuffled a little on the marble floor as they waited. They did a couple of pliés. They kept their guns pointed at the security guard, who had been asleep on a chair by the door. He stayed asleep.

In about a minute, the other bank robbers came back through the door again, with the teller. They looked satisfied. The teller looked confused, and he went and sat on the floor next to you. The bank robbers left. Witnesses say they got in a red van with something written in gold on the side and drove away. The driver was an older woman. She looked stern.

Police are on the lookout for this woman, for this van. When they arrived, what did they find inside the vault? Nothing was missing. In fact, things appeared to have been left behind. Several tons of mismatched socks, several hundred pairs of prescription glasses, retainers, a ball python six feet long, curled decoratively around the bronze vault dial. Also a woman claiming to be Amelia Earhart. When police questioned this woman, she claimed to remember very little. She remembers a place, police suspect that she was held hostage there by the bank robbers. It was dark, she said, and people were dancing. The food was pretty good. Police have the woman in protective custody, where she has reportedly received serious proposals from lonely men and major publishing houses.

In the past two months the tap-dancing robbers have kept busy. Who are these masked women? Speculation is rife. All dance performances, modern, classical, even student rehearsals, are well-attended. Banks have become popular places to go on dates or on weekdays, during lunch. Some people bring roses to throw. The girl detective is reportedly working on the case.

Secret origins of the girl detective.

Some people say that she doesn't exist. Someone once suggested that I was the girl detective, but I've never known whether or not they were serious. At least I don't think that I am the girl detective. If I were the girl detective, I would surely know.

Things happen.

When the girl detective leaves her father's house one morning, a man is lurking outside. I've been watching him for a while now from my tree. I'm a little stiff, but happy to be here. He's a fat man with pouched, beautiful eyes. He sighs heavily a few times. He takes the girl detective by the arm. Can I tell you a story, he says.

All right, says the girl detective politely. She takes her arm back, sits down on the front steps. The man sits down beside her and lights a smelly cigar.

The girl detective saves the world.

The girl detective has saved the world on at least three separate occasions. Not that she is bragging.

The girl detective doesn't care for fiction.

The girl detective doesn't actually read much. She doesn't have the time. Her father used to read fairy tales to her when she was little. She didn't like them. For example, the twelve dancing princesses. If their father really wants to stop them, why doesn't he just forbid the royal shoemaker to make them any more dancing shoes? Why do they have to go underground to dance? Don't they have a ballroom? Do they like dancing or are they secretly relieved when they get caught? Who taught them to dance?

The girl detective has thought a lot about the twelve dancing princesses. She and the princesses have a few things in common. For instance, shoe leather. Possibly underwear. Also, no mother. This is another thing about fiction, fairy tales in particular. The mother is usually missing. The girl detective imagines, all of a sudden, all of these mothers. They're all in the same place. They're far away, some place she can't find them. It infuriates her. What are they up to, all of these mothers?

The fat man's story.

This man has twelve daughters, says the fat man. All of them lookers. Nice gams. He's a rich man but he doesn't have a wife. He has to take care of the girls all by himself. He does the best he can. The oldest one is still living at home when the youngest one graduates from high school. This makes their father happy. How can he take care of them if they move away from home?

But strange things start to happen. The girls all sleep in the same bedroom, which is fine, no problem, because they all get along great. But then the girls start to sleep all day. He can't wake them up. It's as if they've been drugged. He brings in specialists. The specialists all shake their heads.

At night the girls wake up. They're perky. Affectionate. They apply makeup. They whisper and giggle. They eat dinner with their father, and everyone pretends that everything's normal. At bedtime they go to their room and lock the door, and in the morning when their father knocks on the door to wake them up, gently at first, tapping, then harder, begging them to open the door, beside each bed is a worn-out pair of dancing shoes.

Here's the thing. He's never even bought them dancing lessons. They all took horseback riding, tennis, those classes where you learn to make dollhouse furniture out of cigarette boxes and doilies.

So he hires a detective. Me, says the fat man—you wouldn't think it, but I used to be young and handsome and quick on my feet. I used to be a pretty good dancer myself.

The man puffs on his cigar. Are you getting all this? the girl detective calls to me, where I'm sitting up in the tree. I nod. Why don't you take a hike, she says.

Why we love the girl detective.

We love the girl detective because she reminds us of the children we wish we had. She is courteous, but also brave. She loathes injustice; she is passionate, but also well-groomed. She keeps her room neat, but not too neat. She feeds her goldfish. She will get good grades, keep her curfew when it doesn't interfere with fighting crime. She'll come home from an Ivy League college on weekends to do her laundry.

She reminds us of the girl we hope to marry one day. If we ask her, she will take care of us, cook us nutritious meals, find our car keys when we've misplaced them. The girl detective is good at finding things. She will balance the checkbook, plan vacations, and occasionally meet us at the door when we come home from work, wearing nothing but a blue ribbon in her hair. She will fill our eyes. We will bury our faces in her dark, light, silky, curled, frizzed, teased, short, shining, long, shining hair. Tangerine, clove, russet, coal-colored, oxblood, buttercup, clay-colored, tallow, titian, lampblack, sooty, scented hair. The color of her hair will always inflame us.

She reminds us of our mothers.

Dance with beautiful girls.

The father hides me in the closet one night, and I wait until the girls, they all come to bed. It's a big closet. And it smells nice, like girl sweat and cloves and mothballs. I hold onto the sleeve of someone's dress to balance while I'm looking through the keyhole. Don't think I don't go through all the pockets. But all I find is a marble and a deck of cards with the Queen of Spades missing, a napkin folded into a swan maybe, a box of matches from a Chinese restaurant.

I look through the keyhole, maybe I'm hoping to see one or two of them take off their clothes, but instead they lock the bedroom door and move one of the beds, knock on the floor and guess what? There's a secret passageway. Down they go, one after the other. They look so demure, like they're going to Sunday School.

I wait a bit and then I follow them. The passageway is plaster and bricks first, and then it's dirt with packed walls. The walls open up and we could be walking along, all of us holding hands if we wanted to. It's pretty dark, but each girl has a flashlight. I follow the twelve pairs of feet in twelve new pairs of kid leather dancing shoes, each in its own little puddle of light. I stretch my hands up and I stand on my toes, but I can't feel the roof of the tunnel anymore. There's a breeze, raising the hair on my neck.

Up till then I think I know this city pretty well, but we go down and down, me after the last girl, the youngest, and when at last the passageway levels out, we're in a forest. There's this moss on the trunk of the trees, which glows. It looks like paradise by the light of the moss. The ground is soft like velvet, and the air tastes good. I think I must be dreaming, but I reach up and break off a branch.

The youngest girl hears the branch snap and she turns around, but I've ducked behind a tree. So she goes on and we go on.

Then we come to a river. Down by the bank there are twelve young men, Oriental, gangsters by the look of 'em, black hair slicked back, smooth-faced in the dim light, and I can see they're all wearing guns under their nice dinner jackets. I stay back in the trees. I think maybe it's the white slave trade, but the girls go peaceful, and they're smiling and laughing with their escorts, so I stay back in the trees and think for a bit. Each man rows one of the girls across the river in a little canoe. Me, I wait a while and then I get in a canoe and start rowing myself across, quiet as I can. The water is black and there's a bit of a current, as if it knows where it's going. I don't quite trust this water. I get close to the last boat with the youngest girl in it and water from my oar splashes up and gets her face wet, I guess, because she says to the man, someone's out there.

Alligator, maybe, he says, and I swear he looks just like the waiter who brought me orange chicken in that new restaurant downtown. I'm so close, I swear they must see me, but they don't seem to. Or maybe they're just being polite.

We all get out on the other side and there's a nightclub all lit up with paper lanterns on the veranda. Men and women are standing out on the veranda, and there's a band playing inside. It's the kind of music that makes you start tapping your feet. It gets inside me and starts knocking inside my head. By now I think the girls must have seen me, but they don't look at me. They seem to be ignoring me. "Well, here they are," this one woman says. "Hello, girls." She's tall, and so beautiful she looks like a movie star, but she's stern-looking too, like she probably plays villains. She's wearing one of them tight silky dresses with dragons on it, but she's not Oriental.

"Now let's get started," she says. Over the door of the nightclub is a sign. **DANCE WITH BEAUTIFUL GIRLS**. They go in. I wait a bit and go in, too.

I dance with the oldest and I dance with the youngest and of course they pretend that they don't know me, but they think I dance pretty fine. We shimmy and we grind, we bump and we do the Charleston. This girl she opens up her legs for me but she's got her hands down in an X, and then her knees are back together and her arms fly open like she's going to grab me, and then her hands are crossing over and back on her knees again. I lift her up in the air by her armpits and her skirt flies up. She's standing on the air like it was solid as the dance floor, and when I put her back down, she moves on the floor like it was air. She just floats. Her feet are tapping the whole time and sparks are flying up from her shoes and my shoes and everybody's shoes. I dance with a lot of girls and they're all beautiful, just like the sign says, even the ones who aren't. And when the band starts to sound tired, I sneak out the door and back across the river, back through the forest, back up the secret passageway into the girls' bedroom.

I get back in the closet and wipe my face on someone's dress. The sweat is dripping off me. Pretty soon the girls come home too, limping a little bit, but smiling. They sit down on their beds and they take off their shoes. Sure enough, their shoes are worn right through. Mine aren't much better.

That's when I step out of the closet and while they're all screaming, lamenting, shrieking, scolding, yelling, cursing, I unlock the bedroom door and let their father in. He's been waiting there all night. He's hangdog. There are circles under his eyes. Did you follow them? he says.

I did, I say.

Did you stick to them? he says. He won't look at them.

I did, I say. I give him the branch. A little bit later, when I get to know the oldest girl, we get married. We go out dancing almost every night, but I never see that club again.

There are two kinds of names.

The girl detective has learned to distrust certain people. People who don't blink enough, for example. People who don't fidget. People who dance too well. People who are too fat or too thin. People who cry and don't need to blow their noses afterwards. People with certain kinds of names are prone to wild and extravagant behavior. Sometimes they turn to a life of crime. If only their parents had been more thoughtful. These people have names like Bernadette, Sylvester, Arabella, Apocolopus, Thaddeus, Gertrude, Gomez, Xavier, Xerxes. Flora. They wear sinister lipsticks, plot world destruction, ride to the hounds, take up archery instead of bowling.

They steal inheritances, wear false teeth, hide wills, shoplift, plot murders, take off their clothes and dance on tables in crowded bars just after everyone has gotten off work.

On the other hand, it doesn't do to trust people named George or Maxine, or Sandra, or Bradley. People with names like this are obviously hiding something. Men who limp. Who have crooked, or too many teeth. People who don't floss. People who are stingy or who leave overgenerous tips. People who don't wash their hands after going to the bathroom. People who want things too badly. The world is a dangerous place, full of people who don't trust each other. This is why I am staying up in this tree. I wouldn't come down even if she asked me to.

The girl detective is looking for her mother.

The girl detective has been looking for her mother for a long time. She doesn't expect her mother to be easy to find. After all, her mother is also a master of disguises. If we fail to know the girl detective when she comes to find us, how will the girl detective know her mother?

She sees her sometimes in other people's dreams. Look at the way this woman is dreaming about goldfish, her mother says. And the girl detective tastes the goldfish and something is revealed to her. Maybe a broken heart, maybe something about money, or a holiday that the woman is about to take. Maybe the woman is about to win the lottery.

Sometimes the girl detective thinks she is missing her mother's point. Maybe the thing she is supposed to be learning is not about vacations or broken hearts or lotteries or missing wills or any of these things. Maybe her mother is trying to tell the girl detective how to get to where she is. In the meantime, the girl detective collects the clues from other people's dreams and we ask her to find our missing pets, to tell us if our spouses are being honest with us, to tell us who are really our friends, and to keep an eye on the world while we are sleeping.

About three o'clock this morning, the girl detective pushed up her window and looked at me. She looked like she hadn't been getting much sleep either. "Are you still up in that tree?"

Why we fear the girl detective.

She reminds us of our mothers. She eats our dreams. She knows what we have been up to, what we are longing for. She knows what we are capable of, and what we are not capable of. She is looking for something. We are afraid that she is looking for us. We are afraid that she is not looking for us. Who will find us, if the girl detective does not?

The girl detective asks a few questions.

"I think I've heard this story before," the girl detective says to the fat man.

"It's an old story."

The man stares at her sadly and she stares back. "So why are you telling me?"

"Don't know," he says. "My wife disappeared a few months ago. I mean, she passed on, she died. I can't find her is what I mean. But I thought that maybe if someone could find that club again, she might be there. But I'm old and her father's house burned down thirty years ago. I can't even find that Chinese restaurant anymore."

"Even if I found the club," the girl detective says, "if she's dead, she probably won't be there. And if she is there, she may not want to come back."

"I guess I know that too, girlie," he says. "But to talk about her, how I met her. Stuff like that helps. Besides, you don't know. She might be there. You never know about these things."

He gives her a photograph of his wife.

"What was your wife's name?" the girl detective says.

"I've been trying to remember that myself," he says.

Some things that have recently turned up in bank vaults.

Lost pets. The crew and passengers of the Mary Celeste. More socks. Several boxes of Christmas tree ornaments. A play by Shakespeare, about star-crossed lovers. It doesn't end well. Wedding rings. Some albino alligators. Several tons of seventh-grade homework. Ballistic missiles. A glass slipper. Some African explorers. A whole party of Himalayan mountain climbers. Children, whose faces I knew from milk cartons. The rest of that poem by Coleridge. Also fortune cookies.

Further secret origins of the girl detective.

Some people say that she was the child of missionaries, raised by wolves, that she is the Princess Anastasia, last of the Romanovs. Some people say that she is actually a man. Some people say that she came here from another planet and that some day, when she finds what she is looking for, she'll go home. Some people are hoping that she will take us with her.

If you ask them what she is looking for, they shrug and say, "Ask the girl detective."

Some people say that she is two thousand years old.

Some people say that she is not one girl but many—that is, she's actually a secret society of Girl Scouts. Or possibly a sub-branch of the FBI.

Whom does the girl detective love?

Remember that boy, Fred, or Nat? Something like that. He was in love with the girl detective, even though she was smarter than him, even though he never got to rescue her even once from the bad guys, or when he did, she was really just letting him, to be kind. He was a nice boy with a good sense of humor, but he used to have this recurring dream in which he was a golden retriever. The girl detective knew this, of course, the way she knows all our dreams. How could she settle down with a boy who dreamed that he was a retriever?

Everyone has seen the headlines. "Girl Detective Spurns Head of State." "I Caught My Husband in Bed with the Girl Detective." "Married Twenty Years, Husband and Father of Four, Revealed to Be the Girl Detective."

I myself was the girl detective's lover for three happy months. We met every Thursday night in a friend's summer cottage beside a small lake. She introduced herself as Pomegranate Buhm. I was besotted with her, her long legs so pale they looked like two slices of moonlight. I loved her size eleven feet, her black hair that always smelled like grapefruit. When we made love, she stuck her chewing gum on the headboard. Her underwear was embroidered with the days of the week.

We always met on Thursday, as I have said, but according to her underwear, we also met on Saturdays, on Wednesdays, on Mondays, Tuesdays, and once, memorably, on a Friday. That Friday, or rather that Thursday, she had a tattoo of a grandfather clock beneath her right breast. I licked it, surreptitiously, but it didn't come off. The previous Thursday (Monday according to the underwear) it had been under her left breast. I think I began to suspect then, although I said nothing and neither did she.

The next Thursday the tattoo was back, tucked discreetly under the left breast, but it was too late. It ended as I slept, dreaming about the waitress at Frank's Inland Seafood, the one with Monday nights off, with the gap between her teeth and the freckles on her ass. I was dreaming that she and I were in a boat on the middle of the lake. There was a hole in the bottom of the boat. I was putting something in it—to keep the water out—when I became aware that there was another woman watching us, an older woman, tall with a stern expression. She was standing on the water as if it were a dance floor. "Did you think she wouldn't find out?" she said. The waitress pushed me away, pulling her underwear back up. The boat wobbled. This waitress's underwear had a word embroidered on it:

Payday.

I woke up and the girl detective was sitting beside me on the bed, stark naked and dripping wet. The shower was still running. She had a strange expression on her face, as if she'd just eaten a large meal and it was disagreeing with her.

"I can explain everything," I said. She shrugged and stood up. She walked out of the room stark naked and the next time I saw her, it was two years later and she was disguised as an Office Lady in a law firm in downtown Tokyo, tapping out Morse code on the desk with one long petal-pink fingernail. It was something about expense accounts, or possibly a dirty limerick. She winked at me and I fell in love all over again.

But I never saw the waitress again.

What the girl detective eats for dinner.

The girl detective lies down on her bed and closes her eyes. Possibly the girl detective has taken the fat man's case. Possibly she is just tired. Or curious.

All over the city, all over the world, people are asleep. Sitting up in my tree, I am getting tired just thinking about them. They are dreaming about their children, they are dreaming about their mothers, they are dreaming about their lovers. They dream that they can fly. They dream that the world is round like a dinner plate. Some of them fall off the world in their dreams. Some of them dream about food. The girl detective walks through these dreams. She picks an apple off a tree in someone's dream. Someone else is dreaming about the house they lived in as a child. The girl detective breaks off a bit of their house. It pools in her mouth like honey.

The woman down the street is dreaming about her third husband, the one who ran off with his secretary. That's what she thinks. He went for takeout one night five years ago and never came back. It was a long time ago. His secretary said she didn't know a thing about it, but the woman could tell the other woman was lying. Or maybe he ran away and joined the circus.

There is a man who lives in her basement, although the woman doesn't know it. He's got a television down there, and a small refrigerator, and a couch that he sleeps on. He's been living there for the past two years, very quietly. He comes up for air at night. The woman wouldn't recognize this man if she bumped into him on the street. They were married about twenty years and then he went to pick up the lo mein and the wontons and the shrimp fried rice, and it's taken him a while to get back home. He still had his set of keys. She hasn't been down in the basement in years. It's hard for her to get down the stairs.

The man is dreaming too. He's working up his courage to go upstairs and walk out the front door. In his dream he walks out to the street and then turns around. He'll walk right back up to the front door, ring the bell. Maybe they'll get married again someday. Maybe she never divorced him. He's dreaming about their honeymoon. They'll go out for dinner. Or they'll go down in the basement, down through the trapdoor into the underworld. He'll show her the sights. He'll take her dancing.

The girl detective takes a bite of the underworld.

Chinese restaurants.

I used to eat out a lot. I had a favorite restaurant, which had really good garlic shrimp, and I liked the pancakes, too, the scallion pancakes. But you have to be careful. I knew someone, their fortune said, "Your life right now is like a rollercoaster. But don't worry, it will soon be over." Now what is that supposed to mean?

Then it happened to me. The first fortune was ominous. "No one will ever love you the way that you love them." I thought about it. Maybe it was true. I came back to the restaurant a week later and I ordered the shrimp and I ate it and when I opened the fortune cookie I read, "Your friends are not who you think they are."

I became uneasy. I thought I would stay away for a few weeks. I ate Thai food instead. Italian. But the thing is, I still wasn't safe. No restaurants are safe—except maybe truckstops, or automats. Waiters, waitresses—they pretend to be kind. They bring us what we ask for. They ask us if there is anything else we want. They are solicitous of our health. They remember our names when we come back again.

They are as kind to us as if they were our own mothers, and we are familiar with them. Sometimes we pinch their fannies.

I don't like to cook for myself. I live alone, and there doesn't seem to be much point to it. Sometimes I dream about food—for instance, a cake, it was made of whipped cream. It was the size of a living room. Just as I was about to take a bite, a dancing girl kicked out of it. Then another dancing girl. A whole troop of dancing girls, in fact, all covered in whipped cream. They were delicious.

I like to eat food made by other people. It feels like a relationship. But you can't trust other people. Especially not waiters. They aren't our friends, you see. They aren't our mothers. They don't give us the food that we long for—not the food that we dream about—although they could. If they wanted to.

We ask them for recommendations about the menu, but they know so much more than that—if only they should choose to tell us. They do not choose to tell us. Their kindnesses are arbitrary, and not to be counted as lasting. We sit here in this world, and the food that they bring us isn't of this world, not entirely. They are not like us. They serve a great mystery.

I returned to the Chinese restaurant like a condemned man. I ate my last meal. A party of women in big hats and small dresses sat at the table next to me. They ordered their food and then departed for the bathroom. Did they ever come back? I never saw them come back.

The waiter brought me the check and a fortune cookie. I uncurled my fortune and read my fate. "You will die at the hands of a stranger." As I went away, the waiter smiled at me. His smile was inscrutable.

I sit here in my tree, eating takeout food, hauled up on a bit of string. I put my binoculars down to eat. Who knows what my fortune will say?

What color is the girl detective's hair?

Some people say that the girl detective is a natural blonde. Others say that she's a redhead, how could the girl detective be anything else? Her father just smiles and says she looks just like her mother. I myself am not even sure that the girl detective remembers the original color of her hair. She is a master of disguises. I feel I should make it clear that no one has ever seen the girl detective in the same room as the aged housekeeper. She and her father have often been seen dining out together, but I repeat, the girl detective is a master of disguises. She is capable of anything.

Further secret origins of the girl detective.

Some people say that a small child in a grocery store bit her. It was one of those children who are constantly asking their parents why the sky is blue and are there really giant alligators—formerly the pets of other small children—living in the sewers of the city and if China is directly below us, could we drill a hole and go right through the center of the earth and if so would we come up upside down and so on. This child, radioactive with curiosity, bit the girl detective, and in that instant the girl detective suddenly saw all of these answers, all at once. She was so overcome she had to lie down in the middle of the aisle with the breakfast cereal on one side and the canned tomatoes on the other, and the store manager came over and asked if she was all right. She wasn't all right, but she smiled and let him help her stand up again, and that night she went home and stitched the days of the week on her underwear, so that if she was ever run over by a car, at least it would be perfectly clear when the accident had occurred. She thought this would make her mother happy.

Why did the girl detective cross the road?

Because she thought she saw her mother.

Why did the girl detective's mother cross the road?

If only the girl detective knew!

The girl detective was very small when her mother left. No one ever speaks of her mother. It causes her father too much pain even to hear her name spoken. To see it written down. Possibly the girl detective was named after her mother and this is why we must not say her name.

No one has ever explained to the girl detective why her mother left, although it must have been to do something very important. Possibly she died. That would be important enough, almost forgivable.

In the girl detective's room there is a single photograph in a small gold frame of a woman, tall and with a very faint smile, rising up on her toes. Arms flung open. She is wearing a long skirt and a shirt with no sleeves, a pair of worn dancing shoes. She is holding a sheaf of wheat. She looks as if she is dancing. The girl detective suspects that this is her mother. She studies the photograph nightly. People dream about lost or stolen things, and this woman, her mother, is always in these dreams.

She remembers a woman walking in front of her. The girl detective was holding this woman's hand. The woman said something to her. It might have been something like, "Always look both ways," or "Always wash your hands after you use a public bathroom," or maybe "I love you," and then the woman stepped into the street. After that the girl detective isn't sure what happened. There was a van, red and gold, going fast around the corner. On the side was "Eat at Mom's Chinese Restaurant." Or maybe "Eat at Moon's." Maybe it hit the woman.

Maybe it stopped and the woman got in. She said her mother's name then, and no one said anything back.

The girl detective goes out to eat.

I only leave my tree to go to the bathroom. It's sort of like camping. I have a roll of toilet paper and a little shovel. At night I tie myself to the branch with a rope. But I don't really sleep much. It's about seven o'clock in the evening when the girl detective leaves her house. "Where are you going," I say, just to make conversation.

She says that she's going to that new restaurant downtown, if it's any of my business. She asks if I want to come, but I have plans. I can tell that something's up. She's disguised as a young woman. Her eyes are keen and they flash a lot. "Can you bring me back an order of steamed dumplings?" I call after her, "Some white rice?"

She pretends she doesn't hear me. Of course I follow her. She takes a bus. I climb between trees. It's kind of fun. Occasionally there aren't any trees and I have to make do with telephone poles, or water towers. Generally I keep off the ground.

There's a nice little potted ficus at Mom's Chinese Restaurant. I sit in it and ponder the menu. I try not to catch the waiter's eye. He's a tall, stern-looking man. The girl detective is obviously trying to make up her mind between the rolling beef and the glowing squid. Listed under appetizers, there's scallion pancakes, egg rolls with shrimp, and wantons (which I have ordered many times. But they always turn out to be wontons instead), also dancing girls. The girl detective orders a glass of water, no lemon. Then she asks the waiter, "Where are you from?"

"China," he says.

"I mean, where do you live now?" the girl detective says.

"China," he says. "I commute."

The girl detective tries again. "How long has this restaurant been here?"

"Sometimes, for quite a while," he says. "Don't forget to wash your hands before you eat."

The girl detective goes to the bathroom.

At the next table there are twelve women wearing dark glasses. They may have been sitting there for quite a while. They stand up, they file one by one into the women's bathroom. The girl detective sits for a minute. Then she follows them. After a minute I follow her.

No one stops me. Why should they? I step carefully from table to table. I slouch behind the flower arrangements.

In the bathroom there aren't any trees, so I climb up on the electric dryer and sit with my knees up by my ears and my hands around my knees. I try to look inconspicuous. There is only one stall and absolutely no sign of the twelve women. Maybe they're all in the same stall, but I can see under the door and I don't see any feet. The girl detective is washing her hands. She washes her hands thoughtfully, for a long time. Then she comes over and dries them. "What next?" I ask her.

Her eyes flash keenly. She pushes open the door of the stall with her foot. It swings. Both of us can see that the stall is empty. Furthermore there isn't even a toilet in it. Instead there is a staircase going down. A draft is coming up. I almost think I can hear alligators, scratching and slithering around somewhere further down the stairs.

The girl detective goes to the underworld.

She has a flashlight of course. She stands at the top of the stairs and looks back at me. The light from the flashlight puddles around her feet. "Are you coming or not?" she says. What can I say? I fall in love with the girl detective all over again. I come down off the dryer. "I guess," I say. We start down the stairs.

The underworld is everything I've been telling you. It's really big. We don't see any alligators, but that doesn't mean that there aren't any. It's dark. It's a little bit cool and I'm glad that I'm wearing my cardigan. There are trees with moss on them. The moss glows. I take to the trees. I swing from branch to branch. I was always good at gym. Beneath me the girl detective strides forward purposefully, her large feet lit up like two boats. I am in love with the top of her head, with the tidy part straight down the middle. I feel tenderly towards this part. I secretly vow to preserve it. Not one hair on her head shall come to harm.

But then we come to a river. It's a wide river and probably deep. I sit in a tree at the edge of the river, and I can't make up my mind to climb down. Not even for the sake of the part in the hair of the girl detective. She looks up at me and shrugs. "Suit yourself," she says.

"I'll wait right here," I say. There are cute little canoes by the side of the river. Some people say that the girl detective can walk on water, but I see her climb in one of the canoes. This isn't the kind of river that you want to stick your toes in. It's too spick-and-span. You might leave footprints.

I watch her go across the river. I see her get out on the other side. There is a nightclub on the other side, with a veranda and a big sign over the veranda. **DANCE WITH BEAUTIFUL GIRLS.** There is a woman standing on the veranda. People are dancing. There is music playing. Up in my tree, my feet are tapping air. Someone says, "Mom?" Someone embraces someone else. Everyone is dancing. "Where have you been?" someone says. "Spring cleaning," someone says.

It is hard to see what is going on across the river. Chinese waiters in elegant tuxedos are dipping dancing princesses. There are a lot of sequins. They are dancing so fast, things get blurry. Things run together. I think I see alligators dancing. I see a fat old man dancing with the girl detective's mother. Maybe even the housekeeper is dancing. It's hard to tell if their feet are even touching the ground. There are sparks. Fireworks. The musicians are dancing, too, but they don't stop playing. I'm dancing up in my tree. The leaves shake and the branch groans, but the branch doesn't break.

We dance for hours. Maybe for days. It's hard to tell when it stays dark all the time. Then there is a line of dancers coming across the river. They skip across the backs of the white alligators, who snap at their heels. They are hand in hand, spinning and turning and falling back, and leaping forward. It's hard to see them, they're moving so fast. It's so dark down here. Is that a dancing princess, or a bank robber? Is that a fat old man, or an alligator, or a housekeeper? I wish I knew. Is that the girl detective or is it her mother? One looks back at the other and smiles. She doesn't say a thing, she just smiles.

I look, and in the mossy glow they all look like the girl detective. Or maybe the girl detective looks like all of them. They all look so happy. Passing in the opposite direction is a line of Chinese waiters. They swing the first line as they pass. They cut across and dosey-do. They clap hands. They clutch each other, across the breast and the back, and tango. But the girl detectives keep up towards the restaurant and the bathroom and the secret staircase. The waiters keep on towards the water, towards the nightclub. Down in that nightclub, there's a bathroom. In the bathroom, there's another staircase. The waiters are going home to bed.

I'm exhausted. I can't keep up with the girl detectives. "Wait!" I yell. "Hold it for just a second. I'm coming with you."

They all turn and look back at me. I'm dizzy with all of that looking. I fall out of my tree. I hit the ground. Really, that's all I remember.

When I woke up.

Someone had carried me back to my tree and tucked me in. I was snug as a bug. I was back in the tree across the street from the girl detective's window. This time the blind was down. I couldn't see a thing.

The end of the girl detective?

Some people say that she never came back from the underworld.

The return of the girl detective.

I had to go to the airport for some reason. It's a long story. It was an important case. This wasn't that long ago. I hadn't been down out of the tree for very long. I was missing the tree.

I thought I saw the girl detective in the bar in Terminal B. She was sitting in one of the back booths, disguised as a fat old man. There was a napkin in front of her, folded into a giraffe. She was crying but there was the napkin folded into a giraffe—she had nothing to wipe her nose on. I would have gone over and given her my handkerchief, but someone sat down next to her. It was a kid about twelve years old. She had red hair. She was wearing overalls. She just sat next to him, and she put down another napkin. She didn't say a word to him. The old man blew his nose on it and I realized that he wasn't the girl detective at all. He was just an old man. It was the kid in the overalls—what a great disguise! Then the waitress came over to take their order. I wasn't sure about the waitress. Maybe she was the girl detective. But she gave me such a look—I had to get up and leave.

Why I got down out of the tree.

She came over and stood under the tree. She looked a lot like my mother. Get down out of that tree this instant! she said. Don't you know it's time for dinner?

pansolapia

JEFFREY FORD

Jeffrey Ford is the author of the novels *The Physiognomy*, *Memoranda*, *The Beyond*, *The Portrait of Mrs. Charbuque*, *The Girl in the Glass*, and *The Shadow Year*. His short fiction has been published in three collections: *The Fantasy Writer's Assistant*, *The Empire of Ice Cream*, and *The Drowned Life*. His fiction has won The World Fantasy Award, The Nebula Award, The Edgar Allan Poe Award, and *Gran Prix de l'Imaginaire*. He lives in New Jersey with his wife and two sons and teaches Literature and Writing at Brookdale Community College.

"Pansolapia" is the second story I ever bought from Ford—a wispy tale of mystery, myth, and tragic inevitability.

The woman of the palace, Vashmena, moves with the grace of the hornbills hunting in a sunset lake. Her black gown, like melting night, is studded with chips of quartz that catch the light of the torches and recreate the heavens. She is deep in meditation— now pacing, now swaying slightly, now standing still. When at rest, it is impossible to tell if she is breathing. The only signs that she is more than a statue are the twitch of a nostril and a quivering at the ends of her silken black hair. Then, like an illusion, she moves—slow as thick mist rolling – wide, arcing arm strokes and high, backward steps. She falls through space where speed has lost all meaning, and holds her long middle fingers curled to her palms. When she lands, back into perfect stillness, it is as if she has never moved at all.

Behind her green eyes roars an iron colored ocean. The waves are mountains and the troughs quick trips to hell. The sky is the color of dirt and the wind has a voice. "Sleep," it howls at the men lashed to the rigging of a lone, double masted ship. Nothing could be more frightening to them than its exquisite elocution, for its command is the voice of the woman they saw dance in the courtyard at Pansolapia. It follows them down beneath the waves, swamping their thoughts as the brine bursts their lungs. Their long hair rises up in wavy points toward the distant storm as the ship drifts into darkness. All hands grin. All hands stare at the woman in black, now moving like an eel, now posing like a rock upon a rock.

The stars shiver down her stomach as her hips swing with fluid speed, and the lion-pawed guard at the gates of the palace knows to let the sailors pass. He growls a command to proceed, which the long-haired foreigners take to be a challenge. They draw curved, serrated knives and wait for a fight. The old beast-man, Kilif, laughs at their weapons and steps aside. "Gusmashnease," he says, his only word, which means nothing, and the broadest of the men sheathes his blade and smiles. "Pansolapia?" asks the traveler, scanning the crumbling turrets of the impossible structure. Vashmena breathes out slowly through her nose as she watches, at an incredible distance, Kilif nod and brush away a tear.

Her voice vibrates, filling the courtyard and frightening the vultures into flight. One word, one syllable, gets beneath the bricks and loosens them. Imperceptibly, her ears prick up in response to the echo just as they do when the sailor calls to her down the long hall of columns leading to the carnivorous gardens. Her memory of running is played out in her pulse. A hundred yards away, she feels his breath at the back of her neck. His pursuit is the gentle tapping of her left foot. She crouches and then as quickly stands and begins to spin as the bearded foreigner suddenly wakes before dawn on the day he is to begin his journey to Pansolapia. Ardnith is his name, and he looks at his sleeping wife, wondering if he will return.

They hear a sound, like a sigh, as they pace quietly, so not to draw ghosts, through the corridors of the deserted palace. How could they know it is the sweep and swirl of her dress as she comes to rest in the courtyard of Pansolapia? The place is nothing like what they had wondered when the Shaman commanded them to go in search of the future. Ardnith's wife had wept at the order, for her recent nightmare had shown her their demise. "What is it?" asked Ardnith as he held her. "Gusmashnease," says the loyal Kilif sometime eight years hence, and the widow soon-to-be says less. Ardnith draws his blade as the first hungry blossom descends to devour him.

Her nipples harden as she recalls his touch, creating a new constellation across her chest. The sailors look up one night on their return journey and realize they are lost. "This is not our ocean," they cry after studying the stars. Young Freg holds tightly to the lock of hair he has stolen from the murdered Kilif, as if a lion's courage would now breathe through him. Ardnith knows immediately that they have been cursed by Vashmena. In the courtyard, she again breathes out, this time through her mouth, and the winds begin to trouble the ocean.

As the ship founders, he remembers taking her from behind in a mirrored chamber, and all he remembers is the illusion of her. She hides and watches as he couples with her image, but when he loses his seed it seeps into her reflection and then into her through her eyes. So now, as she dances, her stomach swells with the deception of the foreigner. She dances as she had for the company before they retreated through the phantom palace toward the harbor. As Ardnith sprints for his ship, the snail streaked walls and frayed tapestries disintegrate, bleeding atoms.

Vashmena falls suddenly back on the stones of the courtyard and opens her legs. She breathes now, only through her mouth, rapid, determined breaths. Her cries wake Ardnith's wife as he is preparing to leave. "Please, don't go," she whispers to him. "The Shaman is a fool," she says. "There is nothing beyond the rim of the world." He tells her he must go and heads for the door. He turns back to look at her as his lungs give their last breath to the rising ocean. Vashmena is dancing, she is giving birth. The Shaman is in his cave, chanting a lion-man to life from a scrap of hide, a tooth, a claw.

As the seaweed wraps around Ardnith's neck, his life plays itself out before his eyes. He sees his childhood, his father's battle scars, caribou moving through the early morning frost, icebergs colliding off shore, his wife's long blonde braid like a maze, his decision not to go. In that instant, Pansolapia is born, and Kilif shouts, "Gusmashnease," loud enough to wake the sleeping sailor. Ardnith rubs his eyes and opens them to see the Shaman, cradling the dream child in his arms. The sly old man spins like a woman dancing and steps away into the night. Then Ardnith hears the masts splinter and crack. The blossom consumes him with a maw of thorns, in a mirrored room, at the bottom of the ocean, next to his sleeping wife.

harbingers

SEVERNA PARK

Severna Park is the author of three novels and the winner of the 2001 Nebula Award for short fiction. She earned her Masters Degree from the Johns Hopkins Graduate Writing Seminars in 2004 and has recently completed a novel.

"Harbingers," published in 1999, depicted an Africa in 2006 that's little different from 2009: riven with the bloody civil wars that periodically break out on the continent. So, (unfortunately) the setting of this sf story about aliens and human interaction with them, has not dated at all.

In '06, Navardie and I found the aliens in a salty puddle at the top of a hill in what was, at the time, Tanzania. The hill was the only one for miles, spume from the meteor that had made Ngorongoro Crater Lake. Maybe the meteor had something to do with why they were there to begin with.

We didn't notice the aliens at first. It wasn't like they jumped out at us.

Navardie shaded her eyes against the noon sun and peered down at the blue eye of the lake in the valley below. "Look, AnnMarie," she said. "Lions!"

I was stretched out, belly-down, still breathless from the climb. Maybe she could see lions way down there, but to me they were just little flecks in the colorless dust. I rolled over and wiped the sweat and dirt off the jack in my wrist. I hadn't been online in the six months since I'd been in Tanzania, but rubbing the metal bud was a habit, like fingering a charm.

I squinted down the other side of the hill where our pilot was contemplating the Piper-Nocturne's starboard engine which, for its own reasons, had decided to quit for the day. From where we were, the plane seemed to be floating in a sea of tall grass with only the cockpit and tail fin visible. In a minute it might have sunk out of sight, into the warm earth of the savanna.

Nav looked over my shoulder. "You could've rented a plane that worked, AnnMarie."

"You're the one who wanted to go to Olduvai."

"I thought you wanted to come."

"I did," I said, "I do."

She rubbed her forehead and smeared white dust over her dark skin. "We'll never get back to Dar by sundown," she said. "What if someone finds out we're off base?"

"What're they going to do?" I said. "Kick us out of the country?"

They were going to anyway. Back in the capital, Dar es Salaam, the Tanzanian government was positioning itself to shut down the US YouthCorps, and that was us. Getting rid of us foreigners might appease the New African Congress guerrillas for a while, but everyone knew that US troops were waiting just north, in Kenya. If the NAC decided to flex its muscle in Tanzania like it had in Rwanda, and points south . . . well. Tourist trips to Olduvai would be out of the question for a long time.

Nav sighed and smoothed her short hair. "I'm thirsty," said Nav. "Did you bring a canteen?"

I hadn't. I grinned at her. "Should I run and get you one?" I might have. Nav was the kind of straight girl I get these terrible crushes on. She knew. I'm sure she knew. I angled a thumb at the lake below. "You could go down there."

"And get eaten by the lions?" She peered over the rocky edge of the hilltop. "There's water right here."

I looked. A pool of water cached in a hollow, shallow and hot blue, like the sky. It was just out of reach from where we were. "Probably contaminated," I said.

"Its fine," said Navardie. "It's just rain water."

She edged down over loose stones on her hands and knees. I sat up, deciding whether or not there was any chance of her falling off the hill and plunging to her death. I wouldn't have liked that.

"Wait a sec," I said, and scrambled down after her as she slid out of sight.

Nothing was growing around this puddle, which should have been a warning sign. Aliens below! Hell. I should have seen it coming.

She stuck her fingers in the water.

"Don't drink it," I said. "You know what kind of slime might be in there?"

She tasted her thumb. "It's salty."

"Mineral runoff," I said, and peered down, and saw them.

Just underneath the surface. No bigger than a big potato. Pale, soft, wrinkled like wads of paper. There were eight? Nine? Were they connected to each other?

I thought they were some kind of tuberous plant at first, or molting crustaceans, somehow trapped at 700 feet above sea level. Then I started thinking that these might be shallow-water cousins of those prehistoric fishes which traveling biologists "discover" on dinner dates with the local hunter-gatherers.

I also knew, even then, that the answer was, none of the above.

"What the fuck are those things?" said Nav, her salty thumb frozen, inches from her mouth.

"Hell if I know."

In the distance, the Piper's engine choked, then roared, over-gassed, revving high so we could hear it.

Navardie steadied herself against the gravel slope and stood. "Let's go," she said.

I stared at the things under the water. Polyps? Worms?

I put my hand in the water.

Tepid.

"AnnMarie!"

I reached deeper, and touched the nearest one.

Soft. Withery-feeling. Like the skin of a very old woman. It didn't seem to have any teeth or stingers. I put my hand around it.

"I want to take it back to the plane," I said, and expected her to object. When I looked up, she was rubbing her thumb—the one she'd dipped into the pool.

"It'll die," she said. "You can't take it out of there."

"It'll fit in a canteen," I insisted. "Will you get a canteen?"

She tucked her hand under her other arm. "Leave it, AnnMarie."

I hesitated. And then I felt it.

A twinge of curt refusal where my palm was touching it.

The sensation was like a color, pale violet.

And then it disappeared.

Not that slick, spiny twist of muscle, as in escaping fish. The Grub just faded—and then my hand was numb. The numbness froze around the jack in my wrist and shot up to my elbow. I jerked out of the water—deeper than I'd thought and empty now. The things— the Grubs—were gone.

Navardie grabbed my hand with fingers I couldn't feel. The skin around my jack had puckered and turned blue.

"Let's go," I said, "let's go!"

We ran down the side of the hill, back to the plane. The pilot, who thought we were out of our minds anyway, turned right around and took us home to Dar es Salaam. We never got to Olduvai. Not on that trip, anyway.

The YouthCorps doctor said it was just an allergic reaction to something I'd touched, and the numbness went away after a few hours. He did ask a lot of questions about what exactly we'd put our hands into, but neither Nav nor I gave him very helpful answers.

I'm not sure why. I mean, I never said to myself, Annie-girl, you touched alien flesh back there at Ngorongoro. I'm sure Navardie never said anything of the kind to herself either, or anyone else, but neither of us could shake the experience. The YouthCorps sent us out to do water sampling and crop evaluations for the locals, as usual, but nothing was the same.

Part of it was the planeloads of American troops at President Mwinyi International Airport. Part of it was the dream I was having. Up on the hill. Arm in the water. Thing disappears. Arm goes numb. Over and over and over. In two weeks, when the Tanzanian government decided we were spies and had to get out, I was almost too frazzled to care.

Navardie and I met Renata in the bar at The President Mwinyi Dar es Salaam Haven of Peace International Airport.

We were waiting to be banished and I assumed that Renata

was from the US Department of Foreign Affairs, which was why I answered her questions. She had a clipboard, and a cute little khaki outfit, and a nametag. Renata Frey. She had—I don't know—an aura of authority? It was more than that. The way her knee bumped mine under the table made my heart jump around. Brown eyes, a coffee-with-cream complexion, hair combed down with a minimum of fuss. She was maybe a year or two older than me. I thought she looked pretty darn good.

I could see her see through me and Navardie, deciding which categories we fit into. I could have told her what she wanted to know, but it was more interesting to watch her figure us out. Navardie and AnnMarie. Both left-wing, middle class, US of A rebels. Both suckered into the YouthCorps on the pretext of international good works, and then turned out as spies. Both pissed off about that. Nav; mahogany-red and sunburned. AnnMarie; sunburned-white, and smelling like aloe-gel.

I saw it when Renata came to the conclusion that Nav and I were *not* sleeping together. I saw Nav slide into Renata's heterosexual column.

Renata smiled her sparkly brown eyes at me, and I went into that *other* column.

"A shame you have to leave," she said. "Tanzania's a lovely country. This part of the continent is spectacular, if you know where to go."

"We were at Ngorongoro two weeks ago," said Nav, sipping on her third Kenya Extra Brau.

"Ah." Renata nodded at me. "Stunning, yes?"

"Yes," I said. "It's a shame we have to leave."

Renata flipped the pages on her clipboard. "Its not safe to stay, though. The New African Congress has a dozen nuclear warheads."

"That isn't true," I said. "Its a scare tactic by the guerrillas."

"Or a rumor started by the government," said Nav.

"I wouldn't want to hang around to find out for sure," said Renata.

"The real tragedy is that this is the place where it all began. You know? Cradle of human consciousness. Olduvia, homo erectus, the missing link and all that. A couple of warheads, and it's all gone." She snapped her fingers. "You look around and you just don't see a lot of progress in the last hundred thousand years. We might as well still be hitting each other over the head with rocks."

She gave Nav a challenging smile, and I could feel Nav decide never to be friends with her. If Renata hadn't been of a roundabout African descent, I think Nav would have nailed her right there for what bordered tentatively on racist comments.

"Progress?" I said, because Nav wasn't going to. "You mean the Africans in particular? There're wars like this everywhere."

"Exactly," said Renata. "There *are* wars like this everywhere. Don't you wonder why that is? After a hundred thousand years, shouldn't there be something new in the works?"

I glanced at Nav, who raised an eyebrow over the Extra Brau. This wasn't exactly the type of conversation one might expect to have with someone from the Department of Foreign Affairs.

"Uh," said Nav. "You mean, like, evolution?"

Renata nodded. "A lot of people are about to get killed for no good reason. You can make as many nice speeches about peace as you want. We still end up with dead bodies for the sake of food, mates, and territory."

"That's awfully simplistic," I started to say, but Nav'd had enough and was getting to her feet.

"Look at the time," she said. "When does our flight leave?"

I started to look at my watch, but Renata was taking an envelope off her clipboard. She opened it and put a photo on the table.

"Before you go," she said, "have a look at this."

I looked. The bar wasn't very bright and the picture wasn't very good, but I saw everything, instantly

At the far end of a dark room, was a fish tank—a big one. The Grubs floated, mostly below the surface, greenish, grayish, the color of internal organs. They were shaped like animal carcasses, without heads or legs, or tails. Wide in the middle, narrow at each end. They clung to each other the way elephants do, trunk to tail, trunk to tail, except it was impossible to tell the front from the back.

My arm went numb like it did in my dream.

Navardie rubbed her right hand, her face gone ashy under mahogany red.

"You saw them," said Renata.

We nodded.

"Where?" whispered Renata.

We looked at each other and back at her.

"Ngorongoro," said Renata, answering for us. "Two weeks ago." She got up fast enough to knock her chair over, flipped two business cards on the table, scooped up her photo and clipboard and all but ran out of the bar.

They were calling our flight. Navardie held my hand all the way to the gate. I couldn't figure out why I was so incredibly cold. Somewhere over the Atlantic, I finally looked at Renata's card.

Renata Frey, no phone, no address, no business or anything. Just a v-dress at the bottom—a net I've never heard of.

Brd.Lvndr.

"Board Lavender," said Navardie's crystalline image on my JackMac, via v-mail. "What is that? Some kind of cyberdyke thing? Have you logged on?"

Neither of us had mentioned it before, but I think we were both dwelling on it—them—Renata—for different reasons. It'd been four months since we came home, and now it was the very dead of winter. Almost Christmas. I was living in my mom's house in Arlington, Virginia. Nav was in Baltimore commuting to a civilian job at the Aberdeen Proving Grounds. I'd only seen her once since we'd gotten back, and I wasn't working. I didn't feel like it.

I missed the sun, the dust.

The breathless air of impending war.

I missed all that and my arm hurt. The skin around my jack

looked infected—soft and swollen and hot, but the doc said no. Just an allergic reaction to something I'd touched.

I hadn't logged on to Board Lavender. I'd come close, though.

And today. Well.

Something about Nav's message pushed me into slow motion. I cleared the JackMac's screen and her message vanished. The feeling of metal under my wrist, plug to socket, was cool, a relief. A wet rag to a fever.

I accessed mom's carrier, and typed in Renata's v-dress.

Brd.Lavender.

I felt a shock in the center of my palm.

Terminal Protocol?

I blinked but there was nothing on the screen. The ID request was all in my head, behind my eyes. I knew I was staring into space like a zombie. I certainly didn't know what the terminal protocol was. But there was a twinge in my arm. The air behind my eyes changed color.

And I was.

On Board.

Renata sits calmly on a big stone. Her eyes show the reflection of the landscape around us. The violet glass bowl of the sky. Dry hills and washed out gullies. I look around. This cyber site seems a lot like the scrub desert in southern California, but flatter. And hotter. The heat is curiously real. The stones and the horizon have a crystalline edges like they would in an everyday piece of v-mail, but this locale has more sensory data attached. It's disorienting, like an acid trip. In the distance I see faint traces of archaeological digs.

"This is Olduvai," I say.

Renata leans forward, brown eyes intent. "Come back," she says.

"Come back?" I say. "Where? To Africa?"

"I need you." She's not responding to me. It's a recording. She points to the ground. An airline ticket is lying in the dust. The destinations are; Baltimore to London. London to Cairo. Cairo to Dar es Salaam. Tanzania. My heart pounds. My cyber palms sweat in the cyber heat. If I pick up the ticket, the reservation info will be on my screen when I open my eyes. I can pack in half an hour. I can be there. I kneel down, and touch the ticket.

Olduvai fades to purple, then black.

Nav met me at the Baltimore-Washington International Airport and put a hard-copy of the Baltimore Sun on the lunch counter. The headline on the end-page of the WORLD section was:

Compromise Likely between Tanzanian Factions.

"Don't you believe it," said Nav.

"I don't."

"What're you going to do when you get there?" she asked. "Take that woman up to the hill and show her what we saw?"

"I don't know."

"You'd better figure it out," said Nav, and lowered her voice. "What if she's the wrong person to find them? What if you're—I don't know—betraying them or something?"

"I think they belong to her," I said.

"Why can't she find them without you?"

Because I can feel those things in my arm. I'm like a weather vane or a divining rod. Renata can point me in the right direction and I can lead her right to them. "I have to go back," I said.

"You're going to get shot," she whispered.

"I'll be okay." I got up and gave her a nervous little kiss on the cheek. She walked me to the International gate, crossed her arms and watched me disappear down the corridor.

Tanzanian sunlight streamed into Renata's apartment. It tinted the whitewashed shadows, changing them from dull gray to mauve and made the cheap flat look as opulent as a painting by Delacroix. Outside the window in the marketplace below, biting black flies tormented the black-clad women. Up here on the third floor, we were unmolested, but it was just as hot.

I sat on the bed by the window waiting for the periodic breeze from the fan on the corner table as it buzzed back and forth in the stifling afternoon. Renata sat across the room in the only chair, fidgeting with the dirty white wire that ran from the jack in her wrist to the black box in her lap as she waited for Board Lavender. Her cheeks were flushed with the heat and her eyes were closed, but it seemed as though she was staring intently at the water stain on the wall above the window. The one we both thought looked like a Grub.

Renata jerked in the chair and turned to me. "Jack in," she said. "I'm there."

I opened the JackMac next to me on the mattress and slid the chrome plug into the metal socket in my wrist.

The shock in the center of my palm was the connect signal.

The taste in my mouth was the dust.

Dry hills. Washed out gullies. Olduvai.

Nav hurries toward us, raising puffs of dust, panting. *You left too soon, AnnMarie. The Grub things are at Aberdeen.*

Again, the weird realism. Sweat is beading on Nav's upper lip. It glitters in the tight curls around her forehead. I can almost smell her perfume.

She makes a wildly impatient motion, and I can feel the current in the air as she moves. *I think they know I was at Ngorongoro. I think they know everything and they're waiting to see what I do next.*

How many Grubs do they have? asks Renata.

There were seven to begin with. Something happened to one of them. By the time they got into the big tank—you know—the one you showed us in the picture at the airport—

She's so scared I can almost feel her heart pounding. I take her hand and my arm tingles where her thumb brushes it.

Calm down, says Renata. *Just think about it.* She makes an abstract motion with her hands, as though she's making an adjustment on a keyboard and a big window opens in the violet sky. Through it, I can see a long black table with a dozen people seated around it.

Several are in uniform. One is an Army colonel. Everyone in the room has a three-inch-thick bound report in front of them.

This is the meeting they asked you to attend? says Renata.

Nav swallows, then nods.

Did they tell you why you were invited?

No, says Nav.

In the recording—or whatever it is—I can see Nav sitting uncomfortably at the edge of a wooden chair, a white lab coat over her blue suit. At the far end of the room, there are two fish tanks. One is small, a plexi travel tank on a wheeled cart. The Grubs are in that one, six of them, each about the size of a deflated football, floating mostly below the surface. The other one must be have a hundred gallons salt water in it, and Nav is right. I recognize it from the photo Renata showed us in the airport. The only thing that's different is that the Grubs are in the wrong tank.

I squint at the images, and feel the muscles in my face move uselessly.

The Grubs are the same. Greenish, grayish. The color of internal organs.

There were seven of those things at Ngorongoro, I say.

I know, says Renata.

A rustle of paper as the people around the table fold back the cover page of the report. Navardie quickly does the same.

The first line of the first page reads:

Genetic inconsistencies, anatomical differences, and unfamiliar DNA configurations make for a plausible argument that the Ngorongoro Organisms (N. O.) are not native to this biosphere.

They've done a dissection, says Renata. *At least now we know for sure.*

Nav looks at me, eyes wide. She doesn't say it, but her expression does.

We?

The Colonel steeples his fingers and frowns across the table at Navardie.

I cannot overemphasize the importance of keeping this matter secure, he says. *There is evidence already that the secrecy of this project has been compromised.*

Why is he looking at you like that? I say.

Watch the Grubs, says Renata.

One Grub, one Ngorongoro Organism, quivers in the plexiglass travel tank. It disengages from its neighbor. No one in the room is watching except the recorded Nav, who I can *feel* is holding her breath. The colonel turns to the next page. Everyone else does the same—except for Nav, whose thumb has a twinge in it—a latent ache, like the pain in my arm. As she watches, the disengaged Grub slowly disappears. Just fades from view. And just as slowly, reappears in the big tank, plain as day.

One by one, the Grubs in the travel tank do the same. One by one, eyes around the long black table turn away from the Ngorongoro Organism report, and stare at the silent show at the end of the room.

Disengage. Disappear. Reappear.

No more spectacular than an eyeblink.

One, two, three.

Four, five, six.

The open window vanishes in the violet sky.

You have to get one of them out, says Renata. *They'll kill them all.*

Nav turns to her in disbelief. *How am I supposed to do that? Do you know how tight the security is?*

Don't try anything heroic, says Renata. *The Grubs can "target" a similar saline environment within a 200 mile range and get away from Aberdeen on their own. All you have to do is take a sample of water from the tank and duplicate it in a bathtub—anything about that size—and wait. You'll only get one, but that's all we need. You'll have to hurry. The political situation here is deteriorating.*

You're out of your fucking mind, says Nav, but Renata has disappeared, unplugged, expecting her will to be done.

Nav turns to me, sweat glittering under her lip. *Who the hell is she talking about when she says "we?"*

I don't have any idea.

You're sleeping with her, says Nav accusingly. *Doesn't she let you ask questions?*

The truth is, I'm afraid we'll stop having sex if I start asking questions like, *Renata, are the Grubs some kind of, um, you know, human-alien evolutionary link or something?* She'd laugh in my face and find herself another divining rod.

It just never came up in conversation, I say uneasily.

Jesus, AnnMarie. You're sleeping with an insane woman who wants us to kidnap aliens for her, and you won't ask questions?

What can I say to that? *You're jealous?* But Nav is gone too. I fumble inside my wrist, unplug, and blink into the apartment where the suffocating waft from the corner fan blows across my face.

In the distance, I can hear gunfire.

Tonight the shots came from the next roof over, no more than ten yards away. Stray bullets came through the window, *pok-pok-pok*, embedding themselves in the far wall of our single room as Renata and I huddled together under the table. From the street, a man shouted in shrill Swahili.

Renata pressed against my shoulder, eyes closed. The wire from the black box bobbed against her wrist, moving with her pulse.

"Did they hit the dish?" I whispered. "Can't you connect?"

Renata didn't answer right away. She pushed her body against me, groped for my wrist socket and slid the plug home.

Not Board Lavender this time. We're in Nav's Baltimore apartment.

I look around to be sure. I've only been here once, but it's her place all right. It's a one-room efficiency with a battered green sofa bed, a dining table and two wooden chairs. There's a fake fireplace with carvings from Tanzania arranged on the mantle. Bolts of kinte cloth hang over the nasty peeling paint on the walls. Here and there she's left the plaster uncovered so she can tape up photos. Zebras and lions. There's a big eight by ten of her and me in front of the YouthCorps station in Dar.

There are three doors. One leads to the bathroom, the other to the kitchen. The third, which leads to the staircase outside is flanked by two small suitcases.

I was thinking at first that Nav had set this up as a virtual home-site, but the tech is too high for anything she could afford. I reach out to touch the wall, and it's solid. I turn to Renata, who's standing behind me.

What is all this? I whisper.

We're online, she says, as if that should explain everything. *Listen.*

For what? I can hear sirens outside—perfectly normal for this area. Nav lives three floors above East Baltimore Street. There's traffic day and night. The firetruck or police, or whatever it is, fades, and I hear water running behind the closed bathroom door. I frown at the window shade pulled halfway down. It was night in our Tanzanian apartment. It should be broad daylight here and Nav should be at work. But it's dark outside. According to the clock, it's a little after eleven.

She's here? I ask Renata. *But it should be daylight.*

It's twenty hours later, says Renata.

How? I ask, but she never tells me anything, and doesn't answer this time either.

Shouldn't we knock? I say.

You can try. Renata starts for the bathroom. I scuff nervously along behind her.

Hey Nav, I say. *Guess what?* My voice seems trapped inside my own head, the way it sounds when your ears are plugged. There's no resonance in the room. I don't think Nav can hear us. I realize I'm expecting to be *feel* her presence—not just hear her. The realization is disorienting. For a second, I'm not sure we're here at all.

Renata pauses at the bathroom door, lays her palm against the surface, and then slides through the door without opening it.

Nav—? My palm goes through wood and chipped enamel paint as though it's air. So does the rest of me.

Inside, Nav has no idea we're watching. She's squirting the contents of a syringe into a half-filled bathtub. A fishtank thermometer floats under the faucet, showing ninety eight point six degrees.

Renata nods. *Good. Just like the Aberdeen tank.*

Navardie stirs gingerly with the tip of the needle, swirling over the blue, no-slip flowers which spread like peculiar fungus over the bottom of the tub. The bathroom is blue, with one window which would look out over the busy street if it wasn't painted aquamarine. Nav stands up, puts the empty syringe in the sink and smoothes her hair in the mirror. Dull light from the aqua window edges her dark skin, making bluish tints in her blackness and green flecks in her eyes.

She runs her fingers along the grimy back edge of the mirror where it doesn't quite meet the wall and pulls out her passport. The ticket and list of connecting flights is there too. She spreads the paper open and I peer over her shoulder. From Baltimore, Air Egypt flight 382 to London, to Cairo, to Dar es Salaam.

She rubs at the lettering on the dark blue leatherette of the passport's cover like she could wipe it away with her thumb.

United States of America

YouthCorps Volunteer

She should have a different passport, I whisper, forgetting she can't hear. *She can't fly into Tanzania with that. They'll shoot her as a spy. Can't you get her a new one?*

Too late, says Renata. *There's no time.*

Outside, a police car rushes past, a meteoric, red-shift shriek in the street below.

There's a weird taste in the air, like raw fish and lime. Then the water in the tub ripples and I look down to see the Grub.

Grub in the tub.

Nav stares at it and almost laughs. She crouches down to examine it, but the thing shows no more sign of life than it did at Aberdeen. Its wrinkled grayish skin has dried on top where the salt water doesn't touch it, tinted blue by the streetlight through the painted window. At best, it appears to be some helpless, prematurely born thing.

Nav's JackMac is leaning against the bathroom wastebasket. She unplugs the electric toothbrush, connects the Mac's power cord, then plugs herself in.

AnnMarie?

The bathroom fades to the glaring cyber-brightness of Olduvai. To my surprise, only the two of us are in the desert. Renata is still a plane away in the blue bathroom ghosting through, like a bad image on TV. The bathtub and the Grub floating in it flicker in and out of existence as a trough of water in the arid sand. Renata stands by the sink, half visible, but *I* am solid enough to cast a shadow.

Navardie! Now I can feel her. Sweat is starting under her breasts. She has a headache. I don't think she's slept recently.

There you are. She frowns past me. *There's something wrong. I can still see my bathroom.*

I wonder if she can see Renata. *I know. So can I.*

She looks around. *Where's your girlfriend?*

I point at Renata leaning over the tub. *Over there.*

Nav squinted and shrugged. *Just tell her I've got it. I'm taking it to the airport. Here's the flight number.* She writes it in the air with her finger—a swirl of pink neon. *See you both tomorrow.* She reaches for her socket, but I grab her arm.

Nav, listen-—I have to stop myself. What am I going to say? We're in your apartment? I can feel everything you're doing? Her arm stiffens and she jabs a finger down the shallow hill to the washed-out gully below.

Jesus! Who the hell is that?

Something is moving in the distance. Renata? I shade my eyes but I know there can't be anyone else here except for us. No one has access codes to Board Lavender and Renata has told me those codes are hard-wired, right-brain, non-verbal recalls. We couldn't reveal them if we tried.

But it isn't Renata. She's much darker, broad-faced and naked to the waist. She's walking briskly along the dry riverbed, and seems human but smaller, somehow rougher-looking than she ought to be.

Renata? I say, because it can't be anyone else.

The woman looks up with a flat, almost retarded expression.

Who are you? demands Navardie. *What are you doing on this board?*

Take me home, replies the woman. *And hurry. Someone's coming.*

I feel Nav's heart seize and swell to fill her throat. She yanks the plug out of her arm. The desert blinks away and I'm a ghost again in her dark apartment.

Renata is elbow-deep in bathwater, her hands all over the Grub.

The phone is ringing in the other room, and I have the feeling its been ringing for some time. Nav bolts out of the bathroom as her machine picks up the call, but the line disconnects. Seconds later, the phone rings again. The machine answers, but whoever it is, hangs up.

There was someone on the Board, I say to Renata, trying to yell for emphasis inside the deadened sound of my own head. *I thought it was you, but it was this woman—she wasn't quite—I don't know—she was—*

Renata looks up with an intense, strained expression. *Someone's coming*, she says.

Nav rushes in with an old thermos jug. It's big enough for the Grub, small enough to fit into carry-on luggage. The phone trumpets in the next room. The thermos slips out of her sweaty hands and tumbles to the floor.

The crunching glass inside is a defeating sound.

Navardie stands trembling by the tub while the phone rings, stops, and rings again.

Renata takes my hand. The apartment fades and she pushes me onto my back in the warm sand.

The cut-glass color of Olduvai's sky presses down on me as her hands slide under my shirt.

What're you doing? What're you-—I shove her away, but my fingers slip on her wet arms. Not her arms—the slick porcelain of the tub. In the desert, the water trough in the sand widens, darkens to a bathwater blue, lukewarm in the bright heat of the day. Fingers tangle in my clothes, and I feel Nav taking off her underpants, dropping them next to the sink. Grit inside my socks dissolves into the bottom of the smooth blue tub. Renata is touching and probing the part of me lying oblivious in her desert, while the rest of me slides inside of Nav.

Not the way I've fantasized it, though.

I find myself in Nav's blue dress, in Nav's dark body, standing with one leg knee-deep in warm water, steadying herself—myself— with one hand on the sill of the aquamarine window.

The Grub has drifted to the far end of the tub, near the drain under the chipped chrome faucet. Nav and I put our other foot in. The surface of the water is starting to feel nearly gelatinous. We bunch the skirt up around our thighs, not taking our eyes off the Grub, which is floating, iceberg-like, mostly submerged. We sit down, feeling weightless and ridiculous, stupid, if truth be told. The dress floats for a moment, then sinks, heaping into a warmish mass against the small of our back. Nav has no idea what she's doing in the tub, but *I* have a sneaking suspicion. In the desert, Renata pulls my pants all the way off. Inside Nav, I'm no more solid than a thought, and screaming at her to get *out of the tub* has no effect. She pulls her knees up against her chest, feet together, toes aimed at the mucus-colored glob. It floats closer with some non-existent current, drifts past her knees and touches the inside of her thigh.

I can feel Renata's palms between my legs, cool in the desert heat.

The Grub is warmer than the water, thin and papery. I can feel it against Nav's crotch, not sure where it should go—even with Renata guiding it. Nav's fingers flutter over her belly, but she absolutely cannot bring herself to touch it. It blunders against her labia, then presses her vagina, slick and insubstantial as a menstrual clot. We dare to peer down between our legs, but there's nothing there to see. Nothing in the tub but Navardie and a whitish trail of slime leading out from under her skirt. Inside, I can feel it moving around, and we realize it's searching for the next opening.

A massive cramp rolls through us as it finds the end of Nav's cervix and tries to squeeze through. Navardie shoves one finger and a thumb inside herself, finds the edge of the thin wet membrane and grabs it with her fingernails. The Grub squirms and I can feel it pulling. A spasm twists through us, clamping her uterus like a pair of pliers. I get a pincer grip on the Grub and a gray, damp piece of it comes away with my fingers. Nav lets out a shriek as it roils and blunders inside her. Then the cramps change. Deeper. Her belly swells like a bad cartoon. It's transferred, like it did from in tank at Aberdeen, and abruptly, Renata's gritty hands are gone. I'm out of Nav's swollen body. I'm a ghost in the apartment again.

Navardie leans back in the tub, panting, holding her belly. The saline content of her blood, her various uterine fluids must be within its parameters of survival. She lays her head against the cool porcelain, breathing hard.

At the door to her apartment, someone is knocking, calling her name, now pounding on the flimsy plasterboard. Navardie lurches out of the tub and grabs her passport, awkwardly wringing out the heavy blue fabric of her dress. I follow her helplessly to the bedroom window where she doubles over pushing against fifty years of paint and her own pain. The window opens halfway and she squeezes out onto the fire escape.

Below is a concrete alley, trash cans, garbage everywhere. One end of the alley opens on West Baltimore Street, where, under the sodium orange street lights, I can see the featureless cars the military uses when it wants to be discreet.

I follow her down the black iron grillwork, not sure if the pounding on her door has stopped or if it's being drowned out by the approaching sirens. She scrambles down the wobbly metal stairs. The other end of the alley comes out between two apartment buildings on Pratt, where its easy to catch a cab to the airport.

One flight down. An old man sits inside the window, watching the evening news.

Compromise likely . . .

Two flights down. A light comes on. Dogs bark frantically.

The last flight ends at a fifteen foot drop to the pile of garbage. Navardie stuffs the passport inside the top of the dress and squats. She inches forward until her knees are dangling over the orange-lit darkness and the scurry of startled rats. She slides over the end of the fire escape, scraping the backs of her legs. She turns and makes an ungraceful twist, half falling grabbing the iron bars with both hands. Tires squeal in the street, red and blue lights glare over the somber sodium orange. A police car jerks to a stop at the mouth of the alley. For a moment, she swings there.

I crouch over her as she dangles, soaked and terrified, belly distended. The taste of raw fish is making me nauseous beyond description. I open my mouth to scream for Renata, and a stifling heat envelopes us, thick as dust, pale as violet. The alley brightens. Nav's hands slip on the rough iron and she drops out of sight.

Not into the garbage, or the arms of the police. Just out of sight.

I blink and open my eyes as Renata pulls the plug out of my wrist.

"What was *that?* What do you think you're *doing?*" I jumped up in the Tanzanian night, ready to sock her right in the mouth.

"Get down," she whispered. "You'll get hit."

Automatic weapons rattled in the street. She grabbed my wrists and pulled me onto the floor again. In the dim light from the street outside, she looked exhausted.

In that second I could see through her. She was as alien as the Grub, just as out of place here as it had been in Nav's bathtub. She was just as scared as I was. I would have felt sorrier for her, but she was using me—me *and* Nav for something I had no way to define.

"Where's Nav?" I demanded.

"You can plug in and find out—"

"I don't *want* to plug in and find out. I want *you* to tell me."

Renata's body slumped against the cool plaster wall. "She's at the airport. She's safe. She'll catch her plane in half an hour. We know she lands in Dar tomorrow afternoon."

"We?" I demanded. "Who's we?"

Renata didn't answer. She moved closer, put her arms around me, and let out her breath against my ear.

Far below our window a man let out a rich, satisfied laugh.

The next day the marketplace was deserted except for the flies. Bullet holes stippled the near wall of the building next door. There was a dead body, too, but the angle of the window was wrong, and I couldn't tell if it was a human or some unlucky animal. All I could see were the flies.

Renata took the car keys out of her pocket and checked her watch again. "Are you ready?"

We'd waited as long as we could for Navardie's plane. We knew it took off from BWI on schedule and we knew she was on it. She'd connected in London, and should have taken off from Cairo hours ago. We would have known more about the fighting around us, but our satellite dish had been shot to pieces just before dawn and we couldn't eavesdrop on the BBC anymore. All I could find locally were a few foreign reporters online with their own board, daring each other to go out in the streets. We might have done better if we'd had something primitive, like a radio, or even a walkie talkie.

"They'll cut off the airport," I said for the fiftieth time. "It's the first thing they'll do."

"We'll come around from the other side, by the runway. It's easy."

None of this was going to be easy. "What if the plane doesn't come?" I said. "They must know what's going on. Don't you think they'll land somewhere else? Like Nairobi?"

"No," said Renata. "We know it lands here." She looked at her watch again. "Let's go."

Outside, distant bullets whined though the hot morning air. Somewhere down the street, I heard a woman screaming.

Renata's car was parked in an alley behind our building. She'd shown it to me before, but I'd never thought it worked. It was a roofless old Toyota LandCruiser with an unmuffled engine, and when she started it, it was so loud there was no way to pretend we might casually drive through Dar without being noticed.

I fastened my seatbelt thinking maybe I shouldn't. If armed guerrillas attacked us, I planned to leap from the car and run run run until I found Nav. Nothing would stop me.

Renata shoved the car into gear, but I put a hand on her arm.

"Look," I yelled over the engine. "You're from the future, right? You must have all kinds of doodads and technology. Why do we have to drive through a war zone for you to get your alien? Just zap them out! Why do you have to risk your neck? Or my neck?"

She narrowed her eyes at me. Sweat trickled down her cheek. "Zap?" she shouted.

"You know what I mean."

She wiped her face. Her hand was trembling. "Stay here if you're afraid."

As *if* she'd really let me do that. I had a sudden flash of my body under hers in her desert while the rest of me slid into the tub with Nav. Why was she even letting me argue? "Why the hell am *I* part of this?" I demanded. "And why did you make Nav take that thing inside her body? Why didn't *you* do it?"

Her tidy mask of self control disappeared. She opened her mouth and shrieked at me. "My *real* contacts were executed before I got here! How *else* was I supposed to get it over three thousand miles of water?"

I stared at her while the engine roared. She stopped looking at me, and glared over the steering wheel instead. I watched as she gulped down all that desperation and fury and made her face settle into its usual fearless pragmatism.

"We're going to get killed," I said. "Is that right? I mean, do you already know?"

She shook her head. More like a shudder. She slammed the Toyota into gear. "I don't think so."

"You don't *think* so?" I yelled, and we roared out onto the narrow street.

On a good day, in normal traffic, The President Mwinyi Dar es Salaam Haven of Peace International Airport was a good hour away. Now, with most of the shooting on the rooftops along the main streets, Renata gunned the car through the deserted souks, avoiding the fighting downtown. I thought the trip would take hours, except I'd never driven with her before.

She'd punch the accelerator down, yank the handbrake up, and heel the Toyota into screeching right-angle turns. It was too loud to complain, so I just hung on, one hand cemented around the rollbar, one clamped to my side of the windscreen, not trusting the stringy seatbelt as it cut into my vital organs.

I blinked away from the oncoming rush of narrow walls long enough to see the strip of sky above us, interrupted by laundry lines. Smoke from the burning buildings downtown was blowing in like bad weather.

Another corner and the empty alleyways were history. Under the dust and lowering smoke, donkeys and chickens, dogs and bicycles blocked the way ahead. Crowds of burdened women crammed the street, their youngest children slung across their backs, their worldly goods balanced on their heads in baskets.

We inched along until Renata found a narrow drive between two houses and squeezed the Toyota into it, scraping the walls with the stubs of her rearview mirrors. We bumped over a stack of metal poles and came out on the shallow banks of a stream. The stream was apparently open drainage for the neighborhood, and goats wandered through the big stones, searching for trash. There were no people. Only wooden houses patched with corrugated tin and plastic bags cluttering the far side of the bank. Beyond them, the airport fence quivered in the midday swelter.

We both looked up as the plane came into view, tilted ever so slightly for its final approach to the airport.

"Is that the one she's on?" asked Renata.

"Why are you asking me?"

Impatience flickered over her face. "Because you should be able to feel her. You should be able to feel them both."

I looked up at the plane again and across the unprotected stretch of dry gully. Of course I could feel her. I was afraid to close my eyes because if I did I would find myself in the seat next to Nav. I would be able to see our satellite dish shattered like an eggshell, and I would feel Nav's panic solidify. What was she supposed to do if the plane was allowed to land? Show her passport, give her charming smile and move on? She'd already torn the passport to shreds and thrown it into the chemical waters of the toilet. The Grub was making her as sick as a truly pregnant woman, and if I blinked, I'd be able to see the clear combination of vomit and torn paper, floating in viscous blue liquid.

I swallowed against the taste of puke in my throat. "You can't cross here," I said. "It's full of snipers."

"We don't have a choice," said Renata. "Hang on."

She gunned the Toyota over the rocky drainage ditch, and I grabbed whatever I could to keep from being thrown out of the car. The slums of Dar jounced in nauseating, unfocused motion. Up ahead, I could make out the blurry, leaping forms of the goats as they rushed across this ditch to get out of our way.

Rocks scraped the bottom of the car and something came loose with a high-pitched rattle. I turned to Renata, mouth open to tell her. She ducked sideways and bullets chattered through her side of the windshield.

I yanked open the seatbelt, but I didn't jump out of the car and run. I shoved myself under the dashboard, cheek and elbows pressed against the torn vinyl seat. Renata drove like hell unchained, crouched over sideways, her head sticking out the door. She veered in between two high cinderblock walls, hit the brakes and stared at me, jammed under the dashboard. Her dark hair stuck out in all directions. Her face was waxy and damp as fresh bread dough. "Are you hurt?" she whispered, and pulled me up, with slick, quivering hands.

Further ahead, the houses thinned out and we found the maintenance gate for the runway. It had already been broken open by someone with a much larger vehicle. Twisted chainlink hung like a tangle of gray string.

Renata pulled through the rip in the fence, stopped and took a pair of binoculars out from under the seat. Between us and the concrete walls of the blockhouse terminal, soldiers swarmed around a dirty white DC-10. The passengers stood underneath the tail section, the only shade on the asphalt tarmac.

Renata squinted over the black eyepieces and sucked a breath through her teeth. "I think they're collecting passports."

"Can you see her?"

Renata shook her head and gave me the binocs.

The breathless waves of heat made the image about as clear as objects under rushing water. I squinted and focused, searching the blurs for Navardie's face.

I found three or four middle-aged white men. A family from India. Three women, very dark, all too tall to be Navardie.

"She has to be there," said Renata.

"She is." I couldn't see her, but I could feel the Grub. "How're we going to get her out of there? We'll never get her out."

Renata caught my wrist in her sweaty fingers. She pulled me around in the torn vinyl seat so we were facing each other, and pressed her thumb over the socket in my wrist. She clapped her hand over my eyes before I could say anything, pressing my eyelids down like I was a corpse already. A pain like sharp needles stabbed up the length of my arm.

I didn't even need Board Lavender anymore.

I was inside Nav's body, sweating and nauseous in the shadow of the plane. She swayed in the blast-furnace afternoon and I smelled the subtle odor of other peoples' fear as the soldiers moved through the crowd with a satchel of confiscated identity papers.

Can she feel me? Does she know I'm here? *Nav?* I want to shake her, to make her trembling legs *move*. But she'll just get shot in the back if she tries to escape. The most I can do is show her the Toyota, a long way off, quivering like a mirage. She blinks and takes a sharp breath, but we both know it's too far.

At least it is for her.

The Grub twists underneath her blue dress. We're melting like a candle with this *thing* churning inside while the heat penetrates the soles of our shoes, our clothes, her skin. Anyone, she thinks, anyone can tell this creature is not a child. They may shoot her because it's so obvious that she's carrying a monster in her belly.

A soldier steps in front of her. "Passport."

He's taller than she is, but she can't look up because any motion will make her faint. All she can see is his rumpled uniform shirt hanging loosely over dusty farmer's trousers.

"Passport." This time the gun comes up.

She tries to spread her hands and shrug, but her fingers only get as far as her belly. They flutter, not protective, but pointing out the culprit who brought her here.

The soldier in his farmer's trousers grabs her shoulder and shakes her. Behind him, four more men are pointing rifles at her.

The Grub moves back and forth in her womb, like an animal in a cage.

Ngorongoro is a three hundred miles away. It can't make the leap home any more than Nav can make a run for the Toyota.

AnnMarie, says Renata's voice, very clearly. *Take it.*

"What?" I hear myself saying. *What?*

The Grub lunges and Nav shrieks in agony. Hot fluid sluices down her legs. Her belly heaves, unearthly and demonic. The soldier lets go, stepping back in horrified amazement. He brings his rifle up. In very slow motion, we watch him pull the trigger. The second lags, stretching like taffy, and I can feel the Grub separate. A rushing breath of freshly-turned earth invades Nav's lungs and envelopes her, thick and purple as fog.

And that thing was in *me*. It filled me from the inside out, swelling like a water balloon under my clothes, stretching and pressing every organ I had. All I could do was scream my head off as Renata drove down the runway, faster than any bullet. She flew through the tangled gate, past the crumbling urban edge of Dar, and through waist-high grass of the surrounding plains, heading due north, to Ngorongoro.

"Nav!" I shrieked. "Where's Nav?" Because I couldn't feel her anymore.

"She's gone," shouted Renata.

"Shot!" I screamed. "You let them shoot her, you *bitch!*"

"No," she said. "I let it save her."

It took a week to reach the hill at Ngorongoro, driving overland from Dar. The troops on the road kept us off the highway most of the time. We ran out of gas and had to steal more. It all seemed like a useless exercise. We should have headed for the Kenyan border and gone to Nairobi where it was safer. But Renata was driving, not saying much. It was the Grub that was speaking to me, showing me things. Cyber things. It had me up at Ngorongoro and back in the car. It flew me over the points in between—Kilimanjaro, and every little town, from Singida to Oldeani. If the Grub could have had an emotion, I guess I would have said it was excited to be going home.

Finally it showed me Nav, with her toes in the salty pool on top of the hill.

I opened my eyes in the afternoon heat. Renata had stopped under the only tree for fifty miles and was drinking from a canteen.

"I saw her," I pushed myself and my belly up straight in the seat. "I just saw her. Where is she?"

"It'll be easier to explain once we get to Ngorongoro," said Renata. "You can jack in and talk her when we get there."

"But she's dead," I said.

Renata dabbed at a drop of water under her lip. "Not exactly."

"What the hell do you mean by that? I just saw her on your board."

"Its hard to explain," said Renata. "But it's not a board. It's a bridge. Or a tunnel."

"To where?"

"To my time," she said.

I leaned back in the seat to stare at the flawless sky. The ache in my arm, the beating of the hot, dry wind—everything was starting to merge into an unbelievable hallucination where Renata was a time traveler and the Grubs had the power to change—everything.

"I don't believe you," I said.

"I know," said Renata. "It really doesn't matter what you believe. Except that your friend isn't really dead."

Cyber Kilimanjaro rises in the crystalline north and for the first time in a long time, Navardie is relaxing. The gravel slopes of the hill crumble downward, merging far below with the sapphire eye of Ngorongoro crater. Days have passed, she's fairly sure, but she can't decide how long she's been here.

She's keeping an eye out for the Toyota. Annmarie will give birth to whatever it is when she gets here with Renata, so Nav keeps a close watch on the valley below. She's been seeing a lot of things down there in the meantime. Lions. Zebras. A giraffe or two.

As for the Grub . . . as distant as it is inside of Annmarie's body, Nav can tell that it's changed. The indistinct bloat is more defined. It has an arm, a leg, a small, soft skull. It kicks now instead of lunging.

Nav shades her eyes in the low cyber sun. There's that woman again. Navardie can see her clearly from up here. Flat-faced. Dark skinned. She gets closer every day, shambling but purposeful. A midwife, thinks Nav. She looks for all the world like a cross between a chimpanzee and a more fully human being.

Perhaps that's exactly what she is.

frankenstein's daughter

MAUREEN F. McHUGH

Maureen McHugh is an award winning short story writer and novelist. Her books include the Tiptree Award winner, *China Mountain Zhang* and the short story collection, *Mothers & Other Monsters*. Along with Steve Peters and Behnam Karbassi, she is a partner in No Mimes Media, which produces immersive, interactive narratives. She has worked on projects for Nine Inch Nails, the *Watchmen* movie, and the Halo video game franchise. She lives in Austin, Texas.

"Frankenstein's Daughter" deals with the ripple effect of miraculous new technologies on those not directly affected by their use.

I'm at the mall with my sister Cara, doing my robot imitation. *Zzzt-choo. Zzzt. Zzzt.* Pivot on my heel stiffly, 45 degrees, readjust forward, headed toward Sears, my arms stiff and moving with mechanical precision.

"Robert!" Cara says. It's easy to get her to laugh. She likes the robot stuff a lot. I first did it about a year ago, and it feels a little weird to do it in public, in the mall. But I want to keep Cara happy. Cara is six, but she's retarded, so she's more like three or four, and she'll probably never be more than about four or five. Except she's big. She was born big. Big bones like a cow. Big jaw, big knuckles. Big blue eyes. Only her blonde hair is wispy. You have to look really hard to see how she resembles Kelsey. Kelsey was my big sister. I'm fourteen. Kelsey was hit by a car when she was thirteen. She'd be twenty now. Cara is Kelsey's clone, except of course Kelsey wasn't retarded or as big as a cow. In our living room there's a picture of Kelsey in her gymnastics leotard, standing next to the balance beam. You can kind of see how Cara looks like her.

"Let's go in Spencer's," I say.

Cara follows me. Spencer's is like heaven for a retarded girl—all the fake spilled drinks and the black lights and the lava lamps and optical projections and Cara's favorite, the Japanese string lights. They're back with the strings of chili pepper lights and the Coca-Cola lights. They sort of look like weird Christmas lights. If you look right at them, all they do is flicker, but if you look kind of sideways at them, you see all these Japanese letters and shit. Cara just stares at them. I think it's the flicker. While she's staring, I wander toward the front of the store.

Spencer's is shoplifter paradise, so they've got really good security. There's this chubby guy in the back, putting up merchandise and sweating up a storm. There are the cameras. There's a girl at the front cash register who is bored out of her mind and fiddling with some weird Spencer Gifts pen but who can pretty much see anything in the store if she bothers to look. But I've got Cara. That, and I understand the secret of shoplifting, which is to have absolutely no emotions. Be cold about the whole thing. I can switch off everything, and I'm just a thinking machine, doing everything according to plan. If you're nervous, then people notice you. Iceman. That's my name, my tag. That's the nickname I use in chatrooms. That's me.

I look at the bedroom board games. I stand at the shelf so that I pretty much block anything anyone could see in a camera. I don't know exactly where the cameras are, but if I don't leave much space between me and the shelf, how much can they really see? I wait. After a minute or two, Cara is grabbing the light strings, and after another couple of minutes the girl who's watching from the cash register has called someone to go intercept Cara and I palm a deck of *Wedding Night Playing Cards*. They're too small to have an anti-theft thing. I don't even break a sweat, increase my heart rate, nothing. The ice man. I head back to Cara.

Everyone's just watching the weird retarded girl except this one chubby guy who's trying to get her to put down the lights but who's afraid to touch her.

"Not supposed to touch those," he says. "Where's your mom? Is your mom here?"

"Sorry!" I say.

The chubby guy frowns at me.

"Cara," I say. "No hands."

Cara looks at me, looks at the lights. I gently try to take them.

"No!" she wails. "Pretty!"

"I'm sorry," I say, "I'm her brother. She's developmentally delayed. Cara! Cara, no. No hands."

She wails but lets me disentangle her hands.

"I'm sorry," I say again, the concerned big brother. "I was just looking around and thought she was right with me, you know? Our mom's down at Dillard's."

Chubby guy kind of hovers until I get the lights away from Cara, and as soon as I put them on the shelf he grabs them and starts straightening them out and draping them back over the display.

I herd Cara toward the front of the store, mouthing sorry at the front cashier. She's kind of pretty. She smiles at me. Nice big brother with retarded sister.

Back out in the mall, Cara is wailing, which could start an asthma attack, so to distract her I say, "You want a cookie?"

Mom has Cara on a diet, so of course she wants a cookie. She perks up the way Shelby, our Shetland Sheepdog, does when you say "treat." I take her to the food court and buy her an M&M cookie and buy myself a Mountain Dew, and then, while she's eating her cookie, I pull the deck of cards out of my pocket and unwrap it. We've got another fifteen minutes before we have to meet my mom.

The idea is to play fish, except every time you get a match you're supposed to do what it says. *Tie partner's hands with a silk scarf. Kiss anywhere you like and see how long your partner can keep from moving or making any noise. The one who lasts the longest gets to draw an extra card.*

Tame but pretty cool. I can't wait to show Toph and Len.

Cara has chocolate smeared on her mouth, but she lets me wipe her face off.

"You ready to go back to see Mom?" I say.

When we pass Spencer's again, she stops. "Uhhh," she says, pointing to the store. Mom always tries to get her to say what she wants, but I know what she wants and I don't want to fight with her.

"No," I say. "Let's go see Mom."

Cara's face crumples up, and she hunches her thick shoulders. "Uhhh," she says, mad.

"It's okay," I say. "Come on."

She swings at me. I grab her hand and pull her behind me. She tries to sit down, but I just keep on tugging, and she follows me, gulping and wailing.

"What did you do?" my mom says when she sees us. My mom had to buy stuff, like gym shorts for me and underwear for herself, so I told her that I'd take Cara with me while she bought her stuff. She's holding a Dillard's bag.

"She wanted to go in Spencer's," I say. "We went in, but she kept grabbing stuff and I had to take her out and now she's upset."

"Robert," my mom says, irritated. She crouches down. "Ah, Cara mia, don't cry."

We trail out of the store, Cara holding Mom's hand and sniffling.

By the time we get to the car though, Cara's wheezing. Mom digs out Cara's inhaler, and Cara dutifully takes a hit. I tried it once, and it was pretty dreadful. It felt really weird trying to get that stuff in my lungs, and it made me feel a little buzzy, but it didn't even feel good, so it's pretty amazing that Cara will do it.

Cara sits in her booster seat in the back of the car, wheezing all the way home, getting worse and worse, and by the time we pull in the driveway, she's got that white look around her mouth.

"Robert," Mom says, "I'm going to have to take her to the Emergency Room."

"Okay," I say and get out of the car.

"You want to call your dad?" Mom asks. "I don't know how long we'll be." Mom checks her watch. It's three something now. "We may not be home in time for dinner."

I don't want to call my dad, who is probably with Joyce, his girlfriend, anyway. Joyce is always trying to be likable, and it gets on my nerves after a while—she tries way too hard. "I can just make a sandwich," I say.

"I want you to stay at home then," she says. "I've got my cell phone if you need to call."

"Can Toph and Len come over?" I ask.

She sighs. "Okay. But no roughhousing. Remember you have school tomorrow." She opens the garage door so I can get in.

I stand there and watch her back down the driveway. She turns back, watching where she's going, and she needs to get her hair done again because I can really see the gray roots. Cara is watching me through the watery glass, her mouth a little open. I wave good-bye.

I'm glad they're gone.

I watch my daughter try to breathe. When Cara is having an asthma attack she becomes still—conserving, I think. Her face becomes empty. People think Cara looks empty all the time, but her face is usually alive—maybe with nothing more than some faint reflected flicker of the world around her, like those shimmers of light on the bottom of a pool, experience washing over her.

"Cara mia," I say. She doesn't understand why we won't pick her up anymore, but she weighs over sixty-five pounds and I just can't.

She doesn't like the Emergency Room, but it doesn't scare her. She's familiar with it. I steer her through the doors, my hand on her back, to the reception desk. I don't know today's receptionist. I hand her my medical card. When Cara was born, we officially adopted her, just as if we had done a conventional in-vitro fertilization in a surrogate and adopted the child, so Cara is on our medical plan. Now, of course, medical plans don't cover cloned children, but Cara was one of the early ones.

The receptionist takes all the information. The waiting room isn't very full. "Is Dr. Ramanathan on today?" I ask. Dr. Ramanathan, a soft-spoken Indian with small hands, is familiar with Cara. He's good with her, knows the strange idiosyncrasies of her condition—that her lungs are oddly vascularized, that she sometimes reacts atypically to medication. But Dr. Ramanathan isn't here.

We go sit in the waiting room.

The waiting room chairs don't have arms, so I can lay Cara across a chair with her head on my lap and stroke her forehead.

Calming her helps keep the attack from getting too bad. She needs her diaper changed. I didn't think to bring any. We were making some headway on toilet training until about two months ago, but then she just decided she hated the toilet.

I learned not to force things when she decided to be difficult about dinner. She's big, and although she's not terribly strong, when she gets mad she packs a wallop. The last time I tried to teach her about using a fork, I tried to fold her hand round it and she started screaming. It's a shrill, furious scream, not animal at all but full of something terribly human and too old for such a little girl. I grabbed her hand, and she hit me in the face with her fist and broke my reading glasses. So I don't force things anymore.

The nurse calls us at a little after five.

I settle Cara on the examining table. It's cold, so I wrap her in a blanket. She watches me, terribly patient, her mouth open. She has such blue eyes. The same eyes as Kelsey and the same eyes as my ex-husband, Allan. I can hear the tightness in her chest. I sit down next to her and hum, and she rubs my arm with the flat of her hand, as if she were smoothing out a wrinkle in a blanket.

I don't know the doctor who comes in. He is young, and his face seems good-humored and kind. He has a pierced ear. He isn't wearing an earring, but I can see the crease where his ear is pierced, and it cheers me a little. A little unorthodox, and kind. It seems like a good combination. His name is Dr. Guidall. I do my little speech—that she has asthma, that she had an attack and didn't respond to the inhaler, that she is developmentally delayed.

"Have you been to the Emergency Room before?" he asks.

"Many times," I say. "Right, Cara?"

She doesn't answer; she just watches me.

He examines her, and he is careful. He tells her the stethoscope is going to be cold and treats her like a person, which is a good sign.

"She has odd pulmonary vascularization," I say.

"Are you a doctor?" he asks.

When Cara's sister Kelsey had her accident, I was in charge of the international division of Kleinhoffer Foods. Now I sell real estate. "No," I say. "I've just learned a lot with Cara. Sometimes we see Dr. Ramanathan. He's familiar with Cara's problems."

The doctor frowns. Maybe he doesn't care for Dr. Ramanathan. He's young. Emergency Room doctors are usually young, at least at the hospital where I take Cara.

"She's not Down's Syndrome, is she," he says.

"No," I say. I don't want to say more.

He looks at me, and I realize he's pieced something together. "Is your daughter the clone?"

The clone. "Yes," I say. Dr. Ramanathan asked me if he could write up his observations of Cara to publish, and I said yes, because he seems to really care about her. I get requests from doctors to examine her. When she was first born I got hate mail, too. People saying that she should never have been born. That she was an abomination in the sight of God. I'm upset that Dr. Ramanathan would talk about her with someone else.

Dr. Guidall is silent, examining her. I imagine his censure. Maybe I'm wrong. Maybe he's just surprised.

"Is she allergic to anything?"

"She isn't allergic, but she has atypical reactions to some drugs like leukotriene receptor antagonists." I keep a list of drugs in my wallet. I pull it out and hand it to him. The list is worn, the creases so sharp that the paper is starting to tear.

"Do you use a nebulizer?" he asks. "And what drug are you using?"

"Budesonide," I say. I'm not imagining it. He's curt with me.

He puts a nebulizer—a mask rather than an inhaler, so she won't have to do anything but breathe—on her face. The doctor leaves to pull her chart from records.

I know we'll be here a long time. I've spent a lot of time in hospitals.

The doctor wants to punish me, I think. He does a thorough

exam of Cara, who has fallen asleep as the asthma attack waned. He listens to her lungs and checks her reflexes and looks in her ears. He doesn't need to look in her ears. But how many cloned children will he get to examine? Cloning humans is illegal in the United States, although there's no law against having your child cloned in, say, Israel and then bringing the adopted child into the U.S.

"I don't like what I'm hearing in her breathing," he says. "I would like to run some tests."

He has gotten more formal, which means that something is wrong. I want to go home so bad; I don't want things to start tonight. *Things.* The crisis doesn't always come when you're tired and thinking about the house you're going to show tomorrow, but often it does.

The doctor is very young and very severe. It's easy to be severe when you're young. I can imagine what he would like to ask. *Why the hell did you do it? How do you justify it?* Cara's respiratory defects will kill her, probably before she is twelve, almost certainly before she is eighteen.

He is perhaps furious at me. But Cara is right here. What would the angry people have me do, take her home and put a pillow over her face? How do I tell him, tell them, that when Cara was conceived, I wasn't sane? Nothing prepares you for the death of a child. Nothing teaches you how to live with it.

If he says anything, I will ask him, *Do you have any children? I hope you never lose one*, I will say.

He doesn't ask.

Nobody is impressed with the wedding night playing cards because Toph has scored really big. His dad took him along to Computer Warehouse so his dad could buy some sort of accounting software, and while Toph was hanging out playing video games, some salesperson got out *Hacker Vigilante* to show to some customer and then got paged and forgot to lock it back up. "So I just picked it up and slid it under my shirt," Toph says, "and then when my dad and me got to the car, I slid it under the seat before he got in."

We are in awe, Len and me. It's the biggest thing anyone has ever gotten away with. Toph is studying the box like it's no big deal, but we can tell he's really buggin on the whole thing.

I'm not allowed to have *Hacker Vigilante*. In it, you have to do missions to track down terrorists, and you do all these things to raise money, like steal stuff. My mom won't let me have it because one of the things that you can do to get money is pick up two teenaged girls at the bus station and get them to make a porn movie for you and then post it on the Internet. You don't really get to see anything; the girls just start taking off their shirts and the hotel room door closes, but it's hysterical.

I am dying. I can't believe it. "Man, that was lucky," I say, because it was. No salesperson ever left anything that cool out in front of me.

"Hey," Toph says. "You just gotta know how to be casual."

"I'm casual," I say. "I'm way casual. But that just fuckin fell in your lap."

"You loser," Toph says, laughing at me. "Fuck you." Len is laughing at me, too. I can feel my face turning red, and my ears feel hot, and I'm so mad I want to smash their faces in. Toph is just picking up stuff left lying around by dumbass sales droids and I'm setting up scams in fucking Spencer Gifts which everybody knows is really hard to score at because security is like bugfuck tight.

"You wait, asshole," I say. "You wait. I've got an idea for a score. You watch on the bus going to school tomorrow and you'll see."

"What?" Len says. "What are you going to do?"

"You'll see," I say.

By the time they check Cara into a room, it's almost seven. I manage to get to a phone and call Allan. Joyce, his girlfriend, answers the phone. "Hi, Joyce," I say, "this is Jenna. Is Allan around?"

"Sure," she says. "Hold on, Jenna."

Joyce. Jenna. Allan likes "J" women. Actually, Allan likes thin women with dark hair and a kind of relentlessly Irish look. Joyce and I could be cousins. Joyce is prettier than I am. And younger. Every time I talk to her, I use her name too much and she uses mine too much. We are working hard to be friendly.

"Jenna?" says Allan. "What's up?"

"I'm at the hospital with Cara," I say.

"Do you need me to come down?" he says, too fast. Allan is conscientious. He is bracing himself. *Is it a crisis?* is what he wants to know.

"No, it's just an asthma attack, but the doctor in the Emergency Room didn't like her oxygen levels or something, and they want to keep her. But Robert is home by himself, and they want to do some more tests tonight . . . "

"Ah. Okay," he says. "Let me think a moment."

It's Sunday night. What can he be doing on a Sunday night? "Are you busy? I mean, am I calling at a bad time . . . "

"No, no," he says. "Joyce and I were supposed to meet some friends, but I can call them and let them know. It wasn't anything important."

I try to think of what they could be doing on a Sunday night.

"It's just Joyce's church," Allan says into the pause. "They have a social thing, actually a kind of study thing on Sunday nights."

I didn't know Joyce was religious. "Well," I say, "maybe you could just check in on him? I mean, will it take you too far out of your way?"

"No," Allan says, "I'll go over there."

"See how things are. If you think he's all right, maybe you can just call and make sure he's in bed by ten or something?"

"No," Allan says, "I can stay with him. You're going to be there for hours, I know."

"He's fourteen," I say. "Use your judgment. I mean, I hate to impose on you and Joyce."

"It's okay," Allan says. "They're my kids."

I feel rather guilty, so I hang up without saying, "Church?" One

Christmas my dippy older sister was talking about God protecting her from some minor calamity, some domestic crisis involving getting a dent in her husband's Ford pickup, and later, as we drove home, Allan said, grinning, "I'm so glad that God is looking after Matt's pickup. Makes up for whatever he was doing during, you know, Cambodia, or the Black Plague."

He's going to church for Joyce.

Well, he went through the whole cloning thing for me. I don't exactly have the moral high ground.

I go to bed early because my dad and his girlfriend have shown up to baby-sit for me. Toph and Len bug out as soon as Dad shows up. Joyce is being so nice to me that it feels fake, but she's acting weird toward my dad in the same way: being really nice to him. They've brought a movie they rented, and when my dad asks her if she wants popcorn with it, she says things like, "That would be really nice, thank you." Like they barely know each other.

So I play computer games in my room for a while, and then I go to bed. Shelby, our dog, leaps onto the bed with me. She usually sleeps at the foot of my bed. I get under the covers with my jeans on, and I don't mean to fall asleep, but I do. Shelby wakes me up when my mom gets home because she hears Mom and starts slapping the bed with her tail. My mom talks with my dad and Joyce for a few minutes—I can't hear what they're saying, but I can hear the murmur. I pretend to still be asleep when my mom checks in on me. Shelby is all curled up but happy to see Mom, and my mom comes in and says "Shhh" and pets her a minute.

The hard part is staying awake after that. My clock says 11:18 when my mom leaves my room, and I want to give her at least half an hour to be good and sound asleep. But I nod off, and when I wake up with a jerk it's 1:56 a.m.

I almost don't get up. I'm really tired. But I make myself get up. Shelby wakes up and leaps off my bed. Shelby is my big worry about sneaking out. If I lock her in my room, she'll scratch and then she'll bark. So she follows me downstairs, and I let her out back. Maybe Mom will just think that Shelby had to go out, although usually if Shelby has to go out, I sleep right through it, and she goes downstairs and pees in the dining room, and then my mom gets really twisted at me the next morning.

I almost fall asleep on the couch waiting for Shelby to come back in. I could tell Toph and Len that my dad came over and I couldn't sneak out, and do it tomorrow night. But while Shelby is out, I make myself go into the basement and get a can of black spray paint. My mom used black spray paint to repaint the patio furniture, and most of this can is still left.

I have a navy hooded sweatshirt, and I slide open the back door, let Shelby in, and go out the back. That way the door only opened twice: once to let Shelby out, and then to let Shelby in.

The backyard is dark, and the cold is kind of startling. Mom keeps saying that she can't believe that in four weeks it will be Memorial Day and the pools will be open, but I like the cold. I look up at the stars. The only constellation I know is Orion, but if it is up, it's behind the trees or on the other side of the house. I bet Shelby is watching me through the window when I come around the front of the house. I can't see her, but I know what she looks like cause she does it every time people go out in the car; she's standing on the couch so she can look out the window, but all we'd be able to see is just this little miniature Lassie face with her ears up all cute.

I walk down the street, and I feel like people are watching me out the windows, watching me like Shelby. But all the windows are dark. Still, anyone looking out would see me, and it's after curfew. I should cut through the yards, but they're too dark and people's dogs would bark and people would think I was stealing stuff and call the police—and mostly I just don't want to.

It's a couple of miles to the police station—which is past the middle school. After a while I stop feeling like people are looking at me. They're all in their beds, and I'm out here. I'm the only one moving. I can picture them, all cocooned in their beds. Unaware.

I'm aware. All you sleeping people. I'm out here. And you don't know anything about me. I could do stuff while you sleep.

It's so cool. It's great. I'm like some sort of assassin or something. The Iceman. That's me. Moving out here in the dark. I'm a wolf, and you're all just rabbits or something.

I'm feeling so good. I'm not cold, because I'm walking and I'm feeling so good. By the time I get to the police station, I feel better than anything. Better than after I steal something, which up until now has been the best. But this is the best. The Iceman out moving in the dark. The dark is my friend. I watch the police station for a while, but nothing's moving. I shake the paint can, and the ball bearing in it sounds loud, and for a moment my heart hammers, but then I'm okay again.

I'm casual. I'm better than casual. I'm Special Forces. I'm fucking terror in the streets.

I take a minute and look at the wall. I spray the words on the side, really big, big enough to be seen from the bus:

TO REPORT A CRIME CALL 425-1234

I sketch them fast and then carefully fill them in. Then I sketch my tag—"Iceman." I make the letters all sharp and spiky. It's a bitch that I've only got black paint—it should be blue and white with black outline. I carefully start darkening the "I." Toph and Len will just die. It's so funny to me that I've got this grin on my face. They're going to come by on the bus, and there it will be. Tagging the fucking police station. 425-1234 really is the police phone number. First I was going to put **PROTECTED BY NEIGHBORHOOD BLOCK WATCH**, but I thought this was funnier.

Then the squad car coasts up behind me and turns the floodlights on, and the whole world is white.

I had no idea that police stations had waiting rooms, but when I go to pick up Robert, that's where I end up. It's a room with seats along the walls and fluorescent lights and a bulletproof window. The window has one of those metal circles in it, like movie theaters.

I tell the young woman that I'm Robert's mother and I got a call to come down and get my son, and she picks up a phone to tell someone I'm here.

A cop comes out with Robert. Robert looks properly scared. The cop, who has sandy hair and a handlebar moustache and looks rather boyish, introduces himself as Bruce Yoder. Yoder is an Amish name, although Bruce Yoder obviously isn't Amish. I bet his parents are Mennonite, which is less strict than Amish. It's what you do if you're Amish and you don't have any high school education but you want a car. You become Mennonite. And now their son is a cop, the route to assimilation of my Irish ancestors. Why am I thinking this while my son, who is almost as tall as the cop, stands sullen and afraid with his hands jammed in the front pocket of his sweatshirt?

We walk outside and around the building so I can survey Robert's handiwork.

The police station is pale, sandstone-colored brick and the black letters, as tall as me, stand out even in the dim light. I don't know what to say. Finally I say, "What's 'Iceman'?"

When he doesn't answer, I say, "Robert?"

"A nickname," he says.

The cop says to me, "You're the family with the little girl, the clone."

"Yes," I say. "Cara." When people call her "the clone," I always feel compelled to tell them her name. The cop looks a little embarrassed.

We go back inside, and I talk to the cop. Robert has been booked, and he'll have a hearing in front of a family court referee. I say I'm sorry a number of times. A family court referee. That's what we need. That's what everyone needs, someone to tell us the rules. When the phone rang, I thought it was the hospital, that something had happened to Cara, and then I was washed with clear, cold rage. *How can you do this to me?* But it isn't about me, of course.

Allan walks in. I called him before I left the house, and he said, as soon as he understood that it wasn't Cara, as soon as he understood what was going on, "He'll have to come live with me. You can't do this, not with Cara."

I am so glad to see him. There have been times I loved him, times I hated him, but now he is kin. For all his flaws and for all my flaws, seeing Allan walk in wearing an old University of Michigan sweatshirt, with his hair tousled so I can see how thin it is getting, and his poor vulnerable temples, I feel only relief, and my eyes fill with tears. It's unexpected, this crying.

Allan talks to the cop, the ex-Amish cop, while I sniffle into a wadded-up and ancient Kleenex I found in the pocket of my jacket.

We walk back outside. "I think I should take him home with me tonight," Allan says. "We'll follow you to the house, get him some things. I'll call in tomorrow and start arranging for him to go to school in Marshall."

Robert says, "What?"

Allan says, "You're going to come live with me."

Robert says, his voice cracking across the syllables, "For how long?"

"For good, I suppose," Allan says.

"Is Joyce—" I almost say, "Is Joyce at your place," but I can't ask that.

"Joyce left early; she's got to go to work tomorrow," Allan says, and he looks off across the parking lot, his mouth pursed. This is a problem for him, a monkey wrench.

I start to reach out and say "I'm sorry" again, and tears well up, again.

"What about school?" Robert asks. "I've got to go to school tomorrow. I've got an algebra test on Tuesday!"

"That," Allan says quietly, "is the least of your problems."

"What about my friends!" Robert says. "You can't do this to me!" I can see his eyes glistening, too. The family that cries together.

"I can," Allan says, "and I will. Now you've put your mother and me through enough. Get in the car."

"No!" Robert says. "You can't make me!"

Allan reaches for his arm, to grab him, and Robert slips away, dancing, tall and gangly, and then blindly turns and runs.

I open my mouth, drawing in the breath to shout his name, and he is running, long legs like his father's, full of health and desperation, running pointlessly. It's inescapable, what he is running from, but in the instant before I shout his name I am glad, glad to see him running, this boy of mine who will, I think, survive. "Robert!" I shout, at exactly the same time as his father, but Robert is heading down the street, head up, arms pumping. He won't go far.

"Robert!" his father shouts again.

I am glad, oh so glad. *Run,* I think joyfully. *Run, you sweet bastard. Run!*

the pottawatomie giant

ANDY DUNCAN

"The Pottawatomie Giant" won Andy Duncan a World Fantasy Award. He has also won the Theodore Sturgeon Memorial Award for best science-fiction story of the year, as well as been nominated for the Nebula, Hugo, Stoker, and Shirley Jackson awards. His books include the World Fantasy Award-winning collection *Beluthahatchie and Other Stories* and the non-fiction guidebook *Alabama Curiosities*, now in a second edition. A South Carolina native and a Clarion West graduate, he's an assistant professor in the English department at Frostburg State University in western Maryland. He also teaches seminars in 21st-century science fiction and fantasy in the Honors College of the University of Alabama.

O n the afternoon of November 30, 1915, Jess Willard, for seven months the heavyweight champion of the world, crouched, hands on knees, in his Los Angeles hotel window to watch a small figure swaying like a pendulum against the side of the *Times* building three blocks away.

"Cripes!" Willard said. "How's he keep from fainting, his head down like that, huh, Lou?"

"He trains, Champ," said his manager, one haunch on the sill. "Same's you."

Training had been a dispute between the two men lately, but Willard let it go. "Cripes!" Willard said again, his mouth dry.

The street below was a solid field of hats, with an occasional parasol like a daisy, and here and there a mounted policeman statue-still and gazing up like everyone. Thousands were yelling, as if sound alone would buoy the upside-down figure writhing 150 feet above the pavement.

"Attaboy, Harry!"

"Five minutes, that's too long! Someone bring him down!"

"Five minutes, hell, I seen him do thirty."

"At least he's not underwater this time."

"At least he ain't in a milk can!"

"Look at him go! The straitjacket's not made that can hold that boy, I tell you."

"You can do it, Harry!"

Willard himself hated crowds, but he had been drawing them all his life. One of the farm hands had caught him at age twelve toting a balky calf beneath one arm, and thereafter he couldn't go into town without people egging him on to lift things—livestock, Mr. Olsburg the banker, the log behind the fancy house. When people started offering cash money, he couldn't well refuse, having seen Mama and Papa re-count their jar at the end of every month, the stacks of old coins dull even in lamplight. So Jess Willard, at thirty-three, knew something about what physical feats earned, and what they cost. He watched this midair struggle, lost in jealousy, in sympathy, in professional admiration.

"God damn, will you look at this pop-eyed city," Lou said. "It's lousy with believers. I tell you, Champ, this fella has set a whole new standard for public miracles. When Jesus Christ Almighty comes back to town, he'll have to work his ass off to get in the newspapers at all." Lou tipped back his head, pursed his lips, and jetted cigar smoke upstairs.

"Do you *mind*?" asked the woman directly above, one of three crowding a ninth-floor window. She screwed up her face and fanned the air with her hands.

"Settle down, sister, smoke'll cure you soon enough," Lou said. He wedged the cigar back into his mouth and craned his neck to peer around Willard. "Have a heart, will you, Champ? It's like looking past Gibraltar."

"Sorry," Willard said, and withdrew a couple of inches, taking care not to bang his head on the sash. He had already banged his head crossing from the corridor to the parlor, and from the bathroom to the bedroom. Not that it hurt—no, to be hurt, Willard's head had to be hit plenty harder than that. But he'd never forgotten how the other children laughed when he hit his head walking in the door, that day the Pottawatomie County sheriff finally made him go to school. All the children but Hattie. So he took precautions outside the ring, and seethed inside each time he forgot he was six foot seven. This usually happened in hotel suites, all designed for Lou-sized men, or less. Since Havana, Willard had lived mostly in hotel suites.

Leaning from the next-door window on the left was a jowly man in a derby hat. He had been looking at Houdini only half the time, Willard the other half. Now he rasped: "Hey, buddy. Hey. Jess Willard."

Willard dreaded autograph-seekers, but Lou said a champ had to make nice. "You're the champ, now, boy," Lou kept saying, "and a champ has gotta be *seen!*"

"Yeah, that's me," Willard said.

His neighbor looked startled. Most people were, when they heard Willard's bass rumble for the first time. "I just wanted to say congratulations, Champ, for putting that nigger on the canvas where he belongs."

"I appreciate it," Willard said. He had learned this response from his father, a man too proud to say *thanks*. He tried to focus again on Houdini. The man seemed to be doing sit-ups in midair, but at a frenzied rate, jackknifing himself repeatedly. The rope above him whipped from side to side. Willard wondered how much of the activity was necessary, how much for effect.

The derby-hatted guy wasn't done. "Twenty-six rounds, damn, you taught Mr. Coon Johnson something about white men, I reckon, hah?"

Ever since Havana. Cripes. Houdini's canvas sleeves, once bound across his chest, were now bound behind him. Somehow he'd worked his arms over his head—was the man double-jointed?

"Say, how come you ain't had nothing but exhibitions since? When you gonna take on Frank Moran, huh? I know that nigger ain't taken the fight out of you. I know you ain't left your balls down in Cuba." He laughed like a bull snorting.

Willard sighed. He'd leave this one to Lou. Lou wouldn't have lasted ten seconds in the ring, but he loved a quarrel better than any boxer Willard knew.

"Balls?" Lou squawked, right on schedule. "Balls? Let me tell you something, fella."

Now Houdini's arms were free, the long canvas strap dangling. The crowd roared.

"When Moran is ready, we'll be ready, you got me?" Lou leaned out to shake his finger and nearly lost his balance. "Whoa," he said, clutching his hat. "Fella, you're, why, you're just lucky there's no ledge here. Yeah. You think he's taking it so easy, well, maybe you want to spar a few rounds with him, huh?"

Now Houdini had looped the canvas strap across the soles of his feet, and was tugging at it like a madman. More and more of his white shirt was visible. Willard resolved that when he started training again—when Lou got tired of parties and banquets and Keys to the City and let Willard go home to the gymnasium, and to Hattie—he would try this upside-down thing, if he could find rope strong enough.

"Well, how about I spar with *you*, buddy? Who the hell are you, Mr. Milksop?"

"I'm his manager, that's who I am! And let me tell you another thing—"

Houdini whipped off the last of the jacket and held the husk out, dangling, for all to see. Then he dropped it and flung both arms out to the side, an upside-down T. Amid the pandemonium, the jacket flew into the crowd and vanished like a ghost. Trash rained from the windows, as people dropped whatever they were holding to applaud. Willard stared as a woman's dress fluttered down to drape a lamppost. It was blue and you could see through it. Even the guy with the derby was cheering, his hands clasped overhead. "Woo hoo!" he said, his quarrel forgotten. "Woo hoo hoo!"

With a smile and a shake of his head, Lou turned his back on it all. "The wizard of ballyhoo," he said. "Too bad they can't string up *all* the Jews, eh, Champ?" He patted Willard's shoulder and left the window.

As he was winched down, Houdini took inverted bows, and there was much laughter. Willard, who had neither cheered nor applauded, remained motionless at the window, tracking Houdini's descent. Someone's scented handkerchief landed on his head, and he brushed it away. He watched as the little dark-haired man in the ruffled shirt dropped headfirst into the sea that surged forward and engulfed him. His feet went last, bound at the ankles, patent-leather shoes side by side like a soldier's on review. Willard could imagine how they must shine.

That night, as Willard followed Lou up the curving, ever-narrowing, crimson-carpeted stairs leading to the balconies of the Los Angeles Orpheum, the muffled laughter and applause through the interior wall seemed to jeer Willard's every step, his every clumsy negotiation of a chandelier, his every flustered pause while a giggling and feathered bevy of young women flowed around his waist. Hattie didn't need feathers, being framed, in Willard's mind, by the open sky. These women needed plenty. Those going down gaped at him, chins tipping upward, until they passed; those going up turned at the next landing for a backward and downward look of frank appraisal. "We had a whole box in Sacramento," Lou muttered as he squinted from the numbers on the wall to the crumpled paper in his hand. "Shit. I guess these Los Angeles boxes is for the quality." A woman with a powder-white face puckered her lips at Willard and winked. Grunting in triumph, Lou overshot a cuspidor and threw open a door with a brown grin. "Save one of the redheads for me, willya?" Lou hissed, as Willard ducked past him into darkness.

Willard stopped to get his bearings as a dozen seated silhouettes turned to look at him. Beyond, the arched top of the stage was a tangle of golden vines. The balcony ceiling was too low. Willard shuffled forward, head down, as Lou pushed him two-handed in the small of the back. "Hello," Willard said, too loudly, and someone gasped. Then the others began to murmur hellos in return. "So good to meet you," they murmured amid a dozen outstretched hands, the male shapes half-standing, diamond rings and cufflinks sharp in the light from the stage. Willard was able to shake some hands, squeeze others; some merely stroked or patted him as he passed. "A pleasure," he kept saying. "A God's honest pleasure."

Lou made Willard sit in the middle of the front row next to Mrs. Whoever-She-Was, someone important; Lou said her name too fast. She was plump as a guinea hen and reeked of powder. Willard would have preferred the aisle. Here there was little room for his legs, his feet. Plus the seat, as usual, was too narrow. He jammed his buttocks between the slats that passed for armrests, bowing the wood outward like the sides of a firehose. As his hams sank, his jacket rode up in back. Once seated, he tried to work the jacket down, to no avail. Already his face was burning with the certainty that all eyes in the hall were focused not on the stage but on the newly hunchbacked Jess Willard. "Don't worry, he's just now begun," Mrs. Whoever whispered across Willard, to Lou. "You've hardly missed a thing."

His knees cut off the view of the stage below. He parted his knees just a little. Between them, on the varnished planks of the stage far below, Houdini patted the air to quell another round of applause. He was a short, dark, curly-haired man in a tuxedo. At his feet were a dozen scattered roses.

"Thank you, my friends, thank you," the little man said, though it sounded more like "Tank you"—a German, Willard had heard, this Houdini, or was it Austrian? Seen from this unnatural angle, nearly directly above like this, he looked dwarfish, foreshortened. He had broad shoulders, though, and no sign of a paunch beneath his cummerbund. Lou jabbed Willard in the side, glared at Willard's knees, then his face. Sighing, Willard closed his knees again.

"Ladies and gentlemen—are the ushers ready? Thank you. Ladies and gentlemen, I beg your assistance with the following part of the program. I require the services of a committee of ten. Ten good men and true, from the ranks of the audience, who are willing to join me here upon the stage and to watch closely my next performance, that all my claims be verified as accurate, that its every particular be beyond reproach."

The balcony was uncomfortably hot. Sweat rolled down Willard's torso, his neck. Mrs. Whoever opened her fan and worked up a breeze. A woman across the auditorium was staring at Willard and whispering to her husband. He could imagine. *All I can say is, you cannot trust those photographs. Look how they hide that poor man's deformities.*

"Ten good men and true. Yes, thank you, sir, your bravery speaks well for our boys in Haiti, and in Mexico." A spatter of applause. "The ushers will direct you. And you, sir, yes, thank you as well. Ladies, perhaps you could help us identify the more modest of the good men among us?" Laughter. "Yes, madam, your young man looks a likely prospect, indeed. A fine selection you have made—as have you, sir! No, madam, I fear your fair sex disqualifies you for this work. The stage can be a dangerous place."

Willard retreated to his program, to see which acts he missed because dinner with the mayor ran late. Actually, the dinner, a palm-sized chicken breast with withered greens, had been over quickly; you learned to eat fast on the farm. What took a long time was the mayor's after-dinner speech, in which he argued that athletic conditioning was the salvation of America. Willard bribed a waiter for three thick-cut bologna sandwiches, which he munched at the head table with great enjoyment, ignoring Lou. Now, looking at the Orpheum program, Willard found himself more kindly disposed toward the mayor's speech. It had spared him the "Syncopated Funsters" Bernie & Baker, Adelaide Boothby's "Novelty Songs and Travesties" (with Chas. Everdean at the piano), Selma Braatz the "Renowned Lady Juggler," and Comfort & King in "Coontown Diversions," not to mention a trick rider, a slack-wire routine, a mystery titled "Stan Stanley, The Bouncing Fellow, Assisted by His Relatives," and, most happily missed of all, The Alexander Kids, billed as "Cute, Cunning, Captivating, Clever." *And crooked*, thought Willard, who once had wasted a nickel on a midget act at the Pottawatomie County Fair.

"Thank you, sir. Welcome. Ladies and gentlemen, these our volunteers have my thanks. Shall they have your thanks as well?"

Without looking up from his program, Willard joined the applause.

"My friends, as I am sure you have noticed, our committee still lacks three men. But if you will indulge me, I have a suggestion. I am told that here in the house with us tonight, we have one man who is easily the equal of any three."

Lou started jabbing Willard again. "G'wan," Willard whispered. "I closed my knees, all right?"

"Knock 'em dead, Champ," Lou hissed, his face shadowed but for his grin.

Willard frowned at him, bewildered. "What?"

"Ladies and gentlemen, will you kindly join me in inviting before the footlights the current heavyweight boxing champion—*our champion*—Mr. Jess Willard!"

Willard opened his mouth to protest just as a spotlight hit him full in the face, its heat like an opened oven.

Willard turned to Lou amid the applause and said, "You didn't!"

Lou ducked his chin and batted his eyes, like a bright child done with his recitation and due a certificate.

"Ladies and gentlemen, if you are in favor of bringing Mr. Willard onto the stage, please signify with your applause."

Now the cheers and applause were deafening. Willard gaped down at the stage. Houdini stood in a semicircle of frenziedly applauding men, his arms outstretched and welcoming. He stared up at Willard with a tiny smile at the corner of his mouth, almost a smirk, his eyes as bright and shallow as the footlights. *Look what I have done for you*, he seemed to be saying. *Come and adore me.*

The hell I will, Willard thought.

No, *felt*, it was nothing so coherent as thought, it was a gut response to Lou, to the mayor, to Mrs. Whoever pressing herself up against Willard's left side in hopes of claiming a bit of the spotlight too, to Hattie more than a thousand miles away whom he should have written today but didn't, to all these row after row of stupid people, most of whom thought Willard hadn't beaten Jack Johnson at all, that Johnson had simply given up, had *floated* to the canvas, the word they kept using, *floated*, cripes, Willard had been *standing there*, had heard the *thump* like the first melon dropped into the cart when Johnson's head had bounced against the canvas, *bounced*, for cripes' sake, spraying sweat and spit and blood, that fat lip flapping as the head went down a second time and stayed, *floated*, they said, Willard wasn't a *real* fighter, they said, he had just *outlasted* Johnson—an hour and forty-four minutes in the Havana sun, a blister on the top of his head like a brand, Hattie still could see the scar when she parted his hair to look—*outlasted*, the papers said! Beneath the applause, Willard heard a distant *crunch* as he squeezed the armrest, and was dimly aware of a splinter in his palm as he looked down at Houdini's smirking face and realized, clearly, for the first time: *You people don't want me at all, a big shit-kicker from the prairie.*

It's Jack Johnson you want.

And you know what? You can't have him. Because I beat him, you hear? I beat him.

"No, thanks!" Willard shouted, and the applause ebbed fast, like the last grain rushing out of the silo. The sudden silence, and Houdini's startled blink, made Willard's resolve falter. "I appreciate it," he added. He was surprised by how effortlessly his voice filled the auditorium. "Go on with your act, please, sir," Willard said, even more loudly. Ignoring Lou's clutching hand, which threatened to splinter Willard's forearm as Willard had splintered the armrest, he attempted comedy: "I got a good seat for it right here." There was nervous laughter, including someone immediately behind Willard— who must have, Willard realized, an even worse view than he did.

Arms still outstretched, no trace of a smile now, Houdini called up: "Mr. Willard, I am afraid your public must insist?"

Willard shook his head and sat back, arms folded.

"Mr. Willard, these other gentlemen join me in solemnly pledging that no harm will come to you."

This comedy was more successful; guffaws broke out all over the theater. Willard wanted to seek out all the laughers and paste them one. "Turn off that spotlight!" he yelled. "It's hot enough to roast a hog."

To Willard's amazement, the spotlight immediately snapped off, and the balcony suddenly seemed a dark, cold place.

"Come down, Mr. Willard," Houdini said, his arms now folded.

"Jesus Christ, kid," Lou hissed. "What's the idea?"

Willard shook him off and stood, jabbing one thick index finger at the stage. "Pay *me* what you're paying *them*, and I'll come down!"

Gasps and murmurs throughout the crowd. Willard was aware of some commotion behind him, movement toward the exit, the balcony door slamming closed. Fine. Let them run, the cowards.

In indignation, Houdini seemed to have swollen to twice his previous thickness. Must come in handy when you're straitjacketed, Willard thought.

"*Mister* Willard," Houdini retorted, "I am pleased to pay you what I am paying these gentlemen—precisely *nothing*. They are here of their own free will and good sportsmanship. Will you not, upon the same terms, join them?"

"No!" Willard shouted. "I'm leaving." He turned to find his way blocked by Lou, whose slick face gleamed.

"Please, Champ, don't do this to us," Lou whispered, reaching up with both hands in what might have been an attempted embrace. Willard grabbed Lou's wrists, too tightly, and yanked his arms down. "Ah," Lou gasped.

Houdini's drone continued as he paced the stage, his eyes never leaving the balcony. "I see, ladies and gentlemen, that the champ is attempting to retreat to his corner. Mr. Willard, the bell has rung. Will you not answer? Will you not meet the challenge? For challenge it is, Mr. Willard—I, and the good people of this house, challenge you to come forward, and stand before us, like a champion. As Mr. Johnson would have."

Willard froze.

"Or would you have us, sir, doubt the authenticity of your title? Would you have us believe that our champion is unmanned by fear?"

Willard turned and leaned so far over the rail that he nearly fell.

"I'll do my job in the ring, you do your job onstage," he yelled. "Go on with your act, your trickery, you faker, you four-flusher!" The audience howled. He shouted louder. "Make it look good, you fake. That's all they want—talk!" He felt his voice breaking. "Tricks and snappy dialogue! Go on, then, give 'em what they want. Talk your worthless talk! Do your lousy fake tricks!" People were standing up and yelling at him all over the theater, but he could see nothing but the little strutting figure on the stage.

"Mr. Willard."

Willard, though committed, now felt himself running out of material. "Everybody knows it's fake!"

"Mr. Willard!"

"Four-flusher!"

"Look here, *Mister* Jess Willard," Houdini intoned, his broad face impassive, silencing Willard with a pointed index finger. "I don't care what your title is or how big you are or what your reputation is or how many men you've beaten to get it. I did you a favor by asking you onto this stage, I paid you a compliment, and so has everyone in the Orpheum." The theater was silent but for the magician. Willard and those in the balcony around him were frozen. "You have the right, sir, to refuse us, to turn your back on your audience, but you have no right, sir, *no* right whatsoever, to slur my reputation, a reputation, I might add, that will long outlive yours." In the ensuing silence, Houdini seemed to notice his pointed finger for the first time. He blinked, lowered his arm, and straightened his cummerbund as he continued: "If you believe nothing else I do or say on this stage today, Mr. Willard, believe *this*, for there is no need for special powers of strength or magic when I tell you that I *can foresee your future*. Yes, sir."

Now his tone was almost conversational as he strolled toward center stage, picked up a rose, snapped its stem, and worked at affixing it to his lapel. "Believe me when I say to you that one day soon you no longer will be the heavyweight champion of the world." Satisfied by the rose, he looked up at Willard again.

"And when your name, Mr. Millard, I'm sorry, Mr. *Willard*, has become a mere footnote in the centuries-long history of the ring, everyone—*everyone*—even those who never set *foot* in a theater— will know *my* name and know that *I* never turned my back to my audience, or failed to accomplish *every* task, *every* feat, they set before me. And that, sir, is why champions come and champions go, while I will remain, now and forever, the one and only Harry Houdini!" He flung his arms out and threw his head back a half second before the pandemonium.

There had been twenty-five thousand people in that square in Havana, Willard had been told. He had tried not to look at them, not to think about them—that sea of snarling, squinting, sun-peeled, hateful, ugly faces. But at least all those people had been on his side.

"Go to hell, Willard!"

"Willard, you bum!"

"Willard's a willow!"

"Go to hell!"

Something hit Willard a glancing blow on the temple: a paper sack, which exploded as he snatched at it, showering the balcony with peanut shells. Willard felt he was moving slowly, as if underwater. As he registered that Mrs. Whoever, way down there somewhere, was pummeling him with her parasol—shrieking amid the din, "You bad man! You bad, bad man!"—Willard saw a gentleman's silver-handled cane spiraling lazily through the air toward his head. He ducked as the cane clattered into the far corner. Someone yelped. With one final glance at the mob, Willard turned his back on the too-inviting open space and dashed—but oh, so slowly it seemed—toward the door. People got in his way; roaring, he swept them aside, reached the door, fumbled at it. His fingers had become too slow and clumsy—numb, almost paralyzed. Bellowing something, he didn't know what, he kicked the door, which flew into the corridor in a shower of splinters. Roaring wordlessly now, Willard staggered down the staircase. He cracked his forehead on a chandelier, and yanked it one-handed out of the ceiling with a snarl, flinging it aside in a spasm of plaster and dust. His feet slipped on the lobby's marble floor, and he flailed before righting himself in front of an open-mouthed hat-check girl. Beyond the closed auditorium doors Willard could hear the crowd beginning to chant Houdini's name. Willard kicked a cuspidor as hard as he could; it sailed into a potted palm, spraying juice across the marble floor. Already feeling the first pangs of remorse, Willard staggered onto the sidewalk, into the reek of horseshit and automobiles. The doorman stepped back, eyes wide. "I ain't done nothing, Mister," he said. "I ain't done nothing." Willard growled and turned away, only to blunder into someone small and soft just behind him, nearly knocking her down. It was the hat-check girl, who yelped and clutched at his arms for balance.

"What the hell!" he said.

She righted herself, cleared her throat, and, lips pursed with determination, held out a claim ticket and a stubby pencil. "Wouldja please, huh, Mr. Willard? It won't take a sec. My grandpa says you're his favorite white man since Robert E. Lee."

Jess Willard lost the heavyweight title to Jack Dempsey on July 4, 1919, and retired from boxing soon after. When the fight money dried up, the Willards packed up Zella, Frances, Jess Junior, Enid, and Alan, left Kansas for good and settled in Los Angeles, where Willard opened a produce market at Hollywood and Afton. By day he dickered with farmers, weighed oranges, shooed flies, and swept up. Nights, he made extra money as a referee at wrestling matches. He continued to listen to boxing on the radio, and eventually to watch it on television, once the screens grew large enough to decently hold two grown men fighting. He read all the boxing news he could find in the papers, too, until holding the paper too long made his arms tremble like he was punchy, and spreading it out on the kitchen table didn't work so good either because the small print gave him a headache, and there weren't any real boxers left anyway, and thereafter it fell to his grandchildren, or his great-grandchildren, or his neighbors, or anyone else who had the time to spare, to read the sports pages aloud to him. Sometimes he listened quietly, eyes closed but huge behind his eyeglasses, his big mottled fingers drumming the antimacassar at one-second intervals, as if taking a count. Other times he was prompted to laugh, or to make a disgusted sound in the back of his throat, or to sit forward abruptly—which never failed to startle his youngest and, to his mind, prettiest great-granddaughter, whom he called "the Sprout," so that despite herself she always gasped and drew back a little, her beads clattering, her pedicured toes clenching the edge of her platform sandals—and begin telling a story of the old days, which his visitors sometimes paid attention to, and sometimes didn't, though the Sprout paid closer attention than you'd think.

One day in 1968, the Sprout read Jess Willard the latest indignant *Times* sports column about the disputed heavyweight title. Was the champ Jimmy Ellis, who had beaten Jerry Quarry on points, or was it Joe Frazier, who had knocked out Buster Mathis, or was it rightfully Muhammad Ali, who had been stripped of the title for refusing the draft, and now was banned from boxing anywhere in the United States? The columnist offered no answer to the question, but used his space to lament that boxing suddenly had become so political.

"Disputes, hell. I disputed a loss once," Willard told the Sprout. "To Joe Cox in Springfield Moe in 1911. The referee stopped the fight, then claimed I *wouldn't* fight, give the match to Cox. Said he hadn't stopped nothing. I disputed it, but didn't nothing come of it. Hell. You can't win a fight by disputing."

"I thought a fight *was* a dispute," said the Sprout, whose name was Jennifer. Taking advantage of her great-granddad's near-blindness, she had lifted the hem of her mini to examine the pear-shaped peace symbol her boyfriend had drunkenly drawn on her thigh the night before. She wondered how long it would take to wash off. "Boyfriend" was really the wrong word for Cliff, though he *was* cute, in a scraggly dirty hippie sort of way, and it wasn't like she had a parade of suitors to choose from. The only guy who seemed interested at the coffeehouse last week was some Negro, couldn't you just die, and of course she told him to buzz off. She hoped Jess never found out she'd even said so much as "buzz off" to a Negro boy—God knows, Jess was a nut on *that* subject. Nigger this and nigger that, and don't even bring up what's his name, that Negro boxer, Johnson? But you couldn't expect better from the old guy. After all, what had they called Jess, back when—the White Hope?

"No, no, honey," Willard said, shifting his buttocks to get comfortable. He fidgeted all the time, even in his specially made chair, since he lost so much weight. "A fight in the ring, it ain't nothing *personal*."

"You're funny, Jess," Jennifer said. The old man's first name still felt awkward in her mouth, though she was determined to use it—it made her feel quite hip and adult, whereas "Popsy" made her feel three years old.

"You're funny, too," Willard said, sitting back. "Letting boys write on your leg like you was a Blue Horse tablet. Read me some more, if you ain't got nothing else to do."

"I don't," Jennifer lied.

Jess Willard died in his Los Angeles home December 15, 1968— was in that very custom-made chair, as a matter of fact, when he finally closed his eyes. He opened them to find himself in a far more uncomfortable chair, in a balcony at the Los Angeles Orpheum, in the middle of Harry Houdini's opening-night performance, November 30, 1915.

"Where you been, Champ?" Lou asked. "We ain't keeping you up, are we?"

"Ladies and gentlemen, these our volunteers have my thanks. Shall they have your thanks as well?"

Amid the applause, Lou went on: "You ought to *act* interested, at least."

"Sorry, Lou," Willard said, sitting up straight and shaking his head. Cripes, he must have nodded off. He had that nagging waking sensation of clutching to the shreds of a rich and involving dream, but no, too late, it was all gone. "I'm just tired from traveling, is all."

"My friends, as I am sure you have noticed, our committee still lacks three men. But if you will indulge me, I have a suggestion. I am told that here in the house with us tonight, we have one man who is easily the equal of any three."

Lou jabbed Willard in the side. "Knock 'em dead, Champ," he said, grinning.

For an instant, Willard didn't understand. Then he remembered. Oh yeah, an onstage appearance with Houdini—like Jack London had done in Oakland, and President Wilson in Washington. Willard leaned forward to see the stage, the magician, the committee, the scatter of roses. Lou jabbed him again and mouthed the word, "Surprise." What did he mean, surprise? They had talked about this. Hadn't they?

"And so, ladies and gentlemen, will you kindly join me in inviting before the footlights the current heavyweight boxing champion—*our champion*—Mr. Jess Willard!"

In the sudden broil of the spotlight, amid a gratifying burst of cheers and applause, Willard unhesitatingly stood—remembering, just in time, the low ceiling. Grinning, he leaned over the edge and waved to the crowd, first with the right arm, then both arms. Cheered by a capacity crowd, at the biggest Orpheum theater on the West Coast—two dollars a seat, Lou had said! Hattie never would believe this. He bet Jack Johnson never got such a reception. But he wouldn't think of Johnson just now. This was Jess Willard's night. He clasped his hands together and shook them above his head.

Laughing above the cacophony, Houdini waved and cried, "Mr. Willard, please, come down!"

"On my way," Willard called, and was out the balcony door in a flash. He loped down the stairs two at a time. Sprinting through the lobby, he winked and blew a kiss at the hat-check girl, who squealed. The doors of the auditorium opened inward before him, and he entered the arena without slowing down, into the midst of a standing ovation, hundreds of faces turned to him as he ran down the central aisle toward the stage where Houdini waited.

"Mind the stairs in the pit, Mr. Willard," Houdini said. "I don't think they were made for feet your size." Newly energized by the audience's laughter, Willard made a show of capering stiff-legged up the steps, then fairly bounded onto the stage to shake the hand of the magician—who really was a *small* man, my goodness—and then shake the hands of all the other committee members. The applause continued, but the audience began to resettle itself, and Houdini waved his hands for order.

"Please, ladies and gentlemen! Please! Your attention! Thank you. Mr. Willard, gentlemen, if you will please step back, to make room for—The Wall of Mystery!"

The audience *ooh*ed as a curtain across the back of the stage lifted to reveal an ordinary brick wall, approximately twenty feet long and ten high. As Willard watched, the wall began to turn. It was built, he saw, on a circular platform flush with the stage. The disc revolved until the wall was perpendicular to the footlights.

"The Wall of Mystery, ladies and gentlemen, is not mysterious whatsoever in its construction. Perhaps from where you are sitting you can smell the mortar freshly laid, as this wall was completed only today, by twenty veteran members, personally selected and hired at double wages by the management of this theater, of Bricklayers' Union Number Thirty-Four. Gentlemen, please take a bow!"

On cue, a half dozen graying, potbellied men in denim work clothes walked into view stage left, to bow and wave their caps and grin. Willard applauded as loudly as anyone, even put both fingers in his mouth to whistle, before the bricklayers shuffled back into their workingmen's obscurity.

"Mr. Willard, gentlemen, please approach the wall and examine it at your leisure, until each of you is fully satisfied that the wall is solid and genuine in every particular."

The committee fanned out, first approaching the wall tentatively, as if some part of it might open and swallow them. Gradually they got into the spirit of the act, pushing and kicking the wall, slamming their shoulders into it, running laps around it to make sure it began and ended where it seemed to. To the audience's delight, Willard, by far the tallest of the men, took a running jump and grabbed the top of the wall, then lifted himself so that he could peer over to the other side. The audience cheered. Willard dropped down to join his fellow committeemen, all of whom took the opportunity to shake Willard's hand again.

During all this activity, Houdini's comely attendants had rolled onstage two six-foot circular screens, one from backstage left, one from backstage right. They rolled the screens to center stage, one screen stage left of the wall, one screen stage right. Just before stepping inside the left screen, Houdini said: "Now, gentlemen, please arrange yourselves around the wall so that no part of it escapes your scrutiny." Guessing what was going to happen, Willard trotted to the other side of the wall and stood, arms folded, between the wall and the stage-right screen; he could no longer see Houdini for the wall. The other men found their own positions. Willard heard a *whoosh* that he took to be Houdini dramatically closing the screen around him. "I raise my hands above the screen like so," Houdini called, "to prove I am here. But now—I am gone!" There was another *whoosh*— the attendants opening the screen? The audience gasped and murmured. Empty, Willard presumed. The attendants trotted downstage into Willard's view, professionally balanced on their high heels, carrying between them the folded screen. At that moment the screen behind Willard went *whoosh*, and he turned to see Houdini stepping out of it, one hand on his hip, the other raised above his head in a flourish.

Surprised and elated despite himself, Willard joined in the crescendo of bravos and huzzahs.

Amid the din, Houdini trotted over to Willard, gestured for him to stoop, and whispered into his ear:

"Your turn."

His breath reeked of mint. Startled, Willard straightened up. The audience continued to cheer. Houdini winked, nodded almost imperceptibly toward the open screen he just had exited. Following Houdini's glance, Willard saw the secret of the trick, was both disappointed and delighted at its simplicity, and saw that he could do it, too. Yet he knew that to accept Houdini's offer, to walk through the wall himself, was something he neither wanted nor needed to do. He was Jess Willard, heavyweight champion of the world, if only for a season, and that was enough. He was content. He'd leave walking through walls to the professionals. He clapped one hand onto Houdini's shoulder, engulfing it, smiled, and shook his head. Again almost imperceptibly, Houdini nodded, then turned to the audience, took a deep bow. Standing behind him now, feeling suddenly weary—surely the show wouldn't last much longer—Willard lifted his hands and joined the applause. Backstage to left and right, and in the catwalks directly above, he saw a cobweb of cables and pulleys against stark white brick—ugly, really, but completely invisible from the auditorium. On the highest catwalk two niggers in coveralls stood motionless, not applauding. Looking about, gaping, he was sure, like a hick, Willard told himself: *Well, Jess, now you've had a taste of how it feels to be Harry Houdini.* The afterthought came unbidden, as a jolt: *And Jack Johnson, too.* Disconcerted, Willard turned to stare at the stage-right screen, as two of the women folded it up and carted it away.

Jennifer barely remembered her Grandma Hattie, but she felt as if she sort of knew her by now, seeing the care she had lavished for decades on these scrapbooks, and reading the neat captions Hattie had typed and placed alongside each item:

FORT WAYNE, 1912—WORKING THE BAG—KO'd J. Young in 6th on May 23 (Go JESS!)

The captions were yellowed and brittle now, tended to flutter out in bits like confetti when the albums were opened too roughly.

"I'm a good typist, Jess," Jennifer said. "I could make you some new ones."

"No, thanks," Jess said. "I like these fine."

"Where's the Johnson book?"

"Hold your horses, it's right here. There you go. I knew you'd want that one."

Jennifer was less interested in Jack Johnson *per se* than in the fact that one of Hattie's scrapbooks was devoted to one of her husband's most famous opponents, a man whom Jess had beaten for the title and never met again. Jennifer suspected this scrapbook alone was as much the work of Jess as of Hattie—and the aging Jess at that, since it began with Johnson's obituaries in 1946. Hence the appeal of the Johnson scrapbook; this mysterious and aging Jess, after all, was the only one she knew. The last third of the book had no typewritten captions, and clippings that were crooked beneath their plastic. The last few pages were blank. Stuck into the back were a few torn out and clumsily folded newspaper clippings about Muhammad Ali.

"Johnson was cool," she said, turning the brittle pages with care. "It is so cool that you got to fight him, Jess. And that you won! You must have been proud."

"I *was* proud," Willard said, reaching for another pillow to slide beneath his bony buttocks. "Still am," he added. "But I wish I had known him, too. He was an interesting man."

"He died in a car wreck, didn't he?"

"Yep."

"That's so sad." Jennifer knew about the car wreck, of course; it was all over the front of the scrapbook. She was just stalling, making noise with her mouth, while pondering whether now was the time to get Jess talking about Johnson's three wives, all of them white women, all of them *blonde* white women. Jennifer was very interested to know Jess's thoughts about that.

"You fought him in Havana because, what? You weren't allowed to fight in the United States, or something?" She asked this with great casualness, knowing Johnson was a fugitive from U.S. justice at the time, convicted of violating the Mann Act, i.e. transporting women across state lines for "immoral purposes," i.e., white slavery, i.e., sex with a white woman.

"Yeah, something like that," Jess said. He examined the ragged hem of his sweater, obviously uninclined to pursue the conversation further. God, getting an eighty-seven-year-old man to talk about sex was *hard*.

"I was trying to tell Carl about it, but I, uh, forgot the uh, details." She kept talking, inanely, flushed with horror. *Massive* slip-up. She never had mentioned Carl in front of Jess before, certainly not by name. Carl was three years older than she was, and worse yet, a dropout. He was also black. Not Negro, he politely insisted: black. He wanted to meet Jess, and Jennifer wanted that to happen, too— but she would have to careful about how she brought it up. Not this way! Sure, Jess might admire Jack Johnson as a fighter, but would he want his teenage great-granddaughter to date him?

"There was some rule against it, I think," Jess said, oblivious, and she closed her eyes for a second in relief. "I be doggoned but this sweater wasn't worth bringing home from the store." He glanced up. "You didn't give me this sweater, did you, Sprout?"

"No, Jess," Jennifer said. She closed the Johnson scrapbook, elated to avoid *that* conversation one more day.

"I wouldn't hurt you for nothing, you know," Jess said. "Wouldn't let no one else hurt you, neither."

She grinned, charmed. "Would you stand up for me, Jess?"

"I sure would, baby. Anybody bothers you, I'll clean his clock." He slowly punched the air with mottled fists, his eyes huge and swimming behind his glasses, and grinned a denture-taut grin.

On impulse, Jennifer kissed his forehead. Resettling herself on the floor, she opened one of the safer scrapbooks. Here was her favorite photo of Jess at the produce market, hair gray beneath his paper hat. He held up to the light a Grade A white egg that he smiled at in satisfaction. Grandma Hattie had typed beneath the photo: **TWO GOOD EGGS**.

"One hundred and thirteen fights," Jess said. Something in his voice made Jennifer glance up. He looked suddenly morose, gazing at nothing, and Jennifer worried that she had said something to upset him; he was so moody, sometimes. "That's how many Johnson fought. More than Tunney, more than Louis. Twice as many as Marciano. Four times as many as Jeffries, as Fitzsimmons, as Gentleman Jim Corbett. And forty-four of them knockouts." He sighed and repeated, almost inaudibly, "Forty-four."

She cleared her throat, determined, and said loudly: "Hey, you want to write another letter?" About once a month, Jess dictated to her a letter to the editor, saying Ali was the champ fair and square whether people liked it or not, same as Jack Johnson had been, same as Jess Willard had been, and if people didn't like it then let them take Ali on in the ring like men. The *Times* had stopped printing the letters after the third one, but she hadn't told Jess that.

He didn't seem to have heard her. After a few seconds, though, his face brightened. "Hey," he said. "Did I ever tell you about the time I got the chance to walk through a wall?"

Relieved, she screwed up her face in mock concentration. "Well, let's see, about a hundred million billion times, but you can tell me again if you want. Do you ever wish you'd done it?"

"Nah," Jess said, leaning into the scrapbook to peer at the two good eggs. "I probably misunderstood him in the first place. He never let anybody *else* get in on the act, that I heard of. He was too big a star for that." He sat back, settled into the armchair with a sigh. "I must have misunderstood him. Anyway." He was quiet again, but smiling. "Too late now, huh?"

"I guess so," Jennifer said, slowly turning the pages, absently stroking her beads so that the strands clicked together. Beside her Jess began, gently, to snore. She suppressed a laugh: Could you believe it? Just like that, down for the count. Without realizing it, she had turned to a clipping from the *Times*, dated December 1, 1915.

TWO CHAMPIONS MEET

RING ARTIST, ESCAPE ARTIST SHAKE ON ORPHEUM STAGE

Young Jess looked pretty spiffy in his evening wear, Jennifer thought. *Spiffy*, she knew from reading the scrapbooks, had been one of Grandma Hattie's favorite words. Jess was crouched to fit into the photograph, which must have been taken from the front row. The two men looked down at the camera; at their feet a couple of footlights were visible. At the bottom edge of the photo was the blurred top of a man's head. Someone had penciled a shaky arrow from this blur and written, "Lou." The background was murky, but Jennifer could imagine a vaulted plaster ceiling, a chandelier, a curtain embroidered with intricate Oriental designs. Beneath the clipping, Grandma Hattie had typed: **JESS MEETS EHRICH WEISS a.k.a. HARRY HOUDINI (1874–1926).** On the facing page, Houdini's faded signature staggered across a theater program.

Even as a kid, Jennifer had been intrigued by Houdini's eyes. Although the clipping was yellowed and the photo blurred to begin with, Houdini always seemed to look right at her, *into* her. It was the same in the other photos, in the Houdini books she kept checking out of the library. He wasn't Jennifer's type, but he had great eyes.

As she looked at the clipping, she began to daydream. She was on stage, wearing a tuxedo and a top hat and tights cut up to *there*, and she pulled back a screen to reveal—who? Hmm. She wasn't sure. Maybe Carl; maybe not. Daydreaming was a sign, said the goateed guy who taught her comp class, of sensitivity, of creativity. Yeah, right. Sometimes when she was home alone—she told no one this—she put on gym shorts and went out back and boxed the air, for an hour or more at a time, until she was completely out of breath. Why, she couldn't say. Being a pacifist, she couldn't imagine hitting a *person*, no, but she sure beat hell out of the air. She really wanted to be neither a boxer nor a magician. She was a political science major, and had her heart set on the Peace Corps. And yet, when Carl had walked into the coffeehouse that night alone, fidgeting in the doorway with an out-of-place look, considering, maybe, ducking back outside again, what did she say to him? She walked right up to Carl, bold as brass (that was another of Grandma Hattie's, BOLD as BRASS), stuck out her chin and stuck out her hand and said, "Hi, my name is Jennifer Schumacher, and I'm the great-granddaughter of the ex-heavyweight champion of the world." Carl shook her hand and looked solemn and said, "Ali?" and people stared at them, they laughed so hard, and if *I* ever get a chance to walk through a wall, she vowed to herself as she closed the scrapbook, *I'm* taking it—so *there.*

what i didn't see

KAREN JOY FOWLER

Karen Joy Fowler was born in Bloomington, Indiana in 1950. She has won two Nebjula Awards for her short fiction and she won the World Fantasy Award for her collection, *Black Glass*. Fowler is also the author of five novels, including her debut *Sarah Canary* (described by critic John Clute as one of the finest First Contact novels ever written), *Wit's End*, and *The Jane Austen Book Club*. She lives in Santa Cruz, California with husband Hugh Sterling Fowler II. They have two grown children.

"What I Didn't See" provoked a bit of controversy among a few readers who questioned its inclusion in *SCIFICTION*. It wasn't the first story I've published without a direct link to the science fiction and fantasy genres (I published a few in *OMNI*), but it was the first that provoked outrage. Aside from the story's power as *story*, its "conversation" with a famous classic story of the 1960s gives it an extra jolt. I also note that its dark edge enabled me—with no hesitation— to include it my horror half of the *Year's Best Fantasy and Horror*.

I saw Archibald Murray's obituary in the Tribune a couple of days ago. It was a long notice, because of all those furbelows he had after his name, and dredged up that old business of ours, which can't have pleased his children. I, myself, have never spoken up before, as I've always felt that nothing I saw sheds any light, but now I'm the last of us. Even Wilmet is gone, though I always picture him such a boy. And there is something to be said for having the last word, which I am surely having.

I still go to the jungle sometimes when I sleep. The sound of the clock turns to a million insects all chewing at once, water dripping onto leaves, the hum inside your head when you run a fever. Sooner or later Eddie comes, in his silly hat and boots up to his knees. He puts his arms around me in the way he did when he meant business and I wake up too hot, too old, and all alone.

You're never alone in the jungle. You can't see through the twist of roots and leaves and vines, the streakish, tricky light, but you've always got a sense of being seen. You make too much noise when you walk.

At the same time, you understand that you don't matter. You're small and stuck on the ground. The ghosts of paths weren't made for you. If you get bitten by a snake, it's your own damn fault, not the snake's, and if someone doesn't drag you out you'll turn to mulch just like anything else would and show up next as mold or moss, ferns, leeches, ants, millipedes, butterflies, beetles. The jungle is a jammed-alive place, which means that something is always dying there.

Eddie had this idea once that defects of character could be treated with doses of landscape: the ocean for the histrionic, mountains for the domineering, and so forth. I forget the desert, but the jungle was the place to send the self-centered.

We seven went into the jungle with guns in our hands and love in our hearts. I say so now when there is no one left to contradict me.

Archer organized us. He was working at the time for the Louisville Museum of Natural History and he had a stipend from Collections for skins and bones. The rest of us were amateur enthusiasts and paid our own way just for the adventure. Archer asked Eddie (arachnids) to go along and Russell MacNamara (chimps), and Trenton Cox (butterflies), who couldn't or wouldn't, and Wilmet Siebert (big game), and Merion Cowper (tropical medicine), and also Merion's wife, only he turned out to be between wives by the time we left, so he was the one who brought Beverly Kriss.

I came with Eddie to help with his nets, pooters, and kill jars. I was never the sort to scream over bugs, but if I had been, twenty-eight years of marriage to Eddie would have cured me. The more legs a creature had, the better Eddie thought of it. Up to point. Up to eight.

In fact Archer was anxious there be some women and had specially invited me, though Eddie didn't tell me so. This was smart; I would have suspected I was along to do the dishes (though of course there were the natives for this) and for nursing the sick, which we did end up at a bit, Beverly and I, when the matter was too small or too nasty for Merion. I might not have come at all if I'd known I was wanted. As it was, I learned to bake a passable bread on campfire coals with a native beer for yeast, but it was my own choice to do so and I ate as much of the bread myself as I wished.

I pass over the various boats on which we sailed, though these trips were not without incident. Wilmet turned out to have a nervous stomach; it started to trouble him on the ocean and then stuck around when we hit dry land again. Russell was a drinker, and not the good sort, unlucky and suspicious, a man who thought he loved a game of cards, but should have never been allowed to play. Beverly was a modern girl in 1928 and could chew gum, smoke, and wipe the lipstick off her mouth and onto yours all at the same time. She and Merion were frisky for Archer's taste and he tried to shift this off onto me, saying I was being made uncomfortable, when I didn't care one way or the other. I worried that it would be a pattern and every time one of the men was tired on the trail they'd say we had to stop on my account. I told Eddie right away I wouldn't like it if this was to happen. So by the time we were geared up and walking in, we already thought we knew each other pretty well and we didn't entirely like what we knew. Still, I guessed we'd get along fine when there was more to occupy us. Even during those long days it took to reach the mountains—the endless trains, motor cars, donkeys, mules, and finally our very own feet—things went smoothly enough.

By the time we reached the Lulenga Mission, we'd seen a fair bit of Africa—low and high, hot and cold, black and white. I've learned some things in the years since, so there's a strong temptation now to pretend that I felt the things I should have felt, knew the things I might have known. The truth is otherwise. My attitudes toward the natives, in particular, were not what they might have been. The men who helped us interested me little and impressed me not at all. Many of them had their teeth filed and were only ten years or so from cannibalism, or so we were informed. No one, ourselves included, was clean, but Beverly and I would have tried, only we couldn't bathe without the nuisance of being spied on. Whether this was to see if we looked good or only good to eat, I did not wish to know.

The fathers at the mission told us that slaves used to be led through the villages in ropes so that people could draw on their bodies the cuts of meat they were buying before the slaves were butchered, and with that my mind was set. I never did acknowledge any beauty or kindness in the people we met, though Eddie saw much of both.

We spent three nights in Lulenga, which gave us each a bed, good food, and a chance to wash our hair and clothes in some privacy. Beverly and I shared a room, there not being sufficient number for her to have her own. She was quarreling with Merion at the time though I forget about what. They were a tempest, those two, always shouting, sulking, and then turning on the heat again. A tiresome sport for spectators, but surely invigorating for the players. So Eddie was bunked up with Russell, which put me out, because I liked to wake up with him.

We were joined at dinner the first night by a Belgian administrator who treated us to real wine and whose name I no longer remember though I can picture him yet—a bald, hefty man in his sixties with a white beard. I recall how he joked that his hair had migrated from his head to his chin and then settled in where the food was plentiful.

Eddie was in high spirits and talking more than usual. The spiders in Africa are exhilaratingly aggressive. Many of them have fangs and nocturnal habits. We'd already shipped home dozens of button spiders with red hourglasses on their backs, and some beautiful golden violin spiders with long delicate legs and dark chevrons underneath. But that evening Eddie was most excited about a small jumping spider, which seemed not to spin her own web, but to lurk instead in the web of another. She had no beautiful markings; when he'd first seen one, he'd thought she was a bit of dirt blown into the silken strands. Then she grew legs and, as we watched, stalked and killed the web's owner and all with a startling cunning.

"Working together, a thousand spiders can tie up a lion," the Belgian told us. Apparently it was a local saying. "But then they don't work together, do they? The blacks haven't noticed. Science is observation and Africa produces no scientists."

In those days all gorilla hunts began at Lulenga, so it took no great discernment to guess that the rest of our party was not after spiders. The Belgian told us that only six weeks past, a troupe of gorilla males had attacked a tribal village. The food stores had been broken into and a woman carried off. Her bracelets were found the next day, but she'd not yet returned and the Belgian feared she never would. It was such a sustained siege that the whole village had to be abandoned.

"The seizure of the woman I dismiss as superstition and exaggeration," Archer said. He had a formal way of speaking; you'd never guess he was from Kentucky. Not so grand to look at—inch-thick glasses that made his eyes pop, unkempt hair, filthy shirt cuffs. He poured more of the Belgian's wine around, and I recall his being especially generous to his own glass. Isn't it funny, the things you remember? "But the rest of your story interests me. If any gorilla was taken I'd pay for the skin, assuming it wasn't spoiled in the peeling."

The Belgian said he would inquire. And then he persisted with his main point, very serious and deliberate. "As to the woman, I've heard these tales too often to discard them so quickly as you. I've heard of native women subjected to degradations far worse than death. May I ask you as a favor then, in deference to my greater experience and longer time here, to leave your women at the mission when you go gorilla hunting?"

It was courteously done and obviously cost Archer to refuse. Yet he did, saying to my astonishment that it would defeat his whole purpose to leave me and Beverly behind. He then gave the Belgian his own thinking, which we seven had already heard over several repetitions—that gorillas were harmless and gentle, if oversized and over-muscled. Sweet-natured vegetarians. He based this entirely on the wear on their teeth; he'd read a paper on it from some university in London.

Archer then characterized the famous Du Chaillu description—glaring eyes, yellow incisors, hellish dream creatures—as a slick and dangerous form of self aggrandizement. It was an account tailored to bring big game hunters on the run and so had to be quickly countered for the gorillas' own protection. Archer was out to prove Du Chaillu wrong and he needed me and Beverly to help. "If one of the girls should bring down a large male," he said, "it will seem as exciting as shooting a cow. No man will cross a continent merely to do something a pair of girls has already done."

He never did ask us, because that wasn't his way. He just raised it as our Christian duty and then left us to worry it over in our minds.

Of course we were all carrying rifles. Eddie and I had practiced on bottles and such in preparation for the trip. On the way over

I'd gotten pretty good at clay pigeons off the deck of our ship. But I wasn't eager to kill a gentle vegetarian—a nightmare from hell would have suited me a good deal better (if scared me a great deal more.) Beverly too, I'm guessing.

Not that she said anything about it that night. Wilmet, our youngest at twenty-five years and also shortest by a whole head—blond hair, pink cheeks, and little rat's eyes—had been lugging a tin of British biscuits about the whole trip and finishing every dinner by eating one while we watched. He was always explaining why they couldn't be shared when no one was asking. They kept his stomach settled; he couldn't afford to run out and so on; his very life might depend on them if he were sick and nothing else would stay down and so forth. We wouldn't have noticed if he hadn't persisted in bringing it up.

But suddenly he and Beverly had their heads close together, whispering, and he was giving her one of his precious biscuits. She took it without so much as a glance at Merion, even when he leaned in to say he'd like one, too. Wilmet answered that there were too few to share with everyone so Merion upset a water glass into the tin and spoiled all the biscuits that remained. Wilmet left the table and didn't return and the subject of the all-girl gorilla hunt passed by in the unpleasantness.

That night I woke under the gauze of the mosquito net in such a heat I thought I had malaria. Merion had given us all quinine and I meant to take it regularly, but I didn't always remember. There are worse fevers in the jungle, especially if you've been collecting spiders, so it was cheerful of me to fix on malaria. My skin was burning from the inside out, especially my hands and feet, and I was sweating like butter on a hot day. I thought to wake Beverly, but by the time I stood up the fit had already passed and anyway her bed was empty.

In the morning she was back. I planned to talk to her then, get her thoughts on gorilla hunting, but I woke early and she slept late.

I breakfasted alone and went for a stroll around the Mission grounds. It was cool with little noise beyond the wind and birds. To the west, a dark trio of mountains, two of which smoked. Furrowed fields below me, banana plantations, and trellises of roses, curving into archways that led to the church. How often we grow a garden around our houses of worship. We march ourselves through Eden to get to God.

Merion joined me in the graveyard where I'd just counted three deaths by lion, British names all. I was thinking how outlandish it was, how sadly unlikely that all the prams and nannies and public schools should come to this, and even the bodies pinned under stones so hyenas wouldn't come for them. I was hoping for a more modern sort of death myself, a death at home, a death from American causes, when Merion cleared his throat behind me.

He didn't look like my idea of a doctor, but I believe he was a good one. Well-paid, that's for sure and certain. As to appearances, he reminded me of the villain in some Lillian Gish film, meaty and needing a shave, but handsome enough when cleaned up. He swung his arms when he walked so he took up more space than he needed. There was something to this confidence I admired, though it irritated me on principle. I often liked him least of all and I'm betting he was sharp enough to know it. "I trust you slept well," he said. He looked at me slant-wise, looked away again. *I trust you slept well.* I trust you were in no way disturbed by Beverly sneaking out to meet me in the middle of the night.

Or maybe—I trust Beverly didn't sneak out last night.

Or maybe just I trust you slept well. It wasn't a question, which saved me the nuisance of figuring the answer.

"So," he said next, "what do you think of this gorilla scheme of Archer's?" and then gave me no time to respond. "The fathers tell me a party from Manchester went up just last month and brought back seventeen. Four of them youngsters—lovely little family group for the British museum. I only hope they left us a few." And then, lowering his voice, "I'm glad for the chance to discuss things with you privately."

There turned out to be a detail to the Belgian's story judged too delicate for the dinnertable, but Merion, being a doctor and maybe more of a man's man than Archer, a man who could be appealed to on behalf of women, had heard it. The woman carried away from the village had been menstruating. This at least the Belgian hoped, that we'd not to go up the mountain with our female affliction in full flower.

And because he was a doctor I told Merion straight out that I'd been light and occasional; I credited this to the upset of travel. I thought to set his mind at ease, but I should have guessed I wasn't his first concern.

"Beverly's too headstrong to listen to me," he said. "Too young and reckless. She'll take her cue from you. A solid, sensible, mature woman like you could rein her in a bit. For her own good."

A woman unlikely to inflame the passions of jungle apes was what I heard. Even in my prime I'd never been the sort of woman poems are written about, but this seemed to place me low indeed. An hour later I saw the humor in it, and Eddie surely laughed at me quickly enough when I confessed it, but at the time I was sincerely insulted. How sensible, how mature was that?

I was further provoked by the way he expected me to give in. Archer was certain I'd agree to save the gorillas and Merion was certain I'd agree to save Beverly. I had a moment's outrage over these men who planned to run me by appealing to what they imagined was my weakness.

Merion more than Archer. How smug he was, and how I detested his calm acceptance of every advantage that came to him, as if it were no more than his due. No white woman in all the world had seen the wild gorillas yet—we were to be the first—but I was to step aside from it just because he asked me.

"I haven't walked all this way to miss out on the gorillas," I told him, as politely as I could. "The only question is whether I'm looking or shooting at them." And then I left him, because my own feelings were no credit to me and I didn't mean to have them anymore. I went to look for Eddie and spend the rest of the day emptying kill jars, pinning and labeling the occupants.

The next morning Beverly announced, in deference to Merion's wishes, that she'd be staying behind at the mission when we went on. Quick as could be, Wilmet said his stomach was in such an uproar that he would stay behind as well. This took us all by surprise as he was the only real hunter among us. And it put Merion in an awful bind—we'd more likely need a doctor on the mountain than at the mission, but I guessed he'd sooner see Beverly taken by gorillas than by Wilmet. He fussed and sweated over a bunch of details that didn't matter to anyone and all the while the day passed in secret conferences—Merion with Archer, Archer with Beverly, Russell with Wilmet, Eddie with Beverly. By dinnertime Beverly said she'd changed her mind and Wilmet had undergone a wonderful recovery. When we left next morning we were at full complement, but pretty tightly strung.

It took almost two hundred porters to get our little band of seven up Mount Mikeno. It was a hard track with no path, hoisting ourselves over roots, cutting and crawling our way through tightly woven bamboo. There were long slides of mud on which it was impossible to get a grip. And always sharp uphill. My heart and my lungs worked as hard or harder than my legs and though it wasn't hot I had to wipe my face and neck continually. As the altitude rose I gasped for breath like a fish in a net.

We women were placed in the middle of the pack with gun-bearers both ahead and behind. I slid back many times and had to be caught and set upright again. Eddie was in a torment over the webs we walked through with no pause as to architect and Russell over the bearers who, he guaranteed, would bolt with our guns at the first sign of danger. But we wouldn't make camp if we stopped for spiders and couldn't stay the course without our hands free. Soon Beverly sang out for a gorilla to come and carry her the rest of the way.

Then we were all too winded and climbed for hours without speaking, breaking whenever we came suddenly into the sun, sustaining ourselves with chocolate and crackers.

Still our mood was excellent. We saw elephant tracks, large, sunken bowls in the mud, half-filled with water. We saw glades of wild carrots and an extravagance of pink and purple orchids. Grasses in greens so delicate they seemed to be melting. I revised my notions of Eden, leaving the roses behind and choosing instead these remote forests where the gorillas lived—foggy rains, the crooked hagenia trees strung with vines, golden mosses, silver lichen; the rattle and buzz of flies and beetles; the smell of catnip as we stepped into it.

At last we stopped. Our porters set up which gave us a chance to rest. My feet were swollen and my knees stiffening, but I had a great appetite for dinner and a great weariness for bed; I was asleep before sundown. And then I was awake again. The temperature, which had been pleasant all day, plunged. Eddie and I wrapped ourselves in coats and sweaters and each other. He worried about our porters, who didn't have the blankets we had, although they were free to keep a fire up as high as they liked. At daybreak, they came complaining to Archer. He raised their pay a dime apiece since they had surely suffered during the night, but almost fifty of them left us anyway.

We spent that morning sitting around the camp, nursing our blisters and scrapes, some of us looking for spiders, some of us practicing our marksmanship. There was a stream about five minutes walk away with a pool where Beverly and I dropped our feet. No mosquitoes, no sweat bees, no flies, and that alone made it paradise. But no sooner did I have this thought and a wave of malarial heat came on me, drenching the back of my shirt.

When I came to myself again, Beverly was in the middle of something and I hadn't heard the beginning. She might have told me Merion's former wife had been unfaithful to him. Later this seemed like something I'd once been told, but maybe only because it made sense. "Now he seems to think the apes will leave me alone if only I don't go tempting them," she said. "Lord!"

"He says they're drawn to menstrual blood."

"Then I've got no problem. Anyway Russell says that Burunga says we'll never see them, dressed as we're dressed. Our clothes make too much noise when we walk. He told Russell we must hunt them naked. I haven't passed that on to Merion yet. I'm saving it for a special occasion."

I had no idea who Burunga was. Not the cook and not our chief guide, which were the only names I'd bothered with. I was, at least (and I do see now, how very least it is) embarrassed to learn that Beverly had done otherwise. "Are you planning to shoot an ape?" I asked. It came over me all of sudden that I wanted a particular answer, but I couldn't unearth what answer that was.

"I'm not really a killer," she said. "More a sweet-natured vegetarian. Of the meat-eating variety. But Archer says he'll put my picture up in the museum. You know the sort of thing—rifle on shoulder, foot on body, eyes to the horizon. Wouldn't that be something to take the kiddies to?"

Eddie and I had no kiddies; Beverly might have realized it was a sore spot. And Archer had made no such representations to me. She sat in a spill of sunlight. Her hair was short and heavy and fell in a neat cap over her ears. Brown until the sun made it golden. She wasn't a pretty woman so much as she just drew your eye and kept it. "Merion keeps on about how he paid my way here. Like he hasn't gotten his money's worth." She kicked her feet and water beaded up on her bare legs. "You're so lucky. Eddie's the best."

Which he was, and any woman could see it. I never met a better man than my Eddie and in our whole forty-three years together there were only three times I wished I hadn't married him. I say this now, because we're coming up on one of those times. I wouldn't want someone thinking less of Eddie because of anything I said.

"You're still in love with him, aren't you?" Beverly asked. "After so many years of marriage."

I admitted as much.

Beverly shook her golden head. "Then you'd best keep with him," she told me.

Or did she? What did she say to me? I've been over the conversation so many times I no longer remember it at all.

In contrast, this next bit is perfectly clear. Beverly said she was tired and went to her tent to lie down. I found the men playing bridge, taking turns at watching. I was bullied into playing, because Russell didn't like his cards and thought to change his luck by putting some empty space between hands. So it was me and Wilmet opposite Eddie and Russell, with Merion and Archer in the vicinity, smoking and looking on. On the other side of the tents the laughter of our porters.

I would have liked to team with Eddie, but Russell said bridge was too dangerous a game when husbands and wives partnered up and there was a ready access to guns. He was joking, of course, but you couldn't have told by his face.

While we played Russell talked about chimpanzees and how they ran their lives. Back in those days no one had looked at chimps yet so it was all only guesswork. Topped by guessing that gorillas would be pretty much the same. There was a natural order to things, Russell said, and you could reason it out; it was simple Darwinism.

I didn't think you could reason out spiders; I didn't buy that you could reason out chimps. So I didn't listen. I played my cards and every so often a word would fall in. Male this, male that. Blah, blah, dominance. Survival of the fittest, blah, blah. Natural selection, nature red in tooth and claw. Blah and blah. There was an argument then as to whether by simple Darwinism we could expect a social arrangement of monogamous married couples or whether the males would all have harems. There were points to be made either way and I didn't care for any of those points.

Wilmet opened with one heart and soon we were up to three. I mentioned how Beverly had said she'd get her picture in the Louisville Museum if she killed an ape. "It's not entirely my decision," Archer said. "But, yes, part of my plan is that there will be pictures. And interviews. Possibly in magazines, certainly in the museum. The whole object is that people be told." And this began a discussion over whether, for the purposes of saving gorilla lives, it would work best if Beverly was to kill one or if it should be me. There was some general concern that the sight of Beverly in a pith helmet might be, somehow, stirring, whereas if I were the one, it wouldn't be cute in the least. If Archer really wished to put people off gorilla-hunting, then, the men agreed, I was his girl. Of course it was not as bald as that, but that was the gist.

Wilmet lost a trick he'd hoped to finesse. We were going down and I suddenly saw that he'd opened with only four hearts, which, though they were pretty enough, an ace and a king included, was a witless thing to do. I still think so.

"I expected more support," he said to me, "when you took us to two," as if it were my fault.

"Length is strength," I said right back and then I burst into tears, because he was so short it was an awful thing to say. It took me more by surprise than anyone and most surprising of all, I didn't seem to care about the crying. I got up from the table and walked off. I could hear Eddie apologizing behind me as if I was the one who'd opened with four hearts. "Change of life," I heard him saying. It was so like Eddie to know what was happening to me even before I did.

It was so unlike him to apologize for me. At that moment I hated him with all the rest. I went to our tent and fetched some water and my rifle. We weren't any of us to go into the jungle alone so no one imagined this was what I was doing.

The sky had begun to cloud up and soon the weather was colder. There was no clear track to follow, only antelope trails. Of course I got lost. I had thought to take every possible turn to the right and then reverse this coming back, but the plan didn't suit the landscape nor achieve the end desired. I had a whistle, but was angry enough not to use it. I counted on Eddie to find me eventually as he always did.

I believe I walked for more than four hours. Twice it rained, intensifying all the green smells of the jungle. Occasionally the sun was out and the mosses and leaves overlaid with silvered water. I saw a cat print that made me move my rifle off of safe to ready and then often had to set it aside as the track took me over roots and under hollow trees. The path was unstable and sometimes slid out from under me.

Once I put my hand on a spider's web. It was a domed web over an orb, intricate and a beautiful pale yellow in color. I never touched a silk so strong. The spider was big and black with yellow spots at the undersides of her legs and, judging by the corpses, she carried all her victims to the web's center before wrapping them. I would have brought her back, but I had nothing to keep her in. It seemed a betrayal of Eddie to let her be, but that sort of evened our score.

Next thing I put my hand on was a soft looking leaf. I pulled it away full of nettles.

Although the way back to camp was clearly downhill, I began to go up. I thought to find a vista, see the mountains, orient myself. I was less angry by now and suffered more from the climbing as a result. The rain began again and I picked out a sheltered spot to sit and tend my stinging hand. I should have been cold and frightened, but I wasn't either. The pain in my hand was subsiding. The jungle was beautiful and the sound of rain a lullaby. I remember wishing that this was where I belonged, that I lived here. Then the heat came on me so hard I couldn't wish at all.

A noise brought me out of it—a crashing in the bamboo. Turning, I saw the movement of leaves and the backside of something rather like a large black bear. A gorilla has a strange way of walking—on the hind feet and the knuckles, but with arms so long their backs are hardly bent. I had one clear look and then the creature was gone. But I could still hear it and I was determined to see it again.

I knew I'd never have another chance; even if we did see one later the men would take it over. I was still too hot. My shirt was drenched from sweat and rain; my pants, too, and making a noise whenever I bent my knees. So I removed everything and put back only my socks and boots. I left the rest of my clothes folded on the spot where I'd been sitting, picked up my rifle, and went into the bamboo.

Around a rock, under a log, over a root, behind a tree was the prettiest open meadow you'd ever hope to see. Three gorillas were in it, one male, two female. It might have been a harem. It might have been a family—a father, mother and daughter. The sun came out. One female combed the other with her hands, the two of them blinking in the sun. The male was seated in a patch of wild carrots, pulling and eating them with no particular ardor. I could see his profile and the gray in his fur. He twitched his fingers a bit, like a man listening to music. There were flowers—pink and white—in concentric circles where some pond had been and now wasn't. One lone tree. I stood and looked for a good long time.

Then I raised the barrel of my gun. The movement brought the eyes of the male to me. He stood. He was bigger than I could ever have imagined. In the leather of his face I saw surprise, curiosity, caution. Something else, too. Something so human it made me feel like an old woman with no clothes on. I might have shot him just for that, but I knew it wasn't right—to kill him merely because he was more human than I anticipated. He thumped his chest, a rhythmic beat that made the women look to him. He showed me his teeth. Then he turned and took the women away.

I watched it all through the sight of my gun. I might have hit him several times—spared the women, freed the women. But I couldn't see that they wanted freeing and Eddie had told me never to shoot a gun angry. The gorillas faded from the meadow. I was cold then and I went for my clothes.

Russell had beaten me to them. He stood with two of our guides, staring down at my neatly folded pants. Nothing for it but to walk up beside him and pick them up, shake them for ants, put them on. He turned his back as I dressed and he couldn't manage a word. I was even more embarrassed. "Eddie must be frantic," I said to break the awkwardness.

"All of us, completely beside ourselves. Did you find any sign of her?"

Which was how I learned that Beverly had disappeared.

We were closer to camp than I'd feared if farther than I'd hoped. While we walked I did my best to recount my final conversation with Beverly to Russell. I was, apparently, the last to have seen her. The card game had broken up soon after I left and the men gone their separate ways. A couple of hours later, Merion began looking for Beverly who was no longer in her tent. No one was alarmed, at first, but by now they were.

I was made to repeat everything she'd said again and again and questioned over it, too, though there was nothing useful in it and soon I began to feel I'd made up every word. Archer asked our guides to look over the ground about the pool and around her tent. He had some cowboy scene in his mind, I suppose, the primitive who can read a broken branch, a footprint, a bit of fur and piece it all together. Our guides looked with great seriousness, but found nothing. We searched and called and sent up signaling shots until night came over us.

"She was taken by the gorillas," Merion told us. "Just as I said she'd be." I tried to read his face in the red of the firelight, but couldn't. Nor catch his tone of voice.

"No prints," our chief guide repeated. "No sign."

That night our cook refused to make us dinner. The natives were talking a great deal amongst themselves, very quiet. To us they said as little as possible. Archer demanded an explanation, but got nothing but dodge and evasion.

"They're scared," Eddie said, but I didn't see this.

A night even more bitter than the last and Beverly not dressed for it. In the morning the porters came to Archer to say they were going back. No measure of arguing or threatening or bribing changed their minds. We could come or stay as we chose; it was clearly of no moment to them. I, of course, was given no choice, but was sent back to the mission with the rest of the gear excepting what the men kept behind.

At Lulenga one of the porters tried to speak with me. He had no English and I followed none of it except Beverly's name. I told him to wait while I fetched one of the fathers to translate, but he misunderstood or else he refused. When we returned he was gone and I never did see him again.

The men stayed eight more days on Mount Mikeno and never found so much as a bracelet.

Because I'm a woman I wasn't there for the parts you want most to hear. The waiting and the not-knowing were, in my view of things, as hard or harder than the searching, but you don't make stories out of that. Something happened to Beverly, but I can't tell you what. Something happened on the mountain after I left, something that brought Eddie back to me so altered in spirit I felt I hardly knew him, but I wasn't there to see what it was. Eddie and I departed Africa immediately and not in the company of the other men in our party. We didn't even pack up all our spiders.

For months after, I wished to talk about Beverly, to put together this possibility and that possibility and settle on something I could live with. I felt the need most strongly at night. But Eddie couldn't hear her name. He'd sunk so deep into himself, he rarely looked out. He stopped sleeping and wept from time to time and these were things he did his best to hide from me. I tried to talk to him about it, I tried to be patient and loving, I tried to be kind. I failed in all these things.

A year, two more passed, and he began to resemble himself again, but never in full. My full, true Eddie never did come back from the jungle.

Then one day, at breakfast, with nothing particular to prompt it, he told me there'd been a massacre. That after I left for Lulenga the men had spent the days hunting and killing gorillas. He didn't describe it to me at all, yet it sprang bright and terrible into my mind, my own little family group lying in their blood in the meadow.

Forty or more, Eddie said. Probably more. Over several days. Babies, too. They couldn't even bring the bodies back; it looked so bad to be collecting when Beverly was gone. They'd slaughtered the gorillas as if they were cows.

Eddie was dressed in his old plaid robe, his gray hair in uncombed bunches, crying into his fried eggs. I wasn't talking, but he put his hands over his ears in case I did. He was shaking all over from weeping, his head trembling on his neck. "It felt like murder," he said. "Just exactly like murder."

I took his hands down from his head and held on hard. "I expect it was mostly Merion."

"No," he said. "It was mostly me."

At first, Eddie told me, Merion was certain the gorillas had taken Beverly. But later, he began to comment on the strange behavior of the porters. How they wouldn't talk to us, but whispered to each other. How they left so quickly. "I was afraid," Eddie told me. "So upset about Beverly and then terribly afraid. Russell and Merion, they were so angry I could smell it. I thought at any moment one of them would say something that couldn't be unsaid, something that would get to the Belgians. And then I wouldn't be able to stop it anymore. So I kept us stuck on the gorillas. I kept us going after them. I kept us angry until we had killed so very many and were all so ashamed, there would be no way to turn and accuse someone new."

I still didn't quite understand. "Do you think one of the porters killed Beverly?" It was a possibility that had occurred to me, too; I admit it.

"No," said Eddie. "That's my point. But you saw how the blacks were treated back at Lulenga. You saw the chains and the beatings. I couldn't let them be suspected." His voice was so clogged I could hardly make out the words. "I need you to tell me I did the right thing."

So I told him. I told him he was the best man I ever knew. "Thank you," he said. And with that he shook off my hands, dried his eyes, and left the table.

That night I tried to talk to him again. I tried to say that there was nothing he could do that I wouldn't forgive. "You've always been too easy on me," he answered. And the next time I brought it up, "If you love me, we'll never talk about this again."

Eddie died three years later without another word on the subject passing between us. In the end, to be honest, I suppose I found that silence rather unforgivable. His death even more so. I have never liked being alone.

As every day I more surely am; it's the blessing of a long life. Just me left now, the first white woman to see the wild gorillas and the one who saw nothing else—not the chains, not the beatings, not the massacre. I can't help worrying over it all again, now I know Archer's dead and only me to tell it, though no way of telling puts it to rest.

Since my eyes went, a girl comes to read to me twice a week. For the longest time I wanted nothing to do with gorillas, but now I have her scouting out articles as we're finally starting to really see how they live. The thinking still seems to be harems, but with the females slipping off from time to time to be with whomever they wish.

And what I notice most in the articles is not the apes. My attention is caught instead by these young women who'd sooner live in the jungle with the chimpanzees or the orangutans or the great mountain gorillas. These women who freely choose it—the Goodalls and the Galdikas and the Fosseys. And I think to myself how there is nothing new under the sun, and maybe all those women carried off by gorillas in those old stories, maybe they all freely chose it.

When I am tired and have thought too much about it all, Beverly's last words come back to me. Mostly I put them straight out of my head, think about anything else. Who remembers what she said? Who knows what she meant?

But there are other times when I let them in. Turn them over.

Then they become, not a threat as I originally heard them, but an invitation. On those days I can pretend that she's still there in the jungle, dipping her feet, eating wild carrots, and waiting for me. I can pretend that I'll be joining her whenever I wish and just as soon as I please.

daughter of the monkey god

M. K. HOBSON

"Daughter of the Monkey God", which appeared in *SCI FICTION* in 2003, was M.K. Hobson's first professional sale. Since then, her work has appeared in *Realms of Fantasy*, *The Magazine of Fantasy and Science Fiction*, *Strange Horizons*, *Interzone*, and other publications and anthologies. She has a story forthcoming in the anthology *Haunted Legends* edited by Ellen Datlow and Nick Mamatas.

Her first novel, *The Native Star*, is coming out in 2010. She lives in Oregon with her husband and daughter.

"Daughter of the Monkey God" movingly reflects the continued exploitation of developing countries by richer ones.

For the hundredth time, Sel noted the peculiar smell. It poured out of the shattered windows of the Mercedes, borne on licking yellow flames and fat billows of black oily smoke. It was actually three smells tightly knotted: the smell of the car's champagne leather interior roasting and curling, the acrid smell of motor oil sizzling against hot metal, and the smell of burning flesh.

It was a terrible smell.

Sel pressed a tiny phone against her recently shaven cheek, smelling her own whiskey-tainted breath on the plastic. Her throat was raw and coated with something gritty and astringent. Every breath was like inhaling powdered glass. She was screaming into the phone, screaming words in English. She didn't speak English, but she could feel the meaning of the words that were tumbling from her mouth, " . . . you have to get here quickly! My wife . . . my wife is trapped inside and I can't get her out . . . "

Sel did not want to see the old man's wife die again, stretched out on the rain-shiny pavement, dark men in yellow slickers bending over her. She did not want to see the stiff, charred limbs black-bright in the spinning lights of the emergency vehicles. Sel did not want to process this memory any more. But that was her job. She worked in a Solace Factory.

It was not your fault, you must forgive yourself. She repeated it to the old man wearily, for the hundredth time.

While she processed, she was in two places. In one place, the place inside her mind that was rented out to process the traumatic memories of a man named McDermott, James, she was screaming into a tiny cell phone for help that would not come in time. In that place, she could feel the heat from the flames drying out her wrinkled white skin. She could feel her old-man's heart pounding frantically, ready to burst.

In the other place, in her life that was real, she was in a humid old factory in Katunayake, Colombo's big industrial district, sitting in the slanted sunlight that poured down from the high grimy windows. Tears streamed down her cheeks. She reached up and dashed them away. How she hated those bothersome tears. No one else at the Solace Factory cried like she did, and because she wept so much they called her childish. Anda-bala. Crybaby.

Having brought her consciousness out of the Lump far enough to wipe the tears from her face, she noticed that the muscles of her thigh were contracting painfully. Once again, she'd sat too long without moving. All the other workers in the factory remembered to move once in a while, to stretch occasionally. Most didn't even have to stop processing while they did so. But not her. She was slow. She could not think of too many things at once. Her head did not always work right.

She jiggled her leg against the rough mat of woven banana fibers, her fingertips brushing along the edge of the sock that covered the amputated place just above where her knee used to be. She dug her fingers into the muscle, massaging it. She eased carefully back into the processing while she did this; Manuela the floor boss had an eagle eye, and the fat old clayball would be over to poke her with a stick if she sensed any inattention. Manuela was Sinhalese, and she hated Tamils, called them sneaky, cheating blacks, filthy little temple monkeys, uppity low-caste slaves brought from India to sweat for the British.

Every time there was a Black Tiger bombing in Colombo, the words came a little more loudly to Sel's ears. She wondered why the ugly talk did not bother her more. Perhaps it was because she heard so much of it since she'd come to work in the South. Perhaps it was because her father had taught her not to listen too closely to the words of the Sinhalese.

"The Sinhalese are small people, hateful people, jealous people."

She remembered her father's dark face, as smooth and shining as if it had been carved from teak.

"But the Tamils are an ancient race," he said one night long ago, as they'd sat together watching fireflies. "A people with gods and kings as ancestors, with a lineage that can be traced back to the ancient days when shining King Rama sent Hanuman the Monkey God and his vast monkey armies to reclaim his beautiful wife from the devil who had stolen her. The Tamils, my precious gem, are the descendants of Hanuman's divine army. We are beloved of Hanuman, and that is why, even to this day, we are known for our cleverness. Is it not a fact that Tamil children learn to read most quickly? That Tamils take the best grades at university? And is it not always Tamils who leave Sri Lanka to become programmers and engineers in the faraway West? We are the children of the Monkey God, and monkeys are the cleverest of animals."

And that was why the war was being fought, her father said, why the Tamils bombed the Sinhalese and the Sinhalese bombed the Tamils. Jealousy. The jealousy of the small toward the large.

Her father would have hated Manuela, would have hated the fact that his daughter, his precious gem, had to come to the South to work in a Solace Factory. But Sel felt nothing. She did not feel proud to be Tamil, nor did she hate the Sinhalese. She longed to be nothing in particular, simply there, a lump of flesh just like the Lumps of flesh that contained the memories they processed.

She returned to the ruined Mercedes and the raging fire and McDermott, James and his wife who was dying while the old man watched helplessly. Sel took the guilt into herself for the hundredth time, absorbed it like it was greasy fried fish and she the newspaper. She had already tried this a hundred ways, a hundred times. But no matter how hard she worked, the pain that had been born on that terrible night was intractable.

It was not your fault, you must forgive yourself, she told him again, knowing it would do no good.

The only one who did not call her Crybaby was Dhuraimurugan. He was Tamil, too, and Tamils in Colombo stuck together. He always called her by her full name, Selvakumari, which was the name her mother had given her. Her mother still lived in Jaffna, in a hospital. Sel sent her money from her wages at the Solace Factory, but she had not seen her mother for a long time.

Dhuraimurugan was slim and small, like an animal meant to live in a tree. He looked very much like a monkey, and that was why whenever Manuela called him a dirty little macaque, he just smiled at her as if they'd shared a joke. Dhuraimurugan liked jokes.

The first day he had come to work at the Solace Factory, he had come to sit next to her at lunch, perhaps hoping to find a friend in the factory's only other Tamil. He followed her as she hobbled to her own spot under the red jasmine tree at the corner of the trash-strewn back field where the processors ate their lunches.

"You don't mind, do you?" Dhuraimurugan said as he sat down next to her. There was no indication that the question was anything but rhetorical.

She watched him from the corner of her eye as he unpacked his lunch from a many-times-used brown paper bag. He took each item out swiftly, without rustling the paper, then folded the bag into a perfect little square and tucked it back into his pocket. His movements were swift and nimble, beautiful to watch.

She was not the only one who thought so. A little band of monkeys had come to sit on top of the high cinderblock wall that ran around the back of the factory. The monkeys sat in a straight line, looking down at them. Their black eyes were bright above their white cheeks. Usually the creatures were either shrieking at one another or clambering down to beg or steal food. But that day they sat quiet and still. They seemed subdued. Respectful, almost.

Dhuraimurugan had a plastic container of rice and *mallung*. He poked at it with a plastic fork as he scrutinized her. He looked at her hard, as if he were going to try to draw her afterward with an ink pen. That was when he had asked her name. After some thought, as if she were trying to remember it herself, she gave it to him.

"Selvakumari is a very practical name!" he said, highly pleased for no reason Sel could fathom. Dhuraimurugan, as she would discover, followed no logical laws of conversation, preferring instead to always say the first thing that leapt into his mind.

"Analyzed numerically, it demonstrates that you have an efficient and capable nature. But too serious. You are hardheaded. You do not show love and tenderness to those close to you. There is much misunderstanding and unhappiness in your personal life as a result." He paused, pushed a sticky ball of rice into his mouth, chewed it with large white teeth. "You could suffer constipation, growths, or serious female disorders."

He ate cheerfully, robustly, digging with the plastic fork like a farmer turning soil. She was suddenly annoyed, though she hardly knew why.

"What does *your* name mean?" she said, still not looking at him. "Analyzed numerically."

At first she didn't think he'd heard her question. She was used to her words going unnoticed. The explosion that had taken her leg had also scarred her throat, and she could hardly speak above a whisper. But he heard. He winked at her as he used a tine of the fork to pull some *mallung* from between his teeth.

"Dhuraimurugan is a very mercurial name. A name of energy, impatience, mental flexibility. It is a name that can be too outspoken, too conceited. Probably a name you don't want around. Trouble written in large letters."

Without realizing it, she smiled. He saw, and smiled back.

Sel did not know very much about McDermott, James. What she *did* know about him she had pieced together from the brittle scraps of memory contained in the Lump that had been sent from the States for processing. He was rich. He was old. He drank too much. He wasn't a very good driver.

She looked at the Lump. It was a hairy ball of flesh, grown from McDermott, James's own cells. She touched it, let her hand rest on it. It was warm, as if the fires of the night contained within it were banked around its core.

It was not your fault, you must forgive yourself.

Sel found herself thinking again of her father's old stories, told on nights when the moon hung low and golden on the horizon and the air smelled of cardamom and temple flowers. Stories about King Rama's beautiful wife Sita, kidnapped and imprisoned by the devil-king. McDermott, James had been kidnapped, too, Sel realized suddenly. Kidnapped by his own guilt. Kidnapped and imprisoned in a night that leaped with fire and billows of smoke.

But how was she to set him free?

The morning after his first day at the Solace Factory, Dhuraimurugan took a mat next to her, and from then on, that was his mat. It worried Sel, for she found that Dhuraimurugan loved nothing more than talking. He talked constantly, even when he was processing. He talked an incessant stream of nonsense, bad jokes, lines from Bollywood blockbusters, ancient poetry. If Manuela caught them speaking, she would dock their pay. Enough times, and she would fire them. Troublemaking Tamils. Dhuraimurugan did not seem to care.

"You know, they grow these things in vats in laboratories," Dhuraimurugan whispered to her one day, patting his Lump, his current work assignment, in a way that was badly irreverent and overfamiliar. He was processing the trauma of an old woman who'd lost her only daughter to inoperable brain cancer. Dhuraimurugan had taken a liking to the old woman and referred to her as "granny."

"Shh," Sel told him, her hands still on the Lump of McDermott, James. How many days had she been processing his memory! And she wouldn't ever finish it with Dhuraimurugan whispering to her all the time.

"Once we're finished processing the memories, you know what happens to the Lumps?"

"They are sent back," Sel murmured.

"They are sent back, and do you know what the sad people *do* with them?" Dhuraimurugan's voice took on a conspiratorial cast, and he shifted over a little closer to her. "They eat them!"

Sel looked at him sidelong, raising a skeptical eyebrow. Dhuraimurugan nodded once, curtly.

"It is so! They cook up the Lumps and eat them. In that way they absorb the memories we have reconditioned for them. We do all the work, teach them to forgive themselves, and they have only to chew and swallow to obtain absolution." He paused, shaking his head.

Sel pondered his words; they spun through her head despite her best effort to shut them out. Chew and swallow. *It's not your fault, you must forgive yourself.*

"And they are so expensive, Selvakumari!" he continued, his whispered words breaking through her thoughts. "The price of one of these could buy us a house, a farm, and a car. And they have only one use. To suck out sad thoughts and send them to us."

"Shh," Sel said again. Then she returned to McDermott, James.

It was not your fault, you must forgive yourself. Sel repeated the mantra again, dully.

She took the moment they pulled his wife from the car, reconditioned it as she had done so many times before. She concentrated on the sweet smell of her red jasmine tree; its perfume was strong enough to cut through even the thickest, blackest, oiliest emotions. But she'd been working McDermott, James's memories for so many days. They just would not smooth. Every time she climbed herself into the Lump, it was like she hadn't done anything the day before.

Sel's face was wet, and her head was aching.

It was not your fault, you stupid old man.

Sudden rage and frustration burned through her. She wished that she could take the damned fool by the arms and shake him. She wished she could slap his face again and again. *It was not your fault, you arrogant white bastard. That is what you have paid to believe. And even if it was your fault, I will keep telling you it wasn't until you believe it. Until you believe it right down to your cells, you filthy old devil. You must forgive yourself . . . or at least believe that you are forgiven, though you never will be, never should be. Allow yourself to be deluded, old man. You've paid for it. How easy it will be to chew and swallow your guilt away . . . chew and swallow, chew and swallow . . .*

She felt someone touching her arm. She jerked away from the touch and bared her teeth, glaring. It was Dhuraimurugan. His eyes were concerned.

"You'll hurt yourself," he said, quietly. She tasted blood in her mouth. She ran her tongue over her lower lip and realized that she'd bitten deep into it.

Dhuraimurugan cast a furtive look toward Manuela to see if she was watching. Luckily, she wasn't.

"Listen, take granny," Dhuraimurugan whispered hurriedly, pushing his Lump toward Sel. "Take granny, and I'll take that old man off your hands. Granny's easy."

Sel wanted to accept his offer. She felt her hands trembling on McDermott, James's Lump, itching to throw it at Dhuraimurugan, run as far away from it as she could get. But she couldn't. It was strictly forbidden. Dhuraimurugan had no idea of the risk he was suggesting, but wasn't that just like him? He didn't take life seriously. He sat on mats and gossiped and winked and told jokes. He was a silly man, silly and frivolous.

"No," she said, in a low voice, keeping her eyes on Manuela.

"Why is he so hard?"

"His wife died in an accident . . . " She jerked her head angrily. "I have told him again and again that it is not his fault. That he must forgive himself."

"But how can he believe you?" Dhuraimurugan asked softly, "When you will not forgive him? When you have never forgiven anyone, not even yourself?"

Sel wrinkled her forehead distastefully. Silly man.

"I don't know what you mean," she said.

Dhuraimurugan closed his eyes, put his hands back on Granny, and sighed contentedly.

"Yes, you do," Dhuraimurugan said.

Sel wanted to spit at him for thinking he knew so many answers. She slapped her hands down onto McDermott, James and closed her eyes.

I will teach you about forgiveness, old man . . . She sneered, hard and furious.

In the rented part of her mind, there was a flash, and the smell of burning petroleum. Sel relaxed into these with ugly glee. This time, she *wanted* to see the old man's wife die. This time, she wanted to revel in his pain, dance in it with bare feet.

She was staring at a bright, hot light. There was the sound of faraway screams.

But the Mercedes was not there, nor the yellow flames, nor the billowing black smoke. The light was coming from flares, hundreds of flares like little suns, flares that illuminated the movement of jets dragging long fluffy tails . . .

She was in Jaffna.

She tried to backpedal quickly. Not this memory, she thought, her heart thudding. No, not this memory . . .

Her little sister was crying.

They'd run out from their mother's house into the streets, with dozens of their neighbors. Already, and nearby, there were the sounds of explosions, distant rocking thunder. Her little sister was so afraid of those explosions. Sel cradled her in her arms, looking for her mother.

Her little sister clung to her tightly. Sel could feel the bones of her arms, the little ridges of her spine and ribs through her light evening sarong. The last thing Sel remembered seeing was a tear, her own tear, sparkling on the skin of her little sister's shoulder like a perfect diamond in the harsh brilliance of the magnesium flares.

Then nothing: no cries, no pain, no sound at all.

Just white, white light.

She shook the memory off so hard it hurt. Drops flew from her face as if she were a wet dog shaking off water. The thick dusky light of the Solace Factory resolved around her slowly, a jumble of spinning images. She felt sick. She trembled violently, as if the bombs at Jaffna were exploding within her.

But something was strange. Dhuraimurugan was crouched beside her, his entire body tense, but he was not looking at her. He was looking at all the other factory workers. They had gathered at the windows, pushing against each other for a better view. They all stood with the peculiar twitchiness of people ready to duck.

"What happened?" Selvakumari said.

"You didn't hear that?" Dhuraimurugan looked down at her in astonishment. "A big explosion. Loud one; close, too, by the sound of it. A bomb, I think."

There was chatter and talk and then suddenly a young man ran in with an air of great self-importance and spoke in hushed tones with Manuela.

Manuela got up on a rickety chair.

"Work's over today," she said loudly. "Go home now. Go home."

"Come on," Dhuraimurugan said. There was an anxious look on his face. "We'd better go quickly. I'll walk you home."

"You think you know so many answers," Sel spat at him, her teeth clenched. "Walk yourself home, if you are lucky enough to have one. Go climb a tree. Find someone else to chatter to."

And she hobbled away, leaving him standing in the middle of the Solace Factory.

After she was outside, Sel thought about going back to the house she shared with seven other women. The house was a concrete box with a concrete floor where they slept on mats and hauled water from a well for bathing and cooking. Going home was the safe thing to do. But Sel didn't want to go back there. So she hobbled back to sit under her red jasmine tree and watched the emergency trucks coming and going, their lights spinning and flashing.

She felt along the edge of her amputated leg, fingering the thick puckers of flesh along the bottom.

She remembered white trucks, men in white, their dark faces caked with soot and blood. She remembered a feeling of ringing in her entire body, and the feeling that the world had been turned upside down, except that it was really her that had been turned upside down. After the explosion in Jaffna she had landed on her back against a corrugated wall. Blood had streamed down the back of her throat, choking her. Her little sister lay a ways off. Her little sister did not move.

Sel remembered that her mother had come to kneel between them. Her hands had darted out tenuously, as if she wanted to touch them both but dared not. Sel remembered wishing that her mother would touch her. Her mother had sagged like a dead plant, her forehead on the ground. Sel had wished that her mother would not be so still. But then she saw that her mother was not still at all. She was crying, crying silently, each tear falling to the ground in a little explosion of dust.

The little explosions terrified Sel more than the big one had, for her mother had never cried. Her mother had not cried when the soldiers had taken Sel's father and older brothers. She had not cried when the men never came back.

"Did you know, the island of Ceylon is shaped like a teardrop?" Dhuraimurugan's voice came from behind her. Quickly, he slid down next to her. He had food, warm little *ulundu vadai* cakes from a nearby vendor.

"They are doing a brisk business. Everyone likes to hang around when there's been a suicide bombing. They like to see how the body parts scatter themselves out."

Suicide bombing. That meant there would be a curfew. And house-to-house searches.

"You shouldn't have," she said, as he handed her the warm cakes. "You don't have any more money than I do."

"Sure I do," he said. "I don't have to send any money home."

"You don't have any family?"

"No," he said.

She was silent. She ate the cakes; they were hot and spicy and slightly sweet from the coconut oil they'd been fried in. Chew and swallow, she thought. Chew and swallow. In the trees above them, she could hear monkeys moving between the branches.

She leaned against him a little, letting a little more of her shoulder touch his.

"You know why we all process so well?" he said. "You know why there are so many Solace Factories in Sri Lanka? Because it has been shown that children raised in war zones make the best processors. Our brains are damaged in just the right way." His voice was bitter. She had not heard bitterness in his voice before. It made her feel strangely desolate. She felt tears rise in her eyes. Dhuraimurugan saw them and gave her a nudge. The smile came back to his face.

"But that doesn't mean it can't change someday, right? Maybe we can change it for our children, eh?"

He was a silly man, always playing. How could he play when everything around them was forever falling apart? She did not look at him. He was silent for a while, chewing on his lip.

"You want to know a joke?" he said. Sel didn't. But he continued anyway.

"Guess what they tell their rich customers . . . the ones they make the Lumps for. They tell them that we are serene Buddhist monks. We processors, I mean. They tell them we're priests, holy people who can absolve them. Can you imagine me, sitting on a white snowy peak, my face serene and my farts like flowers?"

"You should be inside somewhere," she said. "They will be searching."

"We should both be inside," he said. "That's why I came to find you. I wanted to make sure you were safe."

"They can't take anything from me, so I am always safe."

He looked at her.

"What a thing to say!" he said. "What about the man you will marry, the children you will laugh at? They are who you must protect yourself for."

"I cannot lose what will never be," Sel snapped angrily. She shoved the wrapper of *vadai* cakes back into his hands. She planted her old, worn crutch firmly and struggled to climb up it, but in her haste she slipped and landed heavily on her backside. The humiliation made fresh tears sting her eyes. "You shouldn't make fun. Go play with one of the pretty Sinhalese girls if you want to play games."

"I'm not making fun," Dhuraimurugan said. He was silent for a moment. Then he looked at her sidelong. "You're the only one that weeps, Selvakumari. That makes you the prettiest girl in the Solace Factory."

Sel didn't say anything. Slowly, thoughtfully, Dhuraimurugan ate the *vadai* cakes he had taken from her. Then he put his hand on hers. It was still warm from the cakes. He leaned back against the tree, looked up into the branches where the monkeys hid. Then he closed his eyes, breathing deeply.

It was not your fault. The thoughts were Dhuraimurugan's. His thoughts smelled like mist and vadai cakes. *You must forgive yourself.*

They sat together that way for a while, until Dhuraimurugan started up suddenly, frenetically.

"We must go back," he said. "I will take you home."

Sel said nothing, but rose carefully. She leaned on her crutch, but saw that Dhuraimurugan was offering her his arm. She had never leaned on anyone. But she decided that this time, she would.

When they came to the boarding house in where Sel lived, soldiers were coming out. Dhuraimurugan stopped. Sel felt him take a breath. But they could not run; the soldiers were coming down the walk of the house. The soldiers were speaking between themselves, laughing.

Sel froze, as if that would make them invisible, but it did not. One of the soldiers saw her, and saw Dhuraimurugan. He gestured to the men around him, and they brought their rifles up.

"You're out too late," the soldier said in clipped Sinhala. He put a hand on Dhuraimurugan's shoulder, pulled him forward. Dhuraimurugan fell to the ground, and Sel, still leaning on him, fell, too. Fell heavily onto the damp, cracked pavement. It made the soldiers laugh.

Dhuraimurugan screeched angrily, grabbing one of the soldiers by his leg and toppling him to the ground. He moved so swiftly, Sel hardly saw his fist as it smashed the soldier's nose. The man tried to crawl away, crawl backward like a crab, but everywhere he moved, Dhuraimurugan was there, his little fists flying.

There was the clack of rifle bolts sliding into place. Sel wanted to scream but could not, the sound clamped inside her throat as if a hand were holding it down.

Two soldiers got their arms around Dhuraimurugan and lifted him up, holding him as he scuffled and struggled. Then another soldier hit him across the face with the butt of his rifle. Dhuraimurugan went still, and the soldier hit him again and again, until Sel could smell the blood.

"Crazy animal," the soldier said, breathing hard. "Filthy monkey."

The scream that had been building in Sel's throat tore free, a corporeal thing, meant to lash out and tear the men to bits, flay them, explode them in white light. She threw herself at them, scrabbling uselessly on her hands and knees, but they laughed at her again. One soldier pushed her back down with his foot. Dhuraimurugan stirred, tried to move. A low sound came from the middle of his chest. The soldiers lowered him to his knees. He sagged there, forehead almost touching the ground, little drops of blood gathering on the tip of his nose. One of the soldiers put his gun to the back of Dhuraimurugan's head.

Remember, beloved.

Mist and *vadai* cakes.

Remember who you are.

And then, the sound. The sound of a small echoing pop, tiny as a tear dropping into dust, loud as the explosions at Jaffna that still echoed within her chest. There was the smell of blood, and the sound of something dropping heavily on the ground. She looked up at the trees, so that she would not have to see. And before night closed completely around them, something caught Sel's eye.

A large dark shadow, swift and nimble, moving through the branches of the red jasmine trees above.

The shrieks of the monkeys followed Selvakumari as she limped slowly back to the Solace Factory later that night, after the big golden moon had risen, after the soldiers had gone, after the blood had dried. The tap-shuffle, tap-shuffle of her gait echoed against the dark silent buildings, little lost plosives of sound. There were only one or two following her at first, but as she walked, tap-shuffle, tap-shuffle, the numbers grew, and by the time she reached the factory, there were a hundred monkeys following her, loping along high walls, swinging from trees, clustering at her heels.

When she came to the factory, she broke a window and climbed through it awkwardly, not caring much when she cut her hand. The monkeys clambered after her, agile and swift, tails curling up like incense smoke into the heavy night air.

She watched them moving around her, watched them from the corners of her eyes. She thought of the swift dark shadow, moving through the branches that swayed in the warm wind. She thought of Dhuraimurugan's quick, nimble movements.

She thought of the stories her father had told her. Of King Rama and his wife and the devil who had stolen her. Of Hanuman, the Monkey God, who brought his army of monkeys to set her free.

The devil can only take what we allow him to take. This was what she would tell the old man. *And what he takes, we may reclaim, not with one strong arm, but with a thousand small hands, quick and nimble. A thousand small moments, moments of contentment and cakes, red jasmine and jokes, hope and solace. A thousand small moments put together are strong enough. This is what you have paid to know. This is all I can tell you.*

Inside the factory, it was black as dripping oil. She crawled to her mat and took up the Lump of McDermott, James. The monkeys clustered around her, warm and chattering, brilliant little eyes glowing like fireflies in the darkness.

She clutched the Lump to her chest, held it tight. And in that moment, all the words she'd brought with her flew away like birds, leaving her with only one single message.

Even if it was your fault, I forgive you, she thought, squeezing her eyes tightly shut.

Who are you? McDermott, James asked her as she stood before him, stood between him and the wrecked Mercedes. She saw herself through his eyes. Illuminated in the dying flames, she was small and lithe and whole.

I am the daughter of the Monkey God, she said, extending her arm to him. *I have been sent to save you.*

And she drew the old man in and cradled him, crooning to him in the rain-slicked darkness. In the pine trees overhead, monkeys watched, still and silent. And the old man's tears flooded through her, washing her clean.

tomorrow town

KIM NEWMAN

Kim Newman was born in Brixton (London), grew up in the West Country, went to University near Brighton and now lives in Islington (London).

His most recent fiction books include *Where the Bodies Are Buried*, *The Man From the Diogenes Club* and *Secret Files of the Diogenes Club* under his own name and *The Vampire Genevieve* as Jack Yeovil. His non-fiction books include *Ghastly Beyond Belief* (with Neil Gaiman), *Horror: 100 Best Books* and *Horror: Another 100 Best Books* (both with Stephen Jones), and a host of books on film. He is a contributing editor to *Sight & Sound* and *Empire* magazines and has written and broadcast widely on a range of topics, scripting radio documentaries, role-playing games, and TV programs. He has won the Bram Stoker Award, the International Horror Critics Award, the British Science Fiction Award and the British Fantasy Award. His official web-site, "Dr Shade's Laboratory" can be found at www.johnnyalucard.com.

"Tomorrow Town" is a mystery featuring Richard Jeperson, member of the Diogenes Club, the "least-known branch of the United Kingdom's intelligence and investigative services." It's written with Newman's tongue firmly embedded in his cheek.

TOMORROW TOWN

*T*his way to the Yeer 2000.

The message, in Helvetia typeface, was repeated on arrow-shaped signs.

"That'll be us, Vanessa," said Richard Jeperson, striding along the platform in the indicated direction, toting his shoulder-slung hold-all. He tried to feel as if he were about to time-travel from 1971 to the future, though in practice he was just changing trains.

Vanessa was distracted by one of the arrow-signs, fresh face arranged into a comely frown. Richard's associate was a tall redhead in hot-pants, halter top, beret and stack-heeled go-go boots—all blinding white, as if fresh from the machine in a soap-powder advert. She drew unconcealed attention from late-morning passengers milling about the railway station. Then again, in his lime dayglo blazer edged with gold braid and salmon-pink bell-bottom trousers, so did he. Here in Preston, the fashion watchword, for the eighteenth consecutive season, was "drab."

"It's misspelled," said Vanessa. "Y Double-E R."

"No, it's F O N E T I K,' he corrected. "Within the next thirty years, English spelling will be rationalised."

"You reckon?' She pouted, sceptically.

"Not my theory,' he said, stroking his mandarin moustaches. "*I* assume the lingo will muddle along with magical illogic as it has since "the Yeer Dot". But orthographic reform is a tenet of Tomorrow Town."

"Alliteration. Very Century 21."

They had travelled up from London, sharing a rattly first-class carriage and a welcome magnum of Bollinger with a liberal Bishop on a lecture tour billed as "Peace and the Pill" and a working-class playwright revisiting his slag-heap roots. To continue their journey, Richard and Vanessa had to change at Preston.

The arrows led to a guarded gate. The guard wore a British Rail uniform in shiny black plastic with silver highlights. His oversized cap had a chemical lighting element in the brim.

"You need special tickets, Ms and Mm," said the guard.

"Mm," said Vanessa, amused.

"Ms," Richard buzzed at her.

He searched through his pockets, finally turning up the special tickets. They were strips of foil, like ironed-flat chocolate bar wrappers with punched-out hole patterns. The guard carefully posted the tickets into a slot in a metal box. Gears whirred and lights flashed. The gate came apart and sank into the ground. Richard let Vanessa step through the access first. She seemed to float off, arms out for balance.

"Best not to be left behind, Mm," said the guard.

"Mm," said Richard, agreeing.

He stepped onto the special platform. Beneath his rubber-soled winkle-pickers, a knitted chain-mail surface moved on large rollers. It creaked and rippled, but gave a smooth ride.

"I wonder how it manages corners," Vanessa said.

The moving platform conveyed them towards a giant silver bullet. The train of the future hummed slightly, at rest on a single gleaming rail which was raised ten feet above the gravel railbed by chromed tubular trestles. A hatchway was open, lowered to form a ramp.

Richard and Vanessa clambered through the hatch and found themselves in a space little roomier than an Apollo capsule. They half-sat, half-lay in over-padded seats which wobbled on gyro-gimbals. Safety straps automatically snaked across them and drew tight.

"Not sure I'll ever get used to this," said Richard. A strap across his forehead noosed his long, tangled hair, and he had to free a hand to fix it.

Vanessa wriggled to get comfortable, doing a near-horizontal dance as the straps adjusted to her.

With a hiss the ramp raised and became a hatch-cover, then sealed shut. The capsule-cum-carriage had seat-berths for eight, but today they were the only passengers.

A mechanical voice counted down from ten.

"Richard, that's a Dalek," said Vanessa, giggling.

As if offended, the voice stuttered on five, like a record stuck in a groove, then hopped to three.

At zero, they heard a rush of rocketry and the monorail moved off. Richard tensed against the expected g-force slam, but it didn't come. Through thick-glassed slit windows, he saw green countryside passing by at about 25 miles per hour. They might have been on a leisurely cycle to the village pub rather than taking the fast train to the future.

"So this is the transport of tomorrow?" said Vanessa.

"A best-guess design," explained Richard. "That's the point of Tomorrow Town. To experiment with the lives we'll all be living at the turn of the century."

"No teleportation then?"

"Don't be silly. Matter transmission is a fantasy. This is a reasonable extrapolation from present-day or in-development technology. The Foundation is rigorous about probabilities. Everything in Tomorrow Town is viable."

The community was funded partially by government research grants and partially by private sources. It was projected that it would soon be a profitable concern, with monies pouring in from scientific wonders developed by the visioneers of the new technomeritocracy. The Foundation, which had proposed the "Town of 2000" experiment, was a think tank, an academic-industrial coalition dedicated to applying to present-day life lessons learned from contemplating the likely future. Tomorrow Town's two-thousand odd citizen-volunteers ("zenvols") were boffins, engineers, social visionaries, health-food cranks and science fiction fans.

Three years ago, when the town was given its charter by the Wilson government, there had been a white heat of publicity:

television programmes hosted by James Burke and Raymond Baxter, picture features in all the Sunday colour supplements, a novelty single ("Take Me to Tomorrow" by Big Thinks and the BBC Radiophonic Workshop) which peaked at Number 2 (prevented from being Top of the Pops by The Crazy World of Arthur Brown's "Fire"), a line of "futopian fashions" from Carnaby Street, a heated debate in the letter columns of *New Scientist* between Arthur C. Clarke (pro), Auberon Waugh (anti) and J.G. Ballard (hard to tell). Then the brouhaha died down and Tomorrow Town was left to get on by itself, mostly forgotten. Until the murder of Varno Zhoule.

Richard Jeperson, agent of the Diogenes Club—least-known branch of the United Kingdom's intelligence and investigative services—was detailed to look into the supposedly open-and-shut case and report back to the current Prime Minister on the advisability of maintaining government support for Tomorrow Town.

He had given Vanessa the barest facts.

"What does the murder weapon of the future turn out to be?" she asked. "Laser-beam? Poisoned moon-rock?"

"No, the proverbial blunt instrument. Letting the side down, really. Anyone who murders the co-founder of Tomorrow Town should have the decency to stick to the spirit of the game. I doubt if it's much comfort to the deceased, but the offending bludgeon was vaguely futurist, a stylised steel rocketship with a heavy stone base."

"No home should be without one."

"It was a Hugo Award, the highest honour the science fiction field can bestow. Zhoule won his murder weapon for Best Novelette of 1958, with the oft-anthologised 'Court Martian'."

"Are we then to be the police of the future? Do we get to design our own uniforms?"

"We're here because Tomorrow Town has no police force as such. It is a fundamental of the social design that there will be no crime by the year 2000."

"Ooops."

"This is a utopian vision, Vanessa. No money to steal. No inequality to foster resentment. All disputes arbitrated with unquestionable fairness. All zenvols constantly monitored for emotional instability."

"Maybe being 'constantly monitored' leads to 'emotional instability.' Not to mention being called a 'zenvol.'"

"You'll have to mention that to Big Thinks."

"Is he the boss-man among equals?'

Richard chuckled. "He's an it. A computer. A very large computer."

Vanessa snapped her fingers.

"Ah-ha. There's your culprit. In every sci-fi film I've ever seen, the computer goes power mad and starts killing people off. Big Thinks probably wants to take over the world."

"The late Mm Zhoule would cringe to hear you say that, Vanessa. He'd never have deigned to use such a hackneyed, unlikely premise in a story. A computer is just a heuristic abacus. Big Thinks can beat you at chess, solve logic problems, cut a pop record and make the monorail run on time, but it hasn't got sentience, a personality, a motive or, most importantly, arms. You might as well suspect the fridge-freezer or the pop-up toaster."

"If you knew my pop-up toaster better, you'd feel differently. It sits there, shining sneakily, plotting perfidy. The jug-kettle is in on it too. There's a conspiracy of contraptions."

"Now you're being silly."

"Trust me, Richard, it'll be the Brain Machine. Make sure to check its alibi."

"I'll bear that in mind."

They first saw Tomorrow Town from across the Yorkshire Dales, nestled in lush green and slate grey. The complex was a large-scale version of the sort of back garden space station that might have been put together by a talented child inspired by Gerry Anderson and instructed by Valerie Singleton, using egg boxes, toilet roll tubes, the innards of a broken wireless, pipe-cleaners and a lot of silver spray-paint.

Hexagonal geodesic domes clustered in the landscape, a central space covered by a giant canopy that looked like an especially aerodynamic silver circus tent. Metallised roadways wound between trees and lakes, connecting the domes. The light traffic consisted mostly of electric golf-carts and one-person hovercraft. A single hardy zenvol was struggling along on what looked like a failed flying bicycle from 1895 but was actually a moped powered by wing-like solar panels. It was raining gently, but the town seemed shielded by a half-bubble climate control barrier that shimmered in mid-air.

A pylon held up three sun-shaped globes on a triangle frame. They radiated light and, Richard suspected, heat. Where light fell, the greenery was noticeably greener and thicker.

The monorail stopped outside the bubble, and settled a little clunkily.

"You may now change apparel," rasped the machine voice.

A compartment opened and clothes slid out on racks. The safety straps released them from their seats.

Richard thought for a moment that the train had calculated from his long hair that he was a Ms rather than a Mm, then realised the garment on offer was unisex: a lightweight jump-suit of semi-opaque polythene, with silver epaulettes, pockets, knee- and elbow-patches and modesty strips around the chest and hips. The dangling legs ended in floppy-looking plastic boots, the sleeves in surgeon's gloves.

"Was that 'may' a 'must'?" asked Vanessa.

"Best to go along with native customs," said Richard.

He turned his back like a gentleman and undressed carefully, folding and putting away his clothes. Then he took the jump-suit from the rack and stepped into it, wiggling his feet down into the boots and fingers into the gloves. A seam from crotch to neck sealed with velcro strips, but he was left with an enormous swathe of polythene sprouting from his left hip like a bridal train.

"Like this," said Vanessa, who had worked it out.

The swathe went over the right shoulder in a toga arrangement, passing under an epaulette, clipping on in a couple of places, and falling like a waist-length cape.

She had also found a pad of controls in the left epaulette, which activated drawstrings and pleats that adjusted the garment to suit individual body type. They both had to fiddle to get the suits to cope with their above-average height, then loosen and tighten various sections as required. Even after every possible button had been twisted every possible way, Richard wore one sleeve tight as sausage skin while the other was loose and wrinkled as a burst balloon.

"Maybe it's a futopian fashion," suggested Vanessa, who—of course—looked spectacular, shown off to advantage by the modesty strips. "All the dashing zenvols are wearing the one-loose-one-tight look this new century."

"Or maybe it's just aggravated crackpottery."

She laughed.

The monorail judged they had used up their changing time, and lurched off again.

The receiving area was as white and clean as a bathroom display at the Belgian Ideal Home Exhibition. A deputation of zenvols, all dressed alike, none with mismatched sleeves, waited on the platform. Synthesised Bach played gently and the artificial breeze was mildly perfumed.

"Mm Richard, Ms Vanessa," said a white-haired zenvol, "welcome to Tomorrow Town."

A short oriental girl repeated his words in sign-language.

"Are you Georgie Gewell?" Richard asked.

"Jor-G," said the zenvol, then spelled it out.

"My condolences," Richard said, shaking the man's hand. Through two squeaking layers of latex, he had the impression of sweaty palm. "I understand you and Varno Zhoule were old friends."

"Var-Z is a tragic loss. A great visioneer."

The oriental girl mimed sadness. Other zenvols hung their heads.

"Jesu, Joy of Man's Desiring" segued into the "Dead March" from *Saul*. Was the musak keyed in somehow to the emotional state of any given assembly?

"We, ah, founded the Foundation together."

Back in the 1950s, Varno Zhoule had written many articles and stories for science fiction magazines, offering futuristic solutions to contemporary problems, preaching the gospel of better living through logic and technology. He had predicted decimal currency and the vertical take-off aeroplane. Georgie Gewell was an award-winning editor and critic. He had championed Zhoule's work, then raised finance to apply his solutions to the real world. Richard understood the seed money for the Foundation came from a patent the pair held on a kind of battery-powered circular slide rule that was faster and more accurate than any other portable calculating device.

Gewell was as tall as Richard, with milk-fair skin and close-cropped snow-white hair. He had deep smile and frown lines and a soft, girlish mouth. He was steadily leaking tears, not from grief but from thick, obvious reactalite contact lenses that were currently smudged to the darker end of their spectrum.

The other zenvols were an assorted mix, despite their identical outfits. Most of the men were short and tubby, the women lithe and fit—which was either Big Thinks's recipe for perfect population balance or some visioneer's idea of a good time for a tall, thin fellow. Everyone had hair cut short, which made both Richard and Vanessa obvious outsiders. None of the men wore facial hair except a red-faced chap who opted for the Puritan beard-without-a-moustache arrangement.

Gewell introduced the delegation. The oriental girl was Moana, whom Gewell described as "town speaker," though she continued to communicate only by signing. The beardie was Mal-K, the "senior medico" who had presided over the autopsy, matched some bloody fingerprints and seemed a bit put out to be taken away from his automated clinic for this ceremonial affair. Other significant zenvols: Jess-F, "arbitrage input tech," a hard-faced blonde girl who interfaced with Big Thinks when it came to programming dispute decisions, and thus was the nearest thing Tomorrow Town had to a human representative of the legal system—though she was more clerk of the court than investigating officer; Zootie, a fat little "agri-terrain rearrangement tech" with a bad cold for which he kept apologising, who turned out to have discovered the body by the hydroponics vats and was oddly impressed and uncomfortable in this group as if he weren't quite on a level of equality with Gewell and the rest; and "vocabulary administrator" Sue-2, whom Gewell introduced as "sadly, the motive," the image of a penitent young lady who "would never do it again."

Richard mentally marked them all down.

"You'll want to visit the scene of the crime?" suggested Gewell. "Interrogate the culprit? We have Buster in a secure store-room. It had to be especially prepared. There are no lockable doors in Tomorrow Town."

"He's nailed in," said Jess-F. "With rations and a potty."

"Very sensible," commented Richard.

"We can prise the door open now you're here," said Gewell.

Richard thought a moment.

"If you'll forgive me, Mr Jep—ah, Mm Richard," said Mal-K, "I'd like to get back to my work. I've a batch of anti-virus cooking."

The medico kept his distance from Zootie. Did he think a streaming nose reflected badly on the health of the future? Or was the artificial breeze liable to spread sniffles around the whole community in minutes?

"I don't see any reason to detain you Mm Mal-K," said Richard. "Vanessa might pop over later. My associate is interested in the work you're doing here. New cures for new diseases. She'd love to squint into a microscope at your anti-virus."

Vanessa nodded with convincing enthusiasm.

"Mal-K's door is always open," said Gewell.

The medico sloped off without comment.

"Should we crack out the crowbar, then?" prompted Gewell.

The co-founder seemed keen on getting on with this: to him, murder came as an embarrassment and an interruption. It wasn't an uncommon reaction. Richard judged Gewell just wanted all this over with so he could get on with things, even though the victim was one of his oldest friends and the crime demonstrated a major flaw in the social design of Tomorrow Town. If someone battered Vanessa to death, he didn't think he'd be so intent on putting it behind him—but he was famous for being sensitive. Indeed, it was why he was so useful to the Diogenes Club.

"I think as long as our putative culprit is safely nailed away, we can afford to take our time, get a feel for the place and the set-up. It's how I like to work, Mm Gewell. To me, understanding why is much more important than knowing who or how."

"I should think the why was obvious," said Gewell looking at Sue-2, eyes visibly darkening.

She looked down.

"The arbitration went against Buster, and he couldn't accept it," said Jess-F. "Though it was in his initial contract that he abide by Big Thinks' decisions. It happens sometimes. Not often."

"An arbitration in a matter of the heart? Interesting. Just the sort of thing that comes in a box marked 'motive' and tied with pink string. Thank you so much for mentioning it early in the case. Before we continue the sleuthing, perhaps we could have lunch. Vanessa and I have travelled a long way, with no sustenance beyond British Rail sandwiches and a beverage of our own supply. Let's break bread together, and you can tell me more about your fascinating experiment."

"Communal meals are at fixed times," said Gewell. "The next is not until six."

"I make it about six o'clock," said Richard, though his watch-face was blurred by the sleeve-glove.

"It's only f-five by our clock," said Sue-2. "We're on two daily cycles of ten kronons. Each kronon runs a hundred sentikronons."

"In your time, a kronon is 72 minutes," explained Gewell. "Our six is your . . . "

Vanessa did the calculation and beat the slide-rule designer, "Wwelve minutes past seven."

"That's about it."

Richard waved away the objection.

"I'm sure a snack can be rustled up. Where do you take these communal meals?"

Moana signalled a direction and set off. Richard was happy to follow, and the others came too.

The dining area was in the central plaza, under the pylon and the three globes, with zinc-and-chrome sheet-and-tube tables and benches. It was warm under the globes, almost Caribbean, and some zenvols wore poker-players' eyeshades. In the artificially balmy climate, plastic garments tended to get sticky inside, which made for creaky shiftings-in-seats.

An abstract ornamental fountain gushed nutrient-enriched, slightly carbonated, heavily-fluoridized water. Gewell had Moana fetch a couple of jugs for the table, while the meek Sue-2 hustled off to persuade "sustenance preparation" techs to break their schedule to feed the visitors. Vanessa cocked an eyebrow at this division of labour, and Richard remembered Zhoule and Gewell had been planning this futopia since the 1950s, well before the publication of *The Female Eunuch*. Even Jess-F, whom Richard had pegged as the toughest zenvol he had yet met, broke out the metallised glass tumblers from a dispenser by the fountain, while Gewell and the sniffling Zootie sat at their ease at table.

"Is that the building where Big Thinks lives?" asked Vanessa.

Gewell swivelled to look. Vanessa meant an imposing structure, rather like a giant art deco refrigerator decorated with Mondrian squares in a rough schematic of a human face. Uniformly-dressed zenvols came and went through airlock doors that opened and closed with hisses of decontaminant.

Gewell grinned, impishly.

"Ms Vanessa, that building *is* Big Thinks."

Richard whistled.

"Bee-Tee didn't used to be that size," said Jess-F. "Var-Z kept insisting we add units. More and more complicated questions need more and more space. Soon, we'll have to expand further."

"It doesn't show any telltale signs of megalomania?" asked Vanessa. "Never programs Wagner for eight straight hours and chortles over maps of the world."

Jess-F didn't look as if she thought that was funny.

"Bee-Tee is a machine, Ms."

Sue-2 came back with food. Coloured pills that looked like smarties but tasted like chalk.

"All the nutrition you need is here," said Gewell, "in the water and the capsules. For us, mealtimes are mostly ceremonial, for debate and reflection. Var-Z said that some of his best ideas popped into his head while he was chatting idly after a satisfying pill."

Richard didn't doubt it. He also still felt hungry.

"Talking of things popping into Zhoule's head," he said. "What's the story on Buster of the bloody fingerprints?"

Jess-F looked at Sue-2, as if expecting to be contradicted, then carried on.

"Big Thinks assessed the dispute situation, and arbitrated it best for the community if Sue-2 were to be pair-bonded with Var-Z rather than Buster."

"Buster was your old boyfriend?" Vanessa asked Sue-2.

"He is my husband," she said.

"On the outside, in the past," put in Jess-F. "Here, we don't always acknowledge arbitrary pair-bondings. Mostly, they serve a useful purpose and continue. In this instance, the dispute was more complicated."

"Big Thinks arbitrated against the arbitrary?" mused Richard. "I suppose no one would be surprised at that."

He looked from face to face and fixed on Sue-2, then asked: "Did you leave Buster for Mm Zhoule?"

Sue-2 looked for a cue, but none came.

"It was best for the town, for the experiment," she said.

"What was it for you? For your husband?"

"Buster had been regraded. From 'zenvol' to 'zenpass.' He couldn't vote."

Richard looked to Jess-F for explication. He noticed Gewell had to give her a teary wink from almost-black eyes before she would say anything more.

"We have very few citizen-passengers," she said. "It's not a punishment category."

"Kind of you to clarify that," said Richard. "I might have made a misconclusion otherwise. You say zenpasses have no vote?"

"It's not so dreadful," said Gewell, sipping nutrient. "On the outside, in the past, suffrage is restricted by age, sanity, residence and so on. Here, in our technomeritocracy, to register for a vote—which gives you a voice in every significant decision—you have to demonstrate your applied intelligence."

"An IQ test?"

"Not a quotient, Mm Richard. Anyone can have that. The vital factor is application. Bee-Tee tests for that. There's no personality or human tangle involved. Surely, it's only fair that the most useful should have the most say?"

"I have a vote," said Zootie, proud. "Earned by applied intelligence."

"Indeed he does," said Gewell, smiling.

"And Mm Jor-G has fifteen votes. Because he applies his intelligence more often than I do."

Everyone looked at Zootie with different types of amazement.

"It's only fair," said Zootie, content despite a nose-trickle, washing down another purple pill.

Richard wondered whether the agri-terrain rearrangement tech was hovering near regrading as a zenpass.

Richard addressed Sue-2. "What does your husband do?"

"He's a history teacher."

"An educationalist. Very valuable."

Gewell looked as if his pill was sour. "Your present is our past, Mm Richard. Buster's discipline is surplus."

"Doesn't the future grow out of the past? To know where you're going you must know where you've been."

"Var-Z believes in a radical break."

"But Var-Z is in the past too."

"Indeed. Regrettable. But we must think of the future."

"It's where we're going to spend the rest of our lives," said Zootie.

"That's very clever," said Vanessa.

Zootie wiped his nose and puffed up a bit.

"I think we should hand Buster over to you," said Gewell. "To be taken outside to face the justice of the past. Var-Z left work undone that we must continue."

"Not just yet," said Richard. "This sad business raises questions about Tomorrow Town. I have to look beyond the simple crime before I make my report. I'm sure you understand and will extend full cooperation."

No one said anything, but they all constructed smiles.

"You must be economically self-supporting by now," continued Richard, "what with the research and invention you've been applying intelligence to. If the Prime Minister withdrew government subsidies, you'd probably be better off. Free of the apron strings, as it were. Still, the extra cash must come in handy for something, even if you don't use money in this town."

Gewell wiped his eyes and kept smiling.

Richard could really do with a steak and kidney pie and chips, washed down with beer. Even a Kit-Kat would have been welcome.

"Have you a guest apartment we could use?"

Gewell's smile turned real. "Sadly, we're at maximum optimal zenvol residency. No excess space wastage in the living quarters.'

"No spare beds," clarified Zootie.

"Then we'll have to take the one living space we know to be free."

Gewell's brow furrowed like a rucked-up rug.

"Zhoule's quarters," Richard explained. "We'll set up camp there. Sue-2, you must know the way. Since there are no locks we won't need keys to get in. Zenvols, it's been fascinating. I look forward to seeing you tomorrow."

Richard and Vanessa stood up, and Sue-2 followed suit.

Gewell and Jess-F glared. Moana waved bye-bye.

"What are you looking for?" Vanessa asked. "Monitoring devices."

"No," said Richard, unsealing another compartment, "they're in the light fittings and the communicator screen, and seem to have been disabled. By Zhoule or his murderer, presumably."

There was a constant hum of gadgetry in the walls and from behind white-fronted compartments. The ceiling was composed of translucent panels, above which glowed a steady light.

The communicator screen was dusty. Beneath the on-off switch, volume and brightness knobs and channel selector was a telephone dial, with the Tomorrow Town alphabet (no Q or X). Richard had tried to call London but a recorded voice over a cartoon smiley face told him that visiphones only worked within the town limits. Use of the telephone line to the outside had to be approved by vote of zenvol visioneers.

In a compartment, he found a gadget whose purpose was a mystery. It had dials, a trumpet and three black rubber nipples.

"I'm just assuming, Vanessa, that the co-founder of Tomorrow Town might allow himself to sample the forbidden past in ways denied the simple zenvol or despised zenpass."

"You mean?"

"He might have real food stashed somewhere."

Vanessa started opening compartments too.

It took a full hour to search the five rooms of Zhoule's bungalow. They discovered a complete run of *Town Magazeen*, a microfilm publication with all text in fonetik, and a library of 1950s science fiction magazines, lurid covers mostly promising Varno Zhoule stories as back-up to Asimov or Heinlein.

They found many compartments stuffed with ring-bound notebooks which dated back twenty years. Richard flicked through a couple, noting Zhoule had either been using fonetik since the early 50s or was such a bad speller that his editors must have been driven to despair. Most of the entries were single sentences, story ideas, possible inventions or prophecies. *Tunel under Irish See. Rokit to Sun to harvest heet. Big lift to awbit. Stoopids not allowd to breed. Holes in heds for plugs.*

Vanessa found a display case, full of plaques and awards in the shapes of spirals or robots.

"Is this the murder weapon?" Vanessa asked, indicating a needle-shaped rocket. "Looks too clean."

"I believe Zhoule was a multiple Hugo-winner. See, this is Best Short Story 1957, for "Vesta Interests". The blunt instrument was . . . "

Vanessa picked up a chunk of ceramic and read the plaque, "Best Novelette 1958." It was a near-duplicate of the base of the other award.

"You can see where the rocketship was fixed. It must have broken when the award was lifted in anger."

"Cold blood, Vanessa. The body and the Hugo were found elsewhere. No blood traces in these quarters. Let's keep looking for a pork pie."

Vanessa opened a floor-level compartment and out crawled a matt-black robot spider the size of an armoured go-kart. The fearsome thing brandished death-implements that, upon closer examination, turned out to be a vacuum cleaner proboscis and limbs tipped with chamois, damp squeegee and a brush.

"Oh, how useful," said Vanessa.

Then the spider squirted hot water at her and crackled. Electrical circuits burned out behind its photo-eyes. The proboscis coughed black soot.

"Or maybe not."

" 'I have seen the future, and it works,' " quoted Richard. "Lincoln Steffens, on the Soviet Union, 1919."

" 'What's to become of my bit of washing when there's no washing to do,' " quoted Vanessa. "The old woman in *The Man in the White Suit*, on technological progress, 1951."

"You suspect the diabolical Big Thinks sent this cleaning robot to murder Varno Zhoule? A Frankensteinian rebellion against the Master-Creator?"

"If Bee-Tee is so clever, I doubt it'd use this arachnoid doodad as an assassin. The thing can't even beat as it sweeps as it cleans, let alone carry out a devilish murder plan. Besides, to use the blunt instrument, it would have to climb a wall and I reckon this can't even manage stairs."

Richard poked the carapace of the machine, which wriggled and lost a couple of limbs.

"Are you still hungry?"

"Famished."

"Yet we've had enough nourishment to keep body and spirit together for the ten long kronons that remain until breakfast time."

"I'll ask medico Mal-K if he sees many cases of rickets and scurvy in futopia."

"You do that."

Richard tried to feel sorry for the spider, but it was just a gadget. It was impossible to invest it with a personality.

Vanessa was thinking.

"Wasn't the idea that Tomorrow Town would pour forth 21st Century solutions to our drab old 1970s problems?"

Richard answered her. "That's what Mr Wilson thought he was signing up for.'

"So why aren't Mrs Mopp Spiders on sale in the Charing Cross Road?"

"It doesn't seem to work all that well."

"Lot of that about, Mm Richard. A monorail that would lose a race with Stephenson's Rocket. Technomeroticratic *droit de seigneur*. Concentrated foods astronauts wouldn't eat. Robots less functional than the wind-up ones Fred's nephew Paulie uses to conquer the playground. And I've seen the odd hovercraft up on blocks with 'Owt of Awder' signs. Not to mention Buster the Basher, living incarnation of a society out of joint."

"Good points all," he said. "And I'll answer them as soon as I solve another mystery."

"What's that?"

"What are we supposed to sleep on?"

Around the rooms were large soft white cubes which distantly resembled furniture but could as easily be tofu chunks for the giants who would evolve by the turn of the millennium. By collecting enough cubes into a windowless room where the lighting panels were more subdued, Richard and Vanessa were able to put together a bed-shape. However, when Richard took an experimental lie-down on the jigsaw-puzzle affair, an odd cube squirted out of place and fell through the gap. The floor was covered with warm fleshy plastic substance that was peculiarly unpleasant to the touch.

None of the many compartment-cupboards in the bungalow contained anything resembling 20th Century pillows or bedding. Heating elements in the floor turned up as the evening wore on, adjusting the internal temperature of the room to the point where their all-over condoms were extremely uncomfortable. Escaping from the Tomorrow Town costumes was much harder than getting into them.

It occurred to Richard and Vanessa at the same time that these spacesuits would make going to the lavatory awkward, though they reasoned an all-pill diet would minimise the wasteful toilet breaks required in the past. Eventually, with some co-operation, they got free and placed the suits on hangers in a glass-fronted cupboard which, when closed, filled with coloured steam. "Dekontaminashun Kompleet,' flashed a sign as the cabinet cracked open and spilled liquid residue. The floor was discoloured where this had happened before.

Having more or less puzzled out how the bedroom worked, they set about tackling the bathroom, which seemed to be equipped with a dental torture chamber and a wide variety of exotic marital aids. By the time they were done playing with it all, incidentally washing and cleaning their teeth, it was past ten midnight and the lights turned off automatically.

"Nighty-night," said Richard.

"Don't let the robot bugs bite," said Vanessa.

He woke up, alert. She woke with him.

"What's the matter? A noise?"

"No," he said. "No noise."

"Ah."

The Tomorrow Town hum, gadgets in the walls, was silenced. The bungalow was technologically dead. He reached out and touched the floor. It was cooling.

Silently, they got off the bed.

The room was dark, but they knew where the door—a sliding screen—was and took up positions either side of it.

The door had opened by touching a pad. Now the power was off, they were shut in (a flaw in the no-locks policy), though Richard heard a winding creak as the door lurched open an inch. There was some sort of clockwork back-up system.

A gloved hand reached into the room. It held an implement consisting of a plastic handle, two long thin metal rods, and a battery pack. A blue arc buzzed between the rods, suggesting lethal charge.

Vanessa took the wrist, careful not to touch the rods, and gave a good yank. The killing-prod, or whatever it was, was dropped and discharged against the floor, leaving a blackened patch and a nasty smell.

Surprised, the intruder stumbled against the door.

As far as Richard could make out in the minimal light, the figure wore the usual Tomorrow Town suit. An addition was an opaque black egg-shaped helmet with a silver strip around the eyes which he took to be a one-way mirror. A faint red radiance suggested some sort of infra-red see-in-the-dark device.

Vanessa, who had put on a floral bikini as sleepwear, kicked the egghead in the chest, which clanged. She hopped back.

"It's armoured," she said.

"All who defy Buster must die," rasped a speaker in the helmet.

Vanessa kicked again, at the shins, cutting the egghead down.

"All who defy Buster must die," squeaked the speaker, sped-up. "All who de . . . de . . . de . . . de . . . "

The recorded message was stuck.

The egghead clambered upright.

"Is there a person in there?" Vanessa asked.

"One way to find out," said Richard.

He hammered the egghead with a bed-cube, but it was too soft to dent the helmet. The intruder lunged and caught him in a plastic-and-metal grasp.

"Get him off me," he said, kicking. Unarmoured, he was at a disadvantage.

Vanessa nipped into the en-suite bathroom and came back with a gadget on a length of metal hose. They had decided it was probably a water-pick for those hard-to-clean crannies. She stabbed the end of the device at the egghead's neck, puncturing the plastic seal just below the chin-rim of the helmet, and turned the nozzle on. The tappet-key snapped off in her fingers and a high-pressure stream that could have drilled through cheddar cheese spurted into the suit.

Gallons of water inflated the egghead's garment. The suit self-sealed around the puncture and expanded, arms and legs forced out in an X. Richard felt the water-pressure swelling his captor's chest and arms. He wriggled and got free.

"All who defy Buster . . . "

Circuits burned out, and leaks sprouted at all the seams. Even through the silver strip, Richard made out the water rising.

There was a commotion in the next room.

Lights came on. The hum was back.

It occurred to Richard that he had opted to sleep in the buff and might not be in a decorous state to receive visitors. Then again, in the future taboos against social nudity were likely to evaporate.

Georgie Gewell, the ever-present Moana and Jess-F, who had another of the zapper-prod devices, stood just inside the doorway.

There was a long pause. This was not what anyone had expected.

"Buster has escaped," said Gewell. "We thought you might be in danger. He's beyond all reason."

"If he was a danger to us, he isn't any longer," said Vanessa.

"If this is him," Richard said. "He was invoking the name."

The egghead was on the floor, spouting torrents, super-inflated like the Michelin Man after a three-day egg-eating contest.

Vanessa kicked the helmet. It obligingly repeated 'All who defy Buster must die.'

The egghead waved hands like fat starfish, thumbing towards the helmet, which was sturdier than the rest of the suit and not leaking.

"Anybody know how to get this thing off?" asked Richard

The egghead writhed and was still.

"Might be a bit on the late side."

Gewell and Jess-F looked at each other. Moana took action and pushed into the room. She knelt and worked a few buttons around the chinrim of the helmet. The egghead cracked along a hitherto-unsuspected crooked seam and came apart in a gush of water.

"That's not Buster," said Vanessa. "It's Mal-K, the medico."

"And he's drowned," concluded Richard.

"A useful rule of thumb in open-and-shut cases," announced Richard, "is that when someone tries to murder any investigating officers, the case isn't as open-and-shut as it might at first have seemed."

He had put on a quilted double-breasted floor-length jade green dressing gown with a Blakeian red dragon picked out on the chest in sequins.

"When the would-be murderer is one of the major proponents of the open-and-shut theory," he continued, "it's a dead cert that an injustice is in the process of being perpetrated. Ergo, the errant Buster is innocent and someone else murdered Mm Zhoule with a Hugo award."

"Perhaps there was a misunderstanding," said Gewell.

Richard and Vanessa looked at him.

"How so?" Richard asked.

Wheels worked behind Gewell's eyes, which were amber now.

"Mm Mal-K might have heard of Buster's escape and come here to protect you from him. In the dark and confusion, you mistook his attempted rescue as an attack."

"And tragedy followed," completed Jess-F.

Moana weighed invisible balls and looked noncommittal.

It was sixty-eight past six o'kronon. The body had been removed and they were in Zhoule's front room. Since all the cubes were in the bedroom and wet through, everyone had to sit on the body-temperature floor. Vanessa perched decorously, see-through peignoir over her bikini, on the dead robot spider. Richard stood, as if lecturing.

"Mm Jor-G, you were an editor once," he said. "If a story were submitted in which a hero wanted to protect innocent parties from a rampaging killer, would you have allowed the author to have the hero get into a disguise, turn off all the lights and creep into the bedroom with a lethal weapon?"

"Um, I might. I edited science fiction magazines. Science fiction is about *ideas*. No matter what those New Wavers say. In s-f, characters might do anything."

"What about 'All who defy Buster must die'?" said Vanessa.

"A warning?" Gewell ventured, feebly.

"Oh, give up," said Jess-F. "Mal-K was a bad 'un. It's been obvious for desiyears. All those speeches about 'expanding the remit of the social experiment' and 'assuming pole position in the larger technomeritocracy.' He was in a position to doctor his own records, to cover up instability. He was also the one who matched Buster's fingerprints to the murder weapon. Mm and Ms, congratulations, you've caught the killer."

"Open-and-shut-and-open-and-shut?" suggested Richard.

Moana gave the thumbs-up.

"I'm going to need help to convince myself of this," said Richard. "I've decided to call on mighty deductive brainpower to get to the bottom of the mystery."

"More yesterday men?" said Jess-F, appalled.

"Interesting term. You've been careful not to use it before now. Is that what you call us? No, I don't intend to summon any more plods from the outside."

Gewell couldn't suppress his surge of relief.

"I've decided to apply the techniques of tomorrow to these crimes of the future. Jess-F, I'll need your help. Let's take this puzzle to Big Thinks, and see how your mighty computer does."

Shutters came down behind Jess-F's eyes.

"Computer time is precious," said Gewell.

"So is human life," answered Richard.

The inside of the building, the insides of Big Thinks, was the messiest area Richard had seen in Tomorrow Town. Banks of metal cabinets fronted with reels of tape were connected by a spaghetti tangle of wires that wound throughout the building like coloured plastic ivy. Some cabinets had their fronts off, showing masses of circuit-boards, valves and transistors. Surprisingly, the workings of the master brain seemed held together with a great deal of sellotape, string and blu-tak. Richard recognised some components well in advance of any on the market, and others that might date back to Marconi or Babbage.

"We've been making adjustments," said Jess-F.

She shifted a cardboard box full of plastic shapes from a swivel chair and let him sit at a desk piled with wired-together television sets. To one side was a paper-towel dispenser which coughed out a steady roll of graph-paper with lines squiggled on it.

He didn't know which knobs to twiddle.

"Ms Jess-F, could you show me how a typical dispute arbitration is made. Say, the triangle of Zhoule, Buster and Sue-2."

"That documentation might be hard to find."

"In this futopia of efficiency? I doubt it."

Jess-F nodded to Moana, who scurried off to root through large bins full of scrunched and torn paper.

Vanessa was with Gewell and Zootie, taking a tour of the hydroponics zone, which was where the body of Varno Zhoule had been found. The official story was that Buster (now, Mal-K) had gone to Zhoule's bungalow to kill him but found him not at home. He had taken the Hugo from its display case and searched out the victim-to-be, found him contemplating the green gunk that was made into his favourite pills, and did the deed then and there. It didn't take a computer to decide it was more likely that Zhoule had been killed where the weapon was handy for an annoyed impulse-assassin to reach for, then hovercrafted along with the murder weapon to a public place so some uninvolved zenvol clot could find him. But why ferry the body all that way, with the added risk of being caught?

"Tell you what, Ms Jess-F, let's try BeeTee out on a hypothetical dispute? Put in the set-up of *Hamlet*, and see what the computer thinks would be best for Denmark."

"Big Thinks is not a toy, Mm."

Moana came back waving some sheaves of paper.

Richard looked over it. Jess-F ground her teeth.

Though the top sheet was headed "Input tek: Buster Munro," this was not the triangle dispute documentation. Richard scrolled through the linked print-out. He saw maps of Northern Europe, lists of names and dates, depositions in non-phonetic English, German and Danish, and enough footnotes for a good-sized doctoral thesis. In fact, that was exactly what this was.

"I'm not the first to think of running a hypothetical dispute past the mighty computer," said Richard. "The much-maligned Buster got there before me."

"And wound up recategorised as a zenpass," said Jess-F.

"He tried to get an answer to the Schleswig-Holstein Question, didn't he? Lord Palmerston said only three men in Europe got to the bottom of it—one who forgot, one who died and one who went mad. It was an insanely complicated argument between Denmark and Germany, over the governance of a couple of border provinces. Buster put the question to Big Thinks as if it were a contemporary dispute, just to see how the computer would have resolved it. What did it suggest, nuclear attack? Is that why all the redecoration? Buster's puzzle blew all the fuses."

Richard found the last page.

The words "forgot died mad" were repeated over and over, in very faint ink. Then some mathematical formulae. Then the printer equivalent of scribble.

"This makes no sense."

He showed it to Jess-F, hoping she could interpret it. He really would have liked Big Thinks to have got to the bottom of the tussle that defeated Bismarck and Metternich and spat out a blindingly simple answer everyone should have seen all along.

"No," she admitted. "It makes no sense at all."

Moana shrugged.

Richard felt a rush of sympathy for Jess-F. This was painful for her.

"BeeTee can't do it," said Richard. "The machine can do sums very fast, but nothing else?"

Jess-F was almost at the point of tears.

"That's not true,' she said, with tattered pride. "Big Thinks is the most advanced computer in the world. It can solve any logic problem. Give it the data, and it can deliver accurate weather forecasts, arrange schedules to optimise efficiency of any number of tasks . . . "

"But throw the illogical at it, and BeeTee just has a good cry."

"It's a machine. It can't cry."

"Or arbitrate love affairs."

Jess-F was in a corner.

"It's not fair," she said, quietly. "It's not BeeTee's fault. It's not my fault. They knew the operational parameters. They just kept insisting it tackle areas outside its remit, extending, tampering, overburdening. My techs have been working all the hours of the day . . . "

"Kronons, surely?"

" . . . all the bloody kronons of the day, just trying to get Big Thinks working again. Even after all this, the ridiculous demands keep coming through. Big Thinks, Big Thinks, will I be pretty, will I be rich? Big Thinks, Big Thinks, is there life on other planets?"

Jess-F put her hands over her face.

" 'They'? Who are 'they'?"

"All of them,' Jess-F sobbed. "Across all disciplines."

"Who especially?"

"Who else? Varno Zhoule."

"Not any more?"

"No."

She looked out from behind her hands, horrified.

"It wasn't me," she said.

"I know. You're left-handed. Wrong wound pattern. One more question: what did the late Mm Mal-K want from Big Thinks?"

Jess-F gave out an appalled sigh.

"Now, he *was* cracked. He kept putting in these convoluted specific questions. In the end, they were all about taking over the country. He wanted to run the whole of the United Kingdom like Tomorrow Town."

"The day after tomorrow, the world?"

"He kept putting in plans and strategies for infiltrating vital industries and dedicating them to the cause. He didn't have an army, but he believed Big Thinks could get all the computers in the country on his side. Most of the zenvols thought he was a dreamer, spinning out a best-case scenario at the meetings. But he meant it. He wanted to found a large-scale Technomeritocracy."

"With himself as Beloved Leader?"

"No, that's how mad he was. He wanted Big Thinks to run everything. He was hoping to put BeeTee in charge and let the future happen."

"That's why he wanted Vanessa and me out of the story. We were a threat to his funding. Without the subsidies, the plug is pulled."

"One thing BeeTee can do is keep track of figures. As a community, Tomorrow Town is in the red. Enormously."

"There's no money here, though."

"Of course not. We've spent it. And spent money we don't have. The next monorail from Preston is liable to be crowded with dunning bailiffs."

Richard thought about it. He was rather saddened by the truth. It would have been nice if the future worked. He wondered if Lincoln Steffens had any second thoughts during the Moscow purge trials?

"What threat was Zhoule to Mal-K?" he asked.

Jess-F frowned. "That's the oddest thing. Zhoule was the one who really encouraged Mal-K to work on his coup plans. He did see himself as, what did you call it, 'Beloved Leader.' All his stories were about intellectual supermen taking charge of the world and sorting things out. If anything, he was the visioneer of the tomorrow take-over. And he'd have jumped anything in skirts if femzens wore skirts here."

Richard remembered the quivering Sue-2.

"So we're back to Buster in the conservatory with the Hugo award?"

"I've always said it was him," said Jess-F. "You can't blame him, but he did it."

"We shall see."

Sirens sounded. Moana put her fingers in her ears. Jess-F looked even more stricken.

"That's not a good sign, is it?"

The communal meal area outside Big Thinks swarmed with plastic-caped zenvols, looking up and pointing, panicking and screaming. The three light-heat globes, Tomorrow Town's suns, shone whiter and radiated hotter. Richard looked at the backs of his hands. They were tanning almost as quickly as an instant photograph develops.

"The fool," said Jess-F. "He's tampered with the master controls. Buster will kill us all. It's the only thing he has left."

Zenvols piled into the communally-owned electric carts parked in a rank to one side of the square. When they proved too heavy for the vehicles, they started throwing each other off. Holes melted in the canopy above the globes. Sizzling drips of molten plastic fell onto screaming tomorrow townies.

The sirens shrilled, urging everyone to panic.

Richard saw Vanessa through the throng.

She was with Zootie. No Gewell.

A one-man hovercraft, burdened with six clinging zenvols, chugged past inch by inch, outpaced by someone on an old-fashioned, non-solar-powered bicycle.

"If the elements reach critical," said Jess-F, "Tomorrow Town will blow up."

A bannerlike strip of paper curled out of a slit in the front of Big Thinks.

"Your computer wants to say goodbye," said Richard.

SURKIT BRAKER No. 15.

"Not much of a farewell."

Zootie walked between falling drips to the central column, which supported the three globes. He opened a hatch and pulled a switch. The artificial suns went out. Real sunlight came through the holes in the canopy.

"Now that's what computers can do," said Jess-F, elated. "Execute protocols. If this happens, then that order must be given."

The zenvol seemed happier about her computer now.

Richard was grateful for a ditch-digger who could read.

"This is where the body was?" he asked Zootie. They were by swimming-pool sized tanks of green gunk, dotted with yellow and brown patches since the interruption of the light-source. "Bit of a haul from Zhoule's place."

"The body was carried here?" asked Vanessa.

"Not just the body. The murder weapon too. Who lives in that bungalow?"

On a small hill was a bungalow not quite as spacious as Zhoule's, one of the mass of hutches placed between the silver pathways, with a crown of solar panels on the flat roof, and a dish antennae.

"Mm Jor-G," said Moana.

"So you do speak?"

She nodded her head and smiled.

Gewell sat on an off-white cube in the gloom. The stored power was running down. Only filtered sunlight got through to his main room. He looked as if his backbone had been removed. All the substance of his face had fallen to his jowls.

Richard looked at him.

"Nice try with the globes. Should have remembered the circuit-breaker, though. Only diabolical masterminds construct their private estates with in-built self-destruct systems. In the future, as in the past, it's unlikely that town halls will have bombs in the basement ready to go off in the event that the outgoing Mayor wants to take the whole community with him rather than hand over the chain of office."

Gewell didn't say anything.

Vanessa went straight to a shelf and picked up the only award in the display. It was another Hugo.

"Best Fan Editor 1958," she read from the plaque.

The rocketship came away from its base.

"You killed him here," said Richard, "broke your own Hugo, left the bloody rocketship with the body outside. Then, when you'd calmed down a bit, you remembered Zhoule had won the same award. Several, in fact. You sneaked over to his bungalow—no locks, how convenient—and broke one of his Hugos, taking the rocket to complete yours. You made it look as if he were killed with his own award, and you were out of the loop. If only you'd got round to developing the glue of the future and fixed the thing properly, it wouldn't be so obvious. It's plain that though you've devoted your life to planning out the details of the future, your one essay in the fine art of murder was a rushed botch-up job done on the spur of the moment. You haven't really improved on Cain. At least, Mm Mal-K made the effort with the space-suit and the zapper-prod."

"Mm Jor-G," said Jess-F, "*why*?"

Good question, Richard thought.

After a long pause, Gewell gathered himself and said, "Varno was destroying Tomorrow Town. He had so many . . . so many *ideas*. Every morning, before breakfast, he had four or five. All the time, constantly. Radio transmitters the size of a pinhead. Cheap infinite energy from tapping the planet's core. Solar-powered personal flying machines. Robots to do everything. Robots to make robots to do everything. An operation to extend human lifespan threefold. Rules and regulations about who was fit to have and raise children, with gonad-block implants to enforce them. Hats that collect the electrical energy of the brain and use it to power a personal headlamp. Non-stop, unrelenting, unstoppable. Ideas, ideas, ideas . . . "

Richard was frankly astonished by the man's vehemence. "Isn't that what you wanted?"

"But Varno did the easy bit. Once he'd tossed out an idea, it was

up to *me* to make it work. Me or Big Thinks or some other plodding
zenvol. And nine out of ten of the ideas didn't work, couldn't ever
work. And it was always our fault for not making them work, never
his for foisting them off on us. This town would be perfect if it
hadn't been for his ideas. And his bloody dreadful spelling. Back
in the 50s, who do you think tidied all his stories up so they were
publishable? Muggins Gewell. He couldn't write a sentence that
scanned, and rather than learn how he decreed the language should
be changed. Not just the spelling, he had a plan to go through the
dictionary crossing out all the words that were no longer needed,
then make it a crime to teach them to children. It was something to
do with his old public school. He said he wanted to make gerunds
extinct within a generation. But he had these wonderful, wonderful,
ghastly, terrible *ideas*. It'd have made you sick."

"And the medico who wanted to rule the world?"

"Him too. He had ideas."

Gewell was pleading now, hands fists around imaginary
bludgeons.

"If only I could have had ideas," he said. "They'd have been *good*
ones."

Richard wondered how they were going to lock Gewell up until
the police came.

The monorail was out of commission. Most things were. Some
zenvols, like Jess-F, were relieved not to have to pretend that
everything worked perfectly. They had desiyears—months,
dammit!—of complaining bottled up inside, and were pouring it
all out to each other in one big whine-in under the dead light-heat
globes.

Richard and Vanessa looked across the Dales. A small vehicle
was puttering along a winding, illogical lane that had been laid
out not by a computer but by wandering sheep. It wasn't the police,
though they were on the way.

"Who do you think this is?" asked Vanessa.

"It'll be Buster. He's bringing the outside to Tomorrow Town. He always was a yesterday man at heart."

A car-horn honked.

Zenvols, some already changed out of their plastic suits, paid attention. Sue-2 was excited, hopeful, fearful. She clung to Moana, who smiled and waved.

Someone cheered. Others joined.

"What is he driving?" asked Vanessa. "It looks like a relic from the past."

"For these people, it's deliverance," said Richard. "It's a fish 'n' chip van."

Terms Used in "Tomorrow Town"

Since the Year Dot: since time immemorial.

A **Dalek.** Trundling cyborg giant pepperpot featured in the long-running BBC-TV science-fiction programme *Doctor Who*, introduced in 1963. The Daleks' distinctive mechanical voices were much-imitated by British children in the 1960s. Their catch-phrase: "ex-ter-min-ate!"

The Wilson Government. Harold Wilson was Labour Prime Minister of Great Britain from 1964 to 1970 and again from 1974 to 1976. A Maigret-like pipe-smoking, raincoated figure, he famously boasted of "the white heat of technology" when summing up British contributions to futuristic projects like the Concorde. At the time of this story, he had been succeeded by the Tory Edward Heath, a laughing yachtsman.

James Burke and Raymond Baxter. The hosts in the 1960s of BBC-TV's long-running *Tomorrow's World*, a magazine programme covering the worlds of invention and technology. They were also anchors for UK TV coverage of the moon landings.

The BBC Radiophonic Workshop. The corporation's sound effects department, responsible for Dalek voices and the *Doctor Who* theme. Their consultants included the Pink Floyd and Michael Moorcock.

The Crazy World of Arthur Brown. "I am the God of Hell Fire," rants Arthur on his single "Fire," which was Number One in the UK charts in 1968. An influence on Iron Maiden and other pioneer Heavy Metal groups, Arthur was also a devoted surrealist-cum-Satanist. He never had another hit, but is still gigging.

New Scientist. UK weekly magazine, scientific sister publication to the left-leaning political journal *New Statesman*.

Arthur C. Clarke. Now Sir Arthur C. Clarke, author of *Childhood's End*, screenwriter of *2001: A Space Odyssey*, writer on scientific topics and Sri Lankan resident. Known in the UK as host of *Arthur C. Clarke's Mysterious World*, a TV series about Fortean phenomena that is twenty years on the template for much *X-Files*-ish fringe documentary programming.

Auberon Waugh. Crusty conservative commentator, son of Evelyn Waugh, author of satirical novels. In the 1960s, his waspish journalism was most often found in *The Spectator* and the *Daily Telegraph*.

J.G. Ballard. Major British novelist, a key influence in the so-called New Wave of British s-f in the 1960s and 70s, now better known for more or less mainstream work that is weirder than most genre stuff.

Varno Zhoule. British s-f author, most prolific in the 1950s, when he published almost exclusively in American magazines. His only novel, *The Stars in Their Traces*, is a fix-up of stories first seen in *Astounding*. His "Court Martian" was dramatised on the UK TV series *Out of the Unknown* in 1963.

Gerry Anderson. TV producer famous in collaboration with his wife Sylvia, for 1960s technophilic puppet shows *Fireball XL-5*, *Stingray*, *Thunderbirds* and *Captain Scarlet and the Mysterons*. His 1970s live-action *Space 1999* has not achieved the lasting place in UK pop culture attained by the "supermarionation" shows.

Valerie Singleton. Presenter of the BBC-TV children's magazine programme *Blue Peter*. Well-spoken and auntie-like, she famously showed kids how to make things out of household oddments without ever mentioning a brand-name (a co-host who once said "Biro" instead of "ball-point pen" was nearly fired).

Smarties. Chocolate discs inside shells of various colours, available from Rowntree & Company in cardboard tubes. Still a staple "sweet" (ie: candy) in the UK; similar to M&Ms.

Kit-Kat. A chocolate bar.

The Tomorrow Town Alphabet. Q and X are replaced by KW and KS; the vestigial C exists only in CH and is otherwise replaced by K or S. Eg: THE KWIK BROWN FOKS JUMPED OVER THE LAYZEE DOG.

The Man in the White Suit. Film directed by Alexander Mackendrick, starring Alec Guinness. An inventor develops a fabric that never wears out or gets dirty, and the clothing industry tries to keep it off the market.

Can't even beat as it sweeps as it cleans. The UK slogan for Hoover vacuum cleaners in the 1970s was "it beats as it sweeps as it cleans."

Michelin Man. Cheery advertising mascot of the tire company, he consists of white bloated tires.

The Schleswig-Holstein Question. Bane of any schoolboy studying O level European history in 1975. It's a key plot point in George Macdonald Fraser's novel *Royal Flash*.

Muggins: a sap, a patsy.

there's a hole
in the city

RICHARD BOWES

Richard Bowes has written five novels, the most recent of which is the Nebula Award nominated *From the Files of the Time Rangers*. His most recent short fiction collection is *Streetcar Dreams And Other Midnight Fancies* from PS Publications. He has won the World Fantasy, Lambda, International Horror Guild, and Million Writers Awards.

Recent and forthcoming stories appear in *The Magazine of Fantasy and Science Fiction*, *Electric Velocipede*, *Clarkesworld*, and *Fantasy* magazines and in the *Del Rey Book of Science Fiction and Fantasy*, *Year's Best Gay Stories 2008*, *Best Science Fiction and Fantasy*, *The Beastly Bride*, *Haunted Legends*, *Fantasy Best of the Year 2009*, *Year's Best Fantasy* and *Naked City* anthologies . Several of these stories are chapters in his novel in progress, *Dust Devil on a Quiet Street*.

His home page is: www.rickbowes.com

"There's a Hole in the City" won the International Horror Guild Award, the Million Writers Award and was nominated for the Nebula award.

WEDNESDAY 9/12

On the evening of the day after the towers fell, I was waiting by the barricades on Houston Street and LaGuardia Place for my friend Mags to come up from Soho and have dinner with me. On the skyline, not two miles to the south, the pillars of smoke wavered slightly. But the creepily beautiful weather of September 11 still held, and the wind blew in from the northeast. In Greenwich Village the air was crisp and clean, with just a touch of fall about it.

I'd spent the last day and a half looking at pictures of burning towers. One of the frustrations of that time was that there was so little most of us could do about anything or for anyone.

Downtown streets were empty of all traffic except emergency vehicles. The West and East Villages from Fourteenth Street to Houston were their own separate zone. Pedestrians needed identification proving they lived or worked there in order to enter.

The barricades consisted of blue wooden police horses and a couple of unmarked vans thrown across LaGuardia Place. Behind them were a couple of cops, a few auxiliary police and one or two guys in civilian clothes with ID's of some kind pinned to their shirts. All of them looked tired, subdued by events.

At the barricades was a small crowd: ones like me waiting for friends from neighborhoods to the south; ones without proper identification waiting for confirmation so that they could continue on into Soho; people who just wanted to be outside near other people in those days of sunshine and shock. Once in a while, each of us would look up at the columns of smoke that hung in the downtown sky then look away again.

A family approached a middle-aged cop behind the barricade. The group consisted of a man, a woman, a little girl being led by the hand, a child being carried. All were blondish and wore shorts and casual tops. The parents seemed pleasant but serious people in their early thirties, professionals. They could have been tourists. But that day the city was empty of tourists.

The man said something, and I heard the cop say loudly, "You want to go where?"

"Down there," the man gestured at the columns. He indicated the children. "We want them to see." It sounded as if he couldn't imagine this appeal not working.

Everyone stared at the family. "No ID, no passage," said the cop and turned his back on them. The pleasant expressions on the parents' faces faded. They looked indignant, like a maitre d' had lost their reservations. She led one kid, he carried the other as they turned west, probably headed for another checkpoint.

"They wanted those little kids to see Ground Zero!" a woman who knew the cop said. "Are they out of their minds?"

"Looters," he replied. "That's my guess." He picked up his walkie-talkie to call the checkpoints ahead of them.

Mags appeared just then, looking a bit frayed. When you've known someone for as long as I've known her, the tendency is not to see the changes, to think you both look about the same as when you were kids.

But kids don't have gray hair, and their bodies aren't thick the way bodies get in their late fifties. Their kisses aren't perfunctory. Their conversation doesn't include curt little nods that indicate something is understood.

We walked in the middle of the streets because we could. "Couldn't sleep much last night," I said.

"Because of the quiet," she said. "No planes. I kept listening for them. I haven't been sleeping anyway. I was supposed to be in housing court today. But the courts are shut until further notice."

I said, "Notice how with only the ones who live here allowed in, the South Village is all Italians and hippies?"

"Like 1965 all over again."

She and I had been in contact more in the past few months than we had in a while. Memories of love and indifference that we shared had made close friendship an on-and-off thing for the last thirty-something years.

Earlier in 2001, at the end of an affair, I'd surrendered a rent-stabilized apartment for a cash settlement and bought a tiny co-op in the South Village. Mags lived as she had for years in a run-down building on the fringes of Soho.

So we saw each other again. I write, obviously, but she never read anything I publish, which bothered me. On the other hand, she worked off and on for various activist leftist foundations, and I was mostly uninterested in that.

Mags was in the midst of classic New York work and housing trouble. Currently she was on unemployment and her landlord wanted to get her out of her apartment so he could co-op her building. The money offer he'd made wasn't bad, but she wanted things to stay as they were. It struck me that what was youthful about her was that she had never settled into her life, still stood on the edge.

Lots of the Village restaurants weren't opened. The owners couldn't or wouldn't come into the city. Angelina's on Thompson Street was, though, because Angelina lives just a couple of doors down from her place. She was busy serving tables herself since the waiters couldn't get in from where they lived.

Later, I had reason to try and remember. The place was full but very quiet. People murmured to each other as Mags and I did. Nobody I knew was there. In the background Resphigi's *Ancient Airs and Dances* played.

"Like the Blitz," someone said.

"Never the same again," said a person at another table.

"There isn't even anyplace to volunteer to help," a third person said.

I don't drink anymore. But Mags, as I remember, had a carafe of wine. Phone service had been spotty, but we had managed to exchange bits of what we had seen.

"Mrs. Pirelli," I said. "The Italian lady upstairs from me. I told you she had a heart attack watching the smoke and flames on television. Her son worked in the World Trade Center and she was sure he had burned to death.

"Getting an ambulance wasn't possible yesterday morning. But the guys at that little fire barn around the corner were there. Waiting to be called, I guess. They took her to St. Vincent's in the chief's car. Right about then, her son came up the street, his pinstripe suit with a hole burned in the shoulder, soot on his face, wild-eyed. But alive. Today they say she's doing fine."

I waited, spearing clams, twirling linguine. Mags had a deeper and darker story to tell; a dip into the subconscious. Before I'd known her and afterward, Mags had a few rough brushes with mental disturbance. Back in college, where we first met, I envied her that, wished I had something as dramatic to talk about.

"I've been thinking about what happened last night." She'd already told me some of this. "The downstairs bell rang, which scared me. But with phone service being bad, it could have been a friend, someone who needed to talk. I looked out the window. The street was empty, dead like I'd never seen it.

"Nothing but papers blowing down the street. You know how every time you see a scrap of paper now you think it's from the Trade Center? For a minute I thought I saw something move, but when I looked again there was nothing.

"I didn't ring the buzzer, but it seemed someone upstairs did because I heard this noise, a rustling in the hall.

"When I went to the door and lifted the spy hole, this figure stood there on the landing. Looking around like she was lost. She wore a dress, long and torn. And a blouse, what I realized was a shirtwaist. Turn-of-the-century clothes. When she turned toward my door, I saw her face. It was bloody, smashed. Like she had taken a big jump or fall. I gasped, and then she was gone."

"And you woke up?"

"No, I tried to call you. But the phones were all fucked up. She had fallen, but not from a hundred stories. Anyway, she wasn't from here and now."

Mags had emptied the carafe. I remember that she'd just ordered a salad and didn't eat that. But Angelina brought a fresh carafe. I told Mags about the family at the barricades.

"There's a hole in the city," said Mags.

That night, after we had parted, I lay in bed watching but not seeing some old movie on TV, avoiding any channel with any kind of news, when the buzzer sounded. I jumped up and went to the view screen. On the empty street downstairs a man, wild-eyed, disheveled, glared directly into the camera.

Phone service was not reliable. Cops were not in evidence in the neighborhood right then. I froze and didn't buzz him in. But, as in Mags's building, someone else did. I bolted my door, watched at the spy hole, listened to the footsteps, slow, uncertain. When he came into sight on the second floor landing he looked around and said in a hoarse voice, "Hello? Sorry, but I can't find my mom's front-door key."

Only then did I unlock the door, open it, and ask her exhausted son how Mrs. Pirelli was doing.

"Fine," he said. "Getting great treatment. St. Vincent was geared up for thousands of casualties. Instead . . . " He shrugged. "Anyway, she thanks all of you. Me too."

In fact, I hadn't done much. We said good night, and he shuffled on upstairs to where he was crashing in his mother's place.

THURSDAY 9/13

By September of 2001 I had worked an information desk in the university library for almost thirty years. I live right around the corner from Washington Square, and just before 10 A.M. on

Thursday, I set out for work. The Moslem-run souvlaki stand across the street was still closed, its owner and workers gone since Tuesday morning. All the little falafel shops in the South Village were shut and dark.

On my way to work I saw a three-legged rat running not too quickly down the middle of MacDougal Street. I decided not to think about portents and symbolism.

The big TVs set up in the library atrium still showed the towers falling again and again. But now they also showed workers digging in the flaming wreckage at Ground Zero.

Like the day before, I was the only one in my department who'd made it in. The librarians lived too far away. Even Marco, the student assistant, wasn't around.

Marco lived in a dorm downtown right near the World Trade Center. They'd been evacuated with nothing more than a few books and the clothes they were wearing. Tuesday, he'd been very upset. I'd given him Kleenex, made him take deep breaths, got him to call his mother back in California. I'd even walked him over to the gym, where the university was putting up the displaced students.

Thursday morning, all of the computer stations around the information desk were occupied. Students sat furiously typing e-mail and devouring incoming messages, but the intensity had slackened since 9/11. The girls no longer sniffed and dabbed at tears as they read. The boys didn't jump up and come back from the restrooms red-eyed and saying they had allergies.

I said good morning and sat down. The kids hadn't spoken much to me in the last few days, had no questions to ask. But all of them from time to time would turn and look to make sure I was still there. If I got up to leave the desk, they'd ask when I was coming back.

Some of the back windows had a downtown view. The pillar of smoke wavered. The wind was changing.

The phone rang. Reception had improved. Most calls went through. When I answered, a voice, tight and tense, blurted out,

"Jennie Levine was who I saw. She was nineteen years old in 1911 when the Triangle Shirtwaist Factory burned. She lived in my building with her family ninety years ago. Her spirit found its way home. But the inside of my building has changed so much that she didn't recognize it."

"Hi, Mags," I said. "You want to come up here and have lunch?"

A couple of hours later, we were in a small dining hall normally used by faculty on the west side of the Square. The university, with food on hand and not enough people to eat it, had thrown open its cafeterias and dining halls to anybody with a university identification. We could even bring a friend if we cared to.

Now that I looked, Mags had tension lines around her eyes and hair that could have used some tending. But we were all of us a little ragged in those days of sun and horror. People kept glancing downtown, even if they were inside and not near a window.

The Indian lady who ran the facility greeted us, thanked us for coming. I had a really nice gumbo, fresh avocado salad, a soothing pudding. The place was half–empty, and conversations again were muted. I told Mags about Mrs. Pirelli's son the night before.

She looked up from her plate, unsmiling, said, "I did not imagine Jennie Levine," and closed that subject.

Afterward, she and I stood on Washington Place before the university building that had once housed the sweatshop called The Triangle Shirtwaist Factory. At the end of the block, a long convoy of olive green army trucks rolled silently down Broadway.

Mags said, "On the afternoon of March 25, 1911, one hundred and forty-six young women burned to death on this site. Fire broke out in a pile of rags. The door to the roof was locked. The fire ladders couldn't reach the eighth floor. The girls burned."

Her voice tightened as she said, "They jumped and were smashed on the sidewalk. Many of them, most of them, lived right around here. In the renovated tenements we live in now. It's like those planes blew a hole in the city and Jennie Levine returned through it."

"Easy, honey. The university has grief counseling available. I think I'm going. You want me to see if I can get you in?" It sounded idiotic even as I said it. We had walked back to the library.

"There are others," she said. "Kids all blackened and bloated and wearing old-fashioned clothes. I woke up early this morning and couldn't go back to sleep. I got up and walked around here and over in the East Village."

"Jesus!" I said.

"Geoffrey has come back too. I know it."

"Mags! Don't!" This was something we hadn't talked about in a long time. Once we were three, and Geoffrey was the third. He was younger than either of us by a couple of years at a time of life when that still seemed a major difference.

We called him Lord Geoff because he said we were all a bit better than the world around us. We joked that he was our child. A little family cemented by desire and drugs.

The three of us were all so young, just out of school and in the city. Then jealousy and the hard realities of addiction began to tear us apart. Each had to find his or her own survival. Mags and I made it. As it turned out, Geoff wasn't built for the long haul. He was twenty-one. We were all just kids, ignorant and reckless.

As I made excuses in my mind, Mags gripped my arm. "He'll want to find us," she said. Chilled, I watched her walk away and wondered how long she had been coming apart and why I hadn't noticed.

Back at work, Marco waited for me. He was part Filipino, a bit of a little wiseass who dressed in downtown black. But that was the week before. Today, he was a woebegone refugee in oversized flip-flops, wearing a magenta sweatshirt and gym shorts, both of which had been made for someone bigger and more buff.

"How's it going?"

"It sucks! My stuff is all downtown where I don't know if I can ever get it. They have these crates in the gym, toothbrushes, bras, Bic razors, but never what you need, everything from boxer shorts on out, and nothing is ever the right size. I gave my clothes in to be cleaned, and they didn't bring them back. Now I look like a clown.

"They have us all sleeping on cots on the basketball courts. I lay there all last night staring up at the ceiling, with a hundred other guys. Some of them snore. One was yelling in his sleep. And I don't want to take a shower with a bunch of guys staring at me."

He told me all this while not looking my way, but I understood what he was asking. I expected this was going to be a pain. But, given that I couldn't seem to do much for Mags, I thought maybe it would be a distraction to do what I could for someone else.

"You want to take a shower at my place, crash on my couch?"

"Could I, please?"

So I took a break, brought him around the corner to my apartment, put sheets on the daybed. He was in the shower when I went back to work.

That evening when I got home, he woke up. When I went out to take a walk, he tagged along. We stood at the police barricades at Houston Street and Sixth Avenue and watched the traffic coming up from the World Trade Center site. An ambulance with one side smashed and a squad car with its roof crushed were hauled up Sixth Avenue on the back of a huge flatbed truck. NYPD buses were full of guys returning from Ground Zero, hollow-eyed, filthy.

Crowds of Greenwich Villagers gathered on the sidewalks clapped and cheered, yelled, "We love our firemen! We love our cops!"

The firehouse on Sixth Avenue had taken a lot of casualties when the towers fell. The place was locked and empty. We looked at the flowers and the wreaths on the doors, the signs with faces of the firefighters who hadn't returned, and the messages, "To the brave men of these companies who gave their lives defending us."

The plume of smoke downtown rolled in the twilight, buffeted about by shifting winds. The breeze brought with it for the first time the acrid smoke that would be with us for weeks afterward.

Officials said it was the stench of burning concrete. I believed, as did everyone else, that part of what we breathed was the ashes of the ones who had burned to death that Tuesday.

It started to drizzle. Marco stuck close to me as we walked back. Hip twenty-year-olds do not normally hang out with guys almost three times their age. This kid was very scared.

Bleecker Street looked semiabandoned, with lots of the stores and restaurants still closed. The ones that were open were mostly empty at nine in the evening.

"If I buy you a six-pack, you promise to drink all of it?" He indicated he would.

At home, Marco asked to use the phone. He called people he knew on campus, looking for a spare dorm room, and spoke in whispers to a girl named Eloise. In between calls, he worked the computer.

I played a little Lady Day, some Ray Charles, a bit of Haydn, stared at the TV screen. The president had pulled out of his funk and was coming to New York the next day.

In the next room, the phone rang. "No. My name's Marco," I heard him say. "He's letting me stay here." I knew who it was before he came in and whispered, "She asked if I was Lord Geoff."

"Hi, Mags," I said. She was calling from somewhere with walkie-talkies and sirens in the background.

"Those kids I saw in Astor Place?" she said, her voice clear and crazed. "The ones all burned and drowned? They were on the *General Slocum* when it caught fire."

"The kids you saw in Astor Place all burned and drowned?" I asked. Then I remembered our conversation earlier.

"On June 15, 1904. The biggest disaster in New York City history. Until now. The East Village was once called Little Germany. Tens of thousands of Germans with their own meeting halls, churches, beer gardens.

"They had a Sunday excursion, mainly for the kids, on a steamship, the *General Slocum*, a floating firetrap. When it burst into flames, there were no lifeboats. The crew and the captain panicked. By the time they got to a dock, over a thousand were dead. Burned, drowned. When a hole got blown in the city, they came back looking for their homes."

The connection started to dissolve into static.

"Where are you, Mags?"

"Ground Zero. It smells like burning sulfur. Have you seen Geoffrey yet?" she shouted into her phone.

"Geoffrey is dead, Mags. It's all the horror and tension that's doing this to you. There's no hole . . . "

"Cops and firemen and brokers all smashed and charred are walking around down here." At that point sirens screamed in the background. Men were yelling. The connection faded.

"Mags, give me your number. Call me back," I yelled. Then there was nothing but static, followed by a weak dial tone. I hung up and waited for the phone to ring again.

After a while, I realized Marco was standing looking at me, slugging down beer. "She saw those kids? I saw them too. Tuesday night I was too jumpy to even lie down on the fucking cot. I snuck out with my friend Terry. We walked around. The kids were there. In old, historical clothes. Covered with mud and seaweed and their faces all black and gone. It's why I couldn't sleep last night."

"You talk to the counselors?" I asked.

He drained the bottle. "Yeah, but they don't want to hear what I wanted to talk about."

"But with me . . . "

"You're crazy. You understand."

The silence outside was broken by a jet engine. We both flinched. No planes had flown over Manhattan since the ones that had smashed the towers on Tuesday morning.

Then I realized what it was. "The Air Force," I said. "Making sure it's safe for Mr. Bush's visit."

"Who's Mags? Who's Lord Geoff?"

So I told him a bit of what had gone on in that strange lost country, the 1960's, the naïveté that led to meth and junk. I described the wonder of that unknown land, the three-way union. "Our problem, I guess, was that instead of a real ménage, each member was obsessed with only one of the others."

"Okay," he said. "You're alive. Mags is alive. What happened to Geoff?

"When things were breaking up, Geoff got caught in a drug sweep and was being hauled downtown in the back of a police van. He cut his wrists and bled to death in the dark before anyone noticed."

This did for me what speaking about the dead kids had maybe done for him. Each of us got to talk about what bothered him without having to think much about what the other said.

FRIDAY 9/14

Friday morning two queens walked by with their little dogs as Marco and I came out the door of my building. One said, "There isn't a fresh croissant in the entire Village. It's like the Siege of Paris. We'll all be reduced to eating rats."

I murmured, "He's getting a little ahead of the story. Maybe first he should think about having an English muffin."

"Or eating his yappy dog," said Marco.

At that moment, the authorities opened the East and West Villages, between Fourteenth and Houston Streets, to outside traffic. All the people whose cars had been stranded since Tuesday began to come into the neighborhood and drive them away. Delivery trucks started to appear on the narrow streets.

In the library, the huge TV screens showed the activity at Ground Zero, the preparations for the president's visit. An elevator door opened and revealed a couple of refugee kids in their surplus gym clothes clasped in a passion clinch.

The computers around my information desk were still fully occupied, but the tension level had fallen. There was even a question or two about books and databases. I tried repeatedly to call Mags. All I got was the chilling message on her answering machine.

In a staccato voice, it said, "This is Mags McConnell. There's a hole in the city, and I've turned this into a center for information about the victims Jennie Levine and Geoffrey Holbrun. Anyone with information concerning the whereabouts of these two young people, please speak after the beep."

I left a message asking her to call. Then I called every half hour or so, hoping she'd pick up. I phoned mutual friends. Some were absent or unavailable. A couple were nursing grief of their own. No one had seen her recently.

That evening in the growing dark, lights flickered in Washington Square. Candles were given out; candles were lighted with matches and Bics and wick to wick. Various priests, ministers, rabbis, and shamans led flower-bearing, candlelit congregations down the streets and into the park, where they joined the gathering vigil crowd.

Marco had come by with his friend Terry, a kind of elfin kid who'd also had to stay at the gym. We went to this 9/11 vigil together. People addressed the crowd, gave impromptu elegies. There were prayers and a few songs. Then by instinct or some plan I hadn't heard about, everyone started to move out of the park and flow in groups through the streets.

We paused at streetlamps that bore signs with pictures of pajama-clad families in suburban rec rooms on Christmas mornings. One face would be circled in red, and there would be a message like, "This is James Bolton, husband of Susan, father of Jimmy, Anna, and Sue, last seen leaving his home in Far Rockaway at 7:30 A.M. on 9/11." This was followed by the name of the company, the floor of the Trade Center tower where he worked, phone and fax numbers, the e-mail address, and the words, "If you have any information about where he is, please contact us."

At each sign someone would leave a lighted candle on a tin plate. Someone else would leave flowers.

The door of the little neighborhood Fire Rescue station was open;

the truck and command car were gone. The place was manned by retired firefighters with faces like old Irish and Italian character actors. A big picture of a fireman who had died was hung up beside the door. He was young, maybe thirty. He and his wife, or maybe his girlfriend, smiled in front of a ski lodge. The picture was framed with children's drawings of firemen and fire trucks and fires, with condolences and novena cards.

As we walked and the night progressed, the crowd got stretched out. We'd see clumps of candles ahead of us on the streets. It was on Great Jones Street and the Bowery that suddenly there was just the three of us and no traffic to speak of. When I turned to say maybe we should go home, I saw for a moment a tall guy staggering down the street with his face purple and his eyes bulging out.

Then he was gone. Either Marco or Terry whispered, "Shit, he killed himself." And none of us said anything more.

At some point in the evening, I had said Terry could spend the night in my apartment. He couldn't take his eyes off Marco, though Marco seemed not to notice. On our way home, way east on Bleecker Street, outside a bar that had been old even when I'd hung out there as a kid, I saw the poster.

It was like a dozen others I'd seen that night. Except it was in old-time black and white and showed three kids with lots of hair and bad attitude: Mags and Geoffrey and me.

Geoff's face was circled and under it was written, "This is Geoffrey Holbrun, if you have seen him since Tuesday 9/11 please contact . . . " And Mags had left her name and numbers.

Even in the photo, I looked toward Geoffrey, who looked toward Mags, who looked toward me. I stared for just a moment before going on, but I knew that Marco had noticed.

SATURDAY 9/15

My tiny apartment was a crowded mess Saturday morning. Every towel I owned was wet, every glass and mug was dirty. It smelled like a zoo. There were pizza crusts in the sink and a bag of beer cans at the front door. The night before, none of us had talked about the ghosts. Marco and Terry had seriously discussed whether they would be drafted or would enlist. The idea of them in the army did not make me feel any safer.

Saturday is a work day for me. Getting ready, I reminded myself that this would soon be over. The university had found all the refugee kids dorm rooms on campus.

Then the bell rang and a young lady with a nose ring and bright red ringlets of hair appeared. Eloise was another refugee, though a much better-organized one. She had brought bagels and my guests' laundry. Marco seemed delighted to see her.

That morning all the restaurants and bars, the tattoo shops and massage parlors, were opening up. Even the Arab falafel shop owners had risked insults and death threats to ride the subways in from Queens and open their doors for business.

At the library, the huge screens in the lobby were being taken down. A couple of students were borrowing books. One or two even had in-depth reference questions for me. When I finally worked up the courage to call Mags, all I got was the same message as before.

Marco appeared dressed in his own clothes and clearly feeling better. He hugged me. "You were great to take me in."

"It helped me even more," I told him.

He paused then asked, "That was you on that poster last night, wasn't it? You and Mags and Geoffrey?" The kid was a bit uncanny.

When I nodded, he said. "Thanks for talking about that."

I was in a hurry when I went off duty Saturday evening. A friend had called and invited me to an impromptu "Survivors' Party." In the days of the French Revolution, The Terror, that's what they called the soirees at which people danced and drank all night then went out at dawn to see which of their names were on the list of those to be guillotined.

On Sixth Avenue a bakery that had very special cupcakes with devastating frosting was open again. The avenue was clogged with honking, creeping traffic. A huge chunk of Lower Manhattan had been declared open that afternoon, and people were able to get the cars that had been stranded down there.

The bakery was across the street from a Catholic church. And that afternoon in that place, a wedding was being held. As I came out with my cupcakes, the bride and groom, not real young, not very glamorous, but obviously happy, came out the door and posed on the steps for pictures.

Traffic was at a standstill. People beeped "Here Comes the Bride," leaned out their windows, applauded and cheered, all of us relieved to find this ordinary, normal thing taking place.

Then I saw her on the other side of Sixth Avenue. Mags was tramping along, staring straight ahead, a poster with a black and white photo hanging from a string around her neck. The crowd in front of the church parted for her. Mourners were sacred at that moment.

I yelled her name and started to cross the street. But the tie-up had eased; traffic started to flow. I tried to keep pace with her on my side of the street. I wanted to invite her to the party. The hosts knew her from way back. But the sidewalks on both sides were crowded. When I did get across Sixth, she was gone.

AFTERMATH

That night I came home from the party and found the place completely cleaned up, with a thank-you note on the fridge signed by all three kids. And I felt relieved but also lost.

The Survivors' Party was on the Lower East Side. On my way back, I had gone by the East Village, walked up to Tenth Street between B and C. People were out and about. Bars were doing business. But there was still almost no vehicle traffic, and the block was very quiet.

The building where we three had lived in increasing squalor and tension thirty-five years before was refinished, gentrified. I stood across the street looking. Maybe I willed his appearance.

Geoff was there in the corner of my eye, his face dead white, staring up, unblinking, at the light in what had been our windows. I turned toward him and he disappeared. I looked aside and he was there again, so lost and alone, the arms of his jacket soaked in blood.

And I remembered us sitting around with the syringes and all of us making a pledge in blood to stick together as long as we lived. To which Geoff added, "And even after." And I remembered how I had looked at him staring at Mags and knew she was looking at me. Three sides of a triangle.

The next day, Sunday, I went down to Mags's building, wanting very badly to talk to her. I rang the bell again and again. There was no response. I rang the super's apartment.

She was a neighborhood lady, a lesbian around my age. I asked her about Mags.

"She disappeared. Last time anybody saw her was Sunday, 9/9. People in the building checked to make sure everyone was okay. No sign of her. I put a tape across her keyhole Wednesday. It's still there."

"I saw her just yesterday."

"Yeah?" She looked skeptical. "Well, there's a World Trade Center list of potentially missing persons, and her name's on it. You need to talk to them."

This sounded to me like the landlord trying to get rid of her. For the next week, I called Mags a couple of times a day. At some point, the answering machine stopped coming on. I checked out her building regularly. No sign of her. I asked Angelina if she remembered the two of us having dinner in her place on Wednesday, 9/12.

"I was too busy, staying busy so I wouldn't scream. I remember you, and I guess you were with somebody. But no, honey, I don't remember."

Then I asked Marco if he remembered the phone call. And he

did but was much too involved by then with Terry and Eloise to be really interested.

Around that time, I saw the couple who had wanted to take their kids down to Ground Zero. They were walking up Sixth Avenue, the kids cranky and tired, the parents looking disappointed. Like the amusement park had turned out to be a rip-off.

Life closed in around me. A short-story collection of mine was being published at that very inopportune moment, and I needed to do some publicity work. I began seeing an old lover when he came back to New York as a consultant for a company that had lost its offices and a big chunk of its staff when the north tower fell.

Mrs. Pirelli did not come home from the hospital but went to live with her son in Connecticut. I made it a point to go by each of the Arab shops and listen to the owners say how awful they felt about what had happened and smile when they showed me pictures of their kids in Yankee caps and shirts.

It was the next weekend that I saw Mags again. The university had gotten permission for the students to go back to the downtown dorms and get their stuff out. Marco, Terry, and Eloise came by the library and asked me to go with them. So I went over to University Transportation and volunteered my services.

Around noon on Sunday, 9/23, a couple of dozen kids and I piled into a university bus driven by Roger, a Jamaican guy who has worked for the university for as long as I have.

"The day before 9/11 these kids didn't much want old farts keeping them company," Roger had said to me. "Then they all wanted their daddy." He led a convoy of jitneys and vans down the FDR Drive, then through quiet Sunday streets, and then past trucks and construction vehicles.

We stopped at a police checkpoint. A cop looked inside and waved us through.

At the dorm, another cop told the kids they had an hour to get what they could and get out. "Be ready to leave at a moment's notice if we tell you to," he said.

Roger and I as the senior members stayed with the vehicles. The air was filthy. Our eyes watered. A few hundred feet up the street, a cloud of smoke still hovered over the ruins of the World Trade Center. Piles of rubble smoldered. Between the pit and us was a line of fire trucks and police cars with cherry tops flashing. Behind us the kids hurried out of the dorm carrying boxes. I made them write their names on their boxes and noted in which van the boxes got stowed. I was surprised, touched even, at the number of stuffed animals that were being rescued.

"Over the years we've done some weird things to earn our pensions," I said to Roger.

"Like volunteering to come to the gates of hell?"

As he said that, flames sprouted from the rubble. Police and firefighters shouted and began to fall back. A fire department chemical tanker turned around, and the crew began unwinding hoses.

Among the uniforms, I saw a civilian, a middle-aged woman in a sweater and jeans and carrying a sign. Mags walked toward the flames. I wanted to run to her. I wanted to shout, "Stop her." Then I realized that none of the cops and firefighters seemed aware of her even as she walked right past them.

As she did, I saw another figure, thin, pale, in a suede jacket and bell-bottom pants. He held out his bloody hands, and together they walked through the smoke and flames into the hole in the city.

"Was that them?" Marco had been standing beside me.

I turned to him. Terry was back by the bus watching Marco's every move. Eloise was gazing at Terry.

"Be smarter than we were," I said.

And Marco said, "Sure," with all the confidence in the world.

all of us can almost . . .

CAROL EMSHWILLER

Carol Emshwiller grew up in Michigan and France and currently divides her time between New York and California. She is the winner of two Nebula Awards for her stories "Creature" and "I Live With You." She has also won the Lifetime Achievement award given by the World Fantasy Convention.

She's been the recipient of a National Endowment for the Arts grant and two New York State grants. Her short fiction has been published in many literary and science fiction magazine and her most recent books are the novels *Mr. Boots* and *The Secret City*, and the collection *I Live With You and You Don't Know It*.

"All of Us Can Almost . . . " is one of a series of stories published in *SCIFICTION* about strange, avian-like creatures. Emshwiller depicts their alienness through her deft use of "voice."

. . . fly, that is. Of course lots of creatures can *almost* fly. But all of us are able to match any others of us, wingspan to wingspan. Also to any other fliers. But though we match each other wing to wing, we can't get more than inches off the ground. If that. But we're impressive. Our beaks look vicious. We could pose for statues for the birds representing an empire. We could represent an army or a president. And actually, we are the empire. We may not be able to fly, but we rule the skies. And most everything else too.

Creatures come to us for advice on flying. They see us kick up dust and flap and stretch and are awed.

We croak out what we have to say in quacks. We tell them, "The sky is a highway. The sky is of our time and recent. The sky is flat. It's blue because it's happy." They thank us with donations. That's how we live.

The sound of our clacking beaks carries across the valley. It adds to our reputation as powerful—though what good is it really? It's just noise.

Nothing said of us is true, but must we live by truths? Why not keep on living by our lies?

Soaring! Think of it! The stillness of it. Not even the sound of flapping. They say we once did that. Perhaps we still can and just forgot how to begin. How make that first jump? How get the lift? But we grew too large. We began to eat the things that fell, and lots of things fall.

I could leap off a cliff. Test myself. But I might become one of those things tumbling down. Even my own kind would tear me apart.

Loosely . . . very loosely speaking, I do fly. My sleep is full of nothing but that. The joy of it.

But where's the joy in *almost* doing it? Flapping in circles. Making a great wind for nothing but a jump or two. We don't even look good to ourselves.

I don't know what we're made for. It's neither sky nor water nor . . . especially not . . . the waddle of the land. We can't sing. Actually, we can't do anything. Except look fierce.

Pigeons circle overhead. Meadowlarks sing. Geese and ducks, in Vs, do their seasonal things. We stay. We *have* to. Winter storms come and we're still here. We puff up as much as we can and wrap our wings around ourselves. Perhaps that's what our wings were for in the first place. We're designed merely to shelter ourselves. Even our dreams of flying are yet more lies.

But none others are as strong as we are . . . at least none *seem* to be. We win with looks alone and a big voice. We stand, assured and sure.

When creatures ask me for a ride, I say, "I'd take you up anytime you want—hop and skip and up we go—except you're too heavy. Next time measure wings, mine against some other of us. You'll need a few inches more on each side. Tell a bigger one I said to take you up."

"Take to the air along with us," I say. "Follow me up and up." I'm shameless. But I suspect it's only the young that really believe. The older ones pretend to because of our beaks, because of the wind we can stir up—our clouds of dust.

Still, I go on, "Check out my wingspan. Check out my evil eye. Listen. *My* voice."

They jump at my squawk.

They bring me food just to watch me tear at it. At least I'm good at that. I put on a good show. Every creature backs away.

One of the young ones keeps wanting me to take him up. He won't stop asking. I say, "A sparrow could do better." That's true, but he takes it as a joke. I say, "Why not at least ask a male."

"Males scare me."

Finally, just to shut him up, I say, "Yes, but not until the next section of time."

He runs off yelling, "Whee! Whee! Whee! She's taking me up!"

Now how will I get out of it? I only have from one moon to the other. But who knows? One of the big males may have eaten him by that time. They don't care where their food comes from. He was right to be scared.

Who knows how we lost our ability to fly? Maybe we're just lazy. Maybe we just don't exercise our flying muscles. How could we fly, sitting around eating dead things all the time? If anyone can fly, it seems to me more likely one of us smaller females could than a big male.

That little one keeps coming back and saying, "*Really*? Are you *really* going to take me up?"

And I keep saying, "I said I would, didn't I? When have any of us ever lied?" (Actually, when have we ever told the truth?)

He keeps yelling back and forth to all who'll listen. The way he keeps on with it, I could eat him myself.

But we have to be careful. Sometimes those ground dwellers get together and decide not to feed us. Whoever they don't feed always dies. They waddle around trying to get someone of us to share, but we don't. We're not a sharing kind.

I *should* like these ground dwellers because of the food they bring, but I don't. I pretend to, just like they pretend to believe us. They call us Emperor, Leader, Master, but why are they doing this? It could be a conspiracy to keep us fat and lazy so we won't be lords of the sky anymore. So we're tamed and docile. Maybe they started this whole thing, stuffing us with their leftovers. Maybe they're the real emperors of the sky. Master of the sky though never in it any more than we are. At least they can climb trees.

I wonder what they want us for? Or maybe it's the best way to know where we are and what we're doing.

Feed your enemies. Tame them.

I ask some of us, "Where is that cliff they say we used to soar out from?"

"Was there a cliff? Did there used to be a cliff?"

I'm sure there must have been one. How could birds the size of us get started without one—a high one? Maybe that's our problem: we've lost our cliff. We forgot where it is.

Evenings, when all are in their burrows, and my own kind, wrapped in their wings, are clustered under the lean-tos set out for us by lesser beings, I stretch and flap. Reach. Jump. Only the nightingale sees me flop. It's a joy to be up to hear her and to be flipping and flopping.

I'll take that pesky little one all the way to wherever that cliff of ours is. Wouldn't that be something? See the sights? Be up in what we always call "Our element."

But there's a male, has his eye on me. Has had for quite some time. That's another good reason to take off. I'd like to get out of here before the time is ripe.

Or perhaps he's heard the little one yelling, "Whee, Whee," and likes the idea of me with one of those little ones on my back. Easy pickin's, *both* of us. Little one for one purpose and me for another. I can just see it, me distracted, defending the little, and the big taking care of both things while I struggle, front *and* back.

He may be the biggest, but I don't want him. Maybe that's how we got too big to fly: we kept mating with the biggest. It's our own fault we got so big. I'm not going to do that. Well, also the big ones are the strongest. This biggest could slap down all the other males.

If not for the fact that we hardly speak to each other, we females could get together and stop it. Go for the small and the nice. If there are any nice. Not a single one of us is noted for being nice.

I hate to think what mating will be like with one so huge. I'd ask other females if we were the kind who asked things of each other.

He keeps following me around. I don't know how I'm going to avoid him if he's determined. I won't get any help from any of the others. They'll just come and watch. Probably even squawk him onward. I've done it myself.

I'm thinking of ways to avoid that male, so when that little one comes to ask, yet again, "Why wait for next moon?" I say, "You're right. We'll do it now, but I have to find our platform."

"Why?"

"Have you ever seen any of us take off from down here? Of course you haven't. I need a place to soar from."

"Can't we start flying from right here so everybody can see me?"

"No. I have to have a place to take off from. Get on my back. I'll take you there."

"I can walk faster than this all by myself."

"I know, but bear with me."

"My name is Hobie. What's yours?"

"We don't have names. We don't need them."

The big one comes waddling after us. A few of us follow him, wanting to see what's going to happen. I don't think the big realizes how far I'm going. Nobody does.

When we get to the end of the nesting places, Hobie says, "I've never been this far. Is this all right to do?"

"It's all right."

"Your waddling is making me sick."

"We'll rest in a few minutes."

I don't dare stop now, so near the nests. Everybody will waddle out to us. We have to get out of sight. Out there I could eat Hobie myself if need be. I don't suppose anybody will be feeding us way out here.

I don't stop soon enough. Hobie throws up on my back. It smells of dirt-dweller's food. And we're still not out of sight.

"Hang on. I'll stop at that green patch just ahead."

I waddle a little faster, but that just makes him fall off. I'm thinking, Oh well, go on back and let the big male do what he wants to do. It can't last more than a couple of minutes. If he breaks my legs it might be better than what I'm going through now.

But I wait for Hobie to get back on. I say, "Not much farther." He climbs on slowly. I wonder if he suspects I might eat him.

That big is coming along behind us, but he's slower even that I am. Who'd have thought I was worth so much trouble.

In the green patch there's water—a stream. We both drink, and I start washing my back. Hobie keeps saying, "I couldn't help it."

"I know that. Now stop talking so I can think."

I leave footprints. Maybe best if I go along the stream for a while. Then we can drink anytime we want. I turn toward the high side, where the stream comes down from. If there really is a take-off platform, it's got to be high.

"Where are we going?"

"There's a place in the sky that'll give me a good lift."

"What kind of a place?"

"A cliff."

"How far is it?"

"Oh, for the sky's sake, keep quiet."

"Why does your kind always say 'for the sky's sake'?"

"Because we're sky creatures. Not like you. Now let me think about walking."

Even in this little stream there's fish. Wouldn't it be nice if I could catch one by myself?

"Hang on!"

I dive. But I forgot about the water changing the angle of view. I miss. I say, "Next time."

Hobie says, "I can."

I let him off to stand on the bank and dive, and he does it. Gives the fish to me even though I'll bet he's getting hungry too.

"Thank you, Hobie. Now get one for yourself."

At dusk we find a nice place to nest in among the trees along the stream—soft with leaves. Hobie curls up right beside my beak. Practically under it. I'm more afraid of my bite than he is. I hope I don't snap him up in my sleep.

Toward morning we hear something coming . . . lumbering along. Sounding tired for sure. We both know who. Hobie doesn't like big males any more than I do. He scrambles up on my back and says, "Shouldn't we go?"

Because I'm so much smaller than any male, I waddle a lot faster. It gets steeper, but I'm still doing pretty well. It's so steep I have hopes of finding our cliff. I turn around and look back down and here comes the big, but a long ways off. Staggering, stumbling. Am I really worth all this effort?

"Are we far enough ahead? Are we getting someplace? How long now?"

"Do you ever say anything that isn't a question?"

"You do it. That's a question."

I'm not used to waddling all day long, especially not uphill. It's the hardest thing I've ever done. But the big. . . . He's still coming. It's getting steeper. I hope one as large as he is can't get up here. This is just what I wanted. The launching platform has got to be here. How did it ever come to be that we got stuck down in the flat places?

And finally, here it is, *the* flat place at the top of the cliff. I look over the edge. I'm so scared just looking I start to feel sick. I'm not sure I can even pretend to jump.

"Why are you shaking so much? It's going to make me sick again."

Should I eat Hobie now before he tells everybody I not only can't fly, I can't even get close to the edge without trembling and feeling sick?

But it's been nice having company. I've gotten used to his paws tangled in my feathers, making a mess of them. I'd miss his questions.

I move back and look over the other side. It's steep on that side too, though not so much. This platform is a promontory going off into nothing on all sides but one. It must have been perfect for fliers.

I look around to see if I can see any signs that it was used as a launching place, but there's nothing. I suppose, up here so high, the weather would have worn away any signs of that. I wonder if that big male knows anything more about it than I do.

It's breezy up here. I flap my wings to test myself, but I do it well away from the edges.

Hobie says, "Go, go, go."

Maybe I should just get closer and closer to the edge . . . get used to it little by little . . . until I don't feel quite so scared.

I look over the side again, though from a few feet away. I see the big male is still coming. I see him turn around and look down at exactly the same spot where we did. Then he looks up. Right at us. He spreads his wings at us so I'll see his wingspan. Then he turns side view. That's so I'll get a good look at his profile . . . the big hooked beak, the white ruff. . . . Then he starts up again.

I look over the more sloping side again. I think I might be able to slide down there, though it's a steep slide. At the bottom there's a lot of trees and brush. That would break our fall.

That big one is getting so close I can hear him shuffling and sliding just like I did. I sit over by the less steep side and wait.

Pretty soon I see the fierce head looking up at us, the beady eye, and then the whole body. He has an even harder time than I had lifting himself on to the launching platform.

Hobie says, "I'm scared of males," and I say, "I am too."

As soon as the big catches his breath, he says, "You're beautiful."

I say, "That's neither here nor there."

He says, "I love you." As if any of us knew what that word meant.

I say, "Love is what you feel for a nice piece of carrion."

He looks a mess. I must too. Dusty, feathers every which way. Hobie and I filled up on fish back at the stream, but I don't think he did. He looks at Hobie like the next meal. I back up a little closer to the slide. I say, "This one's mine." *That*, he'll understand.

He's inching closer. He thinks I don't notice. If he grabs me, there's no way I can escape. I back up even more.

And then. . . . I didn't mean to. Off we go. Skidding, sliding, but like flying. Almost! Almost!

Hobie is yelling, "Whee. Whee. Whee." At least he's happy.

When we get down as far as the trees and bushes, I grab at them with my beak to slow us. And then I hear the big coming behind us. I never thought he . . . such a big one . . . would dare follow.

There's a great swish of gravel sliding with us. Even more as the big comes down behind us. Here he is, landed beside us, but, thank goodness, not exactly on.

Hobie and I are more or less fine. Scratched and bruised and dusty, but the big is moaning.

We're in a sort of ditch full of lots of brush and trees. It looks to be up hill on all sides. I wonder if either of us . . . the big and I . . . could waddle out of it. Hobie could.

Hobie and I dust off.

Hobie says. "That was great. I wish the others could have seen me."

He can't, can he? Can't *possibly* think that was flying?

Then I see that the big one's legs slant out at odd angles. His weight was his undoing. My relative lightness saved me.

The big says, "Help me." But why should I? I say, "It's all your fault in the first place."

He's in pain. I brush him off. I even dare to preen him a bit. I don't think he'll hurt me or try to mate. He couldn't with those broken legs, anyway. He needs me. He has to be nice. That'll be a change.

These big males are definitely bigger than they need to be. He's twice my size. Where will all this bigness lead? Just to less and less, ever again, the possibility of flight, that's where.

Hobie doesn't even need to be asked. "I'm hungry. Can I go get us some food?"

"Of course you can."

"After you flew me, I owe you lots."

Off he goes into the brush. I take a look at the big one's legs and wonder what to do. Can I make splints? And what to use to bind them with? Though there's always lots of stringy things in our carrion if Hobie finds us food.

"You're not only never going to fly, you may never waddle either."

He just groans again.

"I'll try to straighten these out." I give him a stick to bite on. And then I do it. After, I look for sticks as splints.

In no time Hobie brings three creatures. I think one for each of us, but he says he ate already. He's says this place is all meals. Nothing has been hunting here in a long time, maybe never. He says, "You could even hunt for yourself."

Now there's a thought. I think I will.

I leave the three creatures for the big male and start out, but the big says, "Don't leave me." Just like a chick.

I say, "If you eat Hobie, that's the last you'll ever see of me." And I go.

Hobie is right, all the little meals are easy to catch. I eat four and keep all the stringy things. I also look around at where we are and if we could ever get out. There's that little stream from below, cool and clear, bubbling along not far from where we fell. Beside it there's a nice place for a nest. I think about chicks. How I'd try to get them flapping right from the start. Even the baby males. And maybe, if we all were thinner and had to scramble for our food like I just had to do, and if all the food would get to know the danger and make us scramble harder and we'd get even thinner and stronger, and first thing you know we wouldn't have to climb out of here, we'd fly. All of us. Could that really come to be?

I throw away the stringy things I was going to make splints with. I have everything under control. I'll tell Hobie he can go on home if he wants to, though I'll tell him I do wish he'd stay, just for the company. And just in case we never do learn to fly again, we'd need his help when the food gets smarter and scarcer.

you go where it takes you

NATHAN BALLINGRUD

Nathan Ballingrud's stories have appeared in *Inferno: New Tales of Terror and the Supernatural*, *The Del Rey Book of Science Fiction and Fantasy*, *Lovecraft Unbound*, and *Naked City: New Tales of Urban Fantasy*, among other places. He won the Shirley Jackson award for his short story "The Monsters of Heaven." He lives with his daughter in Asheville, NC.

Although Ballingrud had a few short stories published soon after his stint as a Clarion student in 1992, he stopped writing for about eight years. I think I may have read something by him before his submission of "You Go Where It Takes You," but *this* is the story that really blew me away. It's been described as what Raymond Carver would have written if he wrote horror.

He did not look like a man who would change her life. He was big, roped with muscles from working on offshore oil rigs, and tending to fat. His face was broad and inoffensively ugly, as though he had spent a lifetime taking blows and delivering them. He wore a brown raincoat against the light morning drizzle and against the threat of something more powerful held in abeyance. He breathed heavily, moved slowly, found a booth by the window overlooking the water, and collapsed into it. He picked up a syrup-smeared menu and studied it with his whole attention, like a student deciphering Middle English. He was like every man who ever walked into that little diner. He did not look like a beginning or an end.

That day, the Gulf of Mexico and all the earth was blue and still. The little town of Port Fourchon clung like a barnacle to Louisiana's southern coast, and behind it water stretched into the distance for as many miles as the eye could hold. Hidden by distance were the oil rigs and the workers who supplied this town with its economy. At night she could see their lights, ringing the horizon like candles in a vestibule. Toni's morning shift was nearing its end; the dining area was nearly empty. She liked to spend those slow hours out on the diner's balcony, overlooking the water.

Her thoughts were troubled by the phone call she had received that morning. Gwen, her three-year-old daughter, was offering increasing resistance to the male staffers at the Daylight Daycare, resorting lately to biting them or kicking them in the ribs when they knelt to calm her. Only days before, Toni had been waylaid there by a lurking social worker who talked to her in a gentle saccharin voice, who touched her hand maddeningly and said, "No one is judging you; we just want to help." The social worker had mentioned the word "psychologist" and asked about their home life. Toni had been embarrassed and enraged, and was only able to conclude the interview with a mumbled promise to schedule another one soon. That her daughter was already displaying such grievous signs of social ineptitude stunned Toni, left her feeling hopeless and betrayed.

It also made her think about Donny again, who had abandoned her years ago to move to New Orleans, leaving her a single mother at twenty-three. She wished death on him that morning, staring over the railing at the unrelenting progression of waves. She willed it along the miles and into his heart.

"You know what you want?" she asked.

"Um . . . just coffee." He looked at her breasts and then at her eyes.

"Cream and sugar?"

"No thanks. Just coffee."

"Suit yourself."

The only other customer in the diner was Crazy Claude by the door, speaking conversationally to a cooling plate of scrambled eggs and listening to his radio through his earphones. A tinny roar leaked out around his ears. Pedro, the short-order cook, lounged behind the counter, his big round body encased in layers of soiled white clothing, enthralled by a guitar magazine which he had spread out by the cash register. The kitchen slumbered behind him, exuding a thick fug of onions and burnt frying oil. It would stay mostly dormant until the middle of the week, when the shifts would change on the rigs, and tides of men would ebb and flow through the small town.

So when she brought the coffee back to the man, she thought nothing of it when he asked her to join him. She fetched herself a cup of coffee as well and then sat across from him in the booth, grateful to transfer the weight from her feet.

"You ain't got no nametag," he said.

"Oh . . . I guess I lost it somewhere. My name's Toni."

"That's real pretty."

She gave a quick derisive laugh. "The hell it is. It's short for Antoinette."

He held out his hand and said, "I'm Alex."

She took it and they shook. "You work offshore, Alex?"

"Some. I ain't been out there for a while, though." He smiled and gazed into the murk of his coffee. "I've been doing a lot of driving around."

Toni shook loose a cigarette from her pack and lit it. She lied and said, "Sounds exciting."

"I don't guess it is, though. But I bet this place could be, sometimes. I bet you see all kinds of people come through here."

"Well . . . I guess so."

"How long you been here?"

"About three years."

"You like it?"

"Yeah, Alex, I fucking love it."

"Oh, hey, all right." He held up his hands. "I'm sorry."

Toni shook her head. "No. *I'm* sorry. I just got a lot on my mind today."

"So why don't you come out with me after work? Maybe I can help distract you."

Toni smiled at him. "You've known me for, what, five minutes?"

"Hey, what can I say, I'm an impulsive guy. Caution to the wind!" He drained his cup in two swallows to illustrate his recklessness.

"Well, let me go get you some more coffee, Danger Man." She patted his hand as she got up.

It was a similar impulsiveness that brought Donny back to her, briefly, just over a year ago. After a series of phone calls that progressed from petulant to playful to curious, he drove back to Port Fouchon in his disintegrating blue Pinto one Friday afternoon to spend a weekend with them. It was nice at first, though there was no talk of what might happen after Sunday.

Gwen had just started going to daycare. Stunned by the vertiginous growth of the world, she was beset by huge emotions; varieties of rage passed through her little body like weather systems, and no amount of coddling from Toni would settle her.

Although he wouldn't admit it, Toni knew Donny was curious about the baby, who according to common wisdom would grow to reflect many of his own features and behaviors.

But Gwen refused to participate in generating any kind of infant mystique, revealing herself instead as what Toni knew her to be: a pink, pudgy little assemblage of flesh and ferocity that giggled or raved seemingly without discrimination, that walked without grace and appeared to lack any qualities of beauty or intelligence whatsoever.

But the sex between them was as good as it ever was, and he didn't seem to mind the baby too much. When he talked about calling in sick to work on Monday, she began to hope for something lasting.

Early Sunday afternoon, they decided to give Gwen a bath. It would be Donny's first time washing his daughter, and he approached the task like a man asked to handle liquid nitrogen. He filled the tub with eight inches of water and plunked her in, then sat back and stared as, with furrowed brow, she went about the serious business of testing the seaworthiness of shampoo bottles. Toni sat on the toilet seat behind him, and it occurred to her that this was her family. She felt buoyant, sated.

Then Gwen rose abruptly from the water and clapped her hands joyously. "Two! Two poops! One, two!"

Aghast, Toni saw two little turds sitting on the bottom of the tub, rolling slightly in the currents generated by Gwen's capering feet. Donny's hand shot out and cuffed his daughter on the side of the head. She crashed against the wall and bounced into the water with a terrific splash. And then she screamed: the most godawful sound Toni had ever heard in her life.

Toni stared at him, agape. She could not summon the will to

move. The baby, sitting on her ass in the soiled water, filled the tiny bathroom with a sound like a bomb siren, and she just wanted her to shut up, shut up, just shut the fuck up.

"Shut up, goddamnit! Shut *up*!"

Donny looked at her, his face an unreadable mess of confused emotion; he pushed roughly past her. Soon she heard the sound of a door closing, his car starting up, and he was gone. She stared at her stricken daughter and tried to quiet the sudden stampeding fury.

She refilled Alex's coffee and sat down with him, leaving the pot on the table. She retrieved her cigarette from the ashtray only to discover that it had expired in her absence. "Well, shit."

Alex nodded agreeably. "I'm on the run," he said suddenly.

"What?"

"It's true. I'm on the run. I stole a car."

Alarmed, Toni looked out the window, but the parking lot was on the other side of the diner. All she could see from here was the Gulf.

"Why are you telling me this? I don't want to know this."

"It's a station wagon. I can't believe it even runs anymore. I was in Morgan City, and I had to get out fast. The car was right there. I took it."

He had a manic look in his eye, and although he was smiling, his movements had become agitated and sudden. She felt a growing disquiet coupled with a mounting excitement. He was dangerous, this man. He was a falling hammer.

"I don't think that guy over there likes me," he said.

"What?" She turned and saw Crazy Claude in stasis, staring at Alex. His jaw was cantilevered in mid-chew. "That's just Claude," she said. "He's all right."

Alex was still smiling, but it had taken on a different character, one she couldn't place and which set loose a strange, giddy feeling inside her. "No, I think it's me. He keeps looking over here."

"Really, Claude's okay. He's harmless as a kitten."

"I want to show you something." Alex reached inside his raincoat, and for a moment Toni thought he was going to pull out a gun and start shooting. She felt no inclination to move, though, and waited for what would come. But instead, he withdrew a crumpled Panama hat. It had been considerably crushed to fit into his pocket, and once freed it began to unfold itself, slowly resuming its original shape.

She looked at it. "It's a hat," she said.

He stared at it like he expected it to lurch across the table with some hideous agenda. "That's an object of terrible power," he said.

"Alex—it's a hat. It's a thing you put on your head."

"It belongs to the man I stole the car from. Here," he said, pushing it across to her. "Put it on."

She did. She turned her chin to her shoulder and pouted her lips, looking at him out of

the corner of her eye, like she thought a model might.

"Who are you?" he said.

"I'm a supermodel."

"What's your name? Where are you from?"

She affected a bright, breathy voice. "My name is Violet, I'm from L.A., and I'm strutting down a catwalk wearing this hat and nothing else. Everybody loves me and is taking my picture."

They laughed, and he said, "See? It's powerful. You can be anybody."

She gave the hat back.

"You know," Alex said, "the guy I stole the car from was something of a thief himself. You should see what he left in there."

"Why don't you show me?"

He smiled. "Now?"

"No. In half an hour. When I get off work."

"But it's all packed up. I don't just let that stuff fly around loose."

"Then you can show me at my place."

And so it was decided. She got up and went about preparing for the next shift, which consisted of restocking a few ketchup packets and starting a fresh pot of coffee. She refilled Crazy Claude's cup and gave him another ten packets of sugar, all of which he methodically opened and dumped into his drink. When her relief arrived, Toni hung her apron by the waitress station and collected Alex on her way to the door.

"We have to stop by the daycare and pick up my kid," she said.

When they passed Claude's table they heard a distant, raucous sound coming from his earphones.

Alex curled his lip. "Idiot. How does he hear himself think?"

"He doesn't. That's the point. He hears voices in his head. He plays the radio loud so he can drown them out."

"You're kidding me."

"Nope."

Alex stopped and turned around, regarding the back of Claude's head with renewed interest. "How many people does he have in there?"

"I never asked."

"Well, holy shit."

Outside, the sun was setting, the day beginning to cool down. The rain had stopped at some point, and the world glowed under a bright wet sheen. They decided that he would follow her in his car. It was a rusty old battle wagon from the seventies; several boxes were piled in the back. She paid them no attention.

She knew, when they stepped into her little apartment, that they would eventually make love, and she found herself wondering what it would be like. She watched him move, noticed the graceful articulation of his body, the careful restraint he displayed in her living room, which was filled with fragile things. She saw the skin beneath his clothing, watched it stretch and move.

"Don't worry," she said, touching the place between his shoulder blades. "You won't break nothing."

About Gwen there was more doubt. Unleashed like a darting

fish into the apartment, she was gone with a bright squeal, away from the strange new man around whom she had been so quiet and doleful, into the dark grottoes of her home.

"It's real pretty," Alex said.

"A bunch of knickknacks mostly. Nothing special."

He shook his head like he did not believe it. Her apartment was decorated mostly with the inherited flotsam of her grandmother's life: bland wall hangings, beaten old furniture which had played host to too many bodies spreading gracelessly into old age, and a vast and silly collection of glass figurines: leaping dolphins and sleeping dragons and such. It was all meant to be homey and reassuring, but it just reminded her of how far away she was from the life she really wanted. It seemed like a desperate construct, and she hated it very much.

For now, Alex made no mention of the objects in his car or the hat in his pocket. He appeared to be more interested in Gwen, who was peering around the corner of the living room and regarding him with a suspicious and hungry eye, who seemed to intuit that from this large alien figure on her mama's couch would come mighty upheavals.

He was a man—that much Gwen knew immediately—and therefore a dangerous creature. He would make her mama behave unnaturally; maybe even cry. He was too big, like the giant in her storybook. She wondered if he ate children. Or mamas.

Mama was sitting next to him.

"Come here, Mama." She slapped her thigh like Mama did when she wanted Gwen to pay attention to her. Maybe she could lure Mama away from the giant, and they could wait in the closet until he got bored and went away. "Come here, Mama, come here."

"Go on and play now, Gwen."

"No! Come here!"

"She don't do too well around men," said Mama.

"That's okay," said the giant. "These days I don't either." He patted the cushion next to him. "Come over here, baby. Let me say hi."

Gwen, alarmed at this turn of events, retreated a step behind a corner. They were in the living room, which had her bed in it, and her toys. Behind her, Mama's darkened room yawned like a throat. She sat between the two places, wrapped her arms around her knees, and waited.

"She's so afraid," Alex said after she retreated out of their sight. "You know why?"

"Um, because you're big and scary?"

"Because she already knows about possibilities. Long as you know there are options in life, you get scared of choosing the wrong one."

Toni leaned away from him and gave him a mistrustful smile. "Okay, Einstein. Easy with the philosophy."

"No, really. She's like a thousand different people right now, all waiting to be, and every time she makes a choice, one of those people goes away forever. Until finally you run out of choices and you are whoever you are. She's afraid of what she'll lose by coming out to see me. Of who she'll never get to be."

Toni thought of her daughter and saw nothing but a series of shut doors. "Are you drunk?"

"What? You know I ain't drunk."

"Stop talking like you are, then. I've had enough of that shit to last me my whole life."

"Jesus, I'm sorry."

"Forget it." Toni got up from the couch and rounded the corner to scoop up her daughter. "I got to bathe her and put her to bed. If you want to wait, it's up to you."

She carried Gwen into the bathroom and began the nightly ministrations. Donny was too strong a presence tonight, and Alex's sophomoric philosophizing sounded just like him when he'd had too many beers. She found herself hoping that the prosaic obligations of motherhood would bore Alex, and that he would leave. She listened for the sound of the front door.

Instead, she heard footsteps behind her and felt his heavy hand on her shoulder. It squeezed her gently, and his big body settled down beside her; he said something kind to her daughter and brushed a strand of wet hair from her eyes. Toni felt something move slowly in her chest, subtly yet with powerful effect, like Atlas rolling a shoulder.

Gwen suddenly shrieked and collapsed into the water, sending a small tsunami over them both. Alex reached in to stop her from knocking her head against the porcelain and received a kick in the mouth for his troubles. Toni shouldered him aside and jerked her out of the tub. She hugged her daughter tightly to her chest and whispered placative incantations into her ear. Gwen finally settled into her mother's embrace and whimpered quietly, turning all of her puissant focus onto the warm familiar hand rubbing her back, up and down, up and down, until, finally, her energy flagged, and she drifted into a tentative sleep.

When Gwen was dressed and in her bed, Toni turned her attention to Alex. "Here, let's clean you up."

She steered him back into the bathroom. She opened the shower curtain and pointed to the soap and the shampoo and said, "It smells kind of flowery, but it gets the job done," and the whole time he was looking at her, and she thought: So this is it; this is how it happens.

"Help me," he said, lifting his arms from his sides. She smiled wanly and began to undress him. She watched his body as she unwrapped it, and when he was naked she pressed herself close to him and ran her fingers down his back.

Later, when they were in bed together, she said, "I'm sorry about tonight."

"She's just a kid."

"No, I mean about snapping at you. I don't know why I did."

"It's okay."

"I just don't like to think about what could have been. There's no point to it. Sometimes I don't think a person has too much to say about what happens to them anyway."

"I really don't know."

She stared out the little window across from the bed and watched slate gray clouds skim across the sky. Burning behind them were the stars.

"Ain't you gonna tell me why you stole a car?"

"I had to."

"But why?"

He was silent for a little while. "It don't matter," he said.

"If you don't tell me, it makes me think you mighta killed somebody."

"Maybe I did."

She thought about that for a minute. It was too dark to see anything in the bedroom, but she scanned her eyes across it anyway, knowing the location of every piece of furniture, every worn tube of lipstick and leaning stack of lifestyle magazines. She could see through the walls and feel the sagging weight of the figurines on the shelves. She tried to envision each one in turn, as though searching for one that would act as a talisman against this subject and the weird celebration it raised in her.

"Did you hate him?"

"I don't hate anybody," he said. "I wish I did. I wish I had it in me."

"Come on, Alex. You're in my house. You got to tell me something."

After a long moment, he said, "The guy I stole the car from. I call him Mr. Gray. I never saw him, except in dreams. I don't know anything about him, really. But I don't think he's human. And I know he's after me."

"What do you mean?"

"I have to show you." Without another word, he got to his feet and pulled on his jeans. He was beginning to get excited about something, and it inspired a similar feeling in her. She followed him, pulling a long t-shirt over her head as she went. Gwen slept deeply in the living room; they stepped over her mattress on the way out.

The grass was wet beneath their feet, the air heavy with the salty smell of the sea. Alex's car was parked at the curb, hugging the ground like a great beetle. He opened the rear hatch and pulled the closest box toward them.

"Look," he said, and opened the box.

At first, Toni could not comprehend what she saw. She thought it was a cat lying on a stack of tan leather jackets, but that wasn't right, and only when Alex grabbed a handful of the cat and pulled it out did she realize that it was human hair. Alex lifted the whole object out of the box, and she found herself staring at the tanned and cured hide of a human being, dark empty holes in its face like some rubber Halloween mask.

"I call this one Willie, 'cause he's so well hung," said Alex, and offered an absurd laugh.

Toni fell back a step.

"But there's women in here too, all kinds of people. I counted ninety-six. All carefully folded." He offered the skin to Toni, but when she made no move to touch it he went about folding it up again. "I guess there ain't no reason to see them all. You get the idea."

"Alex, I want to go back inside."

"Okay, just hang on a second."

She waited while he closed the lid of the box and slid it back into place. With the hide tucked under one arm, he shut the hatch, locked it, and turned to face her. He was grinning, bouncing on the balls of his feet. "Okeydokey," he said, and they headed back indoors.

They went back into the bedroom, walking quietly to avoid waking Gwen.

"Did you kill all those people?" Toni asked when the door was closed.

"What? Didn't you hear me? I stole a car. That's what was in it."

"Mr. Gray's car."

"That's right."

"Who is he? What are they for?" she asked; but she already knew what they were for.

"They're alternatives," he said. "They're so you can be somebody else."

She thought about that. "Have you worn any of them?"

"One. I haven't got up the balls to do it again yet." He reached into the front pocket of his jeans and withdrew a leather sheath. From it he pulled a small, ugly little knife that looked like an eagle's talon. "You got to take off the one you're already wearing, first. It hurts."

Toni swallowed. The sound was thunderous in her ears. "Where's your first skin? The one you was born with?"

Alex shrugged. "I threw that one out. I ain't like Mr. Gray, I don't know how to preserve them. Besides, what do I want to keep it for? I must not have liked it too much in the first place, right?"

She felt a tear accumulate in the corner of her eye and willed it not to fall. She was afraid and exhilarated. "Are you going to take mine?"

Alex looked startled, then seemed to remember he was holding the knife. He put it back in its sheath. "I told you, baby, I'm not the one who killed those people. I don't need any more than what's already there." She nodded, and the tear streaked down her face. He touched it away with the back his fingers. "Hey now," he said.

She grabbed his hand. "Where's mine?" She gestured at the skin folded beside him. "I want one, too. I want to come with you."

"Oh, Jesus, no, Toni. You can't."

"But why not? Why can't I go?"

"Come on now, you got a family here."

"It's just me and her. That ain't no family."

"You have a little girl, Toni. What's wrong with you? That's your life now." He stepped out of his pants and pulled the knife from its sheath. "I can't argue about this. I'm going now. I'm gonna change first, though, and you might not want to watch." She made no move to leave. He paused, considering something. "I got to ask you something," he said. "I been wondering about this lately. Do you think it's possible for something beautiful to come out of an awful beginning? Do you think a good life can redeem a horrible act?"

"Of course I do," she said quickly, sensing some second chance here, if only she could say the right words. "Yes."

Alex touched the blade to his scalp just above his right ear and drew it in an arc over the crown of his head until it reached his left ear. Bright red blood crept down from his hairline in a slow tide, sending rivulets and tributaries along his jawline and down his throat, hanging from his eyelashes like raindrops from flower petals. "God, I really hope so," he said. He worked his fingers into the incision and began to tug violently.

Watching the skin fall away from him, she was reminded of nothing so much as a butterfly struggling into daylight.

She is driving west on I-10. The morning sun, which has just breached the horizon, flares in her rearview mirror. Port Fouchon is far behind her, and the Texas border looms. Beside her, Gwen is sitting on the floor of the passenger seat, playing with the Panama hat Alex left behind when he drove North. Toni has never seen the need for a car seat. Gwen is happier moving about on her own, and in times like this, when Toni feels a slow, crawling anger in her blood, the last thing she needs is a temper tantrum from her daughter.

After he left, she was faced with a few options. She could put on her stupid pink uniform, take Gwen to daycare, and go back to work. She could drive up to New Orleans and find Donny. Or she could say fuck it all and just get in the car and drive, aimlessly and free of expectation, which is what she is doing.

She cries for the first dozen miles or so, and it is such a rare luxury that she just lets it come, feeling no guilt.

Gwen, still feeling the dregs of sleep and as yet undecided

whether to be cranky for being awakened early or excited by the trip, pats her on the leg. "You okay, Mama, you okay?"

"Yes, baby. Mama's okay."

Toni sees the sign she has been looking for coming up on the side of the road. Rest Stop, 2 miles.

When they get there, she pulls in, coming to a stop in the empty lot. Gwen climbs up in the seat and peers out the window. She sees the warm red glow of a Coke machine and decides that she will be happy today, that waking up early means excitement and the possibility of treats.

"Have the Coke, Mama? Have it, have the Coke?"

"Okay, sweetie."

They get out and walk up to the Coke machine. Gwen laughs happily and slaps it several times, listening to the distant dull echo inside. Toni puts in some coins and grabs the tumbling can. She cracks it open and gives it to her daughter, who takes it delightedly.

"Coke!"

"That's right." Toni kneels beside her as Gwen takes several ambitious swigs. "Gwen? Honey? Mama's got to go potty, okay? You stay right here, okay? Mama will be right back."

Gwen lowers the can, a little overwhelmed by the cold blast of carbonation, and nods her head. "Right back!"

"That's right, baby."

Toni starts away. Gwen watches her mama as she heads back to the car and climbs in. She shuts the door and starts the engine. Gwen takes another drink of Coke. The car pulls away from the curb, and she feels a bright stab of fear. But Mama said she was coming right back, so she will wait right here.

Toni turns the wheel and speeds back out onto the highway. There is no traffic in sight. The sign welcoming her to Texas flashes by and is gone. She presses the accelerator. Her heart is beating.

russian vine

SIMON INGS

Simon Ings lives and works in London. His most recent novel is *The Weight of Numbers*, a twisted family saga spread over eighty years and three continents. His first popular science book, *A Natural History of Seeing*, was published in 2008.

I've been publishing Ings' short fiction since the days of *Omni*, but unfortunately he writes far too little of it—he keeps getting sidetracked—into music (he edits www.plushmusic.tv), into games (he has two children) and into space (he is a founder of the Lunacy Corporation). He is finishing a long novel about pirates, and researching a book about forgetfulness.

"Russian Vine" is his homage to the literature of the Raj.

ONE

That afternoon in Paris—a cloudy day, and warmer than the late season deserved—they met for the last time. She wore her red dress. Did she intend to make what he had to say more difficult? (He felt his scribe hand tingle, that he should blame her for his own discomfort.) Perhaps she only meant a kind of closure. For the sake of her self-esteem, she was making it clear to him that nobody ever really changes anybody. Even her hair was arranged the same as on that first day.

"And the king said, Bring me a sword. And they brought a sword before the king."

They sat on the *terrasse*, away from the doors, seeking privacy. The preacher—if that was the right word for him, for he did not preach, but had instead launched into an apparently endless recitation—stabbed them irregularly with a gaze from eyes the colour of pewter.

His testament tangled itself up in the couple's last words to each other.

Connie called for the bill. (He had long since conformed his name to the range of the human palate. Being the kind of animal he was, he was not bothered by its effeminate connotations.) He said to her: "This deadening reasonableness. I wish we had smashed something."

She said: "You wish I had smashed something. I've let you down today."

"And the king said, Divide the living child in two, and give half to the one and half to the other."

She said: "You've left us both feeling naked. We can't fight now. It would be undignified: emotional mud-wrestling."

Connie let the reference slide by him, uncomprehended.

"*Then spake the woman whose the living child was unto the king, for her bowels yearned upon her son, and she said, O my lord, give her the living child, and in no wise slay it. But the other said, Let it be neither mine or thine, but divide it.*"

With a gesture, the girl drew Connie's attention to the man's recitation. "You see?" she said. "Undignified. Like it says in the Bible." She laughed at the apposite verses, a laugh that choked off in a way that Connie thought might be emotion.

But how could he be sure? His ear was not—would never be—good enough. He was from too far away. He was, in the parochial parlance of these people, "alien."

He picked up his cup with his bludgeon hand—a dashing breach of his native etiquette—and dribbled down the last bitter grounds. Already he was preening; showing off his rakish "masculinity." His availability, even. As though this choice he had made were about freedom!

He found himself, in that instant, thinking coldly of Rebecca, the woman who lived with him, and for whom (though she did not know this) he had given up this enchanting girl.

"*Then the king answered and said, Give her the living child, and in no wise slay it: she is the mother thereof.*

"*And all Israel heard of the judgement which the king had judged; and they feared the king: for they saw that the wisdom of God was in him to do judgment.*"

Still listening, the girl smiled, and bobbed her head to Connie, in a mock bow.

She had done nothing, this afternoon, but make light of their parting. He hoped it was a defence she had assembled against sentiment. But in his heart, he knew she had not been very moved by the end of their affair. She would forget him very quickly.

Hadmuhaddera's crass remarks, the day Connie arrived on this planet, seemed strangely poignant now: "Trouble is, my friend, we all look the bloody same to them!"

"*And these were the princes which he had . . .* "

There was no purpose to that man's recitation, Connie thought, with irritation, as he kissed the girl goodbye and turned to leave. There was no reasoning to it; just a blind obedience to the literal sequence. As though the feat of memory were itself a devotional act.

"Ahinadab the son of Iddo had Mahanaim . . . "

In spite of himself, Connie stopped to listen. The "preacher" faced him: was that a look of aggression? It was so impossibly hard to learn the body language of these people—of any people, come to that, other than one's own.

So Connie stood there like a lemon, knowing full well he looked like a lemon, and listened:

"Ahimaaz was in Naphtali; he also took Basmath the daughter of Solomon to wife:

"Baanah the son of Hushai was in Asher and in Aloth:

"Jehoshaphat the son of Paruah, in Issachar:

"Shimei the son of Elah, in Benjamin . . . "

Connie realised that he had given too little mind to these feats of recitation. This was more than a display of the power of human memory. This was more than a display of defiance towards the Puscha invader: "See how we maintain our culture, crippled as we are!"

"Geber the son of Uri was in the country of Gilead, in the country of Sihon king of the Amorites, and of Og king of Bashan; and he was the only officer which was in the land."

Connie bowed his head. Not out of respect, surely, since this was, when you came down to it, absurd: to raise an ancient genealogy to a pedestal at which educated men must genuflect. But it said something about the will of this people, that they should have so quickly recovered the skills and habits of a time before reading and writing.

The man might have been an evangelistic scholar of the 1400s by the Christian calendar, and the subsequent six hundred years of writing and printing and reading no more than a folly, a risky experiment, terminated now by shadowy authorities.

When Connie passed him, on his way to the Gare du Nord and the London train, the man did not cease to speak.

"Judah and Israel were many," he declaimed, from memory, *"as the sand which is by the sea in multitude, eating and drinking, and making merry!"*

It was only twenty years since the Puscha had established a physical presence upon the planet, though their husbandry of the human animal had begun some thirty years before first contact. It took time and care to strike upon the subtle blend of environmental "pollutants" that would engineer illiteracy, without triggering its cousin afflictions: autism in all its extraordinary and distressing manifestations—not to mention all the variform aphasias.

Faced with the collapse of its linguistic talent, the human animal had, naturally enough, blamed its own industrial processes. The Puscha armada had hung back, discrete and undetected, until the accusations dried up, the calumnies were forgotten, and all the little wars resolved—until transmissions from the planet's surface had reduced to what they considered safe levels.

Human reactions to the Puscha arrival were various, eccentric, and localised—and this was as it should be. Concerted global responses, the Puscha had found, were almost always calamitous.

So, wherever Connie appeared along the railway line—and especially at the Suffolk terminus where he drank a cup of milkless tea before driving out in the lorry the thirty miles to his orchard—there was a respect for him that was friendly. He had been travelling back and forth, in the same way, for ten years.

There was a clubhouse at the junction: an old white house with lofty, open rooms, where he sometimes had a quick breakfast before driving onto the orchards. There was also an army station near, and as the pace of Autonomy quickened, the club had become a mere transit camp, with both Puscha and human administrators piling bedrolls in the halls, and noisy behaviour in the compounds. There were often civilian hangers-on there too, and the woman who lived with him now—the woman to whom he was faithful once again (the idea of being "faithful again" made more sense in his culture than hers)—had been one of these.

Her name was Rebecca—a name that translated fluently and comically into his own tongue, as a kind of edible, greasy fish. When he first laid eyes on her, she was drinking cocktails with a party of Puscha newcomers lately recruited to some dismal section of government finance (and who were in consequence behaving like abandoned invaders). Quite how she had fallen in with them wasn't clear. She was simply one of those maddening, iconic figures that turbulent events throw up from time to time: less real people, so much as windows onto impossible futures, no less poignant for being chimerical.

A few days later, on the connecting train to Paris, as he considered where to sit, vacillating as usual, he nearly walked straight past her.

She was sitting alone. She was white-skinned. Her hair was long and straight, gold-brown, and a fold of it hung down over one eye, lending her face an asymmetry that appealed to him.

The seat opposite her was invitingly empty.

He sat and read a while, or pretended to, racking his brain for the correct form, the correct stance, for an introduction. Horror stories abounded in the clubs and classes: a visiting male dignitary of the Fifty-Seventh Improvement, informed that human women are flattered by some moderate reference to their appearance, congratulates the First Lady of the North Americas on the buttery yellowness of her teeth—

And how, after all, could you ever learn enough to insure yourself against such embarrassments?

Eventually, it was she who spoke: "What is it you're reading?"

His scribe hand tingled, that he had left the opening gambit to her.

As for what he was reading—or pretending to read—it was dull enough: a glib verse narrative from his own culture. In his day bag, Connie carried more interesting material: novels from the last great centuries of human literacy; but he had felt that it would be indelicate to read them in front of her.

By the end of the journey, however, she had all too easily teased out his real enthusiasms, persuading him, finally, to fetch from his bag and read to her—eagerly and loudly and not too well—two stories by Saki and some doggerel by Ogden Nash. They were old, battered paperback editions, the pages loose in both, and once a page of Saki fell by her foot. She stooped to pick it up for him. She studied it a moment, while he in turn studied the fold of her hair hanging over her eye; he surprised in himself a strong desire to sweep it behind her ear.

He saw with a pang that she was studying the page upside-down.

"I sing," she told him later, as they passed through the Parisian suburbs. "I am a singer."

He made some callow remark, something she must have heard a hundred times before: how human singing so resembles Puscha weeping (itself never formless, but a kind of glossolalia peculiar to the Puscha species).

"I sing for people," she said, "not for Puscha." (She made the usual mistake, lengthening the "u" in Puscha to an "oo.")

It was not a severe put-down, and anyway, he deserved it. So why did it hurt so much?

It maddened him afterwards to think that she must have drawn him out—she must have got him to admit his interest in her people's literature, and read to her—only so she might sit there quietly despising him: the eloquent invader, drip-feeding the poor native whose own throat he had so effectively glued shut!

But all this was eight years ago, and Connie was too much the newcomer to know what undercurrents might run beneath such stilted conversations.

And on the return journey, the same coincidence! This time, she nearly walked past him—would have done so, had he not called her.

Well, their being on the same train yet again was not much of a fluke. He had travelled to Paris to glad-hand the farmers gathered there, and address their concerns about trade links after Autonomy; Rebecca, for her part, had gone to sing for them.

These days, public events had a tendency to run into each other: a trade fair with a concert tour, a concert tour with a religious festival. They were arranged so to do. A non-literate culture can only sustain so much complexity.

In a society without literacy, the eccentric routines of individuals and cliques cannot be reliably communicated and accommodated; so everything moved now to the rhythm of established social customs—even to the patterns of the seasons.

On their return journey, Connie spoke of these things to Rebecca—and then he wished he hadn't. He had an uneasy sensation of describing to her the bars of her prison.

Suddenly he was aware of wanting to say something to her; to make, as casually as he could, a desperate suggestion.

He began to make it, and then found himself trembling unexpectedly.

"What were you going to say?"

"Oh! It was an idea. But then I remembered it wouldn't—it wasn't possible."

"What?"

"Well—" he said. "Well—I was going to suggest you come to visit the orchard I run, for the weekend I mean. The club house is no place—I mean, it's very crowded just now, and you could breathe. Breathe easier. If you came."

"But why is that impossible?"

"Not impossible. I mean—"

He started telling her about the orchard. About the apples, and what his work with them entailed. The busy-ness of the season. Then, warming to his subject, about the savour apples had upon the Puscha palate, their goodness in digestion. And from that, to the premium his crops might fetch among his kind. And all the time he talked, losing himself in this easy, boastful, well-rehearsed chatter, he wondered at the wastefulness of the world, that animals crossed unimaginable gulfs of interstellar space, only to compare with each other the things that filled their guts, and satisfied their palates.

It was not until she was in the lorry with him, her hands resting lightly on her bare knees, her back arched in an elegant curve, and the fold of gold-brown hair hanging still over her eye, that it dawned on him: she was still with him. Silent. Smiling. Improbably patient. She had said yes.

The orchards fanned east in an irregular patchwork from the outskirts of Woodbridge, gathering finally along the banks of the Alde and the Ore. The rivers—wide, muddy, tidal throats— gathered and ran for some miles parallel to each other, and to the sea, which lay behind a thin band of reclaimed land. This ribbon of land—more a sea defence than anything else—was not given over to agriculture, but retained its ancient fenland garb of broken jetties, disused windmills and high, concealing reeds.

Rebecca glimpsed it only once, as Connie drove her through the deserted town of Orford, with its view over mudflats. Then they turned away from the coast, the road shrinking beneath them to a narrow gravel track, as it wound it way among the apple trees.

The monotony of the view was broken only once, by the Alde and the Ore, mingling indirectly through a knot of winding ditches and narrow (you might jump across them) surgically straight canals. The land here was riddled with old channels and overgrown oxbow lakes, as though someone had scrunched up the land and then imperfectly flattened it.

A pontoon bridge and an even narrower driveway led Connie and his companion, at last, to his house.

Across the front door, someone—a disgruntled worker, or other protester—had painted a sign.

$$\textbf{Qi}_t\textbf{t}$$
$$\textbf{ea}^h\textbf{t}$$

The lettering was predictably feeble: the work of one for whom letters were not carriers of information, but merely designs.

She didn't need to be able to read to see that it didn't belong: "What does it say?"

He pondered it. "It's their slogan, now," he said.

"Whose?" she asked him.

"It says, 'Quit Earth'." He scratched at the paint with his bludgeon hand. It would not come off.

It was late in the season, and the light died early, that first night.

They sat drinking apple brandy in the darkness, on deck chairs in front of the house. Glow bulbs cast a febrile warmth like a tremor through the chill air.

"Read to me," she said.

So he read to her. He wondered how she bore it: all those "V's" for "R's" ("R" was a letter he found barely audible unless it was rolled on the tongue, at which point the sound struck him as faintly obscene). Not to mention the "Z's" he had to insert in place of those wonderful, utterly inimitable "W's." It wasn't just the phonetic habits of his own language getting in the way (as far as that went, the speech of his ethnic group, the so-called Desert No'ivel, was notoriously fluid and sing-song); there were anatomical differences, too.

He studied the line of her mouth. He imagined her tongue, frighteningly prehensile. The relative chill of it (so, at least, he had heard, though he had no experience of it himself; felt still—or told himself he felt—a faint revulsion at the idea.) Her teeth, Their—

What was it again? Yes: "buttery yellowness." He laughed—to the human ear, an all-too-malevolent hiss.

Startled, Rebecca turned to face him. In the light from the warm glow bulbs, her irises were brown grey, like stones under water.

He could hardly bare to sit there, and not touch the fold of her hair.

(In the realm of the erotic, otherness is its own reward.)

Then it came to him: she knew this was what he was feeling.

He wondered at what point he had left off reading.

He considered whether or not she had done this before, with one of his kind, and the thought aroused him. He wondered dizzily whether this made him a "homosexual."

(She resembled his own sex, more than the female of his species. Puscha females are not bipeds. It is only relatively recently in their evolutionary history that they have lost the ability to fly. Their sentience is sudden, traumatic, triggered by pregnancy, and short-lived thereafter. Their abrupt, brief capacity for symbolic thought opens them to the possibilities of language—but they have time only to develop a kind of sing-song idiolect before the shutters come down again over their minds. They are resourceful, destructive of crops, and are routinely culled.)

Rebecca leaned forward in her chair, to touch the feathers about his eyes. The lines of her arm were reassuringly familiar to him, though the tone of her skin was not. He reached out with his bludgeon hand to trace delicately the line of the fold of her hair.

A moment later he heard the voice of Hadmuhaddera calling across the lawn, in the broad Lowland No'ivel accents that he had always faintly loathed:

"Hi there, Connie, where've you been hiding yourself?"

For the rest of the evening, the unctious pedagogy of Hadmuhaddera filled the chair between them. Hadmuhaddera, stiff and small, as though some more elegant version of himself were struggling for release within, spoke volubly of the strange differences and stranger similarities of Puscha and human culture—as though Puschas (or humans, for that matter) were these monolithic, homogenous units!

In the guise of leading Connie through the uncharted shallows of "human" habits ("*pain au chocolat* is a splendid invention, in that it allows you to eat chocolate for breakfast") he patronised Rebecca furiously.

Connie felt all the pulse and tremor of the evening come apart in the tepid, irregular slaps of Hadmuhaddera's tongue against his broad, blue palate.

Rebecca meanwhile stretched out almost flat in her chair, her water-polished eyes wide and black and bored, her arms thin and white like sea-polished wood against the arms of her chair.

"But set against the narrow bounds of the physically possible—" Hadmuhaddera was growing philosophical under the influence of Connie's apple brandy— "nature's infinite variations seem no more than decorative flourishes. Like that poet of yours, dear—what's-his-name? "Tall fish, small fish, red fish, blue fish," yes, yes, yes, but they're all bloody *fish*, aren't they? Every planet we go to: fish, fish, fish! And birds. And crustacea. Insects. Everything is exotic, but nothing is actually *alien*."

"Oh, I don't know. Your womenfolk give us pause," Rebecca countered. "Of course, thanks to your kind Improvements, we will never be able to attain your well-travelled disillusionment." In her quiet way, she was giving as good as she was getting. "Perhaps it is because you are the only aliens we have known—but you seem *fucking* peculiar to us."

Hadmuhaddera gave vent to an appreciative hiss.

In spite of himself, Connie found himself joining in. "Nature is capable of infinite variety," he mused, "but only a handful of really good ideas. Because the rules of physics are constant across the universe, so are the constraints within which living things evolve. Eyes, noses, ears, they're all good ideas. They're economical and effective. Consequently, we all have them. Languages, too—you would think they would be infinitely variable. But the differences aren't nearly as striking as the similarities. The predicating deep grammar—that is universal, or we would not be talking to each other now."

But if he imagined that Rebecca would join in—would become, for a minute, the gossiping groupie he had first seen at the club-house—he was wrong. He watched with something like pride—though he had, he knew, no right to such a sentiment—as Rebecca steered their conversation away from the theory and practice of language—that overwhelming Puscha obsession.

He watched her. Could it be that she, too, longed for the moment when they might restart the shattered pulse of their intimacy? He felt his body once again ache for the fold of her hair, and then Hadmuhaddera said:

"Ah, well, I'll bid you goodnight."

They watched him stagger away across the lawn into the darkness. There was no sound in the garden now, except for the stirring of leaves in distant apple trees: in a few weeks, this sound too would cease.

He thought about the apples, the trees, about his work. He thought about pruning. The act of it. The feel of the secateurs in his hands (he was not above getting his hands dirty, though whether he won any respect for it among his workers, he was never sure). He thought about the sound his workers made, as they set about their seasonal tasks.

He thought about gardening, and the fine line the gardener treads between husbandry and cruelty; between control and disfigurement. He thought about the Improvements his people had made among the planets. The years they had argued and agonised over them. The good and pressing reasons why they had made them.

Their enormity.

Rebecca stood up and wandered off a little way. Softly, she began to sing. She had a good voice, a trained voice (he had already learned the difference). An operatic voice.

He closed his eyes against a sudden, searing melancholy. To him it sounded as though she were weeping for the world.

Before the theme came clear, she stopped.

He opened his eyes.

She was looking at him. "Is this what you wanted?" she said.

It hurt him, that she would think this of him "No," he said, truthfully.

She said nothing more, and after a few moments, she began her song again.

They had been together now for eight years.

———

Every civilisation begins with a garden.

The Puscha, whose numerous cultures have bred and battled away at each other for eons, have founded their present, delicate comity upon this simple truth.

Here is another truth the Puscha take to be self-evident: a flower is simply a domesticated weed.

All Puscha "Improvements" are dedicated to the domestication of language. Over the eons of their recorded history, they have confronted languages too many and too noxious to get very sentimental about pruning them. Let a language develop unimpeded, and it will give rise to societies that are complex enough to destroy both themselves and others. Xenocidal hiveminds, juggernaut AIs, planet-busting self-replicators: the Puscha have faced them all—every variety of linguistic ground elder and rhetorical Russian vine.

The wholesale elimination of literacy is one of the stronger weedkillers in the Puscha horticultural armoury, and they do not wield it lightly. Had they not wielded it here, the inventive, over-complex and unwieldy morass of human society would have long since wiped itself off the planet.

The Puscha care, not for their own self-interest, but only for comity and peace and beauty.

They are beyond imperialism.

They are gardeners.

TWO

He still reads to Rebecca. But over the years, something has shifted between them, some balance has tipped.

At night, in bed, with the light on, he reads to her. Lermontov. Turgenev. Gogol. She laughs at Gogol. He reads and reads. He has perfected a kind of ersatz "R." "W's" will, perforce, always elude him. She lies there beside him, listening, her eyes like pebbles, wide and bored, her arms like stripped and polished apple branches, motionless upon the sheets.

He reads and reads.

He waits for her eyes to close, but they never do.

Defeated, he turns out the light.

Darkness is a great leveller.

In the dark, his books may as well be blank. He is alone. He is worse than alone.

In the dark, he finds himself dispersed and ill-arranged: *looseleafed*. He cannot find himself—he cannot find his *place*.

Every day he commits his self, unthinkingly, to diaries and address books, journals and letters and the essays he writes so very slowly and sends to little magazines.

At night, lying there beside her, he finds he has held back nothing of himself. It is all spilled, all committed elsewhere, unreadable in the dark.

Able as he is to read and write, the world inside his head is grown atrophied and shapeless. Equipped as he is with a diary and a journal, he remembers little. Owning, as he does, so many books, he cannot from them quote a single line. Deluged as he is every day with printed opinions, he finds it wearisome to formulate his own.

When the light goes off, and they lie side by side in the bed, listening to the leaves of the distant apple trees, Rebecca tells Connie stories.

Rebecca's stories are different from Connie's. His stories belong to the light; hers, to the dark..

She does not need light to tell her stories. She does not need to read or write. All she needs to do is remember.

And she remembers everything.

With no diary, Rebecca's mind arranges and rearranges every waking moment, shuffles past and future to discover patterns to live by, grows sensitive to time and light and even to the changes in the smell of the air.

Lacking a journal in which to spill herself, she keeps her self contained. Cogent, coherent, strong-willed and opinionated, her personality mounts and swells behind the walls of her skull.

(As he lies there in the dark, listening to her, Connie reflects on gunpowder. Unconfined, it merely burns; packed tight, it explodes.)

Rebecca's stories come out at night. They are stories of the camp-fire, of the clan gathered against the illiterate night. Hers is the fluid repertoire of the band, the gang, the tribe, reinforcing its identity by telling stories about itself.

Rebecca tells him about his workers, about their loves and their losses, their feuds and betrayals. She tells him:

"They burned an old nigger in Woodbridge last night."

It is not her choice of epithet that distresses him—why would it? He is from too far away to appreciate such nuances.

It is the fact of it: the growing littleness of the people of this world. This gathering into clans. This growing distrust of outsiders. This reinvention of foreignness.

This proliferation of languages.

(Already, in the eight years they have been together here, Rebecca's trained, operatic voice has taken on a deep, loamy Suffolk burr.)

He remembers something his neighbour Hadmuhaddera said, years ago: how everything that lives, wherever it lives, comes up with the same solutions, again and again. Hands, noses, eyes, ears. How everything is exotic but nothing is truly *alien*. He recalls, above all, Hadmuhaddera's frustration, that this should be so.

Now there are many, manifestly reasonable arguments to support the Fifty-Seventh Improvement. But Connie is beginning to wonder if those polished arguments might not conceal darker, perhaps subconscious, motives.

Rob a culture of literacy, and rumour replaces record, anecdotes supersede annals. The drive to cooperation remains, but cooperation itself, on a grand scale, becomes impractical. The dream of universal understanding fades. Nations are reborn, and, within them, peoples—reborn or invented. Models of the world proliferate, and science—beyond a rude natural philosophy—becomes impossible. Religions multiply and speciate, fetishising wildly. Parochialism arises in all its finery, speaking argot, wearing folk dress, dancing its ethnic dance.

Connie thinks: We are good gardeners, but we are too flashy. We succumb again and again to our vulgar hunger for exotica.

He thinks: We have made this place our hot-house.

Rebecca says, "They hung a tyre around his neck. A tyre and a garland of unripe hops. The tyre weighed him down and the hops made him sneeze. They hopped and skipped around him, singing. Nigger. Nigger. Nigger. Tears ran down his nose."

These are the rhythms of a campfire tale. This is the sing-song of a story passed from mouth to mouth. Connie's heart hammers in time to her playful, repetitious, Odysseian phrases.

Connie recalls that Homer, being blind, had no need of books.

He cries out in fear.

Rebecca's hand settles, light and dry as apple leaves, upon his breast. "What is it?"

"I don't want to hear this. I don't want to hear."

She says to him: "The ring-leader ran away in the night. They say he's hiding near. They say he's hiding on our land. Among the apple trees." She says: "It's up to you. It's your responsibility."

A week, this lasts: a week of curfews, false sightings, beatings of the rush beds. At last, exhausted, Connie consults with the military authorities in Ipswich, and abandons the hunt.

At night, with the light on, he reads.

"*Rudin spoke intelligently, passionately, and effectively; he exhibited much knowledge, a great deal of reading. No one had expected to find him a remarkable man . . . He was so indifferently dressed, so little had been heard of him. To all of them it seemed incomprehensible and strange how someone so intelligent could pop up suddenly in the provinces."*

With eyes black-brown and bored, she says:

"I've heard this part before."

Yes, and if he asked her, she could probably recite it to him. (He does not ask her.)

"He spoke masterfully, and entertainingly, but not entirely lucidly . . . yet this very vagueness lent particular charm to his speech."

Connie wonders, dizzily, if Ivan Turgenev's observation, sharp enough in its day, means anything at all now.

"A listener might not understand precisely what was being talked about; but he would catch his breath, curtains would open wide before his eyes, something resplendent would burn dazzlingly ahead of him."

Rebecca does not know what vagueness is. She could not be vague if she tried. Her stories shine and flash like knives. He glances at her eyes. They will not close. They will not close. His bludgeon hand is numb, he is so tired. But still he reads.

". . . But most astounded of all were Basistov and Natalya. Basistov could scarcely draw breath; he sat all the while open-mouthed and pop-eyed—and listened, listened, as he had never listened to anyone in his whole life, and Natalya's face was covered in a crimson flush and her gaze, directly fixed at Rudin, both darkened and glittered in turn . . . "

"Tomorrow," he says to her, when at last he can read no more, "let us go for a walk. Where would you like to go?"

"To the banks of the Alde and the Ore," she says, "where Hadmuhaddera's nephew lost his shoe, and the last man in Orford once fished."

Deprived of records, she remembers everything as a story. Because everything is a story, she remembers everything.

Tonight, in the dark, as he sprawls, formless and helpless beside her, she tells him a story of a beach she has heard tell of, a beach she doesn't know, called Chesil.

"Chesil Beach is a high shingle bank, cut free of the coast by small, brackish waters," she says.

"Like here," he says.

"Like here," she agrees, "but the waters aren't rivers, and the bank that parts them from the sea is much bigger, and made all of stones."

She tells him:

"You could spend your whole day among the dunes and never see the sea. Yet you hear its constant stirring, endlessly, and soon in your mind comes the image of this bank, this barrow-mound, put before you like a dike, to keep the sea from roaring in upon you. The land behind you is melted and steep, and before you the pebbles grind, a vast mill, and you wonder how high the sea water is now. You wonder how high the tide comes, relative to the land. You wonder how long it will take, for the sea to eat through the bank . . . "

In the morning, as you are eating breakfast, she comes down the stairs. She is wearing a red dress. It is a dress you recognise. It belongs to the girl you so recently left. It belongs to your mistress in Paris.

Even her hair is arranged in the way that your mistress's hair was arranged.

You say nothing. How can you? You can hardly breathe.

"Let's go for our walk, then," she says.

So you go for your walk, down the track, past the gate, into lane after lane, and all around stand the apple trees, line upon line. The gravel slides wetly under your feet as you walk, and the leaves of the apple trees whisper and rattle. She scents the air, and you wonder what she finds there to smell, what symptom of weather or season or time of day. She tosses her hair in the breeze. Her hair is crunched and pinned and high, and the fold of it that you so treasured is gone, the fold of gold-brown that once hid her eye.

Your orchards fan east to the banks of the Alde and the Ore. The rivers run wide and muddy and dark, and seabirds pick over them, combing for the blind, simple foods of the seashore.

The rivers, slow, rich and mud-laden, evacuate themselves into each other through a maze of ditches and channels, some natural, and some cut by hand through the furze. On the far banks, where the land is too narrow for tillage, an old fenland persists, all jetties and rotten boardwalks and old broken-down walls, and everything is choked by high, concealing reeds.

She turns away from you where you settle, shapeless in the grass. She bends, and the red dress rides up her calves, and you begin to ask her where the dress comes from, and what has she done to her hair? But all that comes out is:

"I— I— I—"

She takes off her shoes.

"What are you going to do?"

"Paddle." She lifts the edges of her dress and unrolls her stockings, peeling them down her brown smooth legs.

The tide is out, the mud is thick and brown like chocolate.

"There are terrible quicksands," you tell her, knowing that she knows.

Absently, she traces her toe through the yielding mud.

"If I don't come back," she says, "you'll know I'm swimming."

"No," you tell her, agitated. "Don't do that! It's dangerous. Don't do that."

You stand and watch her as she walks slowly upstream, in the shallow edge of the water. Swishing her feet. When she is gone, you wander to the water's edge, and you study the thing she has drawn in the mud.

$$Qi_t$$
$$ea^ht$$

A line from a book comes to you: a book by Marshall McLuhan:

Terror is the normal state of any oral society, for in it everything affects everything all the time.

When the rifle shot comes out from the reeds in the far bank, and hits you full in the chest, you do not fall. The suddenness of it seems to freeze the world, to undo the physical constraints that hold you and your kind and her kind and all kinds to worlds that are never quite alien, never quite home.

You do not even stagger.

You stand, watching old abandoned windmills, listening to the rushes, their susurration clear against rustling of the leaves of the apple trees. You watch the distant figure with the rifle leap from cover behind an old ruined wall and disappear between the reeds.

You choke, and fall backwards. As you lie there, she comes running.

She has taken off the red dress. She has let down her hair. You follow the line of it, and find that it has returned to itself, a fold of gold-brown over one eye. Terrified, you follow the fold of her hair to her neck, to her breast. Blood bubbles in your throat as you try to speak.

She puts her arms about you, holding you upright for a few seconds longer. "Try not to move," she says. She is crying in the soft, calm manner of her people.

When your eyes close, she begins to sing. "*I hate you*," she sings. "*I hate you. Oh, how I hate you!*"

Singing, or weeping. You cannot tell the difference.

You come from too far away.

publication history

about the editor

Ellen Datlow has been editing science fiction, fantasy, and horror short fiction for almost thirty years. She was fiction editor of *OMNI Magazine* and *SCIFICTION* and has edited more than fifty anthologies, including the horror half of the long-running *The Year's Best Fantasy and Horror*, the current *Best Horror of the Year*, *Little Deaths*, *Twists of the Tale*, *Inferno*, *The Del Rey Book of Science Fiction and Fantasy*, *Poe: 19 New Tales Inspired by Edgar Allan Poe*, *Lovecraft Unbound*, *Tails of Wonder and Imagination*, *Troll's Eye View: A Book of Villainous Tales*, *Salon Fantastique*, (the last two with Terri Windling).

Forthcoming are *Naked City: New Tales of Urban Fantasy*, *Darkness: Two Decades of Modern Horror*, *Haunted Legends* (with Nick Mamatas), *The Beastly Bride and Other Tales of the Animal People*, and *Teeth* (these last two with Windling). She has won the Locus Award, the Hugo Award, the Stoker Award, the International Horror Guild Award, the Shirley Jackson Award, and the World Fantasy Award for her editing. She was named recipient of the 2007 Karl Edward Wagner Award, given at the British Fantasy Convention for "outstanding contribution to the genre."

She lives in New York. More information can be found at: www.datlow.com or at her blog: ellen-datlow.livejournal.com